P9-DNL-245

THESE HONORED DEAD

THESE HONORED DEAD

DEAD

A LINCOLN AND SPEED MYSTERY

———◆◆◆———

Jonathan F. Putnam

CROOKED
LANE

NEW YORK

Copyright © 2016 by Jonathan F. Putnam

All rights reserved.

Published in the United States by Crooked Lane Books, an imprint of The Quick Brown Fox & Company LLC.

Crooked Lane Books and its logo are trademarks of The Quick Brown Fox & Company LLC.

Library of Congress Catalog-in-Publication data available upon request.

ISBN (hardcover): 978-1-62953-777-1
ISBN (paperback): 978-1-62953-820-4
ISBN (ePub): 978-1-62953-821-1
ISBN (Kindle): 978-1-62953-822-8
ISBN (ePDF): 978-1-62953-823-5

Cover design by Louis Malcangi
Book design by Jennifer Canzone

Printed in the United States.

www.crookedlanebooks.com

Crooked Lane Books
34 West 27th St., 10th Floor
New York, NY 10001

First Edition: August 2016

10 9 8 7 6 5 4 3 2 1

To Christin, my divine muse

Chapter 1

My general store still bore the name A. Y. Ellis & Co., though Ellis had departed long ago. It was one of a dozen stores that stood around the perimeter of Springfield's central square and served its two thousand inhabitants. We sold dry goods, patent medicines, bedclothes, groceries, books—everything the village needed.

Springfield was thick with lawyers, frequent customers of our more expensive items. The senior member of the local bar was Stephen Logan, a fellow son of Kentucky who had moved to Illinois a decade earlier and built a thriving law practice around the many real estate transactions in the growing village. Nearly forty years of age now, he had magnificent whiskers and an aquiline nose.

Logan bustled into the store one morning in March 1837 and barked out a question that proved to be life changing.

"Aware of any unused beds in town, Speed?"

"Has Mrs. Logan thrown you out again?" I returned.

"Would that I were so lucky," Logan said with a harsh laugh and a shake of his head. "I'm sponsoring a young lawyer who's moving here from New Salem. Not so young a fellow, in point of fact, but new to the bar, and he's nowhere to sleep when he arrives. You seem to keep a close company with the other unmarried men about town. I thought you might have some idea."

I looked up from the stack of pantaloons I had been count-
ing behind the counter. "There may be an empty berth in my
bed just now," I replied cautiously. Since my own arrival in
Springfield almost three years earlier, I had lived in the narrow
second-floor room perched atop the Ellis store proper. The room
contained space for little besides two double beds, each barely
the width of side-by-side pillows, and a decrepit dressing table.
Hurst and Herndon shared one of the beds. I slept in the other
with what had been a rotating rogues' gallery of disreputables:
most recently, a weasel-faced man from Georgia named Simpson
who talked to his mother in his sleep and had decamped for the
Michigan Territory the week prior. None of us had been sorry
to see him go.

"Is the berth available to my man or not?" asked Logan
impatiently.

"You say the fellow's a lawyer?" I was hoping, upon Simpson's opportune departure, to exercise some discretion when
picking his successor.

"He's tried a few trades," Logan replied. "Now he's trying
the law, though his legal career's yet to be written. He has managed to last two terms in the legislature. I'll bring him by and see
if you two can't get along well enough to share a bed at night."

Several weeks later, Logan returned as promised with his
acquaintance. I stared at the newcomer as he ducked to enter
the storeroom. He was several years my senior, very tall, and
very thin, indeed close enough to the point of emaciation that
I would have kept him away from my mother, were she nearby,
lest she swoon from maternal concern. He had wide-set gray
eyes, deep brows, a strong nose, and a lantern jaw. He wore his
hair long, curling over his ears and parted rather severely at the
high peak of his forehead. He was dressed in the black frockcoat,
shiny vest, and thin bow tie of his new profession.

"Joshua Speed, Abraham Lincoln," said Logan, introducing us.

Lincoln put down two small saddlebags and gripped my hand.

"How are you?" he said cordially. "As I was telling Logan, I am in need of bedding but not a bed, as I've recently contracted with a carpenter to have made a single-frame one." His voice was reedy and higher pitched than one would have expected to emerge from so large a being.

"What do you need, then?" I asked, feeling relieved. The stranger's size, if nothing else, marked him as a poor candidate for a bedmate.

"A mattress, blankets, sheets, coverlid, and the hardest, cheapest pillow you've got," Lincoln replied.

I did the figures quickly in my head. "For a good friend of Logan's, I can let you have the lot for seventeen dollars." As I saw his face start to fall, I hastened to add, "You'll not find a better price anywhere on the square. I'm sure of it."

"It is perhaps cheap enough," said Lincoln, "but small as it is, I'm unable to pay it. If you'll credit me until Christmas, I'll pay you then if I do well. But if I fail in this, I do not know that I can ever pay you."

As I looked up at him, I realized I had never seen a sadder face.

"See here, Lincoln," Logan interjected, "I told you you were better off sharing a bed. And this fellow Speed is not your usual frontier shopkeeper. He's a regular gentleman to the manor born. On his father's side he's descended from the sixteenth-century English historian of renown, John Speed. And his great-grandfather on his mother's side was Dr. Thomas Walker, the tutor of young Thomas Jefferson."

"I'm quite sure he has some illustrious forebears," Lincoln said to Logan. "Most men these days do. Or claim to, at least." He gave me a toothy grin. "But you'll pardon me if I'm interested at the moment in more practical matters."

"Such as?"

"Which bothers you more, the tuneless playing of a violin or the butchery of a mouth organ?"

I smiled and said, "I can stand either, I suppose, if played with a pure heart."

"And do you thrash about greatly in your sleep?"

"My bedmates have aired many grievances about me but never that one."

"Smoker?"

"Only cigars, and then only after a few draughts." As he nodded, I added, "And what are your shortcomings?"

Lincoln laughed and shook his head. "There are many, as you'll discover for yourself soon enough. You can hardly expect me to admit to them at the outset. Where's this bed of yours?"

I pointed to a pair of narrow winding stairs leading from the far corner of the store. Without another word, Lincoln grabbed his saddlebags and ascended, the wooden steps squeaking loudly in protest. I asked Logan, "You said he was new to the bar. How long has he been practicing law?"

Logan pulled out a gleaming gold pocket watch and gave it a few winds. "About thirty minutes," he said. "We've come from the courthouse directly. Judge Thomas swore him in this very morning."

The ceiling above us creaked. Lincoln was pacing back and forth, as if measuring out the room. Then the footsteps sounded on the staircase again, and the long, ungainly figure gradually reappeared. The saddlebags were nowhere in sight, and his face was obscured by a broad grin.

"Well, Speed," Lincoln said. "I am moved."

CHAPTER 2

That evening, Lincoln and I sprawled in front of the great stone fireplace in the back room of the store. I set a good-sized blaze to warm us from the April chill and swiped two bottles of mash from underneath my counter. I offered one to my new room-mate but he declined. The fire roared and hissed and spit.

"Logan said you come from New Salem," I said after I'd taken a few pulls from my bottle. The town was a commercial village on a high bluff above the swirling waters of the Sangamon River, about twenty miles downstream from Springfield itself. "What landed you there?"

"The current, as much as anything," said Lincoln. He was lying on his back, his hands interlocked behind his head. "I was a piece of floating driftwood after I reached majority and left my father's house. I was piloting a flatboat with some fellows back in '31, bound for New Orleans with bacon and corn and such, when we got snagged on the milldam at New Salem. We caused such a commotion and it took so long for us to float loose that by the time we left, I felt like I knew half the town. A man named Offutt told me that once I completed the trip down the Mississippi I should return and manage his store for him."

"So you did?"

Lincoln raised himself up on his elbows and laughed. "I returned all right," he said. "Only problem was, there was no store. Offutt was well-meaning, but he was a windy, brain-rattling man when it came down to it. Eventually he did manage to open a store, for a few months, but just as quickly it petered out."

Lincoln watched the playing flames before continuing. "After that, I tried pretty much anything I could to stay clothed and fed. I had a group of fellows there in New Salem who'd treated with me with much generosity, and I desired to remain in their company. I was a storekeeper again and failed at it again. I was an indifferent postmaster. I surveyed land—that was enjoyable enough, except for the brambles. At least it was, until my surveying instruments got seized by the sheriff for failure to pay my overdue notes on the store that'd gone out of business." He chuckled ruefully.

"You must have done something right," I said, "to have been elected twice to the state legislature."

"As I said, I have a lot of friends in New Salem." The modesty of his smile seemed genuine. "But a man can hardly live on the legislative salary warrant alone. Besides, we're in session only a couple of months of each two-year term."

"So now you've hit upon the law," I said. It had once been my chosen profession too.

"So now I've read law," he said, nodding. "*Blackstone's Commentaries*, front to back. Twice. I studied with no one but the mosquitoes."

"There's no prospect of a Mrs. Lincoln as of yet?" I asked. I myself was merely twenty-two years of age, but I guessed Lincoln to be five or six years my senior, getting on in life to remain a bachelor, moving to a new town, and seeking a single accommodation.

Lincoln laughed so hard he was sent into a coughing fit. "Don't beat around the bush, Speed," he shouted when he regained his breath. "Please, do tell me what's truly on your mind."

"My experience in sharing a bed, and a narrow one at that, every night with another man is that it's impossible not to learn of his affairs," I replied seriously. "So you can either pretend and ignore the obvious or acknowledge it straight away."

"I suppose you're right," Lincoln returned, turning serious himself. "I remain unmarried. To my profound sorrow."

His voice trailed off, but I sensed he was gathering his words and so I kept my tongue silent. At length he continued, "I'd formed an understanding with a young woman in New Salem. Two years ago. She was a handsome girl. But . . . we had to delay matters while she waited to inform a former beau of hers who'd gone missing. And then, just when it seemed we would move forward to a promised land of contentment . . ." He went mute, and this time he did not continue.

"I'm sorry," I said quietly.

"Brain fever," he murmured.

We sat in silence and watched the crackling hearth. The yellow-orange light of the fire cast Lincoln's tensed face in sharp relief. I regretted having touched so raw a nerve when I was just getting to know the man.

"I'm afraid we somehow detoured down a maudlin road," said Lincoln after a minute, shaking his head back and forth to rouse himself. "Let's turn back. Have you heard the one about the Baptist preacher from Indiana?"

I hadn't, I said, gesturing for him to relate it and glad for the change of subject.

Lincoln clambered to his feet and began pacing about the room, as if addressing some unseen jury. His posture was a little stooped in the shoulders. "So this preacher, he begins his sermon by telling his parishioners"—here Lincoln adopted a voice of self-important pomposity—"'I am the Christ, whom I shall represent today.' Well, he launches into his sermon, and it's a barn-burner. All fire and brimstone.

"Now at one point, a lizard darts out from the shadows and runs right up the preacher's leg. He doesn't stop the sermon—he merely loosens his pantaloons and kicks them off. But by then the lizard is up on his chest, into the pocket of his shirt, and so the preacher, still midsermon, unfastens his shirt collar and pulls his shirt away too. This rids him of the lizard finally, but the preacher is too consumed by his vigorous speechmaking to notice his state of undress. So he's standing in front of his congregation, his naked, hairy stomach extending over his undershorts, as he comes to his thundering conclusion—'and that is the will of the Lord.'"

Mirth now played at the corners of Lincoln's mouth and around his eyes. He went on: "The congregation is stunned, speechless. Finally, one old lady in the front row rises up and shouts"—Lincoln took on her squeaking, scolding tone—"'If you represent Christ, then I'm done with the Bible.'"

Lincoln slapped his own thigh and I roared with laughter. He threw himself down again on the plank floor in front of the glowing embers, his long legs splayed outward and a wide grin spread across his face.

"I've done nearly all the talking," he said as our merriment died away. "How about you? How did a gentleman like Joshua Speed, with all his illustrious forebears, end up out here on the frontier?"

★ ★ ★

To my everlasting good fortune, a few days before my seventeenth birthday my lungs were afflicted by terrible disease. I was taken by our private carriage to Farmington, my family's estate, where Dr. Mathews bled me for several days running. But when the disease did not relent, the doctor told my resigned parents—who had already lost three children to illness—that it was hopeless. My father ordered our house slaves to prepare a suitable gravesite.

For reasons no earthly soul could hope to comprehend, the doctor proved wrong. I lived. And it was during the long months

I spent convalescing in my childhood bedroom, at first gasping mightily for each breath and then, much later, leaving my bed and learning how to walk again, that I started working out a design for my life.

As the second son and sixth surviving child of the great Judge John Speed of Louisville, my destiny was in my blood. I would not inherit any part of Farmington, where my father and our sixty slaves raised hemp and corn from a land of such splendid virgin fertility that the same fields could be planted, without interruption, year after year.

Accordingly, once the old schoolmaster Smith declared in my fourteenth year that I had learned as much as he and his birch rod had to teach, my father directed me to follow the path worn by my older brother, James, to St. Joseph's College in Bardstown, Kentucky. The two years I spent there under the unimaginative hand of Bishop Reynolds seemed to confirm my fitness for my charted future: a clerkship with a local scrivener and then reading law myself one day. Had the disease not disrupted my studies, I have no doubt the law would have remained my calling, and my millstone.

As it was, as I regained my strength at Farmington, I began to realize I was not actually bound to a future where drafting a fine pleading in chancery by candlelight was the highest possible achievement. One day, my brother James came to visit and found me out of bed and gazing through the window.

"You almost ready to return to Reynolds's dungeon?" James asked with a good-natured shout as he entered my bedroom. "You know how cross the Bishop gets when his boys tarry in their studies." James was nineteen years of age at the time, with a great mop of sandy hair and a perpetual grin. *His* future had never been in doubt.

"I've been thinking," I said. "Perhaps I won't return to Bardstown—not right away, at least. I think the merchant's life suits me better."

"What could possibly be stimulating about that?" asked James with genuine wonder.

"Tell me, what have you done in the past week that held your interest?"

"Old Jenkins has let me organize the papers for an ejectment action all by myself," my brother began excitedly. "An elderly miller has lost his lease, but he's refusing to leave, as he must. And, let's see, I attend daily a class that's reading the whole of Chitty's *Work on Pleading*, and—"

I stared out the window again. Acres of sage-green hemp stalks swayed in the afternoon breeze. I could make out in the distance the moss-covered rock enclosure marking the fountain-head of a small, clear stream. I had spent many afternoons in my youth scrambling down and up the stream's steep banks, amid the aromatic mint and tender, pungent cress. But I realized I had never explored where the stream led when it left our land.

Early one morning the following month, finally freed from my sickroom, I walked along the stream's banks and found it flowed into the mighty Ohio River and from there westward into our bountiful Nation. I broke the news to my father that instead of returning to St. Joseph's, I had secured a clerkship in the large wholesale store of William H. Pope in central Louisville. I learned the business from Pope, finding more pleasure in the hurly-burly of commerce than I ever could have hoped to secure from even the most elegantly crafted pleading.

After several years with Pope, I seized the idea to follow the stream still further west. The Red Man was receding, making increasing room for the inevitable spread of white civilization and enterprise. With the defeat of Black Hawk in the war of 1833, a wide new swath of central Illinois—long the preferred destination of impatient, adventurous young men from Kentucky—suddenly became habitable. Late one evening at a large family gathering at Farmington, an obscure second uncle mentioned that my cousin James Bell was in need of a junior partner for his mercantile business in Springfield, Sangamon County, Illinois.

Thus it was that on an auspiciously warm day in September 1834, I climbed aboard my loyal horse, Hickory, to set off for Springfield. Slung over the horse's back were several saddlebags my mother had stuffed full of fine clothes, though I doubted these would be of much use on the frontier. I was just shy of twenty years of age and six feet of height, with long, curly black locks resting on my shoulders. As she gave me a parting kiss on the cheek, my older sister Lucy teased me that I looked like the poet Byron, heading off to exile.

My younger sister and confidante Martha, at fourteen as gangly as a newborn colt, loped alongside as we trotted toward the main road. "Why must you leave, Joshua?" she called up at me.

"There's a whole continent to discover," I called back.

"Take me with you, won't you?"

Martha threw up her hands toward me, but I merely shook my head and laughed. "You can come visit," I said, "once I've found whatever there is to find." With that, I spurred Hickory on and we left Farmington behind.

Springfield stood on the edge of a vast prairie whose wild grasses rose as high as the late summer wheat in Kentucky. As I rode through the prairie, the grass waved back and forth in the breeze like the billows of the ocean while the shadows of fleeting overhead clouds raced ahead of us. In the distance, a prairie fire burned, and the ribbons of fire along the horizon made it appear as if the clouds themselves were aflame.

My first years in Springfield confirmed the wisdom of my momentous decision to follow that little stream away from my birthplace. My cousin Bell soon tired of the day-to-day affairs of the store and became an absentee owner, and I reveled in the autonomy produced by his long absences.

Better still, Springfield brimmed with unmarried young men, and my nights never lacked for company. There was Billy Herndon, who'd grown up in Springfield and, after a brief and unsuccessful term at Illinois College, had returned to work as a part-time clerk for me at my store; ambitious Matheny, the son of the court clerk and from age fifteen the deputy clerk himself; young, pale Hay, hoping to latch on to an attorney as an office boy for hire; stolid Hurst, a clerk in a rival dry goods store; and many other choice spirits too. It was a sort of social club without organization. We spent our evenings milling about the store-room fireplace or dangling from the rafters of the stables behind the Globe Tavern, bottles in hand and vying to top one another with callow good humor. Lincoln, I assured him, would fit in famously.

★ ★ ★

Despite my boldness in questioning him, I withheld from Lincoln that night one important aspect of my biography. She'd sworn me to silence. Besides, the chapter had so recently closed that I was unwilling yet to reopen it to examination.

CHAPTER 3

It had sparked one sultry summer afternoon two years previous, when I'd walked across the Springfield green to the storefront of the Post Office Department, cater-cornered from my store, to see if the Department's thrice-weekly delivery stagecoach had yet arrived.

The postmaster Clark handed me a thin envelope, covered in the distinctive scrawl of my old employer Pope. I pulled out a single sheet of paper and began reading. As I walked out the door, head down and mind engaged, I nearly collided with someone coming from the opposite direction.

"Excuse me," I mumbled, as I inhaled a fleeting scent of wildflowers in August.

A minute later, while I stood on the green and continued to read Pope's exceptionally smutty and no doubt fictional tale, the scent returned. This time I looked up and met a pair of beautiful blue-gray eyes. My breath caught.

The woman standing before me appeared to be a few years past thirty. She was wearing a fitted calico dress that accented her figure, while a small black lace bonnet rested on her tightly bound hair.

"Good afternoon," I managed. "Sorry for nearly knocking you over."

"It takes more than a little bump to knock me over," she returned in a clear feminine voice. Her face lighted with a small smile, and I saw soft lines radiating from the outside of each of her sparkling eyes. They only enhanced the beauty of her face.

"I'm glad of it. Did your letter arrive?"

She held out her empty hands, palms up.

"Perhaps on the next stage," I said.

"Perhaps. Perhaps not. I've about given up checking. Perhaps it was never written in the first place."

"I can't believe someone would have failed to write you," I said before I could think about my words.

She smiled broadly and said, "I do appreciate your confidence. And your enthusiasm, Mr. . . . ."

"Speed. Joshua Fry Speed. The new sole proprietor of A. Y. Ellis & Co.," I added hastily and not altogether truthfully, but I was eager to continue the conversation any way I could. "Right over there, with the navy-blue facade. The finest general store in Springfield, if you have got any needs."

She laughed out loud. "I'm sure it is. I'll keep it in mind. Well, it was nice to meet you, Mr. Speed." She turned to leave.

"And you as well, Mrs. . . . ."

"Harriman. The 'Widow Harriman,' more properly," she said, adjusting the pin holding her mourning bonnet in place. She opened her mouth again and paused for a moment before adding, "As it happens, I too run a general store, out in Menard."

When I shouted in surprise, she continued: "You say you're new to the trade. I've been in the business for a few years now. If you ever find yourself in Menard, knock on my door and perhaps we can exchange a story or two."

As I stared after her receding form, I wondered how long decency required me to wait before making the trip to Menard, a small frontier settlement that was several hours' ride north of Springfield. I had settled on three weeks when I went to meet up with the fellows.

We gathered that evening in the stables, tossing horseshoes at the stake. Usually my focus held until the hour was late and my bottle almost drained, but I was off my mark from the start.

"I wish you'd had such poor aim last week when I was opposing you," complained Matheny, who was playing on my side that evening.

"Guess I'm preoccupied," I said. The image of the Widow Harriman's figure kept floating in front of my eyes where the stake was supposed to be.

"Whatever's on your mind, it can't be as important as beating these two vagrants." He gestured bitterly at Herndon and Hurst, who'd already amassed a nearly insurmountable lead.

"I wouldn't be sure of that."

Two days later, I set off for Menard at dawn. Hickory and I trotted directly away from the rising sun, the supple, muscular horse resolutely pursuing her own elongated shadow. After a few blocks, the street grid of Springfield petered out and we passed through a number of the farms that ringed the village proper. Then the farms gave way and we were alone on the warming prairie.

The sun was nearing its apex and Hickory was breathing heavily when the plateau on which Menard was set came into view. I had ridden by it before without stopping on the way to Peoria. I now saw the heart of the settlement comprised two dozen structures arranged in a semicircle and facing the village commons. These included a blacksmith, stable, and two public houses, along with a one-story building with a bold-lettered sign perched on the roof proclaiming "Harriman & Co., Public Provisioners." I tied Hickory to the post and walked in.

The store was laid out similarly to A. Y. Ellis & Co., with a small public reception area in front and neatly ordered rows of goods resting on wooden shelves behind a polished counter. The Widow Harriman was standing at the counter and attending to a customer, an old woman in a faded ruffled skirt that fell to the rough-planked floor. When I entered, the widow glanced up, and a look of surprise flickered across her face. But her attention remained focused on her customer until the transaction had been completed and the woman bustled past me, carrying several folds of coarse-woven fabric.

"Good day, Widow Harriman—" I began when we were alone.

"Call me Rebecca," she said, and my heart raced.

"Am I in time for the lessons in frontier shopkeeping?"

"You're a little early, actually," she said with a smile, "but I think I can make an exception in your case."

The following hours passed too quickly. Rebecca patiently explained her merchandise and business methods, stopping only to banter and bargain with the customers who entered periodically. My ardor grew steadily as I watched her mind and figure at work. Before I knew it, the sun was low and I found myself unwilling to leave.

"Your lessons were all most illuminating," I said sincerely, "and most impressive. I think I owe you dinner, at the least."

"You don't owe me a thing," she said, "but the ale Johnson brews next door isn't half bad. And Mrs. Johnson's beef stew is usually passable."

Johnson's public room was dim and dank and reeked of spilled beer. A browbeaten man with thinning hair and a dirty leather apron nodded to Rebecca as we entered, and she led me to a table in the corner that seemed her usual perch. Johnson dropped two foaming tankards on our table and I raised one up.

"To frontier shopkeeping," I offered.

"May the customers pay their credit and the competitors stay clear." And we knocked our tankards together.

During the course of the evening and more draughts than I could keep track of, I told her my history and she told me hers: how she and her late husband had never been blessed by children who survived birth, how he'd been ripped away by a raging river current in front of her eyes some four years prior, how she'd buried his clothes in an otherwise empty coffin. After a few days of mourning, she had gathered herself and taken over operation of his general store. From what I'd seen, it was a fair guess she had more aptitude for commerce than her late husband ever possessed.

"I should be back on the trail to Springfield," I said reluctantly at last. Other patrons had come and gone as we'd talked, some of them sneaking glances in our direction, but now the hour was late and we were the only persons left inside the tavern. Johnson himself had called out a farewell and shuffled off to his lodgings upstairs some time earlier.

"I can't let you," Rebecca said. "For your horse's sake, I mean. One false step on the dark prairie and she'll crack a foreleg. My house is just over the ridge a ways. I can arrange a berth for you and the horse both, in my barn."

I did not protest and we made it outside, a little unsteadily, and found Hickory whinnying impatiently at her post. The moon was three-quarters full and luminous.

"We'll give you a ride," I said. "Though it's not a sidesaddle, so you'll have to balance." I looked left and right, but there was no mounting block in sight. So I turned back to Rebecca and said, "Will you permit me?"

"If you please." The edges of her face were tinged with red, though whether from the drink or some other emotion I could not fathom.

I reached my arms out on either side of her waist. My hands felt her dress and petticoat compress over her firm hips and my blood surged. Rebecca gave a little hop and I lifted her up high and onto Hickory's back. She arranged her skirts and crossed her legs with her hands on her lap and faced forward, composed, erect, and proud, like a figurehead bound for new shores. I led Hickory by her reins and we walked in silence—except for my own breathing, which sounded to me as loud as a great steam engine.

After a few minutes, we came upon a one-story cabin, sheltered by a small stand of birches that straddled a brook. The house was constructed of tightly interlocking logs lined with black tar. No other dwellings were in sight.

I reached up to help Rebecca down, and she put her hands on my shoulders as she slid off the back of the beast and rested them there for a second longer than necessary. My hands remained on her waist. Then I took a deep breath and plunged ahead. I pulled her toward me and my lips tasted hers, firm and a little salty, while my hands caressed the soft skin of her face. I picked her up and carried her through the doorway.

Rebecca took off her mourning bonnet and shook out her long hair. I felt her breath on my face and my veins burned with longing. We fell into her bed together, tearing at each other's clothing. When I entered her, I felt for the first time in my life I might be in the presence of the Divine. And when it was over I was sure of it, for I had seen in the moment of completion the face of God.

Afterward I lay next to her, feeling her electric, naked skin against mine and wishing we could linger forever in this sliver of time.

"We should discuss, I suppose," I said, "when the wedding will take place."

Rebecca pulled away to have a better look at me. Her eyes burned with an intense expression I could not decipher. Then she burst out laughing.

CHAPTER 4

"There isn't going to be any wedding."

"There's not?"

"Women in my position marry for one of two reasons," Rebecca said in a matter-of-fact tone. "Love or money. I've been in love before, once. And watched it get ripped away from me. Have you ever been?"

"Well, I rather think . . ." I gestured vaguely toward the disordered bedclothes and our naked bodies.

She started laughing again, her breasts dancing and her eyes sparkling in merriment. "That wasn't love, Joshua. It was true. It may have provided both of us with a moment of pleasure. But it wasn't love.

"As for money," she continued, pulling a sheet up over her nakedness now, "I've been in the trade plenty long enough to know the *junior* partner in A. Y. Ellis & Co. can't have much. Your cousin Bell would be surprised to learn, I'm sure, that he's been dispossessed from his own store."

I had been caught in my fib, and as I thought about it, I realized Rebecca must have known the real facts from the moment of our first meeting. "How did you . . ." I began, but then interrupted myself with another thought: "Why did you . . ."

Rebecca gave another cry of laughter, but this time she drew me toward her. I felt her breasts pressing against my bare chest and felt her legs intertwining with mine.

"You think too much, Joshua Fry Speed," she whispered into my ear, her breath hot and scented. "No more thinking." And we let our bodies speak for the rest of the evening until I fell asleep, fully spent, pressed against her smoldering skin, feeling her heart beat out an unhurried lullaby.

In what seemed like the next instant, Rebecca was shaking my shoulder. I opened my eyes slowly, my head pounding from the aftereffects of liquor and lust. She held a lit candle close to my face, and as my eyes came into focus, I saw that the sky outside her narrow windows was still dark; perhaps there was a faint glow to the east.

"You have to leave now," she said.

I leaned up to kiss her and she kissed me back, but I could tell at once her manner had changed.

"What happened yesterday evening at Johnson's," she said, "dining together, that was unexceptional. The townsfolk here have gotten used to the notion that as an independent woman of business, I'll interact with other men in the trade. But this"— she gestured toward me lying in her bed—"*this*, I assure you, is most exceptional. And it's not something my reputation as an honest woman of business could endure. No one must know about this."

I was out of bed now, searching around in the candlelight for the clothes I'd thrown off the previous night. I nodded and said, "You have my word. Hickory and I will be on the prairie trail before any of your neighbors' cocks start to stir. Only"—I gave her a smile full of desire—"I feel as if I would benefit from additional lessons. In frontier shopkeeping, of course."

Rebecca did not blush but rather answered with seriousness, "I've been thinking the same thing. Both of us would benefit from more learning, I'm certain. Same day, next month?"

"Set your calendar by it," I said, and we both did.

One afternoon some months later I was lingering in her storeroom, waiting for closing time to arrive, when a stout woman bustled in with two small boys in tow. Rebecca was evidently well acquainted with the children, as they scampered over to her and she reached down and embraced them in turn. She handed each boy a sweetmeat to squeals of delight, and she watched indulgently as they scrambled under the opening in her counter and climbed up and down her shelves. It seemed a miracle neither boy was hurt and that the goods on the shelves were only mildly disordered when the whole family departed a half hour later.

I was still thinking about the merry scene as we sat across the table from each other at Johnson's that evening. "You were kind to those boys," I said, when she asked what was on my mind.

"Anything to give their mother a respite in which to do her marketing," she said with an off-hand shrug.

"It was more than that, I think. They took to you naturally, and you to them. Do you ever wonder . . ." I looked up and saw her jaw was uncharacteristically clenched, her eyes hard and unblinking.

"Sorry," I said quickly. "It's none of my concern."

"In truth, I think about it every night as I lay in bed," she said quietly. "But it wasn't in God's plan for me. That's evident. So there's nothing to be done, nor anything to wonder about."

I let the subject drop and did not raise it again.

I continued to live a double life of sorts, one that gave me no small amount of pleasure. For most of the time, I was fully engaged in the business of my store, attending to the counter, procuring merchandise, riding out to nearby towns to visit customers and make deliveries. Our business prospered as Springfield grew; seemingly every week brought a new immigrant, hoping to farm her rich black loam or exploit her central location near the Sangamon River. And in the evenings, the other fellows of Springfield provided company and good cheer.

Meanwhile, nearly every month, I arranged to spend a night or two lost and found in Rebecca's arms. For those precious hours, we seemed the only people alive in the entire world. And then, inexorably, the sun rose and I was back on the trail to Springfield.

While Rebecca and I usually gathered at her cabin in Menard, one summer's afternoon in 1836 I accompanied her to a village fair in Mount Auburn, a half-day's ride east of Springfield. A dozen merchants had set up stalls ringing the commons, and farmers from the surrounding area arrived on foot or in small gigs to look over the wares—farming implements, ready-made clothing, small decorative items, and the like. I recognized a few of the merchants as hailing from Springfield or its environs; all of them, save Rebecca, were men.

I had brought a selection of ladies hats, newly arrived from Philadelphia, which I spread out on a corner of Rebecca's table. She had been particularly insistent we come to this fair, although from the rough look of the crowd, who were picking through the merchandise with dirt-encrusted hands, I doubted either of us would sell much.

After a few hours had passed, my eye was drawn to a young woman who appeared oddly out of place. She was sixteen or seventeen years of age, although she moved about the crowd with the self-possession of a much more mature woman. Her delicate face, set off by prominent cheekbones, was framed with long curls of vibrant auburn hair. She was wearing a crimson dress with a loose, revealing bodice that contrasted greatly with the drab garb of the conservative farmers' wives mingling about the booths.

As I observed the young woman, it became clear that, whoever she was, she was an accomplished thief. At each stall she visited, she followed a similar pattern. She talked to the merchant about his goods, resting her hand daringly near, or occasionally on, his arm. She'd ask about this trifle or that and bend over to have a closer look. At the moment she was bent over the furthest, when the merchant's eyes were invariably engaged by her figure, she would reach out far to the side and close her hand over some small item on the edge of the table. Then she'd straighten up, thank the merchant for his time, and walk away toward the center of the commons. Once she was far enough away, she'd dip her closed hand into a burlap bag she carried at her side, secreting away the stolen item.

When I turned to point my discovery out to Rebecca, I saw she too was watching the striking young woman.

"It's quite a contrivance she's got," I said. "Works every time."

"Their weaknesses are *so* apparent," Rebecca replied. "One of many reasons why women merchants can prosper even when the superior sex falters."

"Have you seen her around before?"

Rebecca shook her head, her lips pursed.

The young woman glanced over in Rebecca's direction at one point, but when she saw Rebecca's eyes were on her, she looked away quickly. It seemed clear that she knew better than to try her stratagem at Rebecca's stall.

Months after the incident at the market, on a winter's morning in early 1837, I lay in Rebecca's bed and listened as a great snowstorm whipped around outside. I had helped reinforce the pitch between the logs of Rebecca's cabin the prior fall, and the walls held fast admirably against the whistling winds. We'd brought in plenty of wood the night before, and the fire in the hearth glowed. There was no place in the world I'd rather have been.

I looked over to say this to Rebecca and stopped short. She was sitting up, a woolen blanket cinched around her naked body, and staring intently into the fire. I noticed tiny red streaks in the corners of her eyes.

"What's wrong?"

She gave a shake of her head. "I can't find the words."

"To say what?"

"To say our stolen season has reached its end," she said, turning to me with a sad smile.

I realized I had known from the first this day would arrive. My only hope had been to delay it for as long as possible. Perhaps we had.

"Why?" I asked.

"A few women from the settlement have started to make remarks," she said, her voice restored to its usual firmness. "To ask questions I cannot answer. In fact, they started a few months back, but I didn't want to hear it and so I ignored them. But I can't any longer, not if I want to maintain my position."

Later that morning, the storm abated. I stood at Rebecca's door and held her tight one last time, inhaling deeply the scent of the nape of her neck. Then I walked out to saddle up Hickory for the cold ride home. The door closed behind me with a sharp retort.

It was only two months later that Logan walked into my store, seeking a berth for the newly minted lawyer named Lincoln.

CHAPTER 5

Lincoln commenced his law practice with another protégé of Logan's, John Todd Stuart. From what I could glean, their practice consisted of routine matters: stolen livestock, land disputes, a divorce petition or two. My circle of unmarried fellows, long used to accommodating new arrivals, gladly opened to admit the voluble newcomer. If anything, our evenings were even more filled with great good humor than they had been.

But there was unease beneath the surface. The business of A. Y. Ellis & Co. was unexpectedly lower in the spring season—typically our busiest—and off by a third by the time summer arrived. All around the square, my fellow merchants were reporting similar declines.

To make tempers even shorter, the summer of 1837 dawned dry and hot and stayed that way. We hadn't felt a drop of rain in weeks. The owner of every wooden structure in town—which was to say virtually every structure in town—worried his building might fire any day. Preoccupied by my immediate concerns, I thought of Rebecca less and less.

Everything changed one day in late July. Lincoln and I were crowded together on a row of rickety chairs in the front room of a two-room shack. The little hovel was owned by a free Negro with the grand given name of William de Fleurville but known to all as Billy the Barber.

In addition to myself and Lincoln, David Prickett, the state's attorney, was there, as was Lincoln's patron Logan and the rotund newspaperman Simeon Francis, publisher of the *Sangamo Journal*. Young Hay sat hunched over in the dim far corner, knobby knees hugged close to his chest.

Prickett, raw-boned and supremely self-confident, had been sprawled in the reclined barbering chair that stood alone in the center of the room. When Prickett's turn was done, Lincoln rose, stretched, and switched places with him.

"The usual, Billy," Lincoln said, slapping the Negro good-naturedly on the back. "And make sure you take off all this fuzz that's suddenly sprouted on my jaw."

"Yes sir, Mr. Lincoln," he replied. His singsong voice still contained an echo of the native island where he'd been raised. Billy dipped his hand, the color of burnt copper, into the tin pot sitting on a table beside the barbering chair, and it came up dripping with a greasy, soapy mixture. The barber proceeded to spread the froth over Lincoln's prominent chin and cheekbones. Then he unfolded a long, curved razor, wiped it on his apron, and set to scraping Lincoln's face. While he worked, Billy whistled softly to himself.

Beside me, Logan turned to Francis and said, "Did I read in your pages this week another bank in Philadelphia has failed?"

"Two more," Francis replied in a low growl. "Makes five from that city alone—five we know about. I told you all back in May, when the New York banks first stopped redeeming paper money for gold and silver, that the Panic would be heading our way."

"Surely we're insulated here in the West," I said, thinking of my own soft sales figures and hoping they would not suffer further. "It's land that gives people wealth out on the frontier, not gold and silver coins."

Francis gave a derogatory "Hrrumph!" and hoisted himself to his feet. The publisher was an immense man, shaped like an egg, bulging in the middle and with a small, bald head. His weak chin was covered, as usual, by about five days' irregular growth of whiskers.

"Land's creating wealth only if acreage prices keep appreciating," he said with an impatient wave of his short arms. "But that's not happening anymore. If there's less gold and silver in circulation, there's nothing to support the land prices. And the moment they stop rising, they'll fall as if lashed to a paving stone."

Logan nodded next to me and said, "That's what's at the root of your Dr. Patterson's problem, Lincoln."

From the barber's chair, Lincoln turned and grunted his assent. Billy yelped.

I saw a spot of red start to blossom on Lincoln's cheek, where Billy's blade had been held a moment earlier.

"Lie still if you please, Mr. Lincoln," the barber said, resting his long fingers on Lincoln's shoulders.

"I thought you said Patterson was trying to sell some property, not buy it," I said. Allan Patterson, one of the handful of doctors in town, had become Lincoln's first substantial client. Like most men with a profession these days, the doctor turned out to be an avid speculator in real estate.

"Patterson's trying to get out of an agreement he made," said Logan. "It's a bold play by Lincoln. We'll see if the judge lets him get away with it."

"I'd like to make a play for his daughter," sniggered Hay from the back corner.

"It'd be an awfully short one, boy," Lincoln returned. "The doctor wouldn't let you near enough to his precious Jane to touch her with a ten-foot barge pole." The men laughed, and Hay drew himself up tighter.

Billy shoved his razor into a pocket of his pantaloons and said, "That takes care of you, Mr. Lincoln. Mr. Logan, you're next I reckon."

Lincoln stood up from the reclining chair and stretched. His forearms grazed one of the wooden beams running the length of the low ceiling. He moved aside and Logan settled into Billy's chair. The barber took out his shears and resumed his low whistling.

"So how's the crime business, Prickett?" Lincoln asked. As state's attorney, Prickett was the prosecutor for Sangamon County, responsible for bringing all criminal proceedings.

"Well in hand."

"I heard that—"

At that instant there was a great crash and the door to Billy's shack was flung open. A thick-chested man barged into the room, his broad-set shoulders barely clearing the narrow doorframe. The shoulders unmistakably belonged to Humble Hutchason, the sheriff of Sangamon County. Hutchason had led a column of local volunteers into the Winnebago War a decade earlier, and the legend of his successful leadership, as well as his unsurpassed bulk, ensured his subsequent election as sheriff.

Hutchason was heaving for breath and perspiring heavily. "Prickett—at last I've found you," he shouted, his booming voice much too loud for the small chamber.

"What's happened?" asked the prosecutor. He was at attention at once, looking at the sheriff with interest.

"A girl's been killed." A great outcry greeted this pronouncement. "Stabbed in the neck from the sound of it. She was found by her aunt."

"Who?" demanded Prickett.

"Where?" called Francis, who had pulled a pencil out from behind his ear and was scribbling away in a small notebook.

"I'm not sure of the girl's name," the sheriff said. "She's new to the county—at least I think she is. She recently moved in with her aunt up in Menard. The aunt's the widow storekeeper there."

I gasped, although in the general hubbub it seemed only Billy noticed, as he inclined his head toward me slightly while he continued to whittle away at Logan's whiskers. My heart raced. Rebecca had never mentioned having a niece, or any other living family for that matter, but I knew for certain there was only one widow storekeeper in Menard.

"The aunt sent a messenger boy to alert me," the sheriff continued. He was leaning against the doorframe now, his breathing slowly returning to normal. "Her note says she found the girl yesterday morning, out in the hay barn."

"Why'd she wait so long to summon you?" asked Prickett.

"Don't know. You can ask her yourself. I'm on my way right now to have a look. Thought you'd want to be there."

"I'll accompany you," barked Francis, on his feet and halfway to the door. "We can ride in my double-team victoria."

"What's the aunt's name, Humble?" asked Lincoln.

"The Widow Harriman," I said before the sheriff could answer. All the men turned to me in surprise.

"You know her?" asked Prickett.

"The widow, not the girl," I replied.

"How?"

"Through the trade, of course. Fellow storekeeper." I hoped mightily the dim light coming through Billy's dirt-streaked windows was insufficient to show my reddening complexion.

"Let's be off," Prickett said, taking Hutchason's beefy arm.

"I'll come along too," I said, rising from my chair. "And why don't you attend as well, Lincoln. I think Simeon's carriage should have room for us all." My room-mate gave me an inquiring look, which I ignored and instead added, to the group, "As I said, I'm acquainted with the widow, and she with me. Perhaps I can add something to your investigations."

CHAPTER 6

When the group of us arrived at the familiar one-story cabin by the stream, Rebecca was waiting at her front door. She was dressed in black from head to toe. I had rehearsed to myself various forms of salutation on the ride up, but as it turned out, none of them was necessary. Rebecca greeted me with a polite nod and a look in her eyes making it clear she wanted to maintain the notion we had never been anything more than business acquaintances. I nodded blandly in return.

She led the sheriff to the barn at the rear of the house, as the rest of us trailed behind. A dingy blanket was draped atop an inert form in the center of the barn. Rebecca took a deep breath and pulled back the blanket. I stared with revulsion.

The mortal remains of a young woman reclined in horrible repose against a large bale of hay. Her legs splayed outward; her hands rested helplessly at her side, palms up. The corpse was stiff and liverish in color. Lifeless, wide-open eyes stared impotently toward the raftered roof. In life, the girl had possessed attractive, prominent cheekbones, but the corpse's skin was already shrinking away, like wax exposed to the flame, making the cheekbones protrude unnaturally. Her pallid face was framed by curly auburn hair, the vibrant color of which was the only aspect of her appearance that was in any way life-like.

The bone handle of a "Bowie" knife jutted out of the girl's neck just above the collarbone. Only about an inch of the dull silver blade was visible before it disappeared into her skin. A dried wash of dark blood stained her neck and the bodice of her housedress and had pooled by the side of her figure.

Next to me, Prickett swore quietly. Simeon Francis, whom I had never known to have a religious impulse, made the sign of the Cross. Lincoln sucked in his breath. Sheriff Hutchason bent down beside the body and gently prodded at it. Rebecca watched us all impassively. The lines around her eyes seemed deeper than I remembered, and her black mourning bonnet seemed more faded.

I recognized the victim at once as the young woman whom Rebecca and I had observed at the village fair the prior summer. And Rebecca's interest that day immediately came into new focus.

"What was her name?" asked the sheriff.

"Lilly," said Rebecca.

"When did you find her?"

"Yesterday afternoon."

"When yesterday afternoon?"

"Midafternoon, perhaps later. The sun was getting low."

The sheriff looked up from the side of the prostrate figure. "You didn't have reason to come out to your barn before then?"

"Not on a Sunday."

"And you hadn't had any reason to go looking for your niece before then?"

"I figured she was off on her own somewhere," Rebecca replied, after a slight pause. "Girls her age are hard to confine."

The sheriff grunted and continued his close examination.

"You hadn't heard any type of disturbance out here the prior night?" the sheriff asked a minute later.

"No."

The sheriff carefully moved the corpse to the side, and her head flopped from one shoulder to the other. I saw he was examining the pool of dried blood. "She must have been right here when she was stabbed," he said, talking mostly to himself, "because the blood flowed straight down. There's none anywhere else. Why didn't she fight back? Only—what's this?" He leaned down, his nose only inches above the dirt floor of the barn, then looked up at Rebecca. "Is it possible someone lay their head in the blood? A portion of the stain looks like it was matted by hair."

For the first time, emotion showed on Rebecca's face. "Jesse was lying there when I found her," she said. She blinked.

"And Jesse would be whom?"

"Lilly's younger brother. My nephew. They both came to live with me a few months ago. He's inside the cabin just now." She nodded toward the house. When the sheriff opened his mouth again she added, "If you have more questions, can we move outside? I'd like to leave Lilly's memory in peace."

"I think that's a wise course," I said, hoping to give Rebecca a respite. "Are you finished with your examination, Sheriff?"

Hutchason straightened up from the corpse, clearing his throat as he did. "For the time being," he said. He took a deep sniff of the still air inside the barn, which was about ten feet square and lit only by small openings high up on each wall. "Do any of you smell anything unusual?" he asked.

Each of us breathed in. "Hay . . . manure . . . sawdust," said Francis, ticking off on his stubby fingers. "And . . ." He sniffed again.

"Whiskey," said Prickett emphatically, staring down the beak of his sharp nose. Francis pointed at him and said, "Exactly." And he made a note in his book.

As we began to file out of the barn, Rebecca gestured toward her niece's body and asked, "Do you mind?" I understood her meaning at once and grabbed Lincoln's arm. Together we gently arranged the blanket to cover the corpse once more.

As we followed the others back into the bright sunlight, I turned to Lincoln and said quietly, "Look out for her if you can. I don't want her to be tripped up by the sheriff's questioning. Or Prickett's." He nodded.

When we rejoined the group, congregated in the side yard between the house and barn, Prickett was stepping forward. The prosecutor was wearing a high-collared, stiff-necked white shirt beneath his frockcoat, rather in the manner of an English lord—which, behind his back, many citizens of Springfield whispered he had pretensions to be. His eyes glinted and his tongue darted out to moisten his lips. Both actions, I knew at once, boded ill for Rebecca.

"Widow Harriman," he began in a dangerous voice, "perhaps you can enlighten us about how long your nephew was out in the barn, lying in his sister's blood, before you noticed your two wards were missing."

"I was away on Saturday night," she said, her face ashen. "I returned yesterday afternoon. Sunday afternoon. When I got home, I couldn't find either of the children. Eventually I looked out here. Jesse was lying beside Lilly's body, holding her tight." She put her hand to her mouth.

"Why didn't you tell us that in the first place?" demanded Prickett.

"You didn't ask," said Rebecca. Her arms were crossed in front of her chest, which was rising and falling faster than normal.

Prickett gave a glare and said, "In that event, Widow Harriman, let me ask unmistakably now—where were you Saturday evening, at the time someone was evidently putting a knife through your niece's neck?"

"You needn't be hostile, Prickett," Lincoln said, putting a hand on his arm. "I imagine she wants, more than anyone, to find out who committed this terrible crime."

Prickett shook free and said, "This doesn't concern you, Lincoln. Don't interfere." To Rebecca, he added, "Well?"

"I left early Saturday morning to attend a market fair at Buffalo Heart," she said. "I'm trying to make sales wherever I can these days. That's the last time I saw Lilly alive. She was asleep in her bed when I rode off. After the market I—I slept that night on the trail, on the seat of the carriage I'd hired, then made the journey the rest of the way back home on Sunday."

"Slept in your coach along the trail," Prickett repeated skeptically. "Why didn't you stay at an inn?"

"I'm not sure that's any of your concern," Rebecca said. Her eyes were alive with anger now. "I imagine you don't have the first idea of what it's like to lodge as a woman, by yourself, at a public house. Besides, I'd already paid for the carriage. There was no need for additional expense."

"You don't happen to recognize the knife, do you, Widow Harriman?" asked the sheriff.

Rebecca looked at the sheriff without blinking. "Never seen one like it," she said. Prickett scowled.

Hoping it would put her in a better light than the questions thus far, I asked, "Where did your niece and nephew come from?"

"Lilly and Jesse Walker are my older sister's children. The ones that survived infancy. My sister and her husband lived over near Decatur, trying to grow enough food to survive on a scrap of farmland. I didn't see much of them. My brother-in-law was a brute. I couldn't stand to be in his company, and I'm quite sure the feeling was reciprocated."

"How did they come to live with you?" asked Lincoln.

Rebecca reached up with a calloused hand and settled her mourning bonnet. "A long string of misfortunes brought them to my door," she said. "My sister passed on at the end of her next confinement, the one after Jesse. The baby was stillborn. Later that same year, my brother-in-law was trampled by an ox in the field and had his leg mangled. Then, a few years ago, he got ejected from the land he was farming. He'd never managed to scrape together any cash to buy it for himself, and a new landlord came along and had other uses in mind for the plot. They had no place to go, and even if I'd wanted to help him, I couldn't very well take all of them in, not the whole family. They ended up—" Rebecca paused, evidently weighing whether to admit the truth—"in the county poorhouse."

I understood at once why Rebecca had never mentioned these poor relations to me. There was, unavoidably, much shame attached to a man who depended on the public's charity for his family's sustenance.

"What became of your brother-in-law?" Francis asked. He had been scribbling notes constantly since we'd arrived.

"Worked to death by a blacksmith without a conscience," Rebecca said. "The poorhouse warden had hired him out to the lowest bidder."

"The lowest bidder?"

"Since the county pays for the indigent, whoever offers to charge the county the least for superintending them wins the right to their labor. My brother-in-law's labor was purchased by a smithy near Elkhart Grove. Lilly and Jesse were confined to the poorhouse. They saw their father one Sunday a month. Lilly told me Jesse ended up in bed beside her every night, whimpering into her shoulder until he finally fell asleep. Earlier this year, my brother-in-law dropped dead of exhaustion." She paused.

"He *was* a brute, but he didn't deserve that fate. And the children certainly didn't. Lilly wrote to me this spring, after their father passed, asking if I could take them on. I felt I hadn't any other choice, under the circumstances."

"It's a great credit to you that you did," I said. I glanced at Prickett, but from the sour expression on his face, it did not appear he'd been swayed by Rebecca's story.

"Can you think of anyone who might have wanted to harm your niece?" asked Lincoln.

Rebecca frowned. "I suspect there are any number of young men about who think she promised them her heart. Or something else even more desirable. She hadn't had a mother for a very long time, and that became obvious the more I came to know her. I expect one of them came to take and she wouldn't give."

"You expect us to believe some common boy, a frustrated suitor, did *that*?" Prickett said, nodding toward the now-closed barn door.

"I don't much care what you believe," Rebecca said. "It won't do anything to bring Lilly back."

"Can you give us the names of these young men?" asked Prickett.

"Let me ask you—do you have a daughter who's reached that age?" Rebecca said. When the prosecutor shook his head, she continued, "I didn't think so. If you did, you'd know the last thing a young woman wants to do is to share such intimacies with their parent, or aunt for that matter."

Both Prickett and the sheriff looked unsatisfied with Rebecca's answers. Standing beside them, I couldn't say I blamed them. Her independent character had always been one of her most attractive qualities to me. But in the present situation, it was plain her lack of interest in pleasing others did her no favors.

"We need to talk to the boy," Prickett said. "Now," he added, when he saw Rebecca frowning.

"Surely not," I protested. "Not after what he's gone through. Wouldn't it be better to wait—"

Sheriff Hutchason held up his hand. "We've a job to do, Speed. Can you bring him out, please, Widow Harriman? I'll be gentle."

She nodded, her lips pursed, and went inside her cabin. A minute later she returned, her hand on the narrow shoulder of a small boy with straight dark hair. He appeared to be somewhere shy of eight years of age. As Rebecca guided him toward us, I saw his pinched face was covered with freckles and his little teeth were unusually crooked.

The sheriff lowered himself to one knee and gestured toward the boy. "Come here, son," he said quietly. Rebecca embraced Jesse and gave him a little push. He wandered hesitantly toward the sheriff.

"My name's Humble," Hutchason said. "What's yours?"

"Jesse." Even standing five feet away, I had to strain to hear the boy's voice.

"I need to ask you some questions about your sister."

"My sister's sleeping," Jesse whispered. "She's gone to visit the doctor."

"Has she now. Who told you that?"

"Auntie. Auntie says the doctor's gonna help Lill wake up." The sheriff looked up at Rebecca, who nodded.

"Do you know who made your sister tired?" the sheriff asked. Jesse shook his head.

"Two nights ago, when your Auntie had gone to the fair, did you see anyone, any stranger?" The boy shook his head again. "Or hear anything unusual?" Another shake.

"When's the last time you saw your sister on the night your Auntie was gone?"

Jesse wrinkled his nose. "When she touched out my candle," he said.

"And the next day . . ."

"The next day I was protecting her, waiting for Auntie to come home." Jesse squinted at the sheriff. "When's Lill gonna wake up, Mister?"

The sheriff sighed and got to his feet. "I'm not too sure, young fellow," he said. "I'm not too sure."

The boy looked on the brink of tears, and this time Lincoln knelt down beside him. He rested his hands on either side of the boy's shoulders. Lincoln's large hands and long frame almost seemed to swallow up the slight boy.

"Can you do us all a favor, son, and take good care of your Auntie in the meantime?" Lincoln said with a kindly smile. "She's going to need all the help you can give her."

Jesse nodded solemnly. Prickett looked as if he wanted to continue the interrogation, but the sheriff said to him, as an aside, "It's best to leave it there for now. We can always come back later if we have more questions."

A few minutes later, the five of us were back in Francis's carriage. As we bounced along the rough track through the rolling prairie, Prickett said, "Don't print this, Francis, but she's guilty. I'm certain of it. We'll find the proof, one way or another."

CHAPTER 7

The prosecutor's words echoed in my mind as I lay in bed that night unable to find sleep. Rebecca's answers had sounded evasive, to be sure, but she was obviously suffering from strain and shock. She was the one who'd taken her relations in out of the kindness of her heart. How could Prickett possibly believe she'd had something to do with her own niece's murder?

"What?" said Lincoln from next to me in our bed.

"Sorry, did I say something aloud?" I said. I looked over and saw through the dim refracted light of the moon that he was lying on his stomach, his head turned toward me on his pillow.

"You've been muttering for a few moments now," he replied. "About the terrible scene in the barn, I think. And the widow."

"I'm awfully sorry if I've woken you," I said, whispering so as to avoid disturbing Hurst and Herndon sleeping in the next bed over. I shifted my frame under our bedsheet, and my foot grazed against Lincoln's bare ankle before finding a new place of repose. "It was terrible, wasn't it? And I can't figure out why Prickett's convinced the Widow Harriman was responsible for the girl's murder."

"She didn't exactly help her own cause by the way she answered their questions," Lincoln said. "Or didn't answer them."

"I know she didn't. But it's obvious she's innocent. Though I can't imagine who could have done such a horrible deed."

"Nor can I," said Lincoln. "There are several mysteries about this afternoon." He blinked his eyes and said with a yawn, "Though one should be easy enough for you to clear up."

I glanced over at him in surprise. "What's that?"

"The basis for your unusual interest in the Widow Harriman."

I looked away and up to the ceiling, determinedly avoiding his gaze for fear that mine would give away the truth. "I don't think it's unusual at all. A fellow storekeeper has suffered a grave loss. Trying to do what I can for her is a simple matter of trade courtesy. Besides . . . that girl . . . she was about the same age as my younger sister Martha."

Suddenly I sat bolt upright in bed and shouted out, "Good God—Martha!"

"What is it?" asked Lincoln, looking alarmed. In the other bed, Hurst sat up, looked over through blank eyes, and collapsed back onto his pillow.

Once I collected myself, I explained quietly to Lincoln. My father had written at the outset of the summer to say he had finally given permission for Martha to visit Springfield. Martha had been clamoring for such a trip for years to see not only me but also her close friend Molly, who had emigrated from Louisville to Springfield as well and had recently married Sheriff Hutchason. But the Springfield area now appeared to harbor a rapacious murderer, a mortal peril to young women. I had to prevent Martha's visit. Apologizing again to Lincoln for waking him, I struck a candle and hurried down the stairs to my storeroom.

It was still to be many years before the railroad or the telegraph reached Springfield. Thus there was no faster means of discourse with my parents in Louisville than the stagecoaches of the Post Office Department. A letter entrusted to the Department in one place could reach the other in ten days, if Fortune was on your side, or as long as three weeks, if she was not.

I spent the night hunched over the counter, composing a suitable letter to my father by candlelight. I did not want to alarm him or my mother, who I knew would search every word of my letter for hidden clues about my well-being. So I decided to keep the letter short and nondescript. It was a busy time at my store, I wrote, and I feared I could not give Martha the necessary attention. Perhaps the following spring would be a propitious time for a visit, but they should delay sending her until then.

When morning came, I was at the doors to the Department's offices the moment Clark opened. While the recipient would, of course, pay for the postage due, I pressed a silver quarter dollar into Clark's palm as I handed over the letter. In turn, he assured me it would be aboard the Terre Haute stage when it departed within the hour. I prayed Fortune would travel with it.

The new edition of the *Sangamo Journal* was resting on my counter when I returned to the store. Simeon's lurid report of Lilly's murder filled the right-hand columns at the top of the front page and spared no detail about the awful condition of the dead girl's body.

In the days that followed, the townspeople coming into my store could talk about little else. Rumors flew wildly with different theories to explain the shocking event. Many citizens sought to blame a member of one of the immigrant groups that had lately been flooding into Illinois, either the Irish drawn to the canal work up north by Lake Michigan or the mysterious "Mormon" people who had recently established a colony along the Mississippi. Others speculated it was the result of a dangerous religious fervor and that Lilly had somehow brought on her own murder.

Simeon reported on these rumors and fanned their flames in his sheet the following week. While I disliked the constant stream of gossip about Rebecca's niece, it was undeniably good for business. I sold more guns and fighting knives in those two weeks than I had in the prior six months combined. And I sold more patent medicines too. Several anxious mothers came in asking for Hooper's Female Pills, a compound said to be able to break the hold of even the most tenacious bout of religious zealotry among young women. Though I harbored my own doubts about its efficacy, I gladly sold out my entire lot.

On Friday afternoon, Simeon Francis himself tramped into the store.

"I imagine your sales figures are up as well," I said.

"I take no pleasure in that, I assure you," he said. When he saw my skeptical look he added, "You sell your goods, I sell the news. When the news is in demand, I sell more of it. You can hardly blame me for the laws of the market."

"I do applaud your discretion in keeping Jesse out of your story," I said. "As well as in refraining from any support for Prickett's wild notion that the Widow Harriman was involved in some way."

Simeon looked around to make sure we were alone. "There's no discretion involved, Speed. Only calculation. I think it likely that those details will emerge over time. After all, I have papers to sell next week, and the week after that as well."

"But the notion she killed her own niece—it's preposterous," I said, feeling the color rise in my face.

The newspaperman contemplated me and rubbed his unshaven chin. "If that's true, help me prove it," he said. "You said you're familiar with the Widow Harriman through the trade. I imagine you're familiar with the other merchants in Menard as well. I'm riding up tomorrow morning hoping to talk to some of them. Come with me and let's see what we find out together."

After breakfast the next morning, I climbed astride Hickory while Francis perched his immense frame awkwardly atop a sturdy black nag, who seemed used to the burden.

We set off in companionable silence through the ripe prairie vibrant with summer wildflowers. About an hour into the journey, the quiet was pierced by an approaching high-pitched whine. The horses surmounted a hillock and we looked down on an enormous flock of prairie chickens, partridges, and blackbirds, all screaming into the morning breeze. There was a sudden fluttering and a vast black-brown carpet flecked with white took off in flight, obscuring the sun as it flew over our heads. And then, mercifully, it was silent again.

When we reached the Menard commons, I rode past Harriman & Co. at once and was relieved to see it shuttered and unoccupied. Rebecca must be off at another market fair. I had come up with a number of things to say to her to explain our presence, but I feared none would have been satisfactory.

At Simeon's suggestion, we started on the far left of the semicircle of businesses and other houses flanking the commons. "Morning, ma'am," he began, addressing an elderly lady in a nondescript housedress who opened the door of a modest home on the literal edge of town. "I'm Francis, publisher of the *Journal*, and I wanted to ask you about what happened over at the Widow—"

The door slammed shut, narrowly missing crushing Simeon's hand, which he pulled back from the doorframe at the last moment.

At the next building, a public house, Simeon got through even less of his introductory sentence before the proprietor pulled a long-barreled pistol from inside his dusty frockcoat.

"You're the one who's writing the filth about the dead girl that's got everyone up in arms?" rasped the man, who had droopy eyes and an enormous, veined nose.

"I report the news, good and bad," replied Simeon, holding his ground.

The man waved his pistol in the air and spat at Simeon's boots. "Unless you want to report on your own death, you'll leave my property in the next ten seconds."

"In that case," said Simeon, "I thank you for your subscription and I wish you a good day." I stifled a laugh as we headed toward the blacksmithy next door.

"Is he actually a subscriber?"

"I know the Department delivers a dozen copies to Menard each week," Simeon said with a casual flick of his hand. "I don't know specifically who takes them. But I always say, a newspaperman who doesn't have more enemies than readers is doing something wrong." He raised his hand to knock but paused and said, "Why don't you try this one, Speed? You're the one who claims to have relations with all these people."

"I used to have good relations with them, before I began associating with you. You go ahead."

We got no further at the smithy nor at the two private houses next in the line. No one wanted to talk about Lilly, especially not to Simeon. The entrance to the stables was a few places along, and I had seen a stable boy moving about, caring for his charges. "Let's try there next," I said, indicating the building. "I wager we're better off finding someone who's not a regular reader of your sheet."

The boy emerged from the stable gates atop a light gray horse. He rode the animal bareback, expertly charting a wide loop around the commons, circling slowly at first but then picking up speed on the last few go-rounds. A half-dozen cows grazed the commons; none of them so much as looked up as horse and boy flew by. We took up a position next to the entrance gates and watched. When they trotted back toward us, the horse glistening with a fine coat of sheen under the midday sun, I called out a greeting.

"Decided you need help with your horses after all, did you?" said the boy. He jumped down and, holding the gray horse's lead, started toward the public post where Simeon and I had tied up our rides when we'd first arrived.

"Water them both, if you please," I said. "Are you the usual boy here?"

"Have been the past few months."

"I've just learned distressing news. A girl I was acquainted with, who lived somewhere about these parts, has turned up dead. Her name was Lilly Walker. Have you heard of her?"

"A little," the boy said without looking up from untying our two horses.

"What have you heard?"

He shrugged. "Dunno."

"Well, did you know her yourself?"

"Only times I ever talked to her was when she'd come collect her brother. Jesse. That little fellow likes to pretend to help me out." I smiled. The stable boy himself was barely larger than the "little fellow" Jesse.

I followed after the stable boy as he led the three horses back into the yard. Simeon trailed behind me.

"Do you know anyone who was angry with Lilly?" I asked. "Anyone who might have wanted to do her harm?"

The boy got to his loose pen and let his horse inside. Then he led Hickory and Simeon's nag over to an open stall with a water trough and small pile of hay. The boy squinted up at me and asked, "Other than the Widow Harriman, you mean?"

My heart raced. Before I could say anything, Simeon stepped in front of me and asked, "What's your meaning, son?"

"I heard Lilly and her arguing all the time. The whole village has. Plenty of days I could hear 'em all the way back here in the yard when they was out on the commons, they was yelling so loud."

"What were they arguing about?" demanded Simeon.

"It ain't my concern," the boy said. "I think this girl Lilly didn't take too kindly to being told how to act by some strange old woman."

"She was no stranger," I protested. "She was her blood, her aunt. She'd saved her from the poorhouse."

"If you say so," the boy said with a shrug. "As I said, it ain't my concern. Now do you want me to keep charge of your horses for the afternoon?"

"That'll be fine," Simeon said. "Come, Speed, let's let the boy get back to his chores. We appreciate your time, young man." He gave the stable hand a half-dime, and the boy touched his own forehead in gratitude.

Another hour of canvassing the settlement yielded no one else who would talk to us. "Why don't we eat before hitting the trail for Springfield?" I said. "We could do worse than that public house over there next to Harriman & Co."

By habit, when we entered Johnson's public room I led us to the small table in the corner where Rebecca and I used to sit. When I realized what I'd done, I turned around to find another, but Simeon was already lowering himself into the small chair, and I figured trying to get him to move would prove more trouble than it was worth.

"It looks like Prickett's suspicions about the Widow Harriman might be on target after all," Simeon said.

"You mean what the stable boy said?" I replied with a dismissive wave. I knew the newspaperman was trying to provoke me. "I don't put stock in that, and I'm sure you don't either. Young people are always thinking the adults around them are bossing them without reason. I know I used to."

"It sounded a good deal more serious," said Simeon.

Johnson came over, nodded with familiarity at me, and promised to return with two ales.

"But it's nothing you could print," I said after he'd left. "That a young woman argued with her guardian—it must happen fifty times a day in Springfield. A hundred. That's not news."

"When the young woman turns up with a knife through her neck it is."

"But surely Lilly Walker—*yeow!*"

Johnson had returned and now stood beside us; one of the tankards that had been in his hand a moment earlier clattered onto the tabletop, the ale cascading out and spilling all over my riding pants. I looked up and saw to my surprise the innkeeper's red face was twisted not in apology but rather in fear.

"I'm going to have to ask the two of you to leave at once," he said, his voice trembling.

"Us? But we've caused no disturbance," I said.

"Nonetheless. If you please." He held out his arm toward the doorway.

"What's the meaning of this?" demanded Simeon.

Johnson glanced nervously toward the door to the kitchen. "If Mrs. Johnson hears you mention that name in our premises," he said softly, "a bit of spilled beer will be the least of your problems. Mine too."

"Lilly Walker? What does your wife have against Lilly Walker?" Simeon asked. With each renewed mention of the girl's name, Johnson's face became more contorted, and he frantically motioned for Simeon to stop talking.

"I've said too much already," the innkeeper said.

"If you won't tell me, I'll have to go ask Mrs. Johnson myself." Simeon rose to his feet, notebook and pencil poised at the ready.

"Sir, if you please." Johnson had a panicked look in his eye. "Won't you leave it alone?"

Simeon did not budge. Johnson sighed.

"Very well, if you must know, Mrs. Johnson thinks there was some encounter between me and that wretched girl. Which there wasn't, of course. I was merely kind to her on one occasion, and she was a friendly sort. Flirtatious, even. But there was never anything else."

Judging by the fervor of the man's reaction, I was skeptical of his profession of innocence. I could tell Simeon was as well. Nonetheless, the newspaperman nodded and resumed his seat.

"We shan't mention her again," Simeon said, "if you'll bring us a towel, a new glass of ale for my friend here, and two bowls of beef stew. You tell Mrs. Johnson we've heard far and wide her stew's the best in the whole entire county."

"As you wish," said Johnson, retreating grudgingly.

"What do you think?" I asked Simeon a half hour later when we had collected our horses from the stables and sat astride them as they grazed in the middle of the Menard commons.

"You heard what the Widow Harriman told the sheriff about the girl's nature," Simeon said. "I wager there is no shortage of men around here who had encounters of one sort or another with the girl."

"And no shortage of wives who bear a grudge," I added.

"But can you imagine any of them doing what someone did to her?" he said, rubbing his rough chin with both palms. "Such intense violence. That's the difficulty." He paused. "Back to Springfield, then. We've learned quite a bit for one day."

"You go ahead," I said. "I've a customer to visit up north near Miller's Ferry. I want to see if I can't get him to increase his take-up for the harvest season."

Simeon stared at me for a moment, then slapped his horse on the backside and headed off on the trail toward Springfield. Hickory and I watched until man and steed became a small, ungainly speck on the horizon.

CHAPTER 8

There was no customer near Miller's Ferry. Instead, once Hickory and I were out of sight of the Menard commons, I pulled her up and we looped around the woods toward the familiar log cabin by the stream just beyond the main settlement.

Our conversations with Johnson and the stable boy had made it clear there might be a number of persons about who bore ill will toward Lilly. But if my goal had been to establish, for the newspaperman's satisfaction as well as my own, that Rebecca could not be among them, I knew I had not yet succeeded.

Rebecca's house looked deserted when we came upon it. My eyes glanced up to the roof and I saw with pleasure that my patches still held. I'd devised them the prior summer on a sultry evening as Rebecca stood below on the ground, her hair falling beguilingly in front of her eyes, offering alternatively encouragement and direction. She had suggested, laughing, that fixing the new leak in her roof was the price of one more night spent in her bed, and it was a price I happily paid.

I tied Hickory to one of the birches and walked around behind the cabin. The door to the adjoining barn was secured by a rusty padlock. Rebecca used to keep the key in an eye-level hollow in the closest birch. As I walked over to the hollow, I heard a metallic noise from above. I looked up and gave a little jump.

A murder of crows, some three dozen in all, lined the upper branches of the birch tree. Three dozen pairs of steely black eyes stared down at me. Their spokesman was on a low-hanging branch and he reproached me insistently: *caw caw caw.* His fellows clicked their beaks rapidly in concurrence.

"Quiet down," I said.

The birds clicked even louder.

My hand found the key, just where it used to be, and it turned in the padlock. The wooden door to the barn opened reluctantly. I peered in cautiously at first and saw with relief that Lilly's corpse had been removed. I hoped Rebecca had given her a decent burial; whatever the imperfections of her life, the young woman plainly merited as much.

As my eyes adjusted to the dim interior, I gazed around the small enclosure, not sure what I was looking for but looking nonetheless. The slatted walls were bare. Loose bales of hay lined the perimeter of the room. In the center of the dirt floor, like an awful beacon, lingered an irregular dark stain. I gulped and stared at the shadow of Lilly's final moments.

I tried to picture the scene as it had been several weeks earlier. Could someone have attacked the girl outside of the barn and later moved her body inside? The sheriff had dismissed the possibility, and as I looked around now, I couldn't detect any signs of blood underneath the dirty footprints leading in and out of the barn. Surely, given the amount of blood that had flowed from the fatal wound at her final resting place, moving her injured body would have produced some kind of trail.

For the first time, I focused on the fact that the bale of hay against which Lilly had been reclined had been positioned to the side of the barn door, and her body had been facing away from the door when we had found it. Someone walking silently might have entered the barn without her knowing it, especially if her perceptions had been dimmed in some fashion. Perhaps she had fallen asleep in the barn and been set upon before she could awake and react. Or perhaps the whiskey Prickett thought he'd detected had played a role.

I crouched and looked around the barn from Lilly's vantage point in those final moments. What had she seen, sitting there against the bale of hay? *Whom* had she seen?

"Who's there?" shouted a familiar voice.

In one motion, I rose to my feet and turned. Rebecca was standing in the doorway to the barn. There was a shotgun clutched in her hands.

"Hallo," I said with a weak smile.

"What are you doing here?" she demanded. The gun in her hands was pointing toward the ground a few feet from where I stood, and while she didn't shoulder it, she did nothing to lay it down either.

"I needed to see again where Lilly died," I said. There seemed no way around it. "I thought perhaps I could find something, something the sheriff had overlooked, that might show who did this."

"You shouldn't have come onto my property without permission. I heard from a neighbor there were two men walking about today, stirring up trouble about Lilly. From the description, I was afraid it was that corpulent publisher. And you."

I nodded. "I'm on your side, Rebecca," I said. "I'm trying to help—"

"I don't need your help. Or want it."

At that moment, there was a great fluttering behind Rebecca and the crows took the skies as one, screeching in angry tones. Immediately Rebecca swung around, raising the gun to her shoulder and advancing out of the barn as she scanned the horizon. Her finger was coiled on the trigger. I took a few steps forward so I could see out over her.

Someone or something had unnerved the crows. But the cause of their sudden flight was nowhere to be seen. We were all alone.

I was about to say as much when Rebecca swung around again. The shotgun was still at her shoulder and this time it was pointing straight at my heart. Less than ten feet separated us.

"Don't shoot," I said, my hands raised over my head.

There was a beat of silence. The still air between us was fraught.

"No, of course not," Rebecca said softly. She lowered the gun and rested it on the ground.

I became aware that I was breathing very deeply. Rebecca was as well, the captivating curve of her breasts rising and falling with each breath. Her face, made beautiful by the life she'd lived, had a look I hadn't seen in a long time. And I felt sure my face was a mirror of hers. We took a step and then rushed toward each other, arms outstretched.

"I think it was the wind," I whispered as my lips urgently felt for hers. My blood surged; my head pounded. I inhaled the moment deeply.

"The wind . . ."

I pulled her toward the interior of the barn, but she managed to shake her head, our bodies and arms and lips still enmeshed, and I realized her meaning at once. She was right; not there.

So I led her to the back door of her cabin and pushed it open. On the threshold she hesitated, resisting my pull, and said, without conviction, "I can't, Joshua. We can't."

"We have to," I whispered as my lips met hers again fiercely. I drew her inside and she did not resist.

We were silent for a long time afterward, lingering in each other's arms, unwilling to let go of the precious now. I was transported back to those early mornings in her bed. The touch of her bare skin had been like putting my hand over a flaming candle—unbearably hot yet irresistible. But I knew there was no way to resume our prior relationship. Inexorably, the cold-hearted machinery of time only moves forward, never backward.

I felt her starting to stir.

"Rebecca . . . ," I began.

"You're not going to ask me to marry again, are you?" she said, smiling.

I shook my head. "I'm worried about your safety out here, alone. Someone killed Lilly. Who's to say they're not coming for Jesse next? Or you, for that matter."

"If anything happens, I'm prepared," she said. "If it was anyone but you in the barn this afternoon, I would have gladly pulled the trigger. But there's not going to be a next time. Whoever came for Lilly came specifically for her. They don't pose a threat to me or Jesse."

"How can you be sure?"

"She was *my* niece." Rebecca's eyes flashed in anger. "You never knew her. In truth, I saw a lot of me in her. Just two weeks before she was killed, the three of us had ridden into Springfield for supplies. I kept Jesse with me while Lilly wandered around. Springfield was the largest city she'd ever seen. She asked me afterward about this business and that. She was trying to figure out the aspects of the town's economy and resources for herself."

"You must have had to pay off all their remaining debts to redeem them from the poorhouse," I said. "How did you manage, especially these days?"

"I managed," Rebecca said simply. "My ledger's remained decently firm. Fewer and fewer people are paying in cash, of course, but the private drafts I've had to take have held up in value pretty well.

"Lilly was very aware of my situation," she added. "I imagine she was afraid of ending up back in the poorhouse. When we came home from Springfield that day, she assured me she'd earn enough money to pay her and Jesse's expenses. I don't think she had the first idea how, but surely she wished it'd be so."

Thinking back to the village fair the previous summer, I felt confident Lilly would have been skilled in contributing financially to Rebecca's household had she lived.

"Let me help you," I said. "Send some customers your way, perhaps, or give you some goods to sell on consignment. I know you must be low on capital."

"I'll manage on my own, Joshua," she said. "Always have."

"But—"

She put her finger over my lips and let me kiss it without protest. But when I moved to embrace her more fully, she pulled away and started adjusting her petticoat and fixing its laces. I had a final, fleeting glimpse of the softness of her breasts before they disappeared beneath the many folds of her garment. And without further congress, we parted.

CHAPTER 9

The following Monday morning, I sat opposite Lincoln at the heavily scarred common table in the dim public room of the Globe Tavern, waiting for the innkeeper Saunders to bring us our breakfast. The Globe was a ramshackle two-story building that stood around the corner from our lodgings. There were a number of finer places to eat in Springfield, but none was more convenient.

Lincoln held the back page of the *Sangamo Journal* close to his nose as he scanned the small-type columns of legal notices— estates being probated, land sales, tax rolls, debtors' auctions.

"What are you looking for?" I asked.

"Employment," he said, his head still buried in the paper. "All these people need lawyers. A few might even be able to pay for one. I'd be overjoyed to collect a debt for a three-dollar hog."

"I suppose this hasn't been the most favorable time to commence law practice."

Lincoln gave a short laugh and put down the paper. "No, indeed," he said, a lopsided smile creasing his face. "Logan might have warned me, when he was extolling the virtues of Springfield, that a financial panic was coming. Reminds me of a farmer I knew up in New Salem. He'd go on and on about how juicy his peaches were. The man would not shut up about his peaches. Ah, here we go."

Saunders had finally arrived with breakfast. He set down on the table between us a battered metal plate containing several rashers of ham, sausages, boiled potatoes, bread and butter, and two large mugs of coffee. Lincoln and I took up our knives and dug in.

"Of course," Lincoln said after he'd wolfed down a few bites, "that farmer in New Salem? He forgot to mention he'd cut down all the peach trees for firewood the previous winter."

He laughed heartily and I joined him.

"That's more like it," he said.

"What's more like it?"

"You're being quiet. You have been, ever since Saturday evening."

"Perhaps I have."

"I heard you and Simeon rode up to Menard on Saturday."

I nodded as I chewed.

"Is your business so bad you're thinking of taking on the sheriff's job?" Lincoln asked. "Or Simeon's?"

"Of course not. I—"

There was a loud jangling of a bell. Two young boys materialized and sprinted through the public room toward the street. The Globe doubled as the stage line office, and the bell signaled the arrival of a new stage, bringing prospective customers as well as horses needing to be watered. Saunders bustled through the room, and soon we could hear him haggling with the new arrivals over the price of room and board.

Lincoln gestured to me with his knife. "You were saying?"

"I think it's only natural I have an interest in the girl's murder. As I've said, I know the Widow Harriman. Through the trade, of course. And it turns out I had met the niece once previously, or seen her, at least."

"'Through the trade,' yes," Lincoln said with a sly smile. "I believe I've heard you say that before." He gulped down a potato. "In fact, I was speaking to Prickett yesterday about his investigation."

"Do they have any suspects?" I asked quietly, so the soot-faced blacksmith at the far end of the table could not hear.

"Prickett told me he's more convinced than ever that the widow, your acquaintance through the trade, is the one responsible."

I felt my temper flaring. "It's nonsense," I said. "Why would she have wanted to slay her own kin? And gruesomely so. There's no logic to it at all."

"That's not how Prickett sees it," Lincoln returned.

Before I could respond, the proprietor of another store on the square stopped by the table and asked Lincoln a few questions about a dispute he'd been having with a customer over a rotten barrel of beer. Lincoln patiently listened to the merchant's complaints and advised him to split the difference with his customer. The merchant wandered off, still mumbling about the unfairness of the situation.

"That's the sort of free advice that's going to put you under if you're not careful," I said as we watched him go.

"Spoken like a true businessman," Lincoln said with a rueful nod. "I'm sure you're right."

"If you're giving out free advice—" I began, but Lincoln glanced at his pocket watch and pushed his chair back with a groan.

"I'm due in court soon," he said. "Dr. Patterson's case. Walk with me. Last time I was two minutes late for my hearing, I couldn't remember where I'd left my notes. Judge Thomas was awfully hard on me."

Lincoln was dressed in his formal frockcoat and bow tie. He stood and wiped his mouth on the back of his sleeve. Then he checked the pockets of his trousers and coat and, finding nothing, started looking around frantically. Laughing, I pointed to the floor beside his chair, where he'd set down a thin packet of papers when we'd arrived some thirty minutes earlier.

"Why don't you take my hat?" I said. "I think we're the same size. You can keep your notes here, in the band."

I habitually wore a different hat from my inventory each day as a form of walking advertisement. That day, I happened to have a tall, black stovepipe hat with a band of black velvet running circumferentially above the brim. Lincoln looked the hat over quickly, twirling it in his hands, and then tucked his packet of papers into the band. When he settled it atop his head, the combined height of the man and his costume nearly reached to the ceiling.

Outside on the street, the summer sun was already beating down without mercy. I raced to keep up with Lincoln, taking three strides for his two.

"Since you're in the habit of handing out free legal advice," I persisted, "I'll take some myself. What's the best way for me to help the investigation into this wretched girl's death?"

"Is your principal interest finding the killer or merely ensuring the Widow Harriman does not face legal jeopardy?"

I considered this as we turned the corner and headed for the town square. "Both—but mostly the latter, I suppose. Of course, I'm dreadfully sorry about what happened to the young woman. But she's gone now. I don't want the tragedy compounded by an unjust accusation against her aunt, who'd taken her in out of the goodness of her heart."

Lincoln looked over at me skeptically. I was going to have to be more adept in my defense of Rebecca, I realized, if I wanted it to make a difference.

We had reached the town green, and we walked past a large rectangular cornerstone surrounded by unruly weeds. The Illinois state legislature had voted to move the state capital to Springfield some months earlier, and like the rest of the village's merchants, I was eagerly awaiting the arrival of the high aspirations and low business of government.

A grand new capitol building and courthouse was to rise in the center of the town square, and its perimeter was already chalked out in the grassy field. But after an elaborate ceremony to lay the cornerstone of the new building, the town fathers had thought to ask who was going to pay for the project. The town thought the legislature should; the legislature thought the reverse; and the increasingly cash-poor banks announced they would not lend to either group. Construction had come to a halt, and the lonely cornerstone remained the full extent of the state government in Springfield.

In the meantime, the legal business of Sangamon County continued to be conducted in the old courthouse in front of us. It was a two-story brick building, topped by a low, hipped roof and a cupola. The structure had long ago begun to fall into disrepair, and its brick walls bowed outward perilously.

"If I were you," said Lincoln, "I'd start by finding out the basis for Prickett's conjecture. The man's a snake in the grass, but he has some relationship, however distant, with the facts. There must be something he's learned that's caused him to view the widow with heightened suspicion."

We reached the courthouse steps and I pulled open the heavy oak door for Lincoln. At that moment, the senior lawyer Logan, a lit corncob pipe clutched in his hand, hurried up from behind us. None other than Prickett was at his side.

"That's quite a hat," Logan said to Lincoln with a laugh. And the two lawyers pushed past us into the courtroom.

"Did I tell you? Logan's my adversary today," Lincoln said. "The old saw is right. A man who's the only lawyer in town has got nothing to do, but once a second lawyer arrives, neither of them will ever want for work." He chuckled and ducked inside.

I hesitated for a moment then followed him in. Lincoln's advice made sense; I would see what I could learn from Prickett.

The courtroom was a dark, shabby affair, a long, narrow room with six crowded rows of wooden benches in the back for spectators and two counsel tables in the front of the room. At the far end rose a low platform that served as the judge's bench. The entire room was obscured by a thick haze of smoke clinging menacingly to the low ceiling like storm clouds converging on the prairie.

Peering through the smoke, I saw the audience this morning consisted of some two dozen persons, mostly lawyers waiting to be heard on other matters, along with a smatter of village residents who habitually attended court sessions as a form of free entertainment. I spotted Prickett off to the far right of the gallery and headed in his direction.

Lincoln was seated on the other side, conferring in whispered tones with Dr. Patterson. Patterson was a small, precise man with thinning hair and an elaborate moustache. As usual, he was wearing his double-breasted, knee-length surgical coat. Dark splotches on the navy blue coat served to advertise the many surgeries he had conducted. It had occurred to me to wonder whether Patterson chose to display these visual reminders of his craft because of the scarcity of living patients who could testify to his services. Next to Patterson was an attractive young woman with light brown hair: his daughter.

In front of us, Judge Thomas was concluding a prior hearing. As I slid in next to Prickett, the judge dismissed the lawyers with an impatient wave of his hand and said to my friend Matheny, who was working as the clerk today, "Call the next matter."

"*Patterson against Richmond*," shouted Matheny in a voice an octave deeper than his usual one. Logan and Lincoln stepped forward into the well of the courtroom.

"What's this one about, Logan?" the judge asked.

"If I may be heard first—" began Lincoln.

"You may not," Judge Thomas said severely. Jesse B. Thomas Jr. looked like a pugilist, with a brawny body; a wide-set, florid face; and a permanent sneer. I had never seen him without a smoldering cigar clenched in his fist, and he now gestured angrily with it toward Lincoln.

"I appreciate greatly you are on-time today, Mr. Lincoln," the judge continued, "but in my courtroom, you will speak when spoken to, and not before. Now, Logan—"

The judge looked over at the senior lawyer, who had been sucking happily on his pipe stem during the exchange between the judge and Lincoln. In front of me, the doctor and his daughter exchanged worried glances.

"Thank you, Your Honor," Logan began with a flourish of his arms. "Your Honor, this is a case of land fraud. My client, Major Sylvester Richmond, is an esteemed veteran of the Late War with Great Britain. The government granted him his bounty land, over in the Military Tract, and earlier this year he contracted to sell it to Dr. Patterson. But then, over the summer, as land prices began to collapse . . ."

I shifted my focus to Prickett on the wooden bench next to me. The prosecutor had been intently studying several packets of paper in his lap, paying no attention to my presence or to the proceeding in front of us. I knocked against his shoulder and whispered, "Pardon me. I didn't see you there."

"Speed," he said with a nod, then looked down again at his papers.

"I've been meaning to ask you," I whispered, "regarding the murder of the Menard girl—have you made any progress in your inquiries?"

"A good deal," he replied without looking up.

"What have you—"

Suddenly there was a commotion in front of us. An older man had been sitting in the first row of the gallery, directly behind Logan, dressed in full military regalia with a blue coat, white breeches, and a tall plumed hat, all badly faded. This was, presumably, the esteemed Major Richmond. He was on his feet now, pointing at Patterson with a trembling arm.

"We had a contract," Richmond shouted, his prominent nose glistening an angry red. The crowd murmured excitedly.

"No, we didn't," growled Dr. Patterson, turning in his seat to glare at Richmond across the gallery. "We never signed anything. We—"

"Silence!" shouted the judge, banging his gavel with so much force I thought it would split in two. "Only the lawyers may speak in my courtroom. If either of you says another word"—he pointed with the burning end of his cigar toward Patterson and Richmond in turn—"I'll have the sheriff throw you in his jail cell."

Richmond sat down, still shaking his fist in anger and muttering to himself. Patterson and his daughter exchanged self-righteous looks.

"Thank you, Your Honor," Logan resumed smoothly. "As I was saying, the nub of the matter is Dr. Patterson doesn't want to pay the agreed upon price for the land anymore. He doesn't want to fulfill his agreement, given what's been happening to land values, as I'm sure I don't need to tell Your Honor."

An angry shadow passed over Judge Thomas's face and he spit into a tarnished spittoon resting at the side of his bench. I expected the judge carried in his pocket at that very moment a half dozen land deeds; most officials did these days, and in my experience, they were constantly monitoring the prices at which similar properties were exchanging hands.

I turned back to Prickett. "What have you found?" I whispered. "I'd like to help you, if I can."

"You don't want to know where the investigation is going," he replied in a low voice. "Trust me."

"If you mean to suggest you still think the Widow Harriman had some involvement, I'm sure you're wrong," I replied in an urgent whisper. "She's a kindly woman. She'd just rescued her niece and nephew, an act of Christian charity. Why would she have done so if she meant to harm the girl?"

Prickett did not reply. In front of us, Logan had completed his argument and sat down with a self-satisfied smile. Lincoln stood and, reaching a long arm up to his hat, pulled out the thin packet of papers from its band. As he smoothed out the pages, his hands trembled slightly.

"Your Honor," Lincoln began, a little shrilly, "my brother counsel does not state all the facts of the matter. In reality—"

As Lincoln began to lay out his client's position, Dr. Patterson and his daughter whispered back and forth with vigor. His arm rested lightly, comfortingly, on her shoulder. I found myself staring at the daughter. She appeared to be a year or two shy of twenty, about the same age Lilly had been. Her pretty, fresh face was not unlike Lilly's had been in life. Why had Fate rendered one an orphan in a poorhouse and then the prey of some horrible villain, while the other enjoyed the loving attentions of her prosperous father? What grand design, I wondered, what higher purpose was served by such bitter inequality?

Lincoln's final peroration broke into my contemplations. "And so, Your Honor," he said, his voice cracking as it rose, "what the parties had here was an agreement to agree, not an agreement on the ultimate *res* itself. When they came to no final agreement regarding that *res*—the bounty land of Major Richmond—Dr. Patterson was free to walk away, and that's exactly the right he's exercised."

Logan rose to respond, but Judge Thomas waved him back into his chair. "I've heard enough for one day," the judge said. "Save your breath. The clerk will put you down for trial in the September Term.

"In the meantime," the judge continued, "the court takes notice of the evident hostility between the two litigants. Dr. Patterson, Major Richmond"—the judge punched the air with his cigar as if jabbing an invisible opponent—"stay clear of each other. If I hear of either of you disturbing the other before I resolve this dispute at trial, I *will* have you jailed. Understood?"

Each man grumbled it was, and the judge directed the clerk Matheny to call the next matter. Prickett turned to me and said, "Then why did she lie about the murder weapon? She told us she'd never seen one like it. But the sheriff and I were out at her cabin again last week and we found another 'Bowie' knife, an exact match, hidden in her backhouse."

I gaped, my heart pounding, as the prosecutor moved forward and took his position in the well of the courtroom.

CHAPTER 10

To my great frustration, I couldn't figure out what to do next. Any number of possible explanations for the presence of the second knife occurred to me—perhaps the killer had brought two with him and had stowed the second one after committing his horrible deed—but I couldn't see how to prove or disprove any of them. Given Rebecca's insistence that I leave her alone, a return trip to Menard to search around her house, or perhaps to confront her and get her explanation for this new evidence, seemed out of the question.

In the meantime, I felt powerless to help Rebecca avoid the onrushing jeopardy. I hesitated to trouble Lincoln further, at least until I had learned more and could offer him something beyond bald assurances of Rebecca's innocence. For the first time since my bout with near-fatal illness, I found myself wishing I'd read law after all. Perhaps then I would have known how to deflect Prickett's unfounded suspicions.

I was still lost amidst these unproductive ruminations a few days later when my store door was thrown open and a blur of a small child shot inside. As Jesse started spinning around in a circle in the reception area, humming with his arms outstretched, Rebecca hurried in behind him.

I strode forward and took her hands, and I flushed as I felt her warm skin against mine and breathed in her intoxicating scent.

There was the briefest flicker of warmth in her eyes, but then she released my hands and her face hardened. "I'm glad we found you, Joshua," she said. "Can I ask a favor?"

"Of course. Anything."

"We've come from the doctor's. There's a bunion on Jesse's foot I wanted him to look at. But now I have some business to conduct in town. Can you keep an eye on Jesse for an hour or so? He's always running off and I'm losing track of him."

"Certainly," I said. "Has he brought his McGuffey Readers with him?"

She looked at me warily and said, "I left those at home, I'm afraid." She added soundlessly, mouthing the words for my benefit, *He doesn't read.* Aloud, she continued: "He's brought his jacks and a set of dominoes. And he likes little cakes, if you have any, when he's hungry. He'll keep his own company and out of your way, don't worry."

I reached out to give Jesse a friendly pat on his head, but he skittered away, scrambled up and over my counter, and started pawing through the goods on my lower shelves.

"How old is he?" I asked as we watched him play. "He doesn't look eight years yet."

"Just turned ten, actually," she said. I cried out in surprise. "The three of us"—her voice faltered—"celebrated his birthday last month. He's very small for his age, it's true. I don't think he's ever had enough to eat, not in his whole entire life. In fact, his age is what brought them to my door."

"How so?"

"Once Jesse reached ten, the master at the poorhouse would have been able to send him off to the lowest bidder, just like their father. Lilly didn't want him to suffer the same fate. That's why she contacted me when she did and why I felt I couldn't refuse her."

On the other side of the counter, Jesse was trying on a pair of adult pantaloons. There was a distinctive ripping sound as he tried to extricate his leg. He lost his balance, toppled over with a soft thud, then popped up again and, with the pantaloons still twisted around his body, started pulling on a jersey.

Rebecca winced and said, "I'll pay for the damage. He's a good-natured boy, but his whole world's disappeared with his sister gone."

"It's nothing a needle and thread can't fix," I said as another ripping sound erupted from the muddled mass of boy and clothing. "We'll be fine." Loudly, for Jesse's benefit, I added: "Did you say the young man plays dominoes? Have you told Master Jesse I was the Oriental Dominoes youth champion at the state fair of Kentucky for two years running? You leave Jesse in my hands and let me see what kind of skill he's got with the tiles."

Jesse had finally managed to shed the clothing, and he scampered back through the opening in the counter and into Rebecca's arms.

"That's a good lad," Rebecca said, holding the boy tightly to her bosom and stroking his straight, dark hair.

"I had one other question I wanted to raise with you privately," I said, thinking this was my chance to explore Prickett's new allegations.

"Can it wait until I come back to collect Jesse? I'm late as it is."

I nodded. "Go about your business. We'll be here when you return."

Jesse spread out his set of worn, wooden tiles on the shop floor and we played several rounds wordlessly. Then Jesse's attention started to wander. He made a few careless plays.

"Let me show you something," I said. I fetched a small leather bag from underneath my counter and handed it to the boy. He dumped out the contents and his eyes widened. It was a polished set of tiles made from ebony-wood with ivory pips that my brother James had given me for my sixteenth birthday. Jesse picked up a few of the tiles to admire them in turn.

"Shall we play a game with them?" I said, feeling pleased with myself that I was managing to entertain the young boy.

"When's my Auntie gonna be back, Mister?" he said.

"Don't you want to play with my fancy tiles?"

"When's my Auntie gonna be back?"

"Any minute now," I said. I glanced at my pocket watch: fifty minutes remained until Rebecca's promised return. My self-confidence in my caretaking abilities began to ebb. Then I had another idea. "Jesse," I said, "would you like to see my horse Hickory?"

His little head shot around and his face lit up with something approaching pleasure. He nodded once, decisively.

"Come with me," I said. I scribbled out a note to Rebecca, which I propped up in the store's front window, and I took Jesse by the arm and led him around the corner toward the stables behind the Globe. As we walked, the afternoon sun high and hot, I asked, "Do you like your new home with your Aunt, Jesse?"

"It's lonely," he said quietly, without turning to look at me.

"I suppose it is," I said. "I'm sure you'll find a new playfellow up in Menard before long."

He trudged ahead as if he had not heard me.

At the entrance to the stables, I nodded at a stable lad about Jesse's age who was perched on two bales of hay by the gate and awaiting the next stage arrival. Then we proceeded past the carriage shed to the stable building itself, a cavernous wooden structure appended to the back of the tavern.

But on the threshold of the stables, Jesse abruptly stopped, his face contorted. He mumbled something unintelligible.

I got to one knee and put my hand on his shoulder. "What did you say, son?" I asked quietly.

"Don't go into the barn."

"Why not? We're allowed to enter. See, the stable boy back there says we can go in to visit Hickory."

"Don't go into the barn," he insisted.

"It's all right. Truly."

"Don't go into the barn," he said again. He seemed near tears. I searched for a response, when suddenly I realized the problem. "Is that what your Auntie told you, after your sister fell asleep?"

He gave a tight nod. "Don't go into the barn. That's what she said."

"But this is a different barn, son. This is where my horse lives. There's nothing scary in here. Won't you come have a look? We'll go in together." I rose to my feet and extended my hand and the boy took it. Hesitantly, he followed me across the threshold.

On the left of the Globe's stable, there was a row of open stalls, each with a shiny tying-up ring, for the working horses—stage and hire and post horses—enjoying a short respite between tasks. On the right, there was a loose room for the dozen or so horses who boarded there, including Hickory. In between, there was a feed table and a large round haystack, reaching well above my head, the lads used for changing the bedding.

I grabbed a fistful of carrots from the feed table and handed them to Jesse. Hickory came trotting over when she saw me, snorting and prancing, and I opened the gate to the loose room a crack to let Jesse in. I was about to admonish him to watch out for flying hooves, but from the lithe way he moved around the pen it was clear he had spent time in stables before. He reached up and stroked Hickory's muzzle and let her nibble on the carrots. It was nice to see something holding the wretched boy's attention.

"Joshua!?"

I swung around. There was a young woman standing behind me in the doorway to the entrance yard, her hands on her hips, her face burst in a wild grin.

"It *is* you, Joshua!" My sister Martha gave a high-pitched squeal as she ran forward and flung her arms around my neck. She giggled into my ear, and at once I was transported back to Farmington and the hours we had spent rolling down the lawns together in gay laughter.

Only, the woman who embraced me did not look anything like Martha. When I had left Farmington, Martha had been a fourteen-year-old girl, precocious in thought but painfully awkward in appearance. A beautiful young woman now stood before me, light brown hair resting on her shoulders, a full, womanly figure blossoming below. But for the familiar voice and the unquenchable enthusiasm, I surely would not have recognized her.

"Did our father actually send you here after I'd warned him not to?" I asked.

"Of course not, silly," Martha said, breaking into a broad smile. "I wasn't about to let him—or you—spoil my adventure."

"But I wrote to him," I persevered, "and told him—"

"—that you were too busy to take care of me. Which is no problem at all, Joshua. I am fully able to care for myself. I won't bother you one bit."

"But why did the Judge ever agree—"

Martha burst into giggles again. "I never gave him the chance," she said. "Your letter arrived the very day I was packing for my journey. I recognized your handwriting on the envelope at once, of course. I was the first one to read it, and I made sure I was the only one to read it. I asked my Lettie to burn it, and that's *exactly* what she did."

Before I could respond, Martha looked over my shoulder and shouted, "Hickory!" She raced over to the fence surrounding the loose room and greeted the animal. She scratched the narrow, jagged white stripe running down Hickory's face from her forehead to the top of her nostrils. The horse whinnied and nuzzled her like an old friend. Jesse watched her with wide eyes.

"Who's this young man?" my sister asked.

"A friend of mine named Jesse," I replied.

"It's nice to meet you, Master Jesse," Martha said with a proper curtsy. Then she turned back to me and said, "Let's be off." She linked her arm with mine and began steering me toward the carriage shed, where I saw two of the stable lads struggling to unload several wooden traveling trunks from the back of our father's lacquered carriage.

"I have half a mind to send you back home at once," I said. "More than half a mind, in fact."

"That's impossible—Molly Hutchason needs me," Martha said. She folded her arms and thrust forward her chin. "This month especially, in her condition. She's written to say her time is near."

Against my will, I nodded. Sheriff Hutchason had not said a word about his wife's circumstance, as it would have been impolite to mention, even in unmixed company. But no one in town could have failed to notice that the sheriff's household would expand by one before long.

"Very well," I said, accepting defeat. "You can stay for a little while. I *am* delighted to see you, though you shouldn't have come without Father's permission."

"He gave me permission. He just didn't know all the facts. What is it lawyers say? *Caveat emptor.*"

I stopped and said, "That's not the right phrase. That one means—"

"*Seriously*, Joshua. The things you find interesting." The expression on her face teetered between amusement and contempt. "We can discuss it another time if you truly insist. Right now, we've got to get my belongings over to Molly's house and get Phillis settled, too."

We had come to a stop next to the mounting stack of Martha's trunks. I perceived for the first time a Negro woman with a heavily lined face and long, gray hair who was lingering uncertainly nearby. I vaguely recognized her as one of my father's slaves, though I doubted I had said five words to her in my whole lifetime.

"What's she doing here?"

"She's a midwife," Martha replied, jabbing me in the ribs, "as you'd know if you'd ever paid attention to anything that actually went on at Farmington. The best midwife in Jefferson County, Momma always said. Momma said I could borrow her, to help out with Molly, of course."

"I suppose so."

"Absolutely so," Martha replied gaily. "No one asked your opinion, Joshua, and it's a good thing we didn't. Now which direction should these boys here carry my trunks?"

I told the stable lads Martha would be lodging with the sheriff and made arrangements with the innkeeper Saunders, who was hovering nearby, for my father's carriage driver to spend the night at the tavern before commencing his return journey to Louisville. I took my sister's arm when Saunders said, with a sharp nod over my shoulder toward the stable, "What about him?"

Jesse was straddling the gate to the loose room, with one leg thrown over either side. I trotted over and said, "Can you stay and keep a watch over Hickory until your Auntie comes to fetch you? I'm sure it won't be long now."

The boy did not protest. *Strangers have been telling him what to do for as long as he can remember,* I thought. I handed Saunders a few silver coins for his trouble, and Martha and I traversed the four blocks to the Hutchason house.

All the while, Martha talked without pause about the goings-on in Louisville society and how her friend Mary Churchill had walked with old one-legged Joseph Bush at the Spring Ball at Galt House but now Aaron Corwine had a fancy for Mary and of course Mary never would have walked with that old cripple Bush if she'd known *Aaron Corwine* of all dashing young men might have a flame for her. The midwife trailed along silently behind us, about five paces back, not looking around at her new surroundings.

When we reached the Hutchason house, a modest one-story dwelling on the west side of town, Molly was standing on the front stoop, her condition concealed as much as was possible by a billowing housedress. The two childhood friends shared a long embrace and many tears of happiness while the stable lads finished lugging Martha's trunks into the house.

"I'll return at sunset to take you to dinner," I told Martha before she went inside.

"When do I get to meet this Mr. Lincoln you've written me about?" she asked. "He sounds most interesting."

"This very evening, I suppose," I returned. "He'll be cross if I don't introduce you to him straight away. We can stop by his offices, and then I thought we'd dine at the American House."

My sister shook her head decisively. "I told Jane we'd join her for dinner tonight."

"Who's Jane?"

"Jane Patterson? The doctor's daughter? Really, Joshua, sometimes I think you're completely hopeless."

"How do you know Jane Patterson?" I asked, dumbfounded. "I don't even know her, not well anyway."

"Well, that's exactly the point, isn't it," said Martha cheerfully. "When we got to town this afternoon, we weren't sure of where the stables were and I spied this *most beautiful* young woman walking along the streets. I got out of the carriage and went up and admired her, and she admired me, and I said I was your sister and asked her to kindly direct us to the stables. And after she pointed us in the correct direction, we started visiting and we realized we already knew of each other, through Molly, of course. And after we'd talked for a while, she said why didn't I come over for dinner this evening and I could bring you as well if I wanted, which I did want to, naturally." Martha paused and squinted at me, before adding: "You'll want to look in the glass before we do, I think.

"Come along, Phillis." And with that, my sister ushered the old Negro slave into the Hutchason house and shut the door firmly in my face.

CHAPTER 11

When I returned to the Globe, Jesse was nowhere to be found. One of the lads assured me an older woman fitting Rebecca's description had been by for him. In his place there was a great hubbub in the stable yard, as a fashionable four-wheeled "Lafayette calèche" carriage with a partially enclosed compartment, pulled by two majestic thoroughbreds, had just arrived and was in need of much attending. I spent a moment trying to identify the owner of this grand conveyance, but when no obvious candidates declared themselves, I headed back to my store so that a whole afternoon's receipts would not be lost.

Several hours later, I sent word to Lincoln, warning him that Martha and I would be by shortly, and then dressed for dinner. Against my better judgment I did, indeed, linger for an extra moment in front of the looking glass before going out to collect my sister.

Lincoln's office was on the upper floor of one of the series of stout, two-story red-brick buildings the landlord Hoffman had recently built a block north of A. Y. Ellis & Co. I led Martha through the door of the second building in the row and up the rickety wooden staircase to the upper floor, where we encountered a closed door announcing, in white-painted lettering, "Stuart and Lincoln, Attorneys and Counselors at Law." I knocked once, loudly.

"At your own peril," called Lincoln's voice from inside.

Pushing open the door, we encountered my friend just as he was rising from his chair by the window and casting off the buffalo-skin cloak he habitually wore around his shoulders. He came forward with a warm smile and took Martha's hands in his. "Miss Speed, it's a pleasure," he said, giving a slightly ungainly bow. "Though I had understood your visit was to be delayed."

"Nobody and nothing can get in my sister's way when she sets her mind to something," I said.

Lincoln looked between her and me and smiled. "I'm sure they can't," he said. "At last, someone who can tell me the truth about Speed here."

"I'll tell you everything about him growing up, Mr. Lincoln," Martha said with a laugh, "If you reveal his present life to me."

"Neither of you will do any such thing," I said sharply.

Lincoln drew us into the room and indicated two places to sit. As he did, he turned to Martha and said in a mock whisper, "We have an arrangement." She giggled, and I glared at her.

"You might have cleaned your office when you knew we were coming by, Lincoln," I said. "I've seen pigsties that were tidier."

Lincoln surveyed the room. Every surface was covered by packets of paper and scrolls of parchment, some in orderly stacks, others strewn around seemingly at random. There was a cluttered square table in the center of the room and a reclining lounge Stuart used by the near wall. In the far, dimly lit corner stood a small bookcase with a chessboard balanced on top of three thick volumes of Blackstone's *Commentaries on the Common Law.*

"As have I," Lincoln admitted, taking in the scene. "Stuart says he leaves straightening to the junior partner and the junior partner is, well, lacking in matters of organization." Lincoln gave a self-deprecating smile, and my sister stifled another giggle.

"Joshua has written about you often in his letters, Mr. Lincoln," Martha said earnestly once she had settled her skirts. She was wearing a long peach-colored dress with a ruffled bodice and billowing silk sleeves. Her hands were sheathed in white silk gloves.

"Don't believe a word he's said, whatever it is," Lincoln replied merrily. "For my part, I must say I'm surprised to have confirmation our Speed has a family. From his utter lack of social grace, I'd become convinced he was an orphan raised by a she-wolf."

"If you heard the howls coming from his bedroom when we were growing up, I'm not sure you could tell the difference."

"Ha! Not only does she have the beauty that passed you by, Speed, but she's quicker than you, too, and by a good margin."

Martha gave a pure smile and blushed.

I cleared my throat unhappily and said, "Perhaps it's time for us to be going, Martha. We don't want to keep Jane and her father waiting, do we?" I took my sister's arm and began to rise from my chair.

"'Jane and her father'—surely you're not dining with my client Dr. Patterson tonight, are you?" Lincoln said. "I didn't think you knew them socially."

Before I could respond, Martha eagerly explained her acquaintance with Jane Patterson. "Why's he your client?" she asked Lincoln. "Is he in some kind of trouble?"

"Not with the criminal law or anything of that nature," Lincoln responded. "It's a business affair gone bad I'm helping him sort out. There's a court case now."

"What kind of business affair?" Martha asked.

"I'm sure that's none of your concern," I said. "And we've already taken too much of Lincoln's time as it is." I tugged on her arm with renewed force, but she shook off my hand and stared at Lincoln earnestly.

"That's more interest in my docket than your brother's ever shown," Lincoln said, his eyes twinkling. "Dr. Patterson doesn't want to go through with a land purchase he discussed with an old veteran in the spring. The price of land has been falling severely all over, so the proposed deal doesn't make sense anymore, not for the doctor anyway."

Martha's face lit up. "The ground the two parties thought they were bargaining over has shifted, hasn't it?" she said with enthusiasm.

"It would be inequitable to hold the doctor to an agreement that didn't contemplate these new facts. Surely your clerk can find a decision from the Lord High Chancellor in England to that effect."

Against my better wishes, I found myself laughing out loud as Lincoln stared with astonishment. "Not for nothing," I said, "is Martha the daughter and younger sister of lawyers."

"I'm afraid *I'm* the clerk, but that's actually not half bad, Miss Speed," Lincoln said. "I'll have a look to see if there's support for such a theory."

"Or perhaps not," Martha said gaily with a shrug. "I'm sure you'll know best, Mr. Lincoln. *Now*, Joshua, we should be on our way. The Pattersons will be waiting. And I assured Molly we wouldn't leave her to Phillis's sufferance for too long on this first night." She rose and gave me her arm.

"Phillis?" asked Lincoln.

"I brought one of our house girls with me," Martha said, "to help out with Molly when her time arrives."

Lincoln's eyes widened as he comprehended Martha's meaning. "You brought a Negro slave with you into Illinois? A free state?"

His sharp tone caused both my sister and I to turn and stare. Martha wrinkled her nose.

"Don't worry," she said, "she won't run off anywhere. How could she? Besides, *why* would she? Her kin's been in our family for generations. And she's got the best lot she could possibly have in life. She's fed, clothed, sheltered—all at our expense."

An awkward silence suffused the formerly jolly room. Lincoln's face had lost its good humor. He seemed to be wrestling with how to respond to Martha. I had a pretty good idea of his true thoughts; after a long night early in his residency that very nearly ended in blows, he and I had consented to disagree on the merits of the peculiar institution so enthusiastically championed by my native land.

"I doubt very much," he said at last, choosing his words carefully, "this woman Phillis would agree fully with your sentiments, Miss Speed—" Martha opened up her mouth to protest, but Lincoln held up his hand—"Though I don't impugn your honesty in expressing them. I'm not suggesting we debate the merits of the practice, not now at least. For the present, I'm concerned with the laws of this state."

"The laws of this state?" I asked. I found my own temper rising. "What could the Illinois law possibly have to say on the matter? It's a simple matter of private property, solemnized by a sister state."

"Slavery's illegal under our state constitution."

"No one's proposing to make anyone a slave in Illinois."

"That's not the point, Speed," Lincoln said. He was pacing the room now, skirting scattered pieces of paper that had fallen from the table, his hands clutched behind his back. "Our constitution specifically provides any slave forced to work in this state is emancipated from his obligation of service. The only exception is if a slave and slave owner are merely passing through Illinois, from one slave state to another."

"I'm not forcing her to work here," Martha said with conviction. "She came willingly. I expect she's pleased, in fact, to have the opportunity to help ease Molly's discomfort. Her soul is simple but kindhearted."

"And besides," I added, "they're as good as passing through. It's not as if Martha has moved here permanently with her."

Lincoln looked unpersuaded. "I'm afraid you've exposed her and yourselves, for that matter, to substantial jeopardy by bringing her. Our laws on this issue are very exacting. Even free Negroes, you know, are required by our Black Code to register with the county clerk and post a substantial bond in order to legalize their residency."

"I thank you for your advice, unsolicited though it was," I said stiffly, facing the door rather than meeting Lincoln's gaze, "but you may be sure we'll take care of all appropriate formalities. We will ensure Phillis's comfort and contentment, as we do for all our bondsmen."

Martha and I linked arms, and on that strained note, we walked from Lincoln's office.

CHAPTER 12

Sunset had come and gone and twilight had settled in. The brooding sky was a crepuscular purple. Still arm in arm, my sister and I walked toward the Pattersons' house.

"I can see why you've found him a convivial friend," Martha said after a few minutes of silence.

I nodded. "I know he was outspoken at the end," I said, "but he meant nothing personal by it. Try not to hold his pique against him. It's an issue he feels strongly about, even though he himself was Kentucky born. Not a few persons around here feel that way. I've found it best to ignore the subject altogether wherever possible."

"I'm sure you're right," Martha returned.

A moment later, she shrieked. A low shadow had suddenly materialized, darted across the street in front of us, and disappeared.

"You'll have to get used to those, too," I said, laughing. "It's merely a feral hog. We've got a bunch of them roaming about. They've outwitted the control efforts of the town fathers at every turn."

We soon arrived at the Patterson house. It was one of the largest in town, two wooden stories painted light brown with bright green shutters bracketing each of the windows. There was a stately brick walkway leading up to the crimson-colored front door, where a brass nameplate identified the master of the mansion.

The Pattersons' hired girl ushered us into the rear parlor, and after several minutes, Jane Patterson entered. She greeted Martha like an old friend and curtsied toward me demurely. Jane was wearing a fashionable dress of light-blue muslin, with a full skirt reaching to the floor and close-fitting bodice flattering her well-rounded bosom. Her beauty was accentuated by a hint of red flush in her cheeks.

"You two know each other, I expect," said Martha.

"Mostly from afar, I'm afraid," I said. "It's a pleasure to encounter you in person, Miss Patterson."

Jane nodded while Martha said, "I beg you'll excuse my brother's poor manners, Miss Patterson, in not making your acquaintance earlier. I had hoped he'd have developed more social grace by now, but alas." Martha sighed dramatically. I smiled indulgently at her.

After Martha and Jane had chattered on for some time, the hired girl appeared again to announce dinner. Jane led us into the dining room, which was dominated by a large chandelier with a dozen candles ablaze. Dr. Patterson was already there, wearing his surgical coat and seated in one of four chairs surrounding a solid, rectangular table. When we entered, he stood and shook my hand gravely, looking me over from top to toe. I introduced my sister, and he greeted her with elaborate formality.

Partway through a very tasty meal—the hired girl had just brought in a china platter heaped with a whole roast duck—Martha turned to Dr. Patterson and asked, "How long have you and your daughter made Springfield your home, sir?"

"It's been almost four years now," Patterson replied.

"Do you like it?" Martha asked. "My brother seems to, very much."

"In that event, I concur with him," the doctor returned as he chewed strenuously. "It's a vital, growing town. The future state capital, as you've no doubt heard."

"Why'd you move here?" Martha continued.

"It was a good time for a change. We'd lived near Decatur for a long time—all of Jane's life, in fact. Her mother's buried there." He paused, as Jane nodded her head silently. "But I hoped there might be more demand for my services, as a modern medical man, here in Springfield, and I've been proven correct."

Martha speared a forkful of duck and asked, "Why'd you become a—"

"Martha!" I exclaimed. "You're not letting the gentleman eat his own dinner."

Martha glared at me while the doctor laughed. "I don't mind, Speed," he said. "In fact, I positively admire a young woman unafraid to speak her mind. It's a story I don't mind telling. Though it began in tragedy. My wife, Jane's mother, passed on shortly after Jane's birth. She didn't receive the treatment her life depended on. The medical arts at the time were positively primitive."

"She drowned herself," said Jane. "In a tub."

"What?" Martha gasped.

The doctor nodded. "It's true. I later came to understand my wife suffered from puerperal insanity. But no one had recognized it at the time, least of all me. That's when I resolved to begin medical training."

I stared at Patterson in disbelief. I could not fathom his callousness in discussing the scandalous nature of his wife's passing so openly in front of Jane. But as I looked over at Jane, I saw her visage was apparently untroubled. This was, I gathered, not the first time her mother's death had become a topic of conversation.

Martha had her hand over her mouth. "How horrible, for both of you," she said. "But what a beautiful tribute to your wife, for you to go into medicine in her memory. So you've raised Jane by yourself, all this time?"

Patterson paused for a moment and then nodded.

"Whenever you find a husband, Miss Patterson," Martha said with sincerity, "he'll have quite a job to live up to the kind attentions of your father, I am most sure."

"Father will ensure I'm well taken care of," said Jane calmly. "As you say, Miss Speed, he always has." She gazed steadily at her father, and he at her, but as I scrutinized them, I thought Patterson's look was somehow more complicated than a simple expression of parental love. I was still trying to decipher its true meaning when the man himself interrupted my thoughts.

"May I inquire, Speed, of your father's position?" Patterson asked.

I quickly cast off my ruminations. "He's a man of the law, but Judge Speed is a farmer, first and foremost," I said. "Our Farmington produced twenty-one tons of hemp last year, enough that my father had to help manufacture the hemp into bags with his own hands."

"Will the estate be yours one day?"

I shook my head and said, "My elder brother's. I considered the law myself, but I settled upon the merchant's life. I've found it a more vigorous, active profession. And I think there's more profit in it, too, in the long run."

"Are you familiar, Miss Patterson, with my brother's store on the square?" asked Martha.

"Of course," Jane said. "Everyone in town finds their way into A. Y. Ellis & Co. at some point or other."

"And do you find it the best-run establishment of its kind in Springfield?" my sister continued. I shot her a warning glance.

"I'm sure I do," Jane answered, her face reddening slightly and her gaze fixed determinedly on Martha.

"With the most pleasing and courteous—*oh!*" I had kicked Martha in the shin, and she bent over in pain.

"I wish you every good fortune in your endeavors, Speed," said Patterson, heedless of my sister's sudden silence. He chewed vigorously on a strand of duck for a few moments, then continued: "Not that the law doesn't have its place. I'm tangled up just now in this spurious lawsuit."

"I share a lodging with your lawyer, Lincoln," I said. "There's not a smarter attorney in the county. If there's a basis for your position, I'm sure he'll find it and argue it to the hilt."

Patterson twirled the ends of his moustache. "I don't know," he said. "There's something stiff about him."

"He can be earnest in the courtroom, perhaps. But he's very good." I paused for a moment before adding, "Though my father always says nothing's certain where a judge or jury's involved."

"What's certain is my opponent in the case, this so-called Major Richmond, is a menace," said Patterson. He waved his knife around. "You should have seen him in the courtroom the other day, yelling at us, unhinged. Mark my words—the man's a certified lunatic."

"Do you truly think him mad?" I asked. "Can one tell merely by observing from a distance?"

"If you know what to look for, you can," the doctor said. "Anyway, I know this Richmond fellow well. There's not a doubt in my mind. He has the predisposition to madness of Lear, even if, like Hamlet, he sometimes appears rational."

"My father's made quite a study of the furiously insane," said Jane.

"He should be locked up in the poorhouse," the doctor said. He slammed his fist onto the table for emphasis.

"The poorhouse? But surely he's not indigent," I said.

"I'm not sure if you follow the same practice in Kentucky," Patterson replied, "but here in Illinois, when we have men unable to govern themselves, they often end up confined to a small room at the back of the poorhouse. Some European states have lately suggested that these madmen should be removed to special therapeutic hospitals where they may receive *moral treatment*, as a result of which some may be cured of their defect, but here in Illinois we're still locking them away. In most circumstances, I consider our practice a tragedy, a waste of a life. But for Richmond? Nothing would suit him better."

Fortunately, the hired girl appeared at that moment and started clearing the dishes from the table. The doctor seethed silently while the other three of us sat in silence. By the time the girl was done, the doctor's anger had seemed to subside.

"Jane, why don't you and Miss Speed retire to the family parlor," he said. "I want a word with Mr. Speed."

Martha winked at me as she took Jane's arm and escorted her from the room. The hired girl placed two drinking glasses and a long-stemmed, green-glass wine bottle on the table. Patterson filled both glasses.

"Tell me what you think," he said, nodding at me to take one up. "I brew my own medicinal liquors. My formulation's a secret. Those charlatans Gage and Warren"—two of the other doctors in Springfield—"would gladly poison me if they thought I'd give up the recipe on my deathbed. Three slugs of this every night and you'll never have a day's sickness. I guarantee it."

I threw back the liquor and barely managed to keep it down. I had never tasted alcohol so strong or bitter. If I have three slugs of that, I thought, I'll be lying in the corner begging for my mother.

"Good, isn't it?" the doctor murmured as he filled the glasses again.

"Delicious," I managed.

"Mind you, this is the mildest of my formulations. If you'd like, we can sample the stronger brews as well." He started to call for the hired girl, but I hurriedly waved him off.

"Let's savor this one," I said.

"As you wish." He raised up his second glass and tossed it back. I lifted mine and took a tiny sip.

"You seem a sensible young man, Speed," Patterson said, settling back into the deep recess of his chair.

I nodded politely. "I'd like to think so."

"I want to know your intentions are honorable."

"Er—I certainly hope they are," I returned. "Though I confess I'm not altogether sure what you're referring to."

Patterson reached out and poured himself another glass. He put the liquor bottle back onto the tabletop with force, causing my glass to jump. "You're here to court Jane, aren't you?" he asked. His face was suddenly hard, his jaw set and his eyes boring in on mine.

I silently cursed Martha's scheme and took a long drink of the bitter liquor. No holding back this time.

"I hope there's been no misunderstanding," I said, feeling my way slowly over the uncertain terrain. "Any unmarried man of Springfield would be, I'm sure, lucky to court your daughter. You have every reason to be prideful of her." I paused. "But I've dined here tonight at the instigation of my sister, who's made your daughter's acquaintance through a mutual friend. It wasn't my intention to signal anything deeper to you, or her, by my presence. I certainly hope I haven't inadvertently done so."

Patterson deliberately tipped back his glass and drank deeply, while I wondered if my words had been sufficient to extricate myself. But at that instant, there was a loud pounding on the dining room door and the hired girl barged in.

"Not now—" began Patterson with a loose wave of his arm.

"I'm sorry, sir, but she said it was urgent," said the girl breathlessly. "One of your patients, sir, one who was here this afternoon. She's returned and she says she needs to see you at once. She says it's a matter of life or death."

The doctor jumped up, swayed, and hurried toward the entrance hall, his steps slightly unsteady and the tails of his surgical coat fluttering behind him. I followed a few steps back. Standing at the open front door, the flickering candlelight showing her face wrought and her mourning bonnet askew, was Rebecca Harriman.

She had grabbed the doctor's arm when she saw me come into view behind him, and we stared at each other in wonder.

"Mr. Speed? But what are you doing here?" she said.

"I was about to ask the same question."

"You two know each other?" said the doctor, looking back and forth between us.

"Never mind that," Rebecca said. She wrung her hands together frantically. "I'm glad I found both of you. I need help. Jesse's missing."

Chapter 13

"What happened?" the doctor and I each demanded, more or less in unison.

"I collected him at the Globe, right where you left him, Mr. Speed. We headed for Torrey's inn. As it was getting toward evening, I decided it made sense to lodge there overnight before riding home at sunrise." Rebecca's voice was much less steady than usual, and her hands worked against each other anxiously as she spoke.

"We were in the public room there, and Jesse said he'd like to go outside for some fresh breaths. After a while, I noticed he hadn't come back. I went to look for him, but he was—" Her voice caught, and she gasped for breath—"nowhere. He'd . . . he'd vanished."

"How long ago was this?" I asked.

"The sun had just set when I went out looking for him."

That was well over two hours ago, I thought. Why had it taken her so long to sound the alarm?

Rebecca had one hand to her forehead and with the other she tore at her black dress. "Oh—if only we'd ridden home to Menard tonight," she wailed. "None of this would have happened. First Lilly and now . . . I cannot bear it." She wobbled on her feet and reached out to the wall to steady herself.

"We don't know anything's happened, Widow Harriman," Dr. Patterson said. "He's probably hiding somewhere, the little devil. We'll find him safe and sound, I've no doubt."

"Let's fan out at once," I said. "He can't have gone far. Doctor, perhaps you and the Widow Harriman should go to Torrey's. Most likely he's still in the vicinity." I turned to Rebecca and asked, "Where else might he have run off to?"

She raised her arms helplessly.

"What about the stables?" came Martha's voice from behind us. I swung around and saw Martha and Jane standing back in the hallway, clutching each other's arms in worry. "This is the little boy who was in the loose room with Hickory when I arrived earlier, right, Joshua? Maybe he's visiting the horses again."

"Good idea," I said. "I'll head to the Globe to look for him there."

"I'm coming with you," Martha said. "Jane and I both will help with the search." Jane nodded resolutely.

We all hurried down the front steps of the house. At the bottom of the red-brick walk I turned to Rebecca and said, with as much confidence as I could muster, "We'll find him." She gave me a stricken look in response.

Patterson grabbed the lapel of my coat and hissed into my ear, "I haven't yet finished with you, Speed." Without waiting for a reply, he turned around, took Rebecca by one arm and Jane by the other, and hurried off in the direction of Torrey's.

"Who's Lilly and what's happened to her?" asked Martha as soon as we were alone, striding swiftly in the direction of the stables.

"I should have told you earlier," I said. "It's the real reason I wrote the letter to Father to forestall your visit." Quickly, I explained about Lilly's death, as Martha's face grew pale in the moonlight. "So stick close by me tonight," I concluded. "Who knows who could be lurking about in the dark, especially if something's happened to the boy now?"

"That's a terrible tragedy, but I can take care of myself," my sister said with assurance.

"I imagine Lilly thought the same."

I prayed Patterson and Rebecca would find Jesse near the inn. Torrey's Temperance Hotel was the oldest and shabbiest public accommodation in Springfield, an odd place for Rebecca to have chosen to spend the night with her young nephew. The public room there was notably rough and the liquor its barkeep served notably harsh. That the self-proclaimed "temperance" hotel had become the quickest and cheapest place in town to get stinking drunk was a fact so accepted by the local populace that no one noticed the irony anymore.

Why was Rebecca lodging there? Was she so short on funds after having paid off the debts of her late brother-in-law that she could better afford the sixty cents Torrey's charged for one night's room and board rather than the seventy-five cents charged by the Globe? For that matter, why had she decided to spend the night in Springfield? She should have had plenty of time to ride back to Menard before nightfall.

Whatever her reasoning, I hoped her decision hadn't been a fatal one. I would have said with a fair level of confidence there was no man in Springfield depraved enough to do harm to a small and defenseless ten-year-old boy; but if by horrible chance such a man did exist, I had even greater confidence he would have been drinking at Torrey's tonight.

As we neared the town square, which we needed to cut across to reach the Globe, I heard the strains of an off-key mouth organ in the wind, interspersed with good-humored shouting. I led Martha toward the commotion.

"Is that you, Speed?" called Lincoln's voice as we approached a group of shadowy forms sprawled in the tall grasses near the capitol cornerstone. He blew a comic fanfare into his organ. "Ah, it's the both of you. I told the boys Miss Speed had arrived intent on marrying you off before harvesttime. So when's the happy day to be?" He laughed loudly, and the forms around him shared his merriment.

"Speed and the doctor's daughter—that's an unlikely match," called a voice, which I recognized as belonging to my store clerk and room-mate Herndon.

"Come now," Lincoln returned. "Speed could do worse than Jane Patterson. Much worse." A pause. "Though I'm not sure *she* could." The fellows exploded with laughter again.

Along with Lincoln and Herndon, I could make out the bulky shadow of Simeon Francis and the much skinnier one of the court clerk Matheny. Several discarded bottles littered the grass around them.

Lincoln was the first to stop laughing as we came upon him and he saw the look on my face. "What's wrong?" he asked.

I explained our urgent errand. At once the fellows were on their feet, offering to help. Matheny and Herndon were soon trotting toward Torrey's to join the doctor in his canvass, while Simeon lurched off in search of Sheriff Hutchason. Lincoln volunteered to accompany us to the Globe. We hurried in step across the green.

"Sorry if I spoke out of turn earlier, Miss Speed," Lincoln said.

My sister waved her hand in the negative and said, "I know you had our interests at heart."

"Martha's got thick skin," I added. "Growing up at Judge Speed's dinner table will do that to anyone."

It soon became clear news of Jesse's disappearance was spreading through town like a prairie fire. Men in small groups began to materialize from the night, racing this way and that across our path, shouting out for the boy. Several of them carried blazing torches. The streets and alleyways thrummed with activity, while the distinctive fishy odor of burning whale oil swirled about.

But when we reached the entrance to the stables, just beyond the tavern itself, they were dark and abandoned. None of the other searchers had thought to come here yet, it seemed. Even more surprisingly, there were no stable lads at the gate awaiting a stage arrival.

"Wait a moment," said Lincoln. He dashed into the tavern, knees and elbows flying, and a minute later returned, dragging along a reluctant Saunders.

"I'm enjoying a quiet supper with the missus," the innkeeper protested, trying to wriggle out of Lincoln's grasp. "What's the meaning of this?"

"Where're your lads?" I demanded. "We need to question them, to learn if they've seen that young fellow I was here with earlier, name of Jesse. He's gone missing."

"I sent them home early," Saunders said. He finally managed to break free of Lincoln, and he glared at both of us as he straightened the fraying collar of his frockcoat.

"Why'd you do that?" I demanded. "What if another stage arrives tonight?"

"There ain't going to be another stage tonight," Saunders said. When I opened my mouth to challenge him, he added, "I'll be at the Ellis store at sunrise tomorrow, Speed, instructing you how to run your business. Or—tell you what—how about you let me govern my affairs and I'll let you govern yours?" He spat on the ground not far from my feet.

Before I could rise further to the challenge, Lincoln put a restraining hand on my arm and said, "We need to search your stables for the missing boy. He was here earlier, as you know. He might have returned. Fetch us some lanterns." When the innkeeper wavered, Lincoln added, in a shrill shout, "*Now*, if you please."

Saunders gave me one more unfriendly look and slunk inside. He returned shortly with three lanterns, each a five-sided glass box containing a burning candle stub.

"Take good care with these," Saunders said, handing the lanterns over. "With how long it's been since we've last had rain, if a single blade of straw catches, the whole thing will go up in a blink. McWorter was left with a complete loss last spring when his stables fired. And you three'll go up with it."

We thanked him and hurried around the corner to the stables' entrance. Once there, Lincoln used his lantern to light the long-fused torches positioned on either side of the entrance gate. The courtyard was instantly lit by the flickering torchlight.

"Jesse!" I called. "Jesse? Come out, boy, if you're hiding. Your Auntie's plenty worried."

We could hear a few of the horses shifting in their stalls. Otherwise, there was no response.

The three of us exchanged grim nods and advanced through the rutted courtyard together, dodging loose paving stones where we could. On the left was the carriage shed. When the yard was full, the stable boys would park carriages inside the shed, but as there were only two coaches present tonight—my father's black lacquered carriage and the large calèche coach whose arrival I had seen later in the afternoon—the boys had left them in front of the shed to save time on their departure. I walked up to the carriages.

"Jesse!" I called again. "Jesse?"

Silence.

"Back in the stables perhaps," said Martha. I nodded. I was about to follow her when I looked again at one of the rear wheels of my father's carriage. There was a small object balanced atop the hub.

"What's this?" I exclaimed, swinging my lantern to have a look.

"What is it, Joshua?" called Martha.

"I just found a little cake," I said, holding a small, half-eaten pastry. It crumbled in my palm. "The widow told me Jesse loved to eat these." I paused. "I know other boys eat them too, of course, but I think he's been here. Recently."

A moment later, Lincoln called from the other side of the yard, "Quiet. What's that noise?"

I listened intently. Nothing. Then, at the far reaches of my hearing, an insidious sound, a sort of crackling. I scanned the stable enclosure in front of us and there it was, off in a corner: a faint glow.

Fire.

The glow got brighter and larger. I saw a tongue of flame flicker along a wooden wall and then retreat, like a deadly snake poised to strike.

"Fire! Get help at once! The stable's on fire!"

"The horses!" shrieked Martha. She dropped her lantern, and before I could stop her, she raced into the burning barn.

CHAPTER 14

"I'm going after her," I shouted to Lincoln, who was standing with his mouth agape on the other side of the courtyard. "You'll have to sound the alarm."

But as I sprinted toward the barn door, now swinging in Martha's wake, I feared a general alarm would do little good. Springfield had no fire company. The town's fire warden was Tilman Hornbuckle, but it was a certainty he was passed out in an alleyway near Torrey's by this hour. Fire hooks, ladders, and buckets were supposed to be available at all hours in the market house. But I knew the implements had been liberated one or two at a time in recent months by cash-poor farmers in need of tools.

I threw the stables door open and immediately gagged. The acrid smoke inside the unventilated building was already thick. It was hard to breathe and even harder to see. The shrieking of the horses competed with the crackle and spit of the flames. Both sounds were awful.

"Martha?" I shouted. "Martha?"

"Over here, in the loose room."

"You've got to get out. At once."

"Not without the horses."

"Now, Martha!"

"No!"

I propped open the door with a paving stone. Then I took a deep breath and raced toward Martha's voice.

"Go! Get out!" I heard her yelling.

I reached the loose room and through my watering eyes saw the gate open and Martha inside the pen trying to urge the horses out. Six or eight horses snorted and stomped and screamed, milling all around us in a mass of fear and confusion. The heat blasting from the far side of the barn was like a giant smithy's hearth. I saw a flash of a familiar white stripe next to me. Hickory.

"Come, girl," I said, grabbing her mane. I breathed in smoke and gagged again.

Hickory resisted at first, twisting her head away from me. But I kept one fist clenched in her mane while I reached up with the other to her muzzle. "It's all right," I said, with a great deal more calm than I felt. "Come with me."

Hickory swung her head back toward me and I felt her resistance faltering. "Have them follow us," I shouted, choking, in the direction I hoped Martha was in. "And you too. We need to leave."

My eyes all but closed now, trying not to breathe, my hand resting on the back of Hickory's neck, I led her through the loose room gate and toward where the entrance door to the stables should be. I couldn't see. Couldn't hear. And then—somehow—we were through the door and outside in the courtyard.

Bent over double, I tried to cough the smoke out of my lungs and then took several huge gulps of fresh air. I slapped Hickory on the rump and she galloped away across the yard. Turning, I saw a soot-blackened line of horses following Hickory through the door and away from the burning building.

Four . . . five . . . six. Then no more. Martha. Where was Martha?

"Martha!" I screamed.

I took a deep breath and then a step toward the door when I saw the head of another horse emerging from the conflagration. And miraculously, my sister at its flank, her dress torn and singed, her face sooty, a silk glove, no longer white, clutched in front of her mouth and nose. She was falling forward as she burst through the door beside the horse and I leapt and caught her. I dragged her away, shaking with fear and relief.

Panting, we sat on the cobblestones about twenty feet back from the burning barn. My arms were still clutched around her waist.

After a few moments, Martha startled struggling to escape my grasp. "We've got to go back in for the others," she cried, over the roar of the blaze. "The ones tied up to rings on the other side. They've got no chance without us."

I squeezed her tighter and shouted, "No!"

At that same moment, I suddenly became aware Martha and I were not the only two persons in the courtyard. In fact, as my perceptions returned, I saw the stable complex had become a hive of activity.

Several dozen men jostled around us in the courtyard, carrying water toward the fire and moving anything flammable away from it. Looking up, I saw a line of men standing across the roof of the Globe Tavern to the point where it adjoined the stable building. They were passing buckets of varying shapes and sizes from hand to hand, and the men closest to the stable were pouring them out, keeping the roof and walls of the inn wet. As my eyes came into full focus, I perceived that the blaze was concentrated on the side of the stables opposite from the inn. The stable building was sure to be a complete loss, but it seemed possible the tavern itself would escape destruction.

"There you are!" called a voice from above us. Gratefully, I felt a familiar large hand rest on my shoulder.

"We got the horses out of the loose room," Martha called up to Lincoln. "But we need to go back for the work horses. Joshua isn't letting me go."

"He's right not to, Miss Speed," Lincoln said. "But you can rest easy. I've been around back of the stables, looking for you two. A couple other fellows were back there already. They'd untied the work horses and led them through the back door. They're all out, I think."

"What were they doing back there?" I asked. "For that matter, where'd everyone come from?" I gestured around the bustling yard and up toward the roof, where the bucket brigade continued to work with surprising efficiency.

"I wager the search for Jesse saved the Globe, and the horses, too," said Lincoln. "There were so many men already out and about on the streets looking for him. As soon as I ran out to warn Saunders and spread the word, we had dozens of volunteers to fight the fire."

"Has the boy been found yet?"

"I don't think so." Lincoln gave a glance toward the ruined stables.

Saunders bustled up at that moment. His face was ashen. "I warned you to be careful with those lanterns," he said, his voice quaking, more with fright than anger.

"It wasn't us," I exclaimed.

"It wasn't," echoed Lincoln. "The flames broke out in front of us. We hadn't even set foot in the stables when they began to fire."

As Saunders wandered off, mumbling to himself in a daze, Patterson, Jane, and Rebecca all materialized out of the crowd, seemingly from three different directions. Patterson looked at Martha and me, still huddled next to each other on the ground, with a professional gaze. "What happened to the two of you?" he asked.

I explained. Looking over at Rebecca, I saw her face remained troubled. "Any sign of Jesse yet, Widow Harriman?" I asked.

"None."

"Then he's run off somewhere by himself," I said. "With how many men joined in the search"—I gestured around—"if he was lying about somewhere . . . incapacitated . . . he would have been found."

"Perhaps he was in there," said Rebecca, pointing with a trembling hand toward the barn. Most of the flames had been extinguished by now, though one or two ravenous licks of orange still leapt about and great quantities of gray-black smoke poured out of the ruins. Half of the stables' roof was missing.

"I don't think so," I replied. "When Martha and I were in there helping the horses out, we didn't see him, did we?" Martha shook her head. "He'll turn up at daybreak, I'm certain of it."

A gust of wind blew through the courtyard. Out of the corner of my eye, I saw a streak of light, like a shooting star.

"What will Saunders do with the—"

An urgent call cut through Jane's question: "Fire! The carriage shed has caught!"

I scrambled to my feet and looked around. The thatched roof of the shed, some fifty feet distant from the stable building, was smoking violently. If the shed collapsed, it would fall on the two carriages parked in front of it. I saw my father's driver, Genser, in his underclothes moving about frantically next to his carriage. Hickory was lingering nearby. With Lincoln by my side, I raced over to them.

"Let's pull the carriage out of the way at once," I shouted. "Hickory will do. Hitch her up and I'll drive."

Genser nodded and got to work expertly, fastening a harness around Hickory and coaxing her back toward the carriage so he could run its shafts through the loops of the saddle.

Meanwhile, Lincoln set about organizing a new line of water buckets to be passed toward the carriage shed. With his unsurpassed height, he positioned himself at the end of the line, ready to fling the water up onto the roof of the shed.

I climbed the mounting step and jumped into the body of my father's carriage on my way to the driver's box. The worn leather bench held a familiar smell, and at once I was struck by a vivid memory of my younger self sitting on the very same seat as we bounced along the rutted road toward Smith's schoolhouse, bound for an examination in mathematics for which I was ill-prepared as usual. I shook off the memory, hurled back to the present by the urgent task at hand.

Atop the box, I called down to Genser: "Ready when you are."

"What about that one?" he said as he finished setting the shaft. He gestured toward the other carriage near the shed. The roof of the shed continued to smolder, although Lincoln's human chain was working quickly, passing a line of buckets to my friend, who hurled their contents toward the roof one after the other. The fire fought back, crackling and hissing.

"Do you know who its owner is?" I called down. Genser shook his head. It seemed odd in the extreme the other owner hadn't come to check on his grand carriage in the midst of the inferno.

Genser quickly walked around Hickory, making sure all the buckles were sound. He took her by the bridle and, whispering encouragingly into her ear, began leading her away from the shed. The horse strained against the weight of the carriage, usually pulled by two horses, and at first we did not budge. But eventually Hickory found purchase and the wheels began turning slowly. We clattered through the courtyard. For good measure, we drove the carriage completely out of the yard and onto the street, crowded with men and women gawking at the blaze.

I jumped down as Genser began unfastening Hickory from her load.

"Let's move the other one as well," I said.

Returning to the yard, I glanced up nervously at the roof of the carriage shed, which was simultaneously smoking and dripping from all the water that had been flung upon it. Judging I was safe enough, I climbed onto the upholstered driver's seat. The ornate calèche carriage, ruby red with black trim and gold-painted wheels, was of the style the legendary French general Lafayette had made famous during his triumphal tour of all twenty-four states the previous decade. It had no roof but four side panels to keep out the dust and dirt of the trail.

What was taking Genser so long? I turned impatiently and looked over the compartment of the carriage to try to locate our man in the crowded courtyard. Then, sickeningly, I realized what I had just seen. I stood on the driver's seat and looked down into the compartment itself.

A limp figure lay on the carpeted floor of the carriage, hidden from any angle of view but mine. Jesse's face was frozen, his mouth half-open as if he had been trying to say something. His skull had been caved in above his left temple, and blood and gore covered his face and smock. Blades of straw stuck out at grotesque angles from each of the sticky surfaces. A paving stone, glistening a bright, sickly red, lay on the floor not far from his ruined head.

I shouted in horror and looked away, trying to fight a wave of nausea. Eventually my eyes fell on the corpse again. This time I saw that Jesse's little fist was clenched impotently by his side. Clutched between his tiny, rigid fingers was a single ebony domino.

CHAPTER 15

It was said more people attended Jesse's funeral at the Episcopalian Church on Monroe Street than had ever attended any religious gathering in the two-decade history of Springfield. One hundred and fifty people jammed the small, rickety benches of the church, while several hundred more clamored for a view from the churchyard outside. The Rev. Batchelder, sensing the chance to increase his small flock of high church communicants, ordered that the doors and windows of the church remain open during the service such that the persons outside as well could hear his fine words of joy, sorrow, and holy contemplation.

Of course, virtually none of the mourners knew the dead boy or even had laid eyes on him during his brief life. Yet the frantic search for Jesse on the night of his murder had enlisted many in his cause, and others were doubtless drawn by the spectacle of a brother and sister, orphans already, who had been—there was no other conclusion to draw—struck down one after the other by the same murderous hand.

Death was everywhere on the frontier. Every man and woman knew it might make its awful approach at any time and for any reason or for no reason at all. Children were disproportionately its victims. And yet even grown men who had seen more than their share of death were moved by the double tragedy that had befallen this broken family.

Rebecca Harriman sat alone in the front pew of the church during the funeral service. I did not think it my place to join her. She remained motionless during the Rev. Batchelder's fine words. And if she heard any of the many uncharitable remarks about her that the other mourners whispered back and forth, she gave no indication of such.

After the Rev. Batchelder had pronounced his benediction on Jesse's soul, the small casket was loaded onto an open carriage to be driven up to Menard so he could be laid to eternal rest next to his sister. Lincoln, Martha, and I stood together in the town square and watched as the carriage, Jesse's casket and Rebecca its only passengers, drove out of town.

"Has the sheriff questioned the owner of the calèche carriage where Jesse was found?" I asked Lincoln.

"Extensively," said Lincoln. "He claims he's completely innocent, as shocked as the rest of us. No idea how the body got there."

"But does he have any way to prove he wasn't the one who murdered the innocent little boy?" asked Martha. Her eyes were still rimmed with red from all the weeping she'd done since Jesse had been found.

"The sheriff told me the fellow said he went into the public room as soon as he arrived at the Globe that afternoon and he never once left, not even during the fire," Lincoln said. He paused as several of the persons filtering away from the funeral service walked close by us. "Saunders supports the story, at least part of it. Saunders says the fellow was so drunk he couldn't get him to move when all the other guests evacuated. The blasted fellow would have burned down with the tavern if the fire hadn't been put out in time."

"Surely he could have been feigning intoxication," I said. "The whole thing sounds suspicious."

"Sheriff Hutchason asked him to remain in town while he investigates and the man's agreed. If the alibi's actually a lie, I'm sure the sheriff will sniff it out."

"What about the fire?" asked Martha. "Does anyone know how it started?"

"Or why?" I added.

"No one's come forward to confess," said Lincoln. "As you know, there were dozens of men about that night, many of them with torches, all looking for Jesse. There was such chaos and confusion. I imagine someone touched it off by accident, but I doubt Hutchason could possibly recreate who was where and when, not at any point during the evening."

"Maybe it was set by the killer to cover his tracks," I said. "To try to destroy the evidence, the body."

"But if that was the plan," said Martha, "why move the body to the carriage in the first place? Why not keep it in the stables, where the killing took place, and then set the fire?"

None of us had a good answer. But it was true the only thing that appeared certain about the night of the murder was Jesse had been attacked in the stables and not in the coach itself. There seemed no other way to explain the presence of straw about his person.

Lincoln departed for Hoffman's Row. Martha and I walked back to my store alone. The square had cleared, the spectacle of the funeral giving way to another prosaic, sweltering summer's day. For a change, the sun was obscured by a thick layer of cloud.

"How is the widow bearing up?" asked my sister.

"She's distraught," I said. I had spent thirty minutes trying without success to comfort Rebecca on the night we discovered Jesse's body. "All her life she's been childless, to her great sorrow. Then two children come into her home and, just as suddenly, now they're both gone."

Martha sighed and wiped a tear from her eye.

If Rebecca had managed to avoid overhearing the malicious gossip passed about during the funeral service, I had not. More than a few of the would-be mourners were convinced the deaths were explained by the arrogance of the childless widow who, to make matters worse, held herself out as an independent woman of business. Others whispered she could not account for her whereabouts at the time of either murder.

I worried growing suspicion would focus on Rebecca. And I feared even more that the actual killer would turn his murderous intentions to her. It was no longer possible to suppose Lilly had been killed by a frustrated suitor. Some monster, it seemed, was intent on killing the members of this accursed family, of which Rebecca was now the sole survivor. Both to ensure Rebecca's freedom and to safeguard her life, it was imperative that I help Prickett and the sheriff identify the killer.

I was working out a concrete plan to accomplish this as Martha and I took inventory inside the store an hour later. Suddenly there was a scream from outside, followed immediately by the sounds of a terrifying crash. Several men started shouting all at once and a horse began shrieking. I took Martha's arm and rushed through the door.

A tangle of men, beasts, and carriage parts littered the street in front of the store. An injured man was sprawled on the street in a muddy, bloody heap, pinned beneath the tongue of a large open carriage, which lay on its side in ruins. A horse still tethered to the overturned carriage pranced around wildly, while another horse, untethered, ran about the street and village green in wild circles. Meanwhile, a feral hog was trapped under a dislodged carriage wheel and several overturned trunks. The hog was squealing and wriggling fiercely for its freedom. Spectators converged on the fantastical scene from all directions.

My friend Hurst, who ran a dry goods store two doors down from mine, waved me over. "Quickly," he said. "We've got to get him out from underneath the carriage before he's crushed to death."

The trapped man, blood trickling down his face, was crying miserably for help. I turned to Martha and said, "He's going to need a doctor. Run and fetch Patterson." As she hurried off, I joined Hurst and several other men beside the wagon tongue.

"You four lift on the count of 'three' and I'll pull him out," I suggested. With a coordinated heave, they managed to raise the carriage remains up a few inches. I grabbed the injured man under his armpits and dragged him away from the wreck. He screamed as I moved him, and I saw his right leg was bent unnaturally below the knee.

"It's all right, friend," I said, pulling out my kerchief and trying to stem the flow of blood from his brow. "A doctor's on his way." I scrutinized the man's face, but he was a stranger to me. His clothing, though covered now with Springfield's black loam, was well-stitched and fashionable.

Hurst squatted beside us. "What happened?" I asked.

"That hog must have ran out from an alleyway and spooked the horses," said Hurst. "One of them broke free from his tether and in the process threw this fellow out and tipped the carriage over on him."

Now that the horses had been calmed, the infernal squealing of the trapped animal came to the fore. "Will you please quiet that beast," Hurst shouted over his shoulder. A moment later a shot rang out. "Someone will eat well this week," he said.

I nodded. "What's your name, friend," I asked the injured man.

"Frederick . . . Julius . . . Gustorf," he managed through labored breaths. "I . . . come from . . . Westphalia."

"Is that near Peoria?" asked Hurst.

The man started to rise up to answer, but I urged him back to the ground. Turning to Hurst, I said, "It's one of the old Napoleonic Kingdoms, you fool. In Europe. It's now part of Prussia."

I looked again at the man's ruined carriage, strewn about the street. In a jolt, I realized it was the Lafayette-calèche carriage, the very one in which I had found Jesse's body. Far from staying put at the Globe, as he had assured the sheriff, the owner of this grand conveyance had been hurrying out of town immediately after Jesse's funeral.

"Where are you going, friend?" I asked the prone man.

The stranger swallowed and drew in and exhaled a deep breath. "I've been . . . inspecting . . . your country," he said. His English was excellent, with only a hint of the characteristic harsh German accent. "I'm heading . . . to Alton . . . next destination. I have . . . a steamboat . . . to catch."

"It looks like your stay in Springfield has been extended instead," I said, gesturing toward his leg. "Here's the doctor now. He'll put you back together."

Dr. Patterson had arrived, with Martha and Jane close at his heels. Patterson took a quick look at the injured man and announced, "We need to get him to my parlor at once. Speed, organize a litter. I think one of those dislodged running boards from the carriage should serve the purpose." Without waiting for a response, Patterson strode back toward his home, the tails of his surgical coat flying out grandly behind him.

Thirty minutes later, the other fellows and I had managed to convey Herr Gustorf to the Pattersons' front parlor, which doubled as the doctor's surgery. It was a long, narrow room with tall windows looking out onto the street. We lay Gustorf on the couch that ran along one wall. Against the opposite wall stood a wooden bureau splattered with wax drippings. A dozen squat red candles burned brightly on the bureau, even in the mid-day light; this was Patterson's attempt to burn away any disease-causing miasma.

The doctor handed Gustorf a deep purple-colored bottle. "Have a few good swigs of this," he said. "It will help with the pain." Gustorf leaned forward and swallowed several long pulls. Then he lay back gingerly.

"Sew up that cut on his head, Jane," the doctor ordered, "while I have a look at his leg."

"Yes, Father." Jane reached under the couch and pulled out a leathern pouch. She took off her silk gloves, loosened the draw-strings of the pouch, and withdrew several needles and a spindle of silk.

"I didn't know you also include 'surgeon' among your talents, Miss Patterson," said Martha, sneaking a look in my direction.

Jane blushed slightly, though whether at Martha's praise or her attempt to interest me, it was hard to tell. "I assist my father when I can be useful, nothing more," she said in a very serious tone. She examined Gustorf's forehead, where I could see he had a three-inch gash running diagonally above his left eyebrow.

"This will only take a few minutes," Jane said to the foreigner. "Don't pay any attention to what I'm doing. Miss Speed, favor us and hold his head just so, with his hair out of the way like this." My sister took her place beside the prone man.

Meanwhile, Dr. Patterson was cutting the cloth off Gustorf's crippled lower leg. It was plain the bone was shattered, and I knew amputation would prove the only suitable treatment. Patterson began manipulating the leg gently and Gustorf screamed out again in pain.

"Distract him while I attend to the leg, won't you, Speed?" Patterson said from his end of the body. If the doctor still bore a grudge from our after-dinner conversation of the other night, he was showing no sign of it.

I positioned myself so the Prussian could meet my eyes without moving his head, which Martha was now holding in place while Jane threaded her surgical needle. I knew I'd been given the opportunity to question a prime suspect in a time of weakness and I intended to seize it.

"What brought you to Illinois, Herr Gustorf?" I began.

"After the defeat of the Emperor, my father's bank failed," he said, "so I was obliged to seek employment far from home. I found your country very much to my liking." Gustorf's breathing was returning to normal, and his voice, though labored, was deep and clear. He appeared to be about thirty, with attractive features and a strong nose. His whiskers were narrow and well-trimmed.

"I secured positions as a private teacher in German, first at Harvard and then at a school in New Haven," Gustorf continued. "This winter—" He suddenly shouted out a vigorous Teutonic oath.

"I told you to ignore me," Jane said. She had just sewed her first stitch in the Prussian's forehead, and the needle was poised in her hand to make another loop.

"I'll do my best," Gustorf responded, gritting his teeth. "I spent the past winter in Philadelphia and I happened to talk at a gather—*oh!*—gathering with an Englishwoman, a Mrs. Martineau, who is collecting material for a book on your young nation for her . . . *ah!* . . . home country, and of course there's Mrs. Trollope's towering success, and Monsieur de Tocqueville's new book about America has sold very well throughout Europe . . . *ahhh!* . . . and I concluded perhaps I could write about my own travels, for the German readership. So, after the final snows melted, I set off to the West, first by rail and then steamer down the Ohio and up the Illinois."

"Where have you been in our state, before reaching Springfield?" I asked. "I want to make sure you haven't missed any place of note for your book."

Jane was sewing another stitch at that moment, so the Prussian took several deep breaths before continuing.

"I started up north in Galena, to see your iron mines. It was there I obtained my carriage and steeds. From Galena—*oh!*—I've driven due south, more or less, some twenty or thirty miles a day, stopping where I find places of interest."

"Did you happen to see a settlement named Menard?" I said casually. My sister lifted her eyes to stare at me, but I ignored her look. "There's a most interesting, er, blacksmith there. Very unusual method of heating the furnace."

"I think I may have done," Gustorf said. "About a day's carriage drive north? I passed through it, I'm sure, now that you mention. Charming outpost. Though I confess I missed the smithy if that was the principal attraction of interest." My heart started beating fast. So he had also been at the site of the first murder.

Gustorf gritted his teeth expectantly and looked up at Jane and Martha. "How many more?" he asked.

"We've been done for a few minutes now," said Jane.

Gustorf relaxed from his clenched pose. "Your touch is agreeably light, *Fräulein*," he said. "Yours as well," he added with a nod and a particularly winning smile toward Martha. My sister blushed. The color was returning to Gustorf's face, a development, I noted without pleasure, that made him look even more manly.

"How are you coming with that leg, Doctor?" I called out. "You'll be wanting to sharpen your saw, I suspect. Shall I keep him talking while you do?"

The doctor shook his head. "I have something else in mind," he said. "Drink the rest of this bottle, won't you, Herr Gustorf," he added, handing the purple bottle back to the prone man. Gustorf sat up partway and swallowed the remaining liquor in several long swigs, which he followed with a loud belch.

"You'll have to stay for a spell, Herr Gustorf," Dr. Patterson said. "I promise we'll take good care of you."

"I shall be delighted," he replied, casting a warm smile toward Martha and Jane. As I looked on, I could not figure out what to make of the mysterious foreigner. His behaviors were simultaneously suspicious and as uncomplicated as a child's.

"You'll be feeling the full effects of my medicinal liquor shortly," Patterson said, nodding. "There's a new treatment for fractured limbs I've been wanting to try out, and your case presents an excellent opportunity. Those inscrutable Turks have finally shared something of use with the rest of the world."

The doctor called out for the hired girl, and when she materialized, he started giving her a complex series of instructions. He seemed to be directing her to soak cotton bandages in "Plaster of Paris," though how this would facilitate the amputation of the Prussian's shattered leg I could not fathom.

I turned back to Gustorf and saw his eyelids fluttering rapidly. "The day you arrived in Springfield," I said, talking loudly in order to try to hold his attention. "Where did you dine that evening? Did you happen to venture to a place called Torrey's?"

"There's no need to keep distracting him, Speed," the doctor said. "He's almost out." And, indeed, Gustorf's eyes fluttered shut for a final time. "He won't wake up until morning at this point, not with the whole bottle in his belly."

Patterson called out to the hired girl again and interrogated her about the state of the cotton bandages. Then he turned back to me and said, "It'll be two hours until she's got them all ready for me. That'll give Herr Gustorf time to find his deepest ebb of sleep. Your mention of Torrey's has me thirsty. Join me there for some refreshment."

I started to protest that I needed to return to my store, but Patterson grabbed my arm with a surprisingly powerful grip and leaned in close. His breath smelled like sour onions. "It wasn't a question, Speed," he hissed. "Let's go."

CHAPTER 16

Even though the sun hadn't yet set, Torrey Temperance Hotel was oozing with ne'er-do-wells when I heaved open the door and let Patterson enter before me. Together we pushed through the crowd in the public room, a low rumble of discontent, toward the bar, where the moon-faced Torrey presided in a filthy apron and a permanent scowl. Torrey greeted Patterson with a familiar nod, while the innkeeper and I glared at each other warily. Early in my tenure at A. Y. Ellis & Co., he'd passed me a private note that proved uncollectable; since then I'd typically stayed clear of his establishment and he of mine.

An open barrel of busthead whiskey sat on the bar. A tray of chipped glasses rested to the side and a large wooden dipper hung from a nail in the wall. I thrust the dipper into the barrel and filled up a glass for the doctor and one for me.

"I've no cause to mince words, Speed," Patterson said once we'd squeezed next to each other on one of the tightly packed benches that lined either side of the room. "Have you an interest in my daughter?"

My hesitation evidently told Patterson everything he needed to know. "I figured as much," he said, nodding, before I could formulate a response. He swallowed half of his glass at a gulp.

"I'm not yet in a position to support a wife," I said. "Someday I hope to buy my cousin Bell out of his share of the store, but I can't yet, and if the Panic hits us with full force, as some are suggesting, it may be some time still. Until I can stand firmly on my own feet, I'm not in a position to support another, certainly not another as virtuous and worthy as your daughter."

The doctor grunted and drained the rest of his glass. He gestured at me to do the same and said, "Your caution is a credit to your name, I'm sure. I don't bear you ill."

I expelled my breath and took a tentative sip. Torrey's mash was actually better than I recalled. I finished the glass and did not object when Patterson offered to refill it.

"How old is your daughter, may I ask?" I said when Patterson had returned with fresh glasses and a pair of soggy bread rolls Torrey had fished out of the pockets of his apron.

"Seventeen."

"There's plenty of time then. She'll have her pick of suitors before long."

"I hope you prove right," Patterson returned. He swallowed half his new glass in a long gulp. "I'd been hoping—well, to settle matters for her sooner rather than later."

I wondered what the doctor's hurry was. My sister Martha was the same age, and I knew our father would not worry about finding a good match for several more years, at the least.

"I wager they're already lining up for her and merely trying to hide it from you," I said. "No doubt they're scared of you, being an eminent man of medicine."

He grunted and gnawed on a roll.

Now that I had evidently avoided the doctor's wrath, my thoughts returned to his newest patient. "How long will Herr Gustorf be laid up in your surgery?" I asked.

"Two weeks? A month?" Patterson ran his fingers over his neat moustache. "I don't have the first idea, to be honest. The Turks told us how to perform the operation, but they haven't bothered to write down what comes next. I shall be most interested to learn for myself how the whole thing proceeds."

"That'll give the sheriff plenty of time to investigate Jesse's death more fully," I said. "Don't you think it dubious Gustorf was fleeing Springfield right after the funeral for the boy whose body was found in his carriage?"

Patterson looked at me with interest. He seemed to have forgotten about his daughter's plight. "I find it *most* suspicious," he said. "It was such a tragedy, the boy struck down just as his life was so full of new promise."

"I know you'd attended him that very afternoon," I said. "Had you known him before—"

Suddenly there was a tapping on my shoulder and a gruff voice said, "Move aside, young man."

An older man with a bulbous nose and a tall plumed hat was two feet away, trying get past me to reach Patterson. It took me a moment to place him without the full military regalia, but I realized it was Major Richmond, the doctor's adversary in the land suit. At the same moment I came to this realization, the doctor muttered loud enough for the men surrounding us to hear, "The Devil himself."

"I need my money, Patterson," Richmond said, his face red and angry. "The money you owe me for the land." His lips kept moving, but no further words issued.

"Have you ever been treated by a psychiater, Richmond?" Patterson returned. He rose and faced the major. "You don't need money. You need help—with your head." He pointed with a forefinger to his own temple.

Richmond's lips moved in silent rebuke. Then he pulled from his pocket a clasp knife. In turn, Patterson drew a surgical knife out of one of the pockets of his heavy coat.

I leapt to my feet. In the crowded tavern, I found myself wedged precariously between the two adversaries. Richmond had the advantage of three inches and fifty pounds or more, but Dr. Patterson had the advantage of somewhat less advanced age. It might be a fair fight if it came to that, I thought. Looking around, it seemed none of Torrey's other customers were paying us any notice; incipient brawls, even between elderly combatants, were about as noteworthy here as men drunk as lords.

"I wondered when you'd show your stinkin' face again after the judge put you in your place, you scoundrel," Richmond sneered.

"You know where to find me at all hours," Patterson shot back.

"That's right, your grand manse," Richmond returned. He grumbled to himself insensibly and spat near Patterson's boots before adding, "The house that desecrates Sarah's memory."

"How dare you!" Patterson shouted. He raised his knife and took a step toward Richmond, although I pushed him back, out of self-preservation more than anything else.

"Who was Sarah?" I asked.

"My sister," Richmond said, "whom he sent to an early grave."

That explained the animosity between the two men. Patterson had cared for Richmond's sister but had been unable to save her life. Still trying to quell the confrontation, I said to Richmond, "The medical arts are never certain, are they, friend?"

"She wasn't a patient," said Richmond. "She was his wife. Disappeared without so much as a trace four years ago. Met her Good Lord at his evil hands, I haven't a doubt." He waved around his own knife not far from my face, though he made no effort to advance on Patterson.

"Jane's mother?" I said, turning to Patterson in surprise. Patterson had said at dinner Jane's mother died shortly after her birth.

"Her stepmother," said Patterson. "My second wife. Vanished one morning. Richmond here and I searched side by side for her for days, to no avail."

"We didn't find her because she wasn't there to be found," Richmond said. "You hid her body somewhere. My greatest regret in life is I never figured out where."

"You have no proof," Patterson replied, his face as red as a beet.

At that moment, Torrey bustled up. "Are you causing trouble, Speed?" he sputtered. "This is a respectable establishment. There's no drawn knives allowed."

"Trying to defuse it," I said. Looking at Patterson and Richmond I added, "No matter who's right, the both of you are reckless for arguing like this in public. Remember what Judge Thomas said about keeping apart from one another."

"The judge's writ doesn't run to Torrey's," Patterson replied with a growl.

"Yes it does," said Torrey. He surveyed his wretched domain through narrowed eyes. "He's right over there." Torrey pointed to the far corner of the room.

"Oh, Your Honor," he called shrilly.

A man who had been seated with his back to us and a cap pulled low over his head turned and stared. Through the haze of the tavern, I could make out the wide-set, florid face and telltale sneer. The judge squinted and shook his cigar hand, although I guessed he was in no condition to recognize the litigants, to say nothing of halting their altercation. Nonetheless, Richmond and Patterson sheathed their weapons and took a step back from each other.

"That's more like it," Torrey said. "Now let me bring you both a fresh glass and you can drink to old times together."

CHAPTER 17

Lincoln was already seated at the Globe's common table the next morning, a half-eaten plate of breakfast in front of him, when Martha and I entered the tavern. An odor of stale smoke lingered about the place.

"I'll wager you a month's rent," I said by way of greeting as we slid in across from him, "you don't know the source of the animosity between your client Patterson and that old veteran Richmond."

"You mean other than their being former brothers-in-law who had the great misjudgment to think they could engage in land speculation with one another?" he said. When he saw my disappointed expression he added, "I was just wondering where next month's payment was coming from. I've solved a major problem before finishing breakfast. You've made my day already, Speed."

I recounted for Lincoln and Martha the confrontation between the two men from the previous night. "It does explain the depth of hard feelings, I suppose." I paused. "You're not actually going to insist on payment, are you? It's poor sport to accept a bet with superior knowledge."

"It's precisely what you yourself were attempting," Lincoln said with a grin. "If only you'd displayed your sister's curiosity about my docket from the outset, you could judge better where to lay down your wagers."

He turned to my sister. "Has Speed shown you around town, Miss Speed? I'm afraid there's nothing in our little frontier village that compares with the finery and grandeur of Louisville."

"Oh, no, you're wrong," Martha replied earnestly. "I've discovered so many interesting things already. Did you know the iron nutgall ink sold at McHendry's on the other side of the square is especially useful for writing long letters? It dries in less than a minute when held over the candle flame."

"I had no idea," said Lincoln, his eyes twinkling.

I told Lincoln about Gustorf's attempt to flee Springfield and the long period of recovery the doctor said would follow his accident. "So the sheriff will have plenty of time to question him. I'd think he's the most likely suspect, especially if we can establish he'd encountered Lilly as well."

"We?" said Lincoln, his eyebrows raised. "I thought you said you weren't after the sheriff's job."

"Of course I'm not. But that doesn't mean I can't be of help to him and Prickett in finding the blackguard. I was with the little fellow Jesse on the day he was killed. In fact, I was probably one of the last men on earth to speak to him. Are you going to tell me I don't have a stake in finding his killer?" And I need to do it, most of all, for Rebecca's sake, I added silently to myself.

"Gustorf might be a potential suspect," Lincoln said. "So could a number of other men, I imagine. But first you need a theory of the case."

"Meaning what?"

"Two young people whom no one in Sangamon County had heard of up until a few months ago have been murdered in close succession. One in Springfield, one in Menard. One by a blow from a paving stone, one by a knife. Why? Why would somebody have wanted to kill two orphans, and penniless ones at that? Before you—or the sheriff and Prickett, for that matter—can start to answer the *who*, you need a good hypothesis as to the *why*."

"Have you any guess at the *why*?" I asked.

Lincoln chewed and shook his head.

"Maybe there is no *why*," said Martha.

"What are you saying?"

"Maybe there's a madman on the loose. No sane, rational person could possibly want to murder two innocent souls." She turned to Lincoln and said, "Madmen are often confined in the poorhouse here, isn't that right? We know Lilly and Jesse were lodged inside one for several years. Perhaps they encountered some raver there and now he's gotten away and come after them."

"That's brilliant," I said.

"It's certainly worth investigating," agreed Lincoln. "How is it, Miss Speed, you've become an expert on poorhouses in addition to nutgall ink?"

Martha blushed.

"Patterson mentioned them to us at dinner the other night," I said.

"Were you talking about his legal action?" asked Lincoln. I nodded. "Figures. The good doctor's been fixated on the issue from the start, this idea that the major's insane. He thinks it's the key to prevailing."

"Isn't it?" I asked. "If Major Richmond's mad, surely he can't get an order from the judge enforcing their agreement."

"If the court adjudges him insane or a lunatic, you're correct."

"But what makes someone insane?" asked Martha.

"It's a person who's deranged, who doesn't speak or act with any sense," I said. "I'm not at all sure it applies to Richmond, though Patterson certainly thinks so."

"I've known lots of men, and women too, who don't make any rational sense when you talk to them," Martha persisted. "Not to me, anyway." She turned toward Lincoln. "Does that make them insane? It could be nearly the whole population of the country, more or less, depending on how you look at it."

Lincoln laughed. A bell sounded in the distance. "I'm going to be late again," he muttered. He took a final bite of sausage and stood up as he chewed, straightening his frockcoat and then reaching to the floor for his stovepipe hat.

Lincoln had taken two steps away from the table when he looked over his shoulder at Martha. "I'm not ignoring your question, Miss Speed, about what makes someone insane in the eyes of the law. It's a good one. I'll see if I can give you a satisfactory answer the next time we're together."

After Lincoln had departed, Saunders put plates of food in front of us and we began to eat in silence. I found my thoughts fixated on Rebecca. I saw again in my mind's eye her weary, heartbroken face as she drove out of town after Jesse's funeral with the boy's small coffin at her side.

"How do people end up in the poorhouse?" asked Martha suddenly. "I don't mean the insane but normal people, like Lilly and Jesse. How do they end up there?"

"The county decided it was spending too much supporting paupers," I said. "It figured it would be cheaper to house all of them together. The idea is they can contribute to their own maintenance by being hired out or working in the fields. There's a master who has the contract to operate the place. He gets to sell for his own account the crops the residents produce, so the county doesn't even have to provide him much in the way of a salary. It works out well for everyone."

"Except the wretched families who are confined inside," Martha cried. She paused, then asked, "Can we visit one?"

"I was thinking the same thing," I said. "Your idea that a madman might be the villain is a good one. I need to mind the counter today, but I'll ride out tomorrow morning. The nearest one, the one where Lilly and Jesse lived, is near Decatur. That's several hours ride to the east."

"I'm coming with you," said Martha. "I cannot bear to contemplate what happened to those children, to imagine their final moments, their fear . . ."

"I'm not sure a poorhouse is a proper place for a young lady like yourself."

My sister punched me in the shoulder, hard enough to sting. "I'm coming too," she insisted. "That phrase, 'not proper for a young lady,' that's an excuse men use when they don't want women to know something important."

I couldn't help but laugh. Looking at Martha's face, creased with determination, I knew further argument was futile. So I detoured by van Hoff's carriage yard—the Globe stables were closed until further notice, and van Hoff had agreed to stable the displaced horses in the meantime—and asked one of the boys there to ready a two-seater for our journey.

The next morning, once Hickory's hitch was set and Martha and I were seated beside each other on the padded cushion of the chaise, we set off. Martha held two bulging saddlebags on her lap. When I asked about their contents, she merely shrugged.

It was an arid August day, and the summer sun beat down in ferocious glory. Even with the heat, there was a great deal of flourishing about in fine hats on the hard-packed streets surrounding the courthouse square. We weaved through an assortment of carriages and buggies and pedestrians out for a stroll. Harvesttime would be here soon enough, at which point man, woman, and beast alike would be consigned to labor in the fields.

"Do you know what I like about Springfield?" Martha asked as I cursed loudly and swerved to avoid a rider who had dismounted his horse suddenly in the middle of the road. "Other than being with you, of course. It's that people take me seriously here."

"People take you seriously at Farmington," I protested. "I know James does. Father, too, most of the time."

Martha shook her head fiercely. "It's not the same," she said. "Both of them still treat me like a child—an intelligent child, maybe, but a child nonetheless. I had to practically beg Father to get him to send me back to school for one more year last fall. And this year, it's out of the question. I'm supposed to sit around and do needlework and go to cotillions and wait for some dim-witted boy with pimples all over his face to ask me to walk with him. It's positively *horrid*."

"I think you're exaggerating," I said. "It's a pretty position to be an eligible young woman, and an attractive one from a wealthy family at that, in Louisville society."

Martha gave me a searching stare. At length she said, "Joshua, you have no idea."

We bounced along the hard-packed path. Even though we were on the principal east–west carriage route through the prairie, the rude road was pockmarked by deep, rocky holes we had to steer around to avoid getting swallowed up.

After we'd been driving for about two hours, we encountered a long train of wagons and horses heading in the opposite direction. I pulled Hickory into the tall grasses to let them pass and the lead rider, a sunburnt man astride an underfed chestnut horse, nodded a greeting.

"Morning," I called. "Where you folks heading?"

"St. Louis," he said. "We're on the move from Kentucky. We've heard there's plenty of first-rate land there. And heaps of money for the taking."

After I'd wished him well, he added, "Be careful on your way. There's a huge slough in the road a few miles ahead of you. Three of our carts got stuck. Took us all night to drag 'em free from the muck."

I thanked the man, and Martha and I watched as the long train rumbled by. We counted seven wagons in total, each pulled by a massive, slovenly ox. The wagons had originally been Conestogas, but the canvas coverings had been reduced to shreds hanging limply from the sidewalls, and the red running gear had been stained rust-brown by the dust.

The first three wagons held an assortment of women and children, looking dirty and tired and almost out of hope. Two wagons behind them were piled high with household belongings, with trunks and furniture jumbled about. And then there were two wagons packed with dark-skinned slaves, seventeen in all, I counted, who looked out on the passing landscape with expressionless eyes. Several men on horseback rode back and forth along the train, keeping the slow-moving oxen apace.

"It's sad," Martha murmured as the travelers passed. "Who'd have thought people would flee Kentucky in search for a better life?"

"People go where the opportunities are, or at least where they think they are. West, more often than not. Worked for me. Maybe they'll have similar fortune."

"I'm not too sure," Martha said as I pulled back onto the road. We soon came upon the slough, crisscrossed with the muddy tracks of cart wheels and desperate hooves, and I carefully steered a wide berth around it through the grasses. A little while later, the farms surrounding Decatur began to come into view.

"There's the poorhouse now," I said, pointing to a two-story house shaped like an *L* that was situated in a shallow valley a few hundred yards below central Decatur. There was a large church with a white steeple located directly uphill from the house. A middle-aged man wearing a straw hat and with a corncob pipe protruding from his mouth was standing on the steps of the poorhouse. As we pulled up at the front gate, he came striding toward us.

"I expect that's the master," I said. "Keep your opinions to yourself, if you please."

"Joshua—"

"I mean it. If you have something to say—and I imagine you'll have lots—save it for the ride home. I promise I'll listen the whole way back if you like."

When the master was five paces from our chaise, I straightened my traveling coat and called out importantly, "I'm looking for the man who owes me money."

"Ain't we all?" he returned, breaking into a jagged, discolored smile.

"Watch your impertinence, sir," I thundered. "I'm out collecting my accounts, and I was told one of my debtors was lately in your care. I demand to see him at once."

"What's his name?"

"Don't know his name. I know him by his lousy, no-good expression. I'll have a look around to see if I can find him." I started to dismount from the chaise.

"And what makes you think," asked the master, "I'm going to let you walk right into my house?" He had taken up position in front of the gate, his arms folded across his chest, his teeth gripping his pipe defiantly.

"We both know it's not your house," I said, nodding at the dwelling. "That's county property. And I'll enter it if I please." I reached up and helped Martha down from the carriage and led her toward the house.

"Who's the lass?" the man sneered as he reluctantly moved aside to let us pass. "Brought your wench out collecting with you?"

It was his misfortune he said this as I was directly abreast of him, and I slammed the back of my hand into his jaw. The man cried out in pain as he fell to the ground, the corncob pipe flying from his mouth.

"Say anything like that again," I said, "and they'll be your last words." Without giving the man another look, I took Martha's arm and proceeded up the walk. I could feel her trembling beside me.

The inside of the house was foul. The walls of the narrow, dim hallway were streaked with grime, and trash lined the passageway. The smell of decay and human suffering was nearly overpowering.

A series of doors led from the long hall, and I walked up to a few, knocking quickly and pushing them open without waiting for a response. The rooms were dark inside, and several sets of anxious eyes peered back at me in each one.

"Joshua," my sister whispered urgently from beside me, "these are people's *homes* we're invading. We've got to allow them some decency."

"In a moment," I said, glancing over my shoulder. "I need to complete the effect first."

The poorhouse master had been following us at a wary distance, as I figured he would. If there was, in fact, any man under his roof who possessed the funds to pay off a debt to me, the master certainly wanted to know so he could extract his own measure of satisfaction.

I pushed open two or three more doors, seeming to get more impatient by the moment. Then I turned and pretended to spot the master for the first time since we had entered the house. I took a menacing step toward him and he took two steps back.

"You there," I shouted. "What did you say your name was?"

"Hathaway."

"I can't find my man, Hathaway."

"Can't say I'm at all surprised," he returned. "There's not a soul with a dime to his name under my care."

"I've heard it said this man I'm looking for has gone stark, staring mad. A candidate for Bedlam, even. All since I advanced him credit, of course. Now where in this cesspool of yours would such a man reside?"

Hathaway cackled. "You should have said so at the outset," he said. "Though you'll sooner get blood from a stone than shake any money loose from my lunatic.

"You want the *man-cage*. Follow me."

CHAPTER 18

Hathaway slid past us in the dank hallway—taking pains to stay as far away from my right hand as possible—and led the way through a closed door and down a narrow flight of stairs. At the bottom of these rested a long room that was apparently some type of infirmary. There were a half-dozen persons lying on the floor, partially covered by threadbare blankets. Each seemed to be suffering from some malady—fever, consumption, broken limbs—and some from more than one. All of them called out to Hathaway when he entered, but he ignored their piteous cries and led us toward a door at the far end of this room.

"You go ahead, Joshua," Martha murmured from behind me. "I'll rejoin you later."

I hesitated, about to argue with her, but Hathaway was plunging ahead and I didn't want to lose him in the labyrinthine building. Hathaway used a key from his pocket to open the door at the end of the infirmary and he and I entered a small, windowless room. Slivers of light filtered in through cracks in the wallboards. A faint trace of fresh air in this room suggested we were in an attached outbuilding.

The master lit a candle. There seemed no exit from the room other than the door we'd entered by. But Hathaway dropped to his knees and pulled on a lever hidden in the floor. He swung a panel open, revealing a pit. The top of a ladder was the only thing visible.

"Lost your nerve yet?" he asked, cackling.

"Lead the way."

As I followed him down the ladder, I was hit by a strong stench of human waste. I held my breath. We were in some sort of dirt cellar. The ceiling was only six feet high at its highest and sloped severely on each side. Hathaway's candle provided the only illumination, and it took a few moments for my eyes to adjust. When they did, I saw a tiny cell had been constructed on one side of the pit, where the inclined ceiling meant there were only a few feet between floor and ceiling. Strong perpendicular bars enclosed a space some five feet by three feet. At first I thought the cage was empty, filled only by a few discarded rags. But then the rags moved, and a filthy, heavily bearded head with bloodshot yellow eyes turned and stared, blinking rapidly.

I gasped.

The poorhouse master cackled again. "Is that your man?" he asked.

I knelt beside the man-cage, which stank of a vile mixture of sweat and urine and waste. My eyes had adjusted to the dim lighting by now and I could make out the creature lying inside. He was naked, save for a soiled cloth secured around his midsection, and on the point of emaciation, with his ribs protruding visibly from his chest. When he saw me staring, he dragged himself into a half-sitting position, which is all he could manage within the tiny confines of his cage. The man pulled back his lips and bared his teeth, like a wild animal threatening a predator.

"What happened to his feet?" I asked in horror. I had just seen that the man's legs ended in shapeless stumps.

"Froze off last winter," said Hathaway. "He was under his sister's care, and I gather he managed to unlock his room and wander off. It took 'em three days to find him, lost in the woods and curled around a tree trunk for the warmth. His feet had shriveled away.

"The sister told me that's when she decided she couldn't care for him any longer. So she dumped him on my doorstep on the basis that he was a pauper, and I had no choice but to house him. He's a complete loss for me—no way I can get any work out of him in the fields."

"Has he been locked away down here the whole time he's been in your charge?" I asked.

"Just about. Once a week, I get my two strongest men to pull him out of there and bind him with ropes while one of the women changes his cloth and cleans the filth out of his cage. Then he's thrown back inside."

I straightened up, taking care to avoid hitting my head on the low ceiling and feeling queasy. "That's not my debtor," I said.

"Didn't think so," said Hathaway. "You don't owe this man money, do you, Fanning?" he continued loudly. Instead of looking at the Idiot he was staring a foot above his head, as if there was some phantasmagoria in the air above him.

"Can he understand you?" I asked.

"You can't communicate with the furiously insane directly," he said. "But sometimes they've got these invisible vapors floating over their heads that can receive messages."

I looked above the Idiot's head and said, doubtfully, "How do you do, Fanning?"

Fanning grabbed the bars of his cage with filthy, gnarled hands and bared his teeth again.

"You said he's been here for several months," I said. "Have you had other madmen here in the last three years or so?"

Hathaway faced me squarely. "What, do they all owe you money?" he sneered. "What's the real reason you've barged in?"

"Let's go up and talk," I said. As we climbed the ladder, leaving Fanning to his cage, I decided I had no choice but to reveal my interest directly. Once I reached the room above, I took several deep breaths, trying to expel the fetid air of the pit from my lungs.

"You had a brother and sister residing in your house until a few months ago named Lilly and Jesse Walker. What can you tell me about them?"

A quick look of surprise flashed through Hathaway's eyes, where it was replaced immediately by one of calculation. "Perhaps I did, perhaps I didn't," he said.

I felt out two silver half-dollars from my pocket and dropped them into his waiting palm, trying my best to avoid making contact with his skin.

"They were here," he said. "Insufferable, both of them. Trouble-makers. The girl most especially. Then it turned out they had some rich relation all along, and one day she shows up and pays off their debts. Good riddance, I said."

"They've both been murdered in the last month."

Hathaway looked taken aback but only for an instant. Then he said: "I've got enough of my own problems. Twenty-five paupers to feed and house, and the state allots me almost nothing for all my efforts. You can't expect me to give two bits about what happens to people once they leave my charge."

"Can you think of anyone they might have come into contact with here who bore them ill?"

"Are you accusing me?" Hathaway said, clenching his fists, although he still took care to remain out of range of my right hand. "Just because you wear a fancy coat don't give you the right to come into my house and spout libel against me."

"I'm hoping to identify the scoundrel who's done mortal harm to two innocent persons," I said, struggling to control my distaste for the man. "I would have thought you'd share that interest. Another madman you housed, perhaps, or someone who quarreled with them during their residency."

"I haven't the first idea," he said. "We haven't had another madman in Fanning's man-cage in years. As for the men who live upstairs, each of them is unbalanced, one way or the other. If they could govern their own affairs, they wouldn't have ended up here."

He paused, then added: "Can't say I'm surprised in the least that wench Lilly met her fate."

"Why do you say that?"

"She could be a hellcat. Made trouble with a few of the married men. Not that she ever did what *I* asked of her, mind you."

"That makes her an even braver and more sensible girl than I'd realized."

"Get out!" he shouted.

"Gladly." I went through the door to the infirmary where I found Martha kneeling and in earnest conversation with a young woman who was lying on the floor, wrapped in a thin shawl. I took my sister by the arm. As we hurried from the room, I had the vague impression of brightly colored clothing and blankets that hadn't been present earlier. Both of us breathed deeply when we finally burst through the front door, grateful to be out of the squalid house at last.

"I'm afraid we didn't learn much of use," I said after we were both seated on our chaise and I prodded Hickory to head back toward Springfield. I relayed what Hathaway had told me.

"Maybe you didn't," Martha returned, a pleased smile on her face, "but I discovered a great deal."

"You? What could you have learned?"

"There's more than one way to gather information, Joshua. It doesn't have to be all battery or bribery. Sometimes kindness goes a long way."

"I suppose."

"There was a girl in the sickroom about my own age. Her name's Abigail. I had a long, interesting talk with her. She came down with fever and ague in the spring, and even though she's all better now, the master won't let her back into her family's apartment upstairs. Abigail told me she knew Lilly and Jesse well. She and Lilly were the only two young women who resided in the house, so naturally they became friends. She was devastated when I told her both of them were gone."

"I don't doubt it," I said. "Did she have anything useful to say that might help us figure out who killed them, or at least why?"

"Abigail said Lilly was very bitter about the circumstances that had landed them in the poorhouse. Apparently their father farmed land belonging to a speculator who lived next door to them. A few years ago, the speculator moved and sold the land and the new owner ejected them. Their father couldn't find a new situation. They'd always managed to scrape by in the past, but when they lost their farm, they had nothing to eat, nowhere to live. That's what led them to the poorhouse."

"What was the name of the speculator?"

"I asked Abigail and she didn't know. Would there be ownership records somewhere?"

"There might be in one of the land offices. The Edwardsville one is probably the one with jurisdiction. That's a long way south, near St. Louis. Or maybe the one in Vandalia would have them. The land offices sprung up patchwork with the land boom, so it's often hard to figure out which has jurisdiction where." I steered the chaise around a particularly large hole in the road. "Did Abigail tell you anything else?"

"Only that that repulsive man, the master, doesn't keep his hands to himself." Martha made a face.

"I gathered as much," I said. "From the sound of it, though, Lilly was able to defend herself."

"Abigail said she was a fighter, every day of her life."

"Which raises the question, again," I said. "Why didn't she fight on her last one?"

Martha was fidgeting with the canvas saddlebags in her lap, and I suddenly realized they were empty. I thought back to the scene in the sickroom as we'd left the poorhouse. "What was in those when we set off this morning?" I asked.

"Smocks, shirts, underclothes. A few blankets. I'd chosen pretty well. I think Abigail and her family and the other families there will make excellent use of them."

"But where had you gotten all those goods?" I asked.

"From your shelves, of course."

"Martha!"

"What? Don't tell me you're opposed to doing charity for your fellow man and woman. Besides, you yourself told me the other day your goods weren't moving as quickly as before with the economic situation. Well, I moved some goods for you."

"But I want to move the goods *and* get paid for them."

She shrugged as if to say that was my concern, not hers.

A little later she exclaimed, "Look how dark it is."

I cast my eyes skyward and saw she was right. A giant dark purple thunderhead rose in the western skies in front of us like a coiled sea monster. I realized the sun had been obscured for the entire trip homeward. After the dim confines of the poorhouse, the cloud cover had not registered. But now the air around us was getting perceptibly heavier and darker by the moment.

"Where do we shelter, in case there's a thunderstorm?" my sister asked, trying hard to keep any worry out of her voice.

Together we surveyed the rolling prairie. The tall grasses waved as a sudden gust blew through from our faces. Hickory whinnied. As far as the eye could see in any direction, there were no signs of human habitation. Indeed, there was not a single tree nor a bush taller than a man's shoulder anywhere within five miles of us.

"There's not going to be a thunderstorm," I said. "It was dark the other afternoon as well and no rain fell. We've been in a drought all summer."

I looked skyward again. A giant drop of rain landed in my eye.

CHAPTER 19

Three fierce thunderbolts arced out of the thunderhead in front of us in quick succession. The first two shot to earth, setting off explosions that reverberated along the darkened prairie. The third seemed to come into contact with a dense cloud, for it smashed into a number of smaller streams, the electric fluid scattering to the ground like dew racing down a spider's web.

Enormous drops of warm rainwater pelted down. The sound of the rain hitting the prairie grasses filled our ears, a constant high-pitched hiss accompanied now and then by deeper expectorations of rolling thunder.

My traveling cloak was soaked through. Martha's long locks were plastered to her cheeks and the back of her neck. A violent wind whipped in our faces. Water streamed off Hickory's coat and down her tail.

"We've no choice but to push ahead," I yelled into Martha's ear. "Perhaps there'll be a farmhouse. I think I remember one from our outward journey."

"Should we lie down in the grasses to avoid the lightning?" Martha shouted back.

"I don't think so. It usually strikes in the woods." My words were punctuated by another lightning strike, closer this time, and accompanied by an urgent growl of thunder.

Hickory put down her head and willingly struggled onward. But the hard-packed path we'd been traversing only minutes earlier was quickly turning liquid. As we went up a gradual rise, rivulets of water coursed down the hill against us. For a moment, the wheels of our carriage seemed to become waterborne, floating away from Hickory until she regained her footing and continued her trudge.

"Hold on to me tight," I shouted to Martha as another blast of wind hurled past.

Hickory came to a halt. It was all she could do to maintain her position against the whipping wind and drenching rain. Martha and I embraced each other, the warmth of her skin providing some comfort against the heartless elements. I began to fear the tempest might outlast us.

And then, just as quickly as the storm had come on, it was over. Concentric circles of yellow and orange appeared on the horizon. Pockets of sunlight, unnaturally bright against the dark clouds, emerged and began muscling the thunderheads out of the way. The rain sputtered and stopped, its constant monotone drumming replaced on the suddenly still prairie by the rhythmic chirping of crickets and the exuberant singing of wrens and vireos and yellow-breasted chats. It was as if the angel of desolation, having amply proven his power and awe-inspiring fury, had abruptly decided to do his terrible bidding elsewhere.

"Are you hurt?" I asked Martha, trying to wipe the water from my eyes so I could see properly again.

"Nothing a warm bath can't heal."

"You may have to wait for that," I said with a laugh. "But let's see if we can't find a farmhouse hearth to warm up by. The Buffalo Heart settlement can't be too far distant."

An hour later, Martha and I sat in borrowed gowns beside a roaring fire while our clothes dried nearby on a rack. Upon reaching Buffalo Heart, nestled on the southern tier of the crescent-shaped Lake Buffalo, I'd made for the cabin of a merchant I knew from the circuit. We were in luck; not only was

Peters, a lively little man with apple cheeks and a cherubic smile, home when we called, but his wife had just placed a large pot of chicken broth into the fire. Peters' liberal hospitality even extended to uncorking a bottle of sparkling catawba wine from Cincinnati. In recognition of Martha's good cheer during the storm, I let Peters pour her half a glass.

As I settled back into my chair, Peters asked what we had been doing caught out in the middle of the prairie.

"Returning to Springfield from Decatur," I said.

"Decatur? I would have thought Knotts has that market pretty well covered."

"He does. We weren't traveling for commercial purposes."

"On a weekday? Do you mean to tell me, Speed, your sales are so firm you can afford to become a man of leisure?"

"Joshua was showing me around the county," Martha said brightly, before I could think of a lie to tell Peters. "I asked him to, as this is my first visit to Illinois."

"That makes more sense," said Peters, as I smiled at my sister gratefully. "My figures are a disaster. They have been ever since springtime."

"Mine as well," I replied.

"We had a market fair a few weekends back—we've organized one for the last Sunday in July for as long as I can remember— and I made a total of eighty-three cents worth of sales. Eighty-three cents. You better enjoy the catawba, because at this rate it's the last I'll ever buy." He raised his glass toward us and gulped it down.

"Things will turn around soon," I said.

"We should drink to that," he said, refilling his glass.

With the suddenness of a thunderclap on a clear day, I realized this was the second reference I'd heard recently to the Buffalo Heart market fair. That same fair was where Rebecca had been on the day Lilly was murdered. Peters should be able to confirm for the sheriff and Prickett, if they still harbored suspicions, that

Rebecca had been miles away from her home at the time of the murder.

"Do you know the Widow Harriman, Peters?" I asked. Martha shot me a look that I ignored. "Harriman & Co., up in Menard."

"Of course."

"Do you recall what she was selling at your July market fair?"

"Nothing."

I looked at the man in surprise. "You mean her sales were even less than yours?"

"No, I mean she didn't show up," Peters returned. "She'd written to say she'd be there, and as a courtesy I'd saved a prime spot on the green for her booth, but she never arrived. Tibbets, that old beast from Jacksonville, moved right into the space, and I could hardly stop him, as I couldn't let the space go to waste. Not that the spot did him any good, mind you."

Peters drank some more catawba, and so did I.

I was still brooding about Peters' revelation as Martha and I drove the final miles back to Springfield the following morning. The merchant seemingly had no reason to lie about Rebecca's failure to appear at the market fair. But what could it mean that she hadn't been there? It made no sense she had engaged in an elaborate ruse merely in order to kill her niece in her own barn. Still, why had she tried to deceive the sheriff and Prickett?

In the wake of the storm, the morning air was crisp and cool, carrying the first faint portent that summer might not last forever. After we'd ridden in silence for a half hour, Martha suddenly turned to me. "Remember I said yesterday how pleased I am people here have been taking me seriously?"

"Uh-huh."

"There's one person who hasn't been. You."

I looked at her in surprise. "Whatever do you mean?"

"It's not like you to take off a whole day from your own work to go chasing down someone else's problem, like we did yesterday. And then there were those questions you asked the merchant last night. It's obvious, to me anyway, that you have a special interest in those wretched children you're not telling me about. And in the Widow Harriman."

She wrinkled her nose with thought. "How well do you truly know the widow, Joshua?"

I shook my head in wonder. "All right, then," I said, drawing in a deep breath, and I proceeded to tell her the whole story.

"If you're certain the widow had nothing to do with the murders," Martha said when I had finished, "you've got to help prove her innocence."

"I've been trying. So far, I seem to be finding more reasons to hold her in suspicion."

"In that case, you're going to have to do a better job," my sister said. "Quickly."

CHAPTER 20

When I returned to A. Y. Ellis & Co. at noon that same day, the urgency of my task came into sharp focus. The new edition of the *Sangamo Journal* was waiting on the counter. Simeon's lead story reported Rebecca Harriman had become the sole suspect in her wards' murders. Simeon also reported that Rebecca's violent arguments with her niece Lilly had been widely known in Menard in the weeks leading up to the girl's death.

My temples pounding, I threw down the paper and rushed over to the *Journal*'s offices on "chicken row," the dilapidated north side of the town square.

"This is an outrage," I roared as I pushed through the door.

The phlegmatic newspaperman did not look up from his composing table. "You do realize," he said, "that shooting the messenger does nothing to change the message."

"Of course. But even so . . ."

"Even so, Speed. That is the message. I'd have thought you'd thank me for passing it along at once, when you still might be able to do something about it."

"If I didn't know it would make you happy, I'd cancel my subscription," I said. The newspaperman was chuckling as I slammed the door shut behind me.

I decided to complete my interrogation of the mysterious Prussian Gustorf. I went straight to Dr. Patterson's house and asked to see him. But the hired girl told me he was still recovering from the doctor's medical procedure on his leg.

"It's a matter of immediacy," I said as I pushed past her into the home.

At that moment, Patterson himself emerged into the hallway from his public parlor, shutting the door carefully behind him. "What's this?" he asked.

"I'm sorry, sir," said the girl. "I told him he couldn't—"

"I need to talk to Gustorf at once," I said.

"Why?"

"A private matter between me and him."

"It'll have to wait, whatever it is. He's in no condition to receive visitors."

"But—"

"When he awakes from sedation, I'll tell him you called," Patterson said, ushering me toward the door.

As I walked back to my store, I tried to build a brief against Gustorf in my mind. He had gone into Rebecca's store in Menard, perhaps, and encountered Lilly there. He'd made roguish advances toward the girl, and when these were rebuffed, he'd attacked her and slit her throat. Later, he'd encountered Jesse in the barn behind the Globe and . . . what? Had he somehow connected Jesse to Lilly? Why had the small boy been a threat, or a prize, worth doing violence to? Did I accuse the Prussian of pederasty as well as murder? I had to admit to myself none of this seemed very plausible. I needed a better theory of the case, as Lincoln had called it.

I was trying to construct one as I sat across the table from Lincoln at the Globe during dinner that evening, staring at the cracked ceiling in search of inspiration while chewing on a roast leg of lamb.

"Did you see Simeon's story?" asked Lincoln, breaking into my thoughts.

"Of course. I imagine everyone in town did."

"For once his reporting hit the mark. I was talking with Humble earlier today about his investigation. Seems the widow can't account for her whereabouts on the evening of the boy's murder. And they think she didn't react with a mother's sorrow when word of his death reached her."

"If they'd actually been with her that evening, as I was, they wouldn't say that. She was hysterical. Inconsolable."

"Perhaps," Lincoln said evenly. "But to make matters worse for her sake, some of her neighbors in Menard have been telling Prickett she's well known to be a woman of loose morals. Prickett is convinced this makes her as good as guilty of murder."

I threw down my leg of lamb with a clatter. "She's a Christian woman," I exclaimed, loudly enough that the men down at the other end of the common table turned to stare at me. Had my own actions, my own desires, contributed to the unjust cloud of suspicion over Rebecca? I could not abide the possibility.

"You've got to take her on as a client," I said more quietly. "Surely you can do something to help her avoid a charge."

"Does she desire my representation?"

"Probably not. She's strong-headed. But she does not, in all likelihood, realize the true jeopardy she's in. Couldn't you talk to her now and understand the full truth of the matter from her? Then convince Prickett and the sheriff their suspicions are misguided."

Lincoln rubbed his smooth jaw for a few moments. "The next time she's in Springfield, why don't you bring her by Hoffman's Row and we'll all have a chat. There's not much of use for me to do until a crime's been charged. But if it will help put your mind at ease, or be of some small assistance, I'm happy to sit down with her."

I wasn't about to take any chances Rebecca might be arrested before Lincoln could provide her with his good counsel. The next morning, I scribbled out a note saying she had to come see me as a matter of urgency. I tracked down Hay, whom I found loitering on the green behind the crumbling courthouse, and bid the boy to ride up to Menard with it and to wait for her reply before returning. Just in case she hadn't seen it yet, I bundled a copy of the *Journal* article with my note.

Hay returned as the sun was setting, his face streaked with sweat and grime from his long ride, and reported that Rebecca was already planning to be in Springfield the very next day and that she'd reluctantly agreed to stop by my store after concluding her other business. I asked Hay to convey the news to Lincoln at once and the boy nodded with a weary, put-upon sigh.

The following afternoon, the door to my store swung open and Rebecca stood at the threshold. She was still wearing her all-black outfit of mourning. Swollen pouches I'd never noticed before hung beneath each of her eyes, and lines of worry creased her forehead.

"You wanted to talk?" she said without ceremony or sentiment.

I did not respond but rather took her by the arm and led her up the street toward Lincoln's office at No. 4, Hoffman's Row. "Where are we going?" she demanded as we climbed the creaking staircase.

We reached the door to Lincoln's office and I pushed it open.

"Good afternoon, Widow Harriman," Lincoln said as he came forward. "Won't you please have a seat—"

"This is your doing?" Rebecca asked Lincoln. She did not move to take Lincoln's outstretched hand and instead remained in the entry to the law office, hands defiantly on her hips.

"No, I'm solely to blame," I said. "See here—I can't stand by and let people think you're guilty. Or not take steps to prepare for your defense, if it comes to that. I asked Lincoln if he'd meet with you and perhaps give you a bit of advice, wisdom. On . . . your situation."

"Meaning no offense to Mr. Lincoln," she replied, looking at me with unfriendly eyes, "I'm in no need of his wisdom."

"You're hardly the first woman to have spoken those words," Lincoln murmured.

Rebecca smiled at this, but when she turned back to me, her face resumed its hardened expression. "I know you mean well, Joshua," she said, "but I'll thank you for letting me attend to my own interests myself. Good day." She took two steps toward the still-open office door.

"Wait," I called. "On the day Lilly died—I know you weren't at the Buffalo Heart fair."

Rebecca stopped in midstep. The expression on her face was unreadable. "What makes you think that?" she asked.

"I encountered the merchant Peters the other day. He told me."

"Why don't you stay for a minute," said Lincoln in a voice free of accusation, "and let's talk about matters more fully."

Rebecca nodded and turned back into the office. Lincoln hurriedly shifted around the debris of his law practice to make two places for us to sit.

"Now, Mrs. Harriman," Lincoln continued, once we were all seated, "I'm going to proceed on the premise you had nothing at all to do with the deaths of your niece and nephew—"

"Of course not," said Rebecca with feeling.

"Of course not," repeated Lincoln reasonably. "Nonetheless, as Speed here says, the sheriff and Prickett have been pursuing inquiries about you. I want to ask the same questions to you directly—not because I think there's any truth to them, but because knowing your answers might help me convince them they're on the wrong track."

Rebecca nodded. Viewing her face in profile, I'd never seen her look so old or so tired.

"On the night of Jesse's murder, they're saying it took several hours after he first went missing for you to raise a general alarm."

"What was I supposed to do?" Rebecca asked, her hands flying up helplessly. "Ten-year-old boys run off and find mischief—Jesse, especially. I'm sure the sheriff did himself, if he can remember that far back. I had every reason to think he'd turn back up, sooner or later."

"You were lodging at Torrey's that night?" he asked.

"That's right."

"And there were people in the public room there who could attest to your presence during the course of the evening, I assume?"

"There were plenty of men who saw me," she said. "Whether they'd swear to it, I suppose that depends whether they were supposed to be somewhere else at the time. And on their state of intoxication."

"By any chance was there an old veteran there, bulbous nose, old plumed hat?" I asked.

Rebecca turned to me in amazement. "How did you know?"

"Lucky guess," I said, feeling pleased we were making some progress. "I've seen him there before. Seemed like a regular. Your opponent in the land case, Lincoln, the esteemed Major Richmond," I added.

"What do you remember about that fellow?" Lincoln asked Rebecca.

"Mostly that he was very drunk. He was wandering in and out of the tavern, talking to himself the whole time. At one point, he made a clumsy advance, but I laughed him off and he didn't bother me thereafter."

"Definitely a possible suspect," I said.

Lincoln nodded. "How about the night Lilly died," he continued. "You weren't home that night or the preceding day?"

"No."

"And I take it, from what Speed said, you weren't at Buffalo Heart either."

"No."

"Can you tell me where you were that day?"

She paused but only for a moment. "No."

Lincoln stroked his chin. "You should think carefully about that," he said. "It's no crime to disappear for a night, of course. But in light of what happened . . ." His voice trailed away.

"The hunting knife that was used to kill Lilly," I said. "Prickett said he found one just like it in your back house."

Rebecca let out a long sigh. "That's my one mistake," she said. "The knife *was* mine, part of a matched pair my late husband gave me as a wedding present. When I saw it had been used to stab dear Lilly I . . . I guess I panicked and didn't want it to be so. So I didn't tell Prickett the truth and I tried to get rid of its mate. I shouldn't have, obviously."

I looked over at Lincoln and saw that his concern about this revelation matched mine. "That's very unfortunate," he said. "But not something we can't deal with. Where was it kept?"

"Out in my barn, mostly. I figure the killer rendered Lilly helpless, somehow, then spotted it and did the terrible deed."

"Who do you think the killer was?" I blurted out. "You must have some notion."

"There's no need to put her on the spot—" Lincoln began.

But Rebecca interrupted him to say, "Actually I do have an idea. A pretty good one. It's one reason for my journey here to Springfield today, in fact."

Both Lincoln and I stared at her but she did not continue. "Well?" I said after a moment.

She shook her head. "I can't say. Maybe—maybe someday soon. But not now."

"But surely you yourself are in jeopardy, Rebecca," I said. "He could come after you next if you don't turn him in immediately. You're being reckless in the extreme."

"I'm in no danger," she said, her arms crossed in front of her chest.

"Speed's advice is sound," said Lincoln. "If you think you know who did it, you should tell the sheriff at once. Even if it's true you're in no physical danger from this blackguard—and I'm not sure how you could have confidence about that—you're certainly in danger of being arrested. I know *that* for a fact."

"Tell me this, Mr. Lincoln," Rebecca said, her voice rising with emotion. "Why would I murder my own kin? The charge is preposterous."

"I haven't heard Prickett or the sheriff give any theories on what motivation you could have had for such terrible acts," Lincoln said. "Perhaps they'd ask if you weren't overwhelmed by the sudden responsibility of having to care for two almost-grown children, where you'd had none before."

Her face darkened. "Those men haven't the first idea of the hardships, the responsibilities I've dealt with all my life. Lilly and Jesse—they were the only children I'll ever have the chance to raise. And now they're . . ." Rebecca had said these last sentences in a croak, and now she blinked her eyes and looked to the floor.

We sat in silence. Lincoln absent-mindedly ran his hands over his buffalo-skin wrap. After an interval, he continued: "Prickett has got it into his head that some of your neighbors up there in Menard have unkind things to say about you."

"I expect they do," Rebecca replied. Her face had hardened into a protective mask again. "Doesn't make me a monster who'd do harm to my own niece and nephew."

"Of course not." He paused. "I'm the first one to say you can't worry about gossip. People will talk about other people behind their backs. It's practically the first rule of society. But until they've arrested the outlaw, you might want to take care not to give your neighbors more reasons to tell tales."

"If I listened to my neighbors' advice, Mr. Lincoln," Rebecca said, getting to her feet, "I'd have long ago remarried a homely widower and given him a new batch of children to support him in his dotage. I live my own life and I don't need advice on how to do it. From anyone. Good day to you both. If I'm in want of further wisdom, I'll know where to find you."

We listened as her footsteps receded down the staircase.

"What do you think?" I asked Lincoln when we could hear them no more.

"I think I won't let you pretend any longer you're not smitten with her," he said. When I started to protest, he held up his hand and turned serious.

"I think she's probably innocent. But it's beyond dispute she's not telling us everything she knows. And she's playing with fire if she truly knows who the villain is. It's obvious she's used to keeping her own counsel, but that habit is going to put her in grave trouble before long, if it hasn't already."

"By the way," I said, making ready to depart myself, "I should have known this before I asked you to intercede. What's your record with murder cases?"

"Haven't lost one yet," he said.

Reassured, I was halfway out the door when I realized his true meaning. I turned back to him and said, "Why do I think that's the same thing the novice surgeon says to his first-ever patient?"

"But no less the truer," Lincoln said with a small smile. "No less the truer."

CHAPTER 21

The following day was a Friday, the first day of September. When Herndon arrived to take his afternoon shift behind the counter, I set off to interview Gustorf again. This time, I came armed with a new stratagem for gaining admittance to the Prussian's sickroom: my sister Martha.

Sure enough, the Pattersons' hired girl led us into the doctor's parlor at once. Herr Gustorf was still on the couch, now in a half-sitting position with several pillows lodged behind him. There was an enormous plaster log resting where his shattered leg used to be.

"What is that damned thing?" I exclaimed as we entered.

"Ah, Miss Speed," Gustorf said, flashing a gleaming smile at my sister. "As soon as the girl said it was you, I knew you were just the tonic my spirits needed." Martha's face colored. Turning to me, he added, "Patterson calls it a 'cast.'"

"Is it supposed to work instead of your leg?"

"It's supposed to *cure* my leg, believe it or not. At least that's what the doctor says. Myself, I don't particularly believe it, but I seem to have been unconscious when he imprisoned me in it, so I have little choice but to see if he proves right. If he does—well, that'll be quite a nice story for my book. Perhaps it will be even if he doesn't."

"So your leg's somewhere inside there? The doctor didn't amputate?"

"So I'm told." The Prussian turned back to Martha. "But I'm terribly bored with my cast. And with the small slice of sky I can see." He gestured toward the window above his resting place. "Tell me something interesting from the outside world, Miss Speed."

Martha obliged him and I let her chatter on. Gustorf's flirtations seemed harmless as long as he was weighed down by the heavy cast. In fact, when the hired girl looked in, I took the liberty of asking her to bring us two glasses of the doctor's liquor and some well water for Martha so we could toast to the Prussian's renewed health. Neither the doctor nor his daughter was in evidence and I did not inquire about them, figuring they would merely serve as obstacles to my design.

Instead, I listened patiently as Gustorf spun stories about his encounters with self-important students at Eastern universities and foul-mouthed alligator men on Mississippi riverboats. He had downed his third glass and just finished relating a story of questionable taste having to do with his half-sister disarming an enraged colonel in Vienna when I decided it was time to proceed.

"Say, Gustorf," I began, "I was thinking about your touring itinerary. We talked about it on the afternoon of your accident. When you passed through Menard—"

"Which village, now?"

"This is the little outpost north of here, with a smithy I suggested you visit."

"If you say so."

"There's also an interesting general store in the same settlement. Harriman & Co. Provisioners. Did you happen to go in there?"

"I don't think so. Where is that girl?" he added, looking around the room with frustration. "The last glass she poured was a miserly one."

"I'm sure she'll return soon," I said. "Do you remember encountering a young woman in Menard, close to my sister's age?"

The Prussian shook his head. "If I had seen another young woman with even half your sister's charms, I would remember her, I assure you." Martha smiled broadly.

At that moment, the girl appeared and Gustorf began negotiating for an additional glass or three.

"Mind yourself," I whispered into Martha's ear. "Remember why we're here."

"He's a cad, not a murderer," she whispered back. "I *can* tell the difference."

"We'll see."

Gustorf's charm seemed to work on the hired girl as well, as she soon returned with a fresh bottle of the doctor's spirits, which she balanced next to the Prussian on his couch. As soon as he'd helped himself to a new glass, I continued.

"I've been looking into the death of that boy, the one whose body was found in your carriage."

"Have you?" he returned with genuine interest. "So shopkeepers in your country also investigate crimes? What an unusual arrangement. I shall certainly have to make a note of *that* in my book."

"I've an interest in the boy," I pressed on. "He was . . . a distant relation of a sort. And he was a friendly, harmless lad. Are you sure you hadn't seen him alive at some point during that day?"

"Quite sure," replied Gustorf, sober for a moment.

"Before the stables began to fire, did you know that he was missing and a search was on for him?"

"Before, during, and after the fire, I was reclined in my chair inside the tavern. I was quite comfortable, as the wine was flowing and it seemed apparent others had a greater interest in the fire than did I."

"But what would you have done if the fire had spread to the tavern itself?" asked Martha.

"Not worrying about things that haven't happened yet gives one much more time to enjoy the things that are already happening," Gustorf said with a smile. He swallowed the remains of his glass and poured himself a new one.

"Have you been to the public room of a place called Torrey's?" I asked. "Torrey's Temperance Hotel?"

"Alas not," he said. "I've been told by more than a few people in town I'd like it. But I never made it through the door, and then my horses got into that brush with the hog and I find myself imprisoned here. I never thought I'd be so unhappy about a *brush*," he added, winking at Martha.

She giggled. I decided it was time to go. I had only one last question: "If you knew nothing about the boy, why did the killer put his body in your carriage as a hiding place?"

"I'd think he was planning to drive away later in the evening, to dispose of the body somewhere, when the fire interrupted those plans. Or perhaps the search did."

"But why your carriage? The other carriage at the shed that night would have provided an equally good hiding place."

"I heard the other carriage was your father's—is that the case?" Gustorf said. "'Speed' was painted on the rear panel?"

"My father's very proud of his coach."

"There's your answer, I wager."

I didn't follow. "Are you suggesting someone wanted to incriminate you?"

"That's unlikely," he said. "I'm a foreigner, just arrived in town. I didn't know a soul here at the time. I mean the opposite—the person who did it wanted to avoid incriminating you."

As I thought about this logic, Gustorf turned his attention back to Martha. "How did it ever happen, my dear, that such a delightful young woman was saddled with such a tedious older brother?"

"I ask myself that question practically every day," Martha replied.

I took her firmly by the arm. "It's time to be going, Sister," I said. "We don't want to tire out Herr Gustorf. And look, it's getting late." As indeed it was. It had turned dusky outside and the windows above the Prussian's couch reflected the dancing lights of the doctor's miasma candles.

Martha and I let ourselves out and headed through the darkening streets toward her temporary residence at the sheriff's house.

"He's very clever, isn't he?" Martha said after a few minutes.

"He's thoroughly unsuit—"

"*Joshua!* You can't possibly think I have an interest in him. A girl likes to be flirted with, but that's all it was."

"Very well," I said with relief. "Still, it appears he had nothing to do with the murders. He didn't react like he's trying to hide something. And I suppose he seems an honest man, though he's quite a rogue."

"I think he's a very good liar," said Martha with a laugh. "But I can't imagine he's a murderer."

We had reached the Hutchason house and Martha went up to the front door. But it proved locked, and no one responded when she knocked loudly.

"Maybe Molly's around back with a prisoner," suggested Martha. She led the way as we went through the gate of the white picket fence surrounding the Hutchasons' large rear yard.

Sheriff Hutchason kept the town's inmates in a rectangular shed adjacent to his barn. The jail was roughly twelve feet deep and six feet across. It had a steeply pitched wooden roof and the long sides featured wooden planks fastened on the outside of an iron skeleton. But the short sides consisted of iron latticework, open to the elements, which allowed rain and wind and—during the long wintertime months—snow easy access to the unfortunate men confined inside. The early morning racket made by Hutchason's two cocks in the neighboring barn tended not to improve the prisoners' overall humor either.

The area around the jail cell was lit by the gibbous moon. Molly Hutchason was standing in front of the cell's grill, and she turned as she heard us coming. I tried to avoid staring at her heavy belly, which was closer to bursting than ever. Can't be long now, I thought.

"There you are, Martha dear," Molly said. "I wondered whether you were coming home for Friday night supper. Humble promised me he'd be home, for once, though I've no sight of him yet."

"You should be inside at this hour," said Martha.

Molly shook her head and said, with a weary sigh, "I've been too busy looking after Amos, in Humble's absence. Or trying to, anyway."

I saw there was a figure slumped on the wooden ledge about two feet off the ground that ran the length of the jail cell. Amos Anderson was one of Springfield's most unrepentant drunkards and thus one of Hutchason's more frequent guests.

At the sound of his name, Anderson groaned and rolled over, falling onto the dirt floor of the jail with a soft thud. "Come now, Amos," Molly said, rattling a tin cup against the bars. "Have a drink of water. It'll get you home quicker." Anderson began snoring loudly in response.

"Fool," Molly said with a sigh. She tipped the tin cup on its side and poured the water through the bars and onto the drunkard's boots. He stirred briefly, rubbing his feet together as if scratching an itch, then relaxed again into a contented snore.

The rear door to the Hutchason house opened and the slave Phillis poked her head out. "Evening, Miss Martha," she said. "I've been telling Miss Molly she's spending too much effort on a man who don't deserve it. And this night air isn't good for her baby."

Martha gave me a quick hug, took Molly by the arm, and led her into the house. Meanwhile, Phillis came out with two large earthenware jugs and started filling them with water from the wellhead that stood a few feet from the door. I was about to take my leave when I heard the sounds of approaching horses and two men talking. One of the voices I recognized at once as the sheriff's. I slid into the shadows cast by the jail shed.

". . . wish we had another choice," the sheriff was saying. The riders pulled up as they reached the barn on the other side of the shed, and I listened to the horses being tied up and a saddle being removed and hung.

"I've told you, we don't," returned the other voice. Prickett, I thought.

The men walked into the yard and stopped a few feet from Phillis at the wellhead, although neither said anything to her nor even seemed to notice her presence. The slave looked up briefly in my direction, though she took pains to avoid direct eye contact. I shook my head. She looked down and continued working the pump handle.

"I still have trouble believing she could commit such vile actions, and against her own kin," the sheriff said to Prickett.

"The widow's guilty for certain," replied Prickett, whose stiff-necked white shirt peeked out from his frockcoat. "All the evidence points that way. And this letter I've intercepted leaves no room for doubt. It's all there in black and white. The jury will have little trouble reaching that conclusion once I'm through laying out the evidence of her actions. And of her character."

The sheriff made a noise of resigned acceptance. Meanwhile, I felt my heart pounding so loudly I worried the men might be able to hear it.

"So we're agreed you'll arrest her tomorrow?" Prickett said. "It'll be convenient for you, at the least. The courthouse will be closed for the weekend, of course, but I'll walk over to Judge Thomas's house in the morning and tell him we've solved the two murders. He'll want to proceed with the trial immediately on Monday morning, just as soon as the clerk can round up a jury."

"Very well," said the sheriff. "I'll send word when I've returned with her." With a curt nod toward Prickett, he headed for his back door. Phillis had filled her jugs and, giving a fleeting final glance in my direction, she followed after him.

Prickett stood alone in the yard, the moon bathing the prosecutor in a soft light. I was silent and still, though my thoughts raced. To whom had Rebecca written? Had she foolishly put into writing something that called into question her sincerity? I had no answers.

After a long minute, Prickett clasped his hands together and shook them above his head—foreseeing victory, I thought— and went to retrieve his horse from the sheriff's barn. I exhaled, then jumped when a soft moan issued next to me.

"Amos," I whispered. The drunkard had turned over on the floor of the jail cell. He rubbed his cheek against the ground until he found a new resting place and resumed his contented snore. I listened as Prickett readied his horse and trotted away. As I leaned my flushed face against the cool iron bars of the jail shed, my mind aflame with dire possibilities, I found myself envying Amos Anderson and the simplicity of his drunken slumber.

CHAPTER 22

I tossed and turned all night, but I awoke before dawn with crystalline clarity of thought. I had to warn Rebecca. I had to get her out of harm's way. And if that meant helping her flee from Prickett's clutches, even at great risk to myself, so be it.

I left our bed, careful not to wake Lincoln, dressed silently, and went to van Hoff's yard to saddle up Hickory. The horse was surprised to see me at that hour but eager for the early morning exercise, and we were out on the prairie just as the sun edged over the horizon. I took an indirect route out of town, and I thought I'd been successful at avoiding witnesses to my departure. If I was about to help Rebecca become a fugitive, I wanted to make it as difficult as possible for the sheriff and Prickett to reconstruct our actions.

My plan was only half formed, because much depended on Rebecca. She was, as I knew better than anyone, a proud, independent woman who would not readily take suggestion, to say nothing of direction. She would be reluctant to abandon her business. But I was hopeful that when presented with the stark reality of the impending arrival of the sheriff and his manacles, she would see there was no course available to her other than flight.

I would help her get to the great Illinois River, two days' ride to the west. From there, she could board a steamer or hitch onto a flatboat and head downriver. I'd arrange for her to obtain a purse full of gold coins from my father's agent in St. Louis. And at that point, the entire length of the Mississippi River would be open to her. I didn't know where she'd go or what she'd do, but I had no doubt there were several avenues of survival available to a woman of her abilities.

Of course, all this meant I'd never lay eyes on Rebecca again. But I felt no sadness at that prospect because I knew the only alternative was to witness her standing trial in Springfield for two horrendous crimes she did not commit. A trial, I realized full well, where my own name might be sullied during the attack on her character. And then—unless Prickett's supreme self-confidence from last night was very much misplaced—to watch her swing from the gallows.

I wasn't sure how much time we had to flee Menard before the sheriff arrived. In reality, I thought as Hickory and I rode through the stillness of the wakening prairie, I might have been better served by riding up to Menard in the moonlight, as soon as I'd overheard the sheriff's conversation with Prickett. But riding through the prairie at night was treacherous. And I knew the sheriff, with his regular evening rounds, to be a late riser. He had no reason to suspect Rebecca would be alert to his design. In all likelihood, he would enjoy a full breakfast at his table before mounting his horse. Even so, I would have less than two hours to convince her of the necessity of my plan and get her on the trail.

I reckoned we were within a few miles of Menard when I spotted in the distance a large white mound, like a huge snowdrift, hard against a stand of dark timber. As the mound came into focus, it took the shape of an enormous tent, and the small forms darting in front of it resolved into soldiers in full military attire. I cursed my misfortune at the presence of witnesses.

I tried to hurry past the soldiers without interaction, but as Hickory and I began to circle around the tent, the closest soldier squinted at us through the risen sun and shouted out a greeting. He was a boy, surely not yet sixteen years of age, with the burnt features of a farmhand. He wore light blue trousers that were much too long and obscured his shoes; a long, darker blue coat with shiny buttons and a golden sash; and a tight-fitting cap, also in a shade of blue.

"What's all this?" I shouted, waving with my straw hat at the several clusters of similarly clad soldiers who were loitering in front of the tent, which I now saw was large enough to have sheltered a couple dozen men.

"Colonel Hinkle has ordered a general muster today, for the field at Menard," the boy replied, his voice cracking with adolescent excitement. "All the regiments of the Illinois Militia will be there, and we hear several columns of veterans of the Indian Wars, the Black Hawk, even some boys who went south to gut the Creek, are marching on as well. Should be a right spree, the lads all think. Brandy and whiskey and women too." He grinned hungrily. "Do you think—"

I spurred Hickory onward before he could finish the sentence. General musters were invariably the site of great public merriment, outdone as an occasion for general drunkenness and debauchery only by election days. It was sure to be hectic at Rebecca's store, with men and women arriving in want of new items of clothing and bagatelles to attract the opposite sex, though scarcely anything beyond the abundant alcohol would be necessary for that trick.

There would be witnesses, and plenty of them, to whatever Rebecca and I decided upon. No matter; the sooner I reached Rebecca, the sooner I could spirit her away from the sheriff's path. The presence of so many onlookers might mean I would have to answer for my role in the affair, but that was a risk I'd already undertaken.

I pressed Hickory into a fast trot. As we neared Menard, we encountered military troops mustering in from all directions. Some groups were well uniformed and coordinated, like the first I had encountered, but many more were ragtag groups of a half-dozen men, a single rifle among them, straggling along the road.

I doubted anyone in these units had ever been within earshot of an actual battle. Many regiments brought along their bands, drums, and fife and an occasional large horn, such that the air soon filled with a discordant jumble. I guessed several hundred men, at least, were converging on the little settlement.

At last Hickory picked her way across the rocky streambed and we were there. The commons was already bustling. Several battalions had erected battle flags to claim a particular portion of the green as their own. Soldiers milled about in boisterous congregation.

I tied Hickory to a post and walked up to the familiar store-front. There was no sign of anyone inside and the door would not budge. I tried pulling it harder when a portly old man came up behind me, his white and blue uniform instantly marking him as a veteran of the Late War with Great Britain.

"The damned widow's not there," he said in a gruff voice reeking of liquor. "I've been trying all morning—need a patch for my topcoat here—but the damn place's never open. Some-one told me she wasn't here yesterday neither. May have to let myself in through the window if she doesn't show her haggard face soon."

Without responding, I raced back to Hickory, who was whinnying at two young soldiers who had started to poke at her fine saddle, and I remounted the animal. Rebecca had been in Springfield two days prior. I realized I had no idea where she'd gone after she left Lincoln's office. What could it mean that she hadn't opened her store yesterday? Had she stayed in Springfield for some reason?

With a jolt, I had the horrible thought that perhaps she had gone back to Torrey's and remained there and that the sheriff and Prickett knew it. Perhaps her presence there was somehow connected to the letter Prickett had mentioned last night. Had I ridden off to Menard only to abandon Rebecca to the sheriff, who might at this very minute be arresting her a mere few blocks from my store? The idea terrified me.

I slapped Hickory's flank and urged her on toward Rebecca's cabin. We arrived there at a gallop two minutes later. The house looked deserted. The iron bar protecting the front door was firmly latched, and I couldn't make out any movement as I peered through the windows. My heart beating faster, I walked around to the rear of the cabin. And then the ground beneath me gave way and I was pitched headlong into the void.

The limp body of the woman who had taught me everything she knew about love lay wedged between the cabin wall and the adjoining stable. I knew at once she was no more. Her arms were thrown out helplessly and her head lay twisted to the side. Her still eyes were open and wide with fear. I sank to my knees, held my head in my hands, and wept.

CHAPTER 23

Time passed. I felt numb. The silence of Rebecca's death roared in my ears, as if I was standing at the seashore and waves were crashing down all around me. I wanted nothing more than to be carried away by one of those waves, carried away into the deep, where I could let go of the visible world and sink slowly to the bottom. Maybe at the bottom—just maybe—would I ever find peace again.

Eventually I found the strength to approach Rebecca's body. Either side of the base of her neck was marred with ugly red bruises. I knelt and reached for her with both arms. Her body was cool and inflexible, and her head lolled back sickeningly when I cradled her and drew her toward me. Her mourning veil remained pinned to the top of her head, a grim reminder of the long hardships of a too-short life.

"Rebecca!" I wailed. "Oh, Rebecca! Oh, how can it be?"

I put my lips on hers, somehow hoping to infuse her body with my breath, but her lips were cold and blue and indifferent to my touch. So I lay her body across my lap and held her tight. I stared at her lifeless blue-gray eyes and tried to remember their shine. I contemplated her calloused fingers and recalled their electric touch as they'd traced patterns on my naked chest, twenty feet and a lifetime away. I felt my eyes stinging with tears.

I knew neither time nor place. The roar of the silent ocean continued unabated.

CHAPTER 24

Some time later, there was movement behind me and a shout: "What's this?" And in the next moment: "Speed? Is that you?"

Roused from my daze, I looked over my shoulder and saw Sheriff Hutchason on foot, leading his horse. His brows were knit in confusion, trying to decipher the scene he'd happened upon.

"I was too late, Sheriff," I said. "She's gone." I gulped. "She's been strangled, I think."

"What?" shouted the sheriff. He dropped the lead from his horse and rushed over. "Are you saying *you* . . ."

"Of course not. I found her like this. Found her lifeless body when I arrived this morning."

The sheriff knelt beside Rebecca's body. He examined her from head to toe, gently prodding her body and moving her clothing around as he did. Meanwhile, I took a few steps away, staring off into the distance and trying very hard not to be sick. At last, the sheriff rose to his feet and let out his breath in a long, low whistle.

"She was strangled, all right," he said. "And she didn't put up a fight for some reason. There aren't any bruises on her hands, as there should have been. I wonder."

"You wonder what?"

He did not elaborate.

"How long do you think she's been dead?" I asked.

"At least twelve hours. Maybe considerably more. I was visiting with the surgeon colonel from the war back at the muster earlier today. I'm going to go fetch him now to have a look."

The sheriff mounted his horse, and as he did, I perceived for the first time he was dressed in the uniform of the Winnebago Wars, with a gray clawhammer coat, pantaloons, and knee-high boots. Both of his shoulders were decorated with gold-braided epaulets of command. I noticed too that the sun had already passed its apex and was arcing into the western skies. I had spent many hours alone with Rebecca's body, I realized, before the sheriff arrived.

The sheriff soon returned with an older man in a tattered version of the same uniform. The man weaved up unsteadily to where I stood, saw the widow's silent form, and stopped short. "Too late, I see," he said. "Don't know why you made me come all this way, General Hutchason." He turned to head back in the direction of the muster.

"Wait and take a look at her body first, will you, Hiram?" the sheriff said. "I only see the strangulation wounds to her neck. But I'd like you to make sure I haven't missed anything. She can't have been dead for too long, as the wolves haven't had at the remains yet."

The medical man bent over Rebecca's body and I looked away again. I stared at one of the nearby birch trees, tall and haughty, and I realized I had last contemplated that particular tree one morning through the window of Rebecca's cabin as I lay beside her in bed, my hand resting on her warm, bare skin as she breathed in and out peacefully. My head pounded with grief.

"I've got nothing to add," the doctor said from behind me. "She's been dead for a while. A few hours—a few days—it's impossible to know. Now I must return. There's to be a tug-of-war and I'm the anchor for our troop."

He teetered off toward the muster. In his wake, the sheriff muttered, "He was almost as useless when we were in pursuit of the Winnebagos. More of a threat to my men than the Red Man ever was."

"She can't have been dead for a few days," I said, "because I saw her Thursday afternoon in Springfield. Lincoln and I met with her at Hoffman's Row."

The sheriff looked at me with interest. "Is that so?" he said. He stared into the sky for so long I thought he might have forgotten about my presence. Then he turned back to me and said, "That might explain a few matters. Except this one—what are you doing here today, Speed?"

"I thought perhaps she could use an extra pair of hands selling to the muster," I said, thinking fast. "Her store was closed when I arrived, though, so I headed out here, to her house. That's when I found her."

"Yesterday evening," he continued, "when I got home, Molly and your sister said I'd just missed you. They said I must have seen you as I rode up. But I didn't. I wonder why."

"I couldn't guess, I'm afraid."

"It is quite a coincidence," the sheriff said, as if puzzling through matters slowly, "because I came here to arrest her after the muster. Prickett had become convinced she killed her niece and nephew."

Even in my grief-stricken state, I had the good sense to gasp in surprise. Nonetheless, the sheriff looked at me with narrowed eyes.

"If there's anything of relevance you haven't told me," he said, "I want to hear it now."

I desperately searched for a plausible response, but my aching head proved barren. I was on the verge of confessing my intent to help Rebecca flee, a design now horribly for naught, when I suddenly hit upon a different answer, one that might actually help the sheriff find her killer.

"Rebecca—the Widow Harriman—wasn't at a market fair at Buffalo Heart on the day her niece Lilly was killed," I said. "A merchant who was there told me as much. I came here this morning to ask her why she'd lied to us. I think perhaps she was covering for someone else. Someone who's now killed her, too.

"I confess I suspected Gustorf, the Prussian traveler," I continued. "But he's laid up under Dr. Patterson's care now. He couldn't have managed to come all the way here from Springfield to attack her, not with the condition of his leg."

The sheriff was looking at the corpse with intense concentration. "I've a fair notion," he said, more to himself than to me.

"What is it?" I demanded.

"I suppose there's no harm in sharing this with you now," he said. "We had thought it evidence of *her* guilt, but now I wonder whether it doesn't still provide the answer, only a different one than we'd originally perceived."

He reached inside the pocket of his commanding officer's coat and pulled out a small packet of paper. As I unfolded it, I recognized Rebecca's looping script. The writing was dated two days earlier, the day we had all met in Springfield. My heart pounding, I read:

Dearest Allan—

I regret having to leave you in such an unsettled state but the sun is getting low and I must be back on the trail. I am sorry we quarreled. I fear I cannot promise I will never again speak my mind. You have known all this time what your future with me would hold. I am and will remain my own mistress; it is my nature. You have desired to move forward with our plans nonetheless. I trust one confrontation will not change all that.

You know how much I want our union to materialize. How, in candor, I need it to do so. It has been an arduous few months but the obstacles are, at last, cleared away. My sister's children sadly no longer present a concern. And your affairs seem settled too. I think it is time to tell the world what we have known since the Spring: that the two of us are destined to spend our final years together. As horrible as the

*present circumstances are, nothing that transpired today
should change months of design.*

Yours forever,

R.

"'Allan,'" I said, looking up. I hadn't taken a breath since I
had started reading the letter. "Dr. Allan Patterson?"

Hutchason nodded. "She'd left it for him with the innkeeper
Saunders, but Prickett managed to intercept it. Regrettably, both
of us misread its import, it seems."

"But how could this letter have made you think she'd killed
her own kin?"

"It's obvious, isn't it?" he returned with a huff. "She speaks
of them as obstacles that have been removed. Obstacles to her
own gratification. Only a cold-hearted woman could write in
those terms. Or so we thought. Now it would appear this same
letter points decisively in a different direction."

It took me a moment to understand his meaning. "Are you
saying you now suspect Patterson of the murders? Of doing *this*?"
I nodded over my shoulder while trying to avoid looking again
at Rebecca's lifeless body.

"I'm saying," the sheriff replied, "that Prickett has already
gone to the judge this morning to tell him we have a murder
trial to commence on Monday morning. That, in all likelihood, Matheny will be at this very moment canvassing on the
green for potential jurors. That the people of Springfield will
be much relieved to hear we have at last identified the wicked
person responsible for these terrible crimes. That if the Widow
Harriman is not the guilty party, then it stands to reason her
secret paramour, Dr. Patterson, is the man we've been seeking all
this time."

I looked again at the letter from Rebecca, which I still
clutched in my hand, and I felt a churn of emotions. Thinking

back to the moment when Rebecca had appeared at the doctor's doorstep on the night of Jesse's disappearance, I couldn't say I was completely surprised to learn of a relationship between the two. But to hold confirmation of the same in her own handwriting was a different matter altogether. It was inescapable that the future she had long ago denied to me she had been prepared to give willingly to Patterson.

At the same time, I had trouble bearing ill against Patterson. Rebecca had written she *needed* the match with him. This was, surely, a reference to her financial straits. I could hardly quarrel with her conclusion that the wealthy, widower doctor could satisfy these far better than could the minority shareholder of a struggling general store. Ever the shrewd woman of business, she had struck the best bargain available. Just as she had written to Patterson, her true nature had been plain to me from the outset.

"That's quite a stretch," I said aloud to the sheriff. "They had some type of tiff two days ago. That's hardly a cause for murder. Especially not if they'd made an arrangement some months back."

"Perhaps so," Hutchason returned. "I suspect Prickett is going to have a different view of the evidence. And I've always wondered about Patterson myself, with all his potions and bleedings and inscrutable arts."

He rested his hand on my shoulder. "I believe you were close to her, Speed. What do you think she would have desired? For a burial, I mean."

The answer came to me at once. "She wouldn't have wanted a funeral," I said. "She's got no kin left at this point. Any neighbors who attended a service, if one took place, would be there to gawk and gossip, not to mourn. Not that she much cared what people said about her, mind you."

I had noticed before a stone marker, covered with a light shadow of moss, on a small mound about twenty feet from the back of the house. "That's where Harriman's remains are interred," I said, pointing. "I think all that was left was his clothing." Next to the marker were two gnarled sticks, stuck upright in the mound above freshly dug earth. Rebecca hadn't even had time to give her niece and nephew proper gravesites.

Sheriff Hutchason went into the barn and came back with a blanket, which he laid over Rebecca's corpse, and a shovel.

"I need to return to Springfield at once," he said. "I wonder if I can ask—"

"Of course."

And so, in a haze of grief I dug a grave for Rebecca alongside the sorry remains of the family she'd never had. The still afternoon air was heavy with regret. My only company was the flock of crows, which watched me silently from their branch. Sweat dripped from my forehead into the deepening hollow. Every now and then I turned and stared at Rebecca's shrouded body, as if expecting her to rise and come stand next to me.

At last, I dug deep enough that I figured her corpse would be safe from scavengers. I laid her body into the open grave, giving her one final embrace before returning her to the dust. I recited the Lord's Prayer aloud. Then I knelt beside the void and began pushing the mound of freshly dug earth on top of her body. And as I did, I promised her soul I would not rest until the blackguard who had taken her had received his full measure of justice in Hell.

CHAPTER 25

The sun was low on the southwestern horizon by the time I mounted Hickory to ride home. I had rinsed my hands and face in the stream by Rebecca's house, but the pall of death remained everywhere about my person. Though I considered bedding down in Menard for the night and getting an early start the next morning, I was in no mood for the boisterousness of the muster. As it was, Hickory and I barely made it through the muster field, stepping carefully over soldiers passed out from drink and weaving our way through a gauntlet of bonfires and bands and bare-knuckle boxing contests.

We raced the sun and then, having lost, rode carefully through the moonlit prairie. A cool breeze ruffled Hickory's chestnut mane and transformed the long grasses into rolling waves. The night sky was very clear. A thousand stars shone down from the heavens.

Rebecca Harriman was dead. I repeated the unthinkable truth over and over in my mind. Her presence in Sangamon County had been inseparable from my own, and I felt keenly that a part of my own history had vanished alongside her. Bringing her killer to justice wouldn't bring her back to life, of course, but it was the only thing I could think of to help salve my loss.

I thought again about the words of Rebecca's letter to Dr. Patterson. Could the sheriff be right that they pointed to the doctor as the murderous culprit? It seemed far-fetched. What possible motive could he have had for killing the two children? I imagined the sheriff, or at least the venal Prickett, responding that he had done so to remove them as "obstacles" to marrying Rebecca. But if that was the case, then why would he have killed her in turn? The doctor fancied himself, above all, as a man of reason, but there was no reason behind the actions they sought to ascribe to him.

That left the question of the identity of the depraved man who had eliminated in turn each member of this tossed-about family. But by the time the farms surrounding Springfield began to materialize from the dark and perilous prairie, I was no further toward answering it.

I took Hickory to her stables, gave her a much-deserved rub-down, and went home and collapsed into bed. Given the horrors of that very long day, it was a blessing I fell asleep immediately and did not dream.

The next morning, Sunday, I awoke to a scribbled note on Lincoln's side of the bed saying there would be a court session at two o'clock in the afternoon I might want to attend. After I dressed, I headed down to the storeroom, thinking I should go find Martha. As it turned out, my sister was at the bottom of the stairs waiting for me, her arms crossed impatiently.

"At last," she exclaimed. "I was about to come rouse you myself."

"I had a ghastly day yesterday," I said, and I started to tell her about it.

"I'm afraid I know all about the Widow Harriman," she said. She put her arms around my shoulders. "I'm ever so sorry. Humble came home yesterday evening very agitated and told me and Molly what'd happened."

I returned Martha's embrace and released her. "Wallowing in her death won't do anyone any good," I said. "I need to find out who did it. Lincoln left a note there's to be a hearing?"

Martha nodded. "Dr. Patterson's been thrown into the jail cell. I caught a glimpse of Lincoln out there early this morning. I think he's defending him."

"I can't believe they actually arrested him."

"I called upon Jane Patterson a few hours ago," Martha said, "and she's devastated. Absolutely devastated. I assured her it's all a mistake and her father would probably be set free this very afternoon."

Martha and I reached the town square several minutes before two. Word of the unusual court session had spread quickly, and large numbers of men and women in Sunday dress milled about in front of the courthouse, trading speculation about the purpose of the hearing. More than a few in the crowd had heard about a commotion at the Patterson house the previous night. Sheriff Hutchason stood at the top of the courthouse steps, holding the door shut against the multitude.

There was a sudden murmur from the crowd, and we saw Jane walking toward us. Her countenance, previously clear and composed, was blotchy and her eyes were streaked with red. Martha hugged her, and I gave her my hand.

"Father's completely innocent," Jane said fiercely.

"I understand he's asked Lincoln to defend him," I said. "Lincoln will do his best, I've no doubt, to rebut the charges."

"He's devoted his whole profession to saving lives," she continued. "How can they think he'd take one?"

Martha squeezed her arm comfortingly. At that moment, Sheriff Hutchason called out from the top of the stairs, "Court's open. The judge says you can all come in now." The crowd surged forward, nearly trampling us in their fervor to secure choice viewing spots for this unexpected but most welcome after-church entertainment.

The public benches at the back of the courtroom were crowded with men in silk top hats and ladies in prodigious lace bonnets and ostrich-plume caps by the time the two young women and I managed to file up the dusty courthouse steps. I was looking around for a place where Martha and Jane could sit when Hutchason gestured toward me. He had saved a small space on the front bench, directly behind the defendant's table. The women and I hurried over and squeezed in beside one another.

Lincoln and Patterson were inclined toward each other in close conversation as we took our seats. Jane called out to her father, and he turned and gave her a smile and gave one toward Martha too. He looked tired and anxious. Several of the men around us muttered angrily at the sight of the doctor's face.

There was a knock on the door of the antechamber and Matheny, the court clerk, shouted for order. Judge Thomas ascended the bench, wearing his dark church suit rather than his judicial robe. The judge had evidently given himself a dispensation to smoke his cigar on Sunday, as it smoldered in his clenched right hand.

"It's the Lord's day, Prickett," the judge began, looking over to the prosecutor, who was seated at the other counsel table in the well of the courtroom. "I understand, though, you have a matter that cannot wait."

"Your Honor," Prickett said, rising confidently, "I am pleased to report to the Court, and to the people of Springfield"—he gestured to the assembled crowd—"we have apprehended the scoundrel responsible for the terrible murders that have lately afflicted our community. Your Honor, the People of the State of Illinois charge this man, Allan Patterson, with three counts of murder with malice aforethought."

Prickett pointed at Patterson with an outstretched arm cloaked in a ruffled sleeve and a long, powerful finger. The crowd around us erupted in jeers and angry shouts. More than a few men called out, "String him up!" Lincoln leaned over and whispered something into the doctor's ear. I saw Jane trembling on the other side of Martha.

From the bench, Judge Thomas puffed on his cigar and watched the crowd howl. Matheny looked over at him for instruction, but the judge gave a quick shake of his head. *Let them rage*, he was saying.

After a minute or two, the crowd's fire began to burn itself out. When it had been reduced to embers—mere growls and angry murmurs—the judge looked at Prickett again.

"Have you confronted the defendant Patterson with your charge?" the judge asked.

"We have, Your Honor. The sheriff and I questioned him together last night, just as soon as we uncovered the final pieces of evidence pointing ineluctably to his guilt."

"And what did he say?"

"He refused to answer our questions," Prickett responded. "Said he'd only talk to his lawyer. Demanded we send for Mr. Lincoln."

Another angry howl arose from the crowd. Most of the spectators, it was clear, viewed the doctor's conduct as an admission of guilt. On the bench, Judge Thomas seemed to concur. He sucked on his cigar and stared at Patterson and Lincoln unsparingly.

"In that case," the judge said, blowing a huge cloud of smoke into the air, "the Court finds there is cause to hold the defendant Patterson on the charge of murder. How do the People wish to proceed?"

"With an immediate trial," Prickett responded. "I note the Court's September Trial Term happens to commence tomorrow. I am quite sure the Court already has an exceptionally busy docket, but I humbly submit this matter take precedence in view of the great interest of the community in the apprehension and punishment of this villain. The People are prepared to begin the murder trial tomorrow morning if the Court is amenable."

This announcement set off a new wave of tumult in the courtroom. Men turned to their wives and said they figured nothing would be harmed by delaying the harvest preparations for a few days. Wives asked husbands what they'd like packed in their picnick lunches. The innkeeper Walters, who was sitting directly behind me, loudly announced to the crowd that his City Hotel would be serving luncheon every day at a time corresponding to the jury's midday recess. Not to be outdone, Saunders climbed atop a bench on the other side of the courtroom and shouted at the top of his voice that persons wishing to lodge at the Globe for the duration of the trial rather than riding in from the outskirts each morning could do so at a special reduced rate.

Once again, the judge let the excitement die away on its own accord. When it had, he turned to Lincoln and asked, "Your plea on behalf of the defendant, Mr. Lincoln?"

Lincoln stood tall, hands clasped behind his back. "Not guilty, Your Honor," he announced in his reedy voice.

"And do you care to comment," the judge said, puffing in and out on his cigar, "on the People's suggestion we proceed with trial tomorrow?"

"That's much too soon," Lincoln said. "The Court will appreciate, I trust, that I was only retained for this charge in the past eight hours."

The judge looked unsympathetic. "You'll have had over twenty-four hours by the time we're finished picking the jury tomorrow, Mr. Lincoln," he said, "Surely that's sufficient." The crowd murmured in concert. Jane grabbed at Martha's arm. In front of us, Patterson looked up at Lincoln with concern.

"With all due respect, it's not, Your Honor," Lincoln returned. "I need more time to investigate my defense. I think two weeks—"

The judge held up his hand and said, brusquely, "You're not getting two weeks. Or one, for that matter."

Sensing his advantage, Prickett rose again. "Your Honor," he said, "if Mr. Lincoln wants an *extra-ordinary* amount of time to prepare, may I suggest he make a preliminary statement of his defense now. The man's as much as admitted to being the killer by his refusal to explain himself."

"We'll put the People to their proof first, Your Honor," Lincoln said. "As is our right."

Judge Thomas scowled at Lincoln over his smoldering cigar, while Prickett said, "I doubt trial will last longer than the morning, in that case. It sounds like Mr. Lincoln has got nothing to say to the jury because his client is guilty. What can he expect?"

"I expect the jury to listen to all the evidence and not to reach any conclusions before they have," Lincoln replied evenly.

Many men, and more than a few women, were calling out angrily again, and this time Judge Thomas directed his clerk to impose order. Matheny hollered for silence, and when this failed, he stalked along the low railing dividing the public section from the well of the courtroom and shouted down the disobeying spectators one by one.

"Trial is set for Tuesday morning," the judge announced when, at length, quiet had been restored. "*This* Tuesday morning, Mr. Lincoln, not the next one. That will give you another full day to find your defense." The judge took two deep pulls on his cigar and expelled a large cloud of smoke, which hung over him like a rain cloud before it slowly dissipated.

"In the meantime, the defendant is to be held without bail. Make sure nothing happens to him, Sheriff," the judge said, looking at the hulking form of Hutchason, who had been standing guard next to Dr. Patterson at Lincoln's table. Hutchason nodded without removing his gaze from his prisoner.

"And listen carefully, all of you out there," the judge added, pointing at the crowd with the burning end of his cigar. "We'll have a verdict before the end of the week. Banish any thoughts of dispensing justice yourselves. That's why we employ the hangman."

As the crowd rumbled its approval and the judge walked off the bench, Jane Patterson reached over and grabbed my arm. "You've got to help Mr. Lincoln save my father," she cried desperately. "You two are his only hope."

CHAPTER 26

That evening, Martha and I were taking our dinner at the Globe's public room when Hay appeared on the threshold. "Lincoln asked you to come by his office when you're finished, Mr. Speed," the boy said. He stole a glance at my sister, but as soon as he saw I was watching, he scampered away.

"I'll walk you home first," I said a few minutes later, once we had finished devouring two large slices of Mrs. Saunders's huckleberry pie.

"You'll do no such thing," Martha said. "I'm coming too."

I knew it would be useless to argue, and so we headed off together toward Hoffman's Row. The public excitement of the afternoon had long since faded; the town was deserted, and the silence was broken only by the crunch of our footsteps on the moonlit dirt-and-gravel streets.

"How is Jane?" I asked as we turned the corner onto Fifth Street. "I know you accompanied her back to her house after the hearing."

"She was on the edge of tears the whole time. She kept asking me what she would do if her father was convicted and actually hung." Martha shuddered.

"What'd you tell her?"

"We'd make sure it didn't happen. You and I. And Lincoln, too, of course."

We were mounting the stairs to No. 4 now. "Do me a favor," I said, "and don't tell Lincoln he's an afterthought in your design to get the doctor acquitted." Without breaking stride, Martha kicked me in the back of my leg. I yelled out in pain.

"That must be the Speeds," Lincoln called from his office.

The door was ajar and the room was, if possible, even more disordered than usual. In addition to widely flung paper and parchment, several half-eaten meals littered the floor. Two candle stubs burned in the middle of the table, perilously close to the scattered papers.

"Good evening to you both," Lincoln said. "I figured, when I sent Hay, I'd end up with two Speeds for the price of one."

"What's your plan for having the doctor acquitted?" Martha asked as Lincoln was still pushing around debris to make two places to sit.

Lincoln gave her a crooked smile. "I only wish," he said, "the doctor's enthusiasm for his own defense matched yours, Miss Speed."

"What do you mean?"

With a great sigh, Lincoln threw himself down onto the buffalo robe draping his chair. "I've spent the better part of the day, before and after the hearing, talking to Patterson through the bars of the jail cell," he said. "Without elucidation. I still don't fully know what his position is. Or, as a consequence, what mine is. That's why I had to dance that jig in front of the judge earlier. I'll tell you—if I'd been wrongly accused of three murders I'd be a lot more outspoken than he's been."

Martha was chewing on her lower lip. "Surely he's still under the shock of the accusation," she said. "I wonder if most men would behave differently. How does he compare with other men accused of murder whom you've defended?"

"I'd say Patterson is about average," Lincoln said casually. I snorted.

"What's funny?" Martha asked, looking back and forth between us.

"Lincoln's made a mathematical joke," I said. "This is his *first* murder case. So, by definition, Patterson's the average thus far."

"You've never done this before?" Martha asked with genuine concern.

"I've represented men accused of various sorts of criminal misconduct," said Lincoln, "but never this severe."

"But then why did he hire you?"

"Watch your impertinence," I said sharply, but Lincoln held up his hand and said, "You needn't defend me, Speed. It's a fair enough question, Miss Speed. I assume it's because the good doctor has familiarity with me from the real estate dispute with Major Richmond."

"I wonder whether the major's the one who should have been arrested," Martha said. She rose and started pacing about, as if it were she who was preparing to address the jury. "We know he bears a grudge against Dr. Patterson, so it makes sense he would have wanted to harm people close to him. Indeed, he might have attacked Patterson himself the other night at Torrey's if you hadn't been there to step between them, Joshua. And we know Richmond was also at Torrey's the night Jesse disappeared. Did you see him at the muster in Menard? It'd certainly make sense, given he wears that sorry uniform around all the time. If he was there, that places him at the scene of at least two of the murders."

"I didn't spot him," I admitted, "though I may have overlooked him. It was a mob's scene, from start to finish."

"Thank you for your opening statement, Miss Speed," Lincoln said with a smile as my sister resumed her seat. "I fully intend to argue at trial Richmond might be the actual killer. Among others. Perhaps it was Speed's favorite suspect, the Prussian Gustorf." Martha started to protest but Lincoln put up his hand. "Perhaps it was the unsavory poorhouse master you encountered in Decatur. Or perhaps it was a madman, as you suggested earlier, Miss Speed, one not locked away in a poorhouse. Who knows for sure?

"Remember, the prosecutor Prickett bears the burden of proving, beyond any reasonable doubt, that Patterson was the killer. I don't need to prove anything myself. Merely suggesting it might have been someone else is enough for me if it causes the jury to have doubts about Prickett's case against Patterson."

"But I want to know who the killer was," I said.

"I know you do," said Lincoln. "And so do I. *After* this week. For this week, my only aim is to ensure Patterson doesn't swing from the gallows. That's all I can manage—quite possibly more than I can manage. If that doesn't suit you, Speed, there's no need for me to involve you in the defense. Defending Patterson is my professional brief after all, not yours."

"Do you think he's guilty?" I asked.

"Nothing's been proven in a court of law," said Lincoln, "and it doesn't make sense he would have wanted to kill them, any of them, even if there's evidence suggesting he could have done so."

"That's good enough for me," I said. "I'd much rather be of use, especially if it helps bring Rebecca's true killer to justice."

"Can't you show the doctor was somewhere else when the murders were committed?" asked Martha. Her face lit up and she added, "In fact, on the night of Jesse's death, we know exactly where he was. Dining at his home with us. So he can't possibly be guilty of that one. Have you told the sheriff?"

"I have," replied Lincoln, "and apparently Prickett intends to try to prove the boy was killed earlier in the evening and then hidden away in the Lafayette carriage for disposal later. The sun had set by the time you got to the Patterson house for dinner?" He looked at me.

I thought back to that night, which seemed so long ago though it was barely two weeks earlier. "That's right," I said. "We came here so I could introduce you to Martha. When we left Hoffman's Row and walked to the Pattersons, it was dark already, as I recall." There was pause, as each of us remembered the argument about Phillis's appearance in Springfield that evening, though none of us said anything about it now.

"I wonder how Prickett obtained the letter?" I thought aloud. Lincoln looked up sharply. "What letter?"

"Prickett or Hutchason didn't tell you?" I asked. I described Rebecca's note and recited its contents from memory. "I don't actually know whether Patterson read it before Prickett intercepted it."

"I'm vexed they've failed to disclose it to me," Lincoln said with a frown. "I wager it will be their central evidence, at least as to the widow's murder. It certainly suggests an argument between the two preceded her murder."

"What about the night of Lilly's murder?" asked Martha. "We know the widow wasn't actually at the market fair that day, where she said she was. How about Patterson?"

"I've asked Patterson repeatedly about that day," said Lincoln. "As near as I can tell, he wasn't at his home in Springfield. But he's been maddeningly vague. Where he actually was, I couldn't tell you."

"Perhaps he was with Rebecca somewhere," I suggested. Even as I said this I flinched.

"I've been wondering the same thing," said Lincoln, "especially in light of the letter you just told me about."

"But if the doctor's not telling you for some reason," Martha said to Lincoln, "and Rebecca's . . . well, how are we going to prove where he was?"

And then, all at once, I was struck by a notion of how to discover if the doctor had an alibi for the night of the first murder.

"Leave this one to me, Lincoln," I said. "I've had an idea."

CHAPTER 27

By the time I got downstairs to prepare the store for opening the next morning, rain was coming down in great sheets. I stood at the front door next to Herndon and watched it fall.

"Doubt we'll do much business today," said Herndon.

"I know it's not your usual shift," I replied, "but will you watch the counter for me? I've an errand to accomplish."

Herndon readily agreed, and in a moment I had thrown on an overcoat and broad-brimmed hat and pushed open the door. Staying close to buildings wherever possible, and avoiding the muddy bogs forming in the low-lying areas of the streets, I wound my way through town. Soon I was knocking on the door of a familiar small shack, the rain pouring off my hat like a downspout.

"You must need a trim something desperate to come out in this weather," Billy the Barber said when he opened the door. "Come in, come in. You ain't got much competition this morning, that's for sure."

I stepped inside and took off my outer gear as a pool of water formed at my feet. Billy started setting up his tools beside his barbering chair, but before I walked over I called out, "Hay? Are you about?"

"Mornin'," came a sleepy voice from Billy's back room. As far as I knew, Hay had no permanent home, but he spent many nights camped on the floor beside Billy's mattress.

"Aren't you due at Lincoln's office?" I asked.

"Not for another hour," said the boy as he wandered into the front room, scratching his scrawny chest. From the look of him, deeply begrimed in his dingy underclothes, he hadn't bathed since the spring.

"Do me a service and leave now," I said, reaching into my pocket. "Head over to van Hoff's and rent a phaeton and hitch Hickory up to it. Tell van Hoff it's for me. Then drive it to Patterson's house and I'll meet you there. Here's a half-dime for your trouble."

"Where're you takin' Patterson's daughter?" Billy asked.

"I'm not taking her anywhere. And I'm not answering your questions. Just go."

"But it's rainin' out."

"Do you want the half-dime or not?"

Hay wavered, then nodded and, throwing on a too-large jacket, went out. Meanwhile, I leaned back into Billy's chair, my eyes closed, and let him comb out my hair.

"This ain't much longer than you usually wear it, Mr. Speed," the barber said. "You sure you want me to cut it?"

"Just a little, then," I said. "It's been bothering me." As he started snipping away, I asked, "How long have you been barbering folks, Billy?"

"'Bout ten years now. Started doing it down in New Orleans. White man keeps the Negro in chains, but for some reason he'll let him hold a sharp blade to his throat so long as there's lather involved."

"When you put it that way, it does seem rash," I replied with a smile. "I imagine you hear all sorts of things while you're cleaning folks up and making them look presentable."

"Mm-hmm."

"I've been thinking," I continued. "About those people who've been killed, the Widow Harriman and her niece and nephew. My younger sister's here for a visit, and all of a sudden

I find myself worried about her safety, about the safety of all the young women in town in particular."

"Mm-hmm."

"So I was wondering whether you might know something about the deaths. Do you, Billy?"

The barber blew out his breath through his teeth, one of which, on the top row, was missing. "That be the sheriff's business, don't you think?" he said. "Or Attorney Prickett's. I've got enough to do tending to people's hair."

"I'm sure you're right," I said.

There were a few minutes of quiet, during which I searched for another approach, while Billy whistled softly to himself in time with the clacking scissor blades. At length I began again.

"Have you been known to trim Dr. Patterson's hair, Billy?"

"I reckon he's been by once or twice."

"So what's your opinion? Do you think he's guilty?"

"Ain't got no opinion. All I've got is these shears." He held them up for a moment, then went back to work on my whiskers.

"Let me ask you another question about Patterson. Maybe you've got an opinion on this. If he wanted an evening away from home, to have a private encounter, say, do you have any idea where he might go?"

Billy's scissors continued to fly around my head, but the whistling stopped. He put down the scissors and said, "Do you consider yourself a religious man, Mr. Speed?"

The question took me aback. "I'm a God-fearing man," I said, "the same as any other good Christian." In truth, it had been many years since I'd attended divine service, but I was not about to admit this to the Negro barber.

"I don't know about yours," Billy continued, "but at the church I attend on Sundays, anything said to the minister is said in private. It's between you and him and the Almighty. The minister'd be run out of town before the sun rose on Monday if he started sharing them secrets around."

"That's true at my church also," I replied with a smile. "Though I'm not sure barbers are held to quite the same standard."

Billy took a step back, squinted at me, and held up his hands. "Do you think," he said in a bold tone I had never heard him use before, "these hands could cut and scape with such skill if the Almighty himself hadn't breathed life into them?"

"I don't imagine they could."

This answer seemed to satisfy Billy, and he picked up his scissors again and resumed his tune. "Besides," he said a few moments later, "you're asking about something that, if I ever knew it, I knew long ago. My mind's not what it used to be." He paused. "Used to be *golden*."

At $2.50 it was a steep price, but with the trial starting tomorrow morning, there was no time to haggle. I felt through the coins in my pocket, located a single gold quarter-eagle, and placed it on the table holding Billy's cutting implements.

Billy made a few last snips and put down his scissors on the table. The gold coin had disappeared. "You're all set now, Mr. Speed," Billy said. "You ever been to Athens?"

"Yes," I said, assuming he meant Illinois, not Greece.

"Ever get wet on the way?"

"Every single time. At least I would if it wasn't for the rope pull ferry at the Salt Creek crossing, the one operated by the keeper of that sorry tavern on the riverbank."

"It's a funny thing," Billy said. "Doc Patterson once said the very same thing to me. You tell me if your feet get wet the next time you're there."

I thanked Billy and hurried out into the elements. The rain had relented, but a light mist was still falling as I made my way through town. Here and there I passed townspeople venturing out onto the soaking streets. Soon I was standing at Patterson's imposing front door. I let myself in.

Gustorf was lying face down on his couch in the parlor, snoring loudly. I tapped his shoulder and he groaned, turned over, and breathed out into my face. The experience was like thrusting my head into a distilling vat. I gagged.

"How can you be drunk at this hour?" I exclaimed.

"How can you be sober at any hour?" Gustorf muttered. "Leave me be."

"I've got a favor to ask," I said. Gustorf groaned again and turned away from me. "It involves a trip outdoors," I continued. "And, unless I'm much mistaken, a woman."

He turned his head toward me again. "Your sister?"

"Better than that for your purposes." When he squinted at me through questioning eyes, I crouched down and told him my plan. The longer I spoke, the broader his smile became. When I had finished explaining, I straightened up and asked, "Will you do it?"

Herr Gustorf pulled himself into a sitting position. "My good friend," he said with a clap of his hands, "it's as if you've been heaven-sent to relieve my tedium. Let's leave at once."

I pulled Gustorf to his feet. Hay was waiting outside, holding Hickory's lead. I helped Gustorf hoist himself up into the light, open-sided carriage. Once he'd positioned his cast to balance himself against toppling out of the conveyance, I gave Hickory a tap.

"How does that damned thing feel?" I asked as we lurched into motion.

"Like I've shoved my leg down the throat of a boar. Or up its arse, more likely. Worse, it's starting to itch."

"Patterson truly thinks you'll be good as new when it's removed?"

"That's what he told me. But I understand the doctor's been saying a lot of fantastical things recently." Gustorf shouted with laughter at his own joke and slapped the cast. It resounded like a hollow log.

The great prairie glistened like an overripe fruit as we drove through it that morning, the sun coming in and out of the clouds. The colors were a little too vivid; the greens even greener than usual, the yellows looking liquid in intensity. Here and there were faint, rusty hints of the reds to come. The grasses were improbably high, and they stood straight at attention in the still, sultry air.

Herr Gustorf shouted out his approval of the setting several times, and he eagerly scribbled down impressions and sketches in his notebook. But I took in the familiar scene with a kind of sadness. When the prairie reached this state, it was a sure sign the end was near, that the decline and death of the fall and winter would arrive before we knew it. The wild beauty would not last. It never did.

The sun was directly overhead when we came upon the lonely tavern beside Salt Creek. As far as I knew, it did not have a name, in part because it had rapidly gone through a series of owners, each having even less good fortune than the last. When I had stayed there a few years earlier, in the middle of a circuit around the county to get to know my new territory, an unsavory drunkard named Esterly had run the place. I'd heard he'd been replaced as proprietor by his spinster daughter, she in turn by a fellow named Dickey, and then he by one Rugg.

An old man bent over on a walking stick hobbled out of the front door as soon as our cart lurched to a stop. He was taking no chances on letting two prospective customers get away, I supposed.

"Can you tend to my horse while we slake our thirst?" I called as the man approached. "It's Rugg, isn't it?"

"Rugg abandoned the place months ago," the man rasped as he took Hickory's reins with a gnarled hand. "My son, Sconce the Younger, took over management. Spruced it up quite nicely, he has." The man looked at the ramshackle one-story inn with pride.

Herr Gustorf and I followed his gaze doubtfully. The inn's dingy white paint was peeling and several of the shutters were off their hinges and hanging at odd angles. Boards had been nailed onto the roof at uneven diagonals, apparently to cover over leaks.

Two scrawny milk cows grazed in the unpenned front yard. Just beyond the inn, Salt Creek trickled by unhappily.

"I can't thank you enough for this expedition," Gustorf murmured with genuine enthusiasm.

The Prussian slid to the ground and limped toward the front door. Meanwhile, I untethered Hickory from the two-wheeled chaise, which we let lean forward onto the ground, and Sconce the Older led the horse into a rickety stable, which stank of moldering manure. Hickory whinnied unhappily, but I scratched her white stripe and whispered assurances she wasn't going to be here for long. Then I followed Gustorf's path into the tavern.

Sconce the Younger, middle-aged and officious, stood behind a reception desk just inside the door, quill pen poised above a bound hotel register. "Will that be two rooms for this evening, sir?" he asked.

I shook my head. "Just a few restorative glasses and then we're back on the trail," I said, my eyes tightly focused on the ledger. Sconce's shoulders sagged as he closed the weathered register and placed it into a bottom drawer of the desk.

I continued past him into the dissolute public room. Discolored shades were drawn over the windows, and the place was lit by a single, foul-smelling whale-oil lamp. Two men, looking like they hadn't moved in weeks, sprawled in chairs next to a decrepit table littered with empty glasses. In the far end of the room, next to the barman's stand, Gustorf was already engaged in animated conversation with a woman.

The Prussian's new companion turned as she heard me approaching and gave me a look of composed sadness. She was middle-aged, dressed in frills and ruffles, and heavily painted. Her hair was pulled back by a band of colored beads. In her younger years, I imagined she would have been very pretty.

"May I introduce Madam Grace Darling," Gustorf said with a grand gesture. I bowed politely.

After a quick glance, Madam Darling returned her attentions to Gustorf, who was already close to the bottom of his glass.

I took a nearby chair, which shuddered as I settled into it, and listened without pretense.

"Why'd you say you were in these parts?" Madam Darling asked Gustorf.

"I'm on a grand tour of your country," he said, speaking with a more pronounced accent than usual. "I'm writing a book, for my homeland."

"Oh, a writer," she replied. She stepped back to squint at him, and I guessed she was assessing the quality of the threads in his jacket. "I like writers—successful ones at least. What country are you from?"

"Prussia."

"I've always wanted to visit Russia," she replied with mustered enthusiasm.

"I've heard that's very nice too," he said. Madam Darling gave Gustorf a confused look while he glanced over her shoulder at me and winked. I rotated my hand like a wagon wheel as if to say, *Get on with it.*

Gustorf drained the remainder of his glass and asked Sconce for two replacements. "The hard stuff, this time," he specified. The Prussian launched into a long disquisition on the Germanic states and their once and future greatness in world affairs. Madam Darling bravely tried to follow the discussion, although once or twice her eyes flicked toward the entrance of the tavern to see if any less long-winded prospects had entered. But no one else came through the door and so Gustorf retained the field unchallenged.

When Gustorf finally finished his lecture, he muttered that he needed to relieve himself, and Madam Darling pointed him through a narrow door at the rear. As he disappeared, she gave a sigh and turned her attention to me.

"What's your tale?" she asked.

"I'm showing my foreign friend around the county," I replied, rising from my chair. "With his leg like it is, he's in need of a driver."

She thrust her shoulders back and her chest forward to accentuate her breasts, which I now realized were readily discernable through her gauzy, lavender dress. "Don't *you* like women?" she asked.

"Very much so," I replied, trying to avoid staring too baldly.

"Well, then . . ."

"It's my friend who's out exploring today, I'm afraid. I have other plans."

At that moment, the rear door banged open and Gustorf tottered back into the room. He was carrying a newly filled glass in each hand as he shuffled along on his cast.

Madam Darling plainly decided the time for alacrity had arrived. "So, my Russian friend," she said, putting her hand boldly on Gustorf's shoulder, "do you want to experience the exotic pleasures of Salt Creek? I think it would make very good reading for that little travel book of yours."

"I'd like that," Gustorf replied with a loose leer. "And so would my readers, I daresay."

"Follow me." Madam Darling turned and Gustorf made as if to go with her. I cleared my throat. Gustorf nodded slightly.

I left Gustorf and his companion and walked quickly toward the reception desk. When I was ten feet from the desk, there was a crash behind me and then a scream. "Help me! My leg!"

Sconce the Younger looked up from his desk. "His father's the Russian Consul in Washington," I said urgently. "A close friend of the Czar himself. If he hears his son was injured in your establishment—"

Sconce rose and hurried toward Gustorf. The Prussian was making a prodigious commotion, carrying on and flailing about on the floor, pulling chairs down on top of himself from all sides. Meanwhile, I pulled open the bottom drawer of the reception desk and grabbed the register, an inch thick with heavily thumbed pages. I slipped it inside my traveling cloak and returned to the scene of Gustorf's performance.

"Too much to drink, Herr Gustorf?" I asked, looking down on him.

"Never," he said, suddenly recollecting his wits. "Too much excitement at Madam Darling's charms. My apologies. Will you help me up?" He reached out his arms. I took one and the bewildered Sconce the Younger the other, and together we pulled Gustorf to his feet.

"Well, it's time to be leaving," I said. "I think we've accomplished what we set out to do."

"Most certainly not," Gustorf replied. He turned to Madam Darling and said, "Now where were we?"

As they walked from the room together, I said to Sconce, "I think I'll take some air. Will you make sure my friend finds his way out safely, after they've completed their business?" I handed Sconce a silver half-dollar and he nodded gratefully.

Outside, I hitched up Hickory with the help of Sconce the Older and drove fifty yards away from the inn. Making sure the old man couldn't see, I took the register out of my cloak and started paging through it. The entries for overnight guests were few and far between, so the one I was looking for was easy to spot. A couple who had registered as "Dr. & Mrs. Patterson" had indeed stayed at the inn the evening of Lilly's death. Leafing backward through the book, I saw another such entry from May of this year. Rebecca's desire to shield this arrangement presumably explained the lie she told Prickett about the day of Lilly's murder.

My breath caught as I realized the full implication of the register, especially when combined with Rebecca's letter to Patterson. Shortly after Rebecca had ended our relations at the turn of the year, two new events had taken place in her life: she assumed custody of her niece and nephew, and she took up with the doctor. And, somehow, the combination had gotten her killed. I was still numb with this thought when Sconce the Younger helped Gustorf into the carriage an hour later.

"*Much* better," Gustorf said, giving me an exuberant slap on the back. "Do you want to hear all about it?"

"Not particularly." I gave the reins a shake and Hickory dutifully began pulling us toward Springfield.

"It was an experience the likes of which I've never had," Gustorf continued as if I had not spoken. "What did she call them—the exotic pleasures of Salt Creek? The crumbling inn, the reeking taproom, the *exotic pleasures*. It was all so perfect. A delicious witch's brew. You must sample it yourself sometime."

"Perhaps," I returned doubtfully.

"Did you find what you were looking for?" he asked after we'd bumped along the trail for a few minutes.

"I did." I tapped the ledger, which I balanced in my lap.

"Then why the long face? It's a glorious day to be alive." He swept his arms toward the horizon, taking in the florid prairie.

"My thoughts are on someone who's not alive to enjoy the day."

"But life is for the living, my friend," he said. "Look at the beauty of God's creation all around us. Do you think the dead want us to dwell on them, when we could dwell instead on this? I don't."

A few miles along, Gustorf added: "You truly don't have any curiosity about how we managed things, with my lower half imprisoned in Dr. Patterson's contraption?"

"I suppose I do."

"Aha!" he exclaimed with a laugh. "It's an amazing tale, a stupendous feat of dexterity."

But when I leaned back toward him to hear he added, "And to learn of it you'll have to buy my book."

Gustorf shouted with laughter. I focused on the trail. A little later, I turned back and saw him slumped against the side of the jangling carriage, a wide grin spread on his face. He was snoring loudly.

CHAPTER 28

I awoke the next morning to bright sunlight streaming into our bedroom through the small window. I lay there for a minute without moving until a church bell began to strike the hour. Eight bells, if I counted them correctly in my somnolent state. Eight o'clock: I was late. *We were late*, I corrected myself, as I felt Lincoln's inert leg jutting out toward me.

I thrust myself up onto my elbows and moved to rouse Lincoln when I saw he was already awake and lying on his back. His forehead was wrinkled, his jaw clenched, and his eyes were wide and expressionless. I'd seen him like this once or twice before, and I knew it would require serious effort to get him moving.

"Lincoln, you've got to rise," I shouted, shaking him with both arms. "Court's starting within the hour. The doctor's case is first on the docket. Don't you remember?"

My friend did not move, nor did his countenance register that he had heard me. His eyelids fluttered once; but for this movement, I would have feared he had turned to stone.

"Lincoln. Now. Get up!" I tried again, shaking him still more vigorously. "Don't tell me your hypos have returned. You don't have time for them, not today you don't."

At last he spoke, although nothing but his lips moved, the words coming out of his mouth with an agonizing slowness. "I am awake, Joshua. You can see that perfectly well."

"You need to get out of bed. Patterson's in the dock. And it won't reflect well on you if poor little Hay is the one who stands up to defend him."

"Yes, I think I will," he replied, still speaking with an unnatural cadence. "I have been contemplating, these past few hours, whether it wouldn't be better to spend the whole day lying in bed. I think it would be better, most probably. But I think you may be right as well and I should get up and go to court."

I sprang into action, with great effort dragging Lincoln out of the bed and starting to feed his hands and legs through his clothes, which I picked up off the floor. His body remained limp at first, but gradually he began animating his limbs. When he was encased in his courtroom attire, and I had quickly thrown on clothes of my own, I turned to look at him.

"Is it safe to take you out into the company of society?"

He smiled, the first display of emotion I'd seen that morning, and when he spoke his voice was almost back to normal. "Good old Speed. I'm not sure how I'd manage without you. Yes, let's be off."

As we took the stairs two at a time, I asked if he had seen the hotel ledger, which I'd left opened to the key page by his side of the bed when I'd gone to sleep the previous night.

"I did. Well done, Speed. I won't ask how you obtained it."

"Better not to."

"I'm not familiar with the inn it's from, though. Could a man—or woman, for that matter—ride on horseback from there to Menard and back in the course of a single night?"

I considered this. "It would be possible, I suppose, if the person rode fast enough, subject to exactly when they left."

Lincoln nodded. "So what you've found is good evidence, but it may not be conclusive. It gives the doctor an alibi for the night of Lilly's murder, depending on when he was actually at the inn. And the problem is—"

"The only person who could attest to that is the very same person whom the doctor is accused of murdering," I said.

We walked the rest of the way to the courthouse in silence.

Precisely at the moment the church bells sounded nine o'clock, Matheny shouted for order in the court. When the boisterous, jostling crowd had finally complied, there was a loud knock and Judge Thomas emerged from his anteroom and ascended the bench. He held a smoldering cigar in one hand and clenched several unlit ones in his other fist. The judge nodded at Matheny.

"Hear-yay, hear-yay," Matheny squeaked, looking from one side of the dim chamber to the other. He was wearing a tightly knotted cravat under his frockcoat. "The September Term of the Circuit Court for Sangamon County is called to session. All persons having business shall approach and be heard." Looking at a scroll of parchment in his hands, he added: "The Court calls as its first case of the day *The People against Allan Patterson*."

Judge Thomas sucked on his cigar and looked out at the counsel table where Prickett sat straight at attention, his high-collared, stiff-necked shirt looking brilliant white against his black frockcoat this morning. I thought he'd likely ordered Mrs. Prickett to launder it with particular care for his starring role this week.

"Are the People ready to proceed?" the judge asked.

Prickett rose and said, with much authority, "We are, Your Honor."

Without looking toward Lincoln or Patterson at the other counsel table in the well, the judge bellowed: "Bring forth the jury box, Clerk."

Matheny lugged forward a heavy wooden cube, some ten inches on all sides, with a great brass latch. Sheriff Hutchason, standing guard near Patterson, helped him settle it on the small clerk's stand at the base of the bench.

"What's in there?" my sister Martha asked quietly from beside me.

"It's got tickets in it with the names of a couple dozen potential jurors for this Term," I whispered back. "Any free white citizen who's a resident of the county, a property holder, and between twenty-one and sixty years is eligible. Matheny will draw twelve names at random for the doctor's jury."

"You mean any free white *male* citizen," said Martha.

"Well, of course."

Martha looked as if she had more to say on the subject, but before she could, Matheny had drawn a key from his pocket, unlocked the latch on the wooden box, and swung open the top panel with a great squeak. Looking off in the other direction, he thrust his hand into the box, swirled it around, and drew out a single scrap of paper. The courtroom leaned forward in anticipation.

"James Short," called Matheny.

A sallow-faced man in loose-fitting canvas trousers and a stained work shirt stood up a few rows behind us. Matheny beckoned him forward and pointed to a crowded row of chairs off to the right of the judge's bench.

"Is he good for the doctor?" Martha whispered frantically as Short walked past our places. Jane Patterson, who was sitting on the other side of Martha, leaned over to hear my answer as well.

"Farmer. Born in Kentucky. Should be open-minded, I think," I replied in a low voice.

"Burton Judson," called Matheny, reading from the next ticket. Jane looked at me.

"Farmer from Tennessee, originally," I whispered as Judson took a seat next to Short. "Not the swiftest fellow. His mill pond overflowed last spring and drowned all his chickens."

"John Alkire," Matheny announced.

"Grain merchant from Pennsylvania," I whispered as he walked past. "Sharp."

"I object, Your Honor," Prickett called as Alkire was opening the gate to the well of the courtroom. "Mr. Alkire has had, I believe, dealings with one of the victims in the course of the trade."

Judge Thomas's face had become tinged with red. He pointed at Alkire with an accusing finger, as if it were he in the dock, and asked, "Any reason you can't be impartial in hearing the evidence in this matter?"

"No, sir."

"Lincoln?" queried the judge.

Lincoln was tipped back in his chair, a look of calm disinterest on his face. "Seems fair enough to me," he said.

"I agree," said the judge. "Overruled." He motioned impatiently for Alkire to continue forward to the jury box. "Next."

And so it went. The twelve-man jury was seated before the bells struck for ten. It comprised six farmers, two merchants, and assorted tradesman—a reasonable selection of the county's population, I thought, and as fair a jury as Lincoln and Patterson could hope to find.

Judge Thomas called for a short recess and stalked off the bench. As soon as the antechamber door closed behind him, the courtroom exploded with noise. The men in the audience cursed their misfortune at not having been selected for the jury; the men in the jury box cursed their misfortune at having been so. Martha and Jane traded nervous conversation. All were expectant.

CHAPTER 29

David Prickett stood alone in the well of the courtroom. He contemplated the jury through intense, unblinking eyes that peered out beneath thick eyebrows. He gave the barest of tosses to his billowing hair. He straightened his already straight back. He gave his shoulders a luxuriant roll. He tugged on the cuffs of his shirtsleeves and stretched out his powerful fingers. With every subtle movement, the jury leaned a little closer in anticipation. Finally, when the courtroom was on a razor's edge, he opened his mouth.

"Gentlemen of the jury," Prickett began, "I am called upon to bring to the view of the court and the jury the circumstances of three murders, each foul and unnatural. Three valuable citizens of our county, each pure in their morals, amiable in their conduct and deportment, and of spotless reputation, have fallen victim to a cruel assassin. Cut off in the prime of life, they have been rudely torn from the embraces of their loved ones. They have been consigned to the silent tomb.

"This is a case of murder three times. Three times the defendant Patterson made the evil decision to take up a deadly weapon. A knife. A paving stone. His own depraved hands. And three times the defendant Patterson made the evil decision to use that weapon to end the life of a treasured member of our community. Three times he committed murder. I regret, and once you've heard the evidence you'll come to regret as well, that he can hang only once for his crimes."

As Jane Patterson gave a gasp from beside me, the crowd murmured its approval. Jane clutched Martha's arm with gloved hands. Her body was rigid with fear. Sitting next to Lincoln in front of us, Dr. Patterson seemed to draw in his breath.

"Let me be more specific," Prickett continued, shifting his weight to his other foot and giving his hair another toss. "Let me be more graphic. It is my duty in this case to bring forth the facts on behalf of the People, and the facts of this case are unavoidably graphic. They are revulsive and graphic and disgusting. I know we have a number of the fair sex in the gallery today, and I have no *right* to tell you to leave, but I say to the gentlemen in the audience that I told Mrs. Prickett she was to stay away this week and I think many of you will want to give the same direction to your own wives."

"Mrs. Prickett would stay away for all time if she had any sense," Martha hissed into my ear. I motioned for her to remain quiet.

Prickett paused, as if giving time for weak-minded wives to decamp, but no one moved. Those lucky enough to have seats had lined up by the courthouse steps starting at seven in the morning. Everyone remained riveted to the prosecutor's words.

"The graphic facts are these," Prickett continued. "The defendant Patterson approached the first victim, the young woman Lilly Walker, in the private setting of her new home. The home she had just found as a shelter, a harbor, for her young, storm-tossed life. The defendant Patterson took up a knife and slashed Lilly's throat. Slashed it with such violence that her life's blood drained right out of her." There were gasps from the crowd.

"The next victim was Lilly's younger brother, a kind little boy, an orphan, a harmless chap by the name of Jesse. What was his crime? What had he done to merit this blackguard's murderous wrath? Not a thing. The boy had never uttered a cross word in his life. And yet, this man, this depraved villain, took a heavy paving stone and crashed it into the boy's skull. Where a moment earlier his happy face had been dotted with freckles, that same face, now frozen into a death mask, was flecked with his blood. And with bits of his brain."

I swallowed hard. The crowd was in an uproar. Several men stood and gestured angrily at Patterson, calling out, "String him up!" or "Let him swing!" A number of women looked faint. Next to Martha, Jane trembled. At least three husbands ordered their wives to leave the courtroom immediately. From their row of chairs in the corner of the well, the jurors watched the upheaval closely. Not one of them looked toward Lincoln or Patterson.

On the bench, Judge Thomas pounded his gavel angrily. Matheny hollered for order. Sheriff Hutchason, who had been standing near to the counsel table where Lincoln and Patterson sat, prowled along the railing, threatening to arrest anyone who was standing and shouting. After several cacophonous minutes, Prickett was finally able to resume.

"I now come to the third murder, the one perhaps most chilling of all because the defendant Patterson executed it with his bare hands. Having killed with weapons, he now decided he could not let any implement come between himself and his victim. His lust for death requires his skin to touch the victim's. His hands must encircle the victim's neck and wring the life from it."

There was another outburst from the crowd, which the judge silenced immediately with a shaking fist. I felt a deep pit growing in my stomach.

"The Widow Harriman was a well-known presence in this county. She was a hardworking woman, a decent woman, who'd persevered after her husband's untimely death. She was part of the soil, the bedrock, of our community. In an act of Christian charity that brings glory to her and to our whole community, she had opened her arms, her home, to bring Lilly and Jesse in from the storm."

Listening to Prickett's apparently heartfelt tribute, I could not help but think of his very different words about Rebecca that I had overheard in the sheriff's backyard. At the same time, I could hardly begrudge the prosecutor for giving Rebecca in death the public praise she'd so fully deserved in life.

"The evidence will show the Widow Harriman had figured out the defendant Patterson was the evil doer who'd struck down her wards. That she had travelled here, to Springfield, to confront him with her knowledge and they had quarreled about her accusation. That, tragically, before she could tell anyone else about her findings, he followed her back to her home and wrung the life out of her pious body."

Prickett moved to stand directly in front of the row of jurors, his back now turned toward the gallery. Even from this angle, his self-righteous posture gave him a commanding look.

"You may be wondering," Prickett continued, "why the three victims allowed Patterson to get close enough to inflict his fatal wounds. Why did they not fight back? Why did they not flee?

"There are two reasons, we will prove, both chilling and both sinister. Patterson was, in each case, a doctor to the victims. They knew him well and they trusted him. If a medical man who has treated you approaches and asks a question, surely it is natural you will listen. Surely your first thought is not flight or fear. You gentlemen of the jury may wish to consider how many of your wives have also been treated by the defendant Patterson. How close may your wife have come to the same unspeakable fate at the hands of this scoundrel?"

Lincoln jumped to his feet and called out, "Objection, Your Honor. My brother counsel should not be able to argue—"

"Overruled," Judge Thomas said without turning to look at Lincoln. The judge was reclined back in his chair, which was orientated toward the spot where Prickett stood, and puffing vigorously on his cigar.

Prickett nodded toward the judge and continued: "The second reason they did not flee is the defendant Patterson gave them, in each case, a foul potion rendering them helpless. Unable to protect themselves. Indeed, unable to move at all as he inflicted the fatal wounds.

"The evidence will be that Patterson often boasted about his special, powerful liquors. That he went so far as to taunt the other medical men in Springfield about the supposed medicinal properties of his brew. About the secret formula, known only to him. Well, what was truly only known to him was his evil use of the potion. It was not an agent of healing. It was an agent of murder."

A round of gasps echoed through the courtroom, although they were more muted this time. I glanced over at the jurors and saw a number of them were whispering to each other and pointing at Patterson. Meanwhile, Prickett walked back to the center of the well.

"After my turn is done," Prickett continued, "my brother Lincoln is going to rise and say a few words. Mr. Lincoln has a folksy nature about him, and I'll admit his stories make even a serious fellow like myself chuckle from time to time." Prickett attempted what I thought was intended to be a self-deprecating smile, but the mood did not suit him and the smile looked more like a grimace. It was the first false note he'd hit.

Prickett seemed to realize as much himself, because he quickly reverted back to his haughty pose and continued: "I want you to listen closely to what he says. Listen to the *substance* of what he says, not merely the amusing digressions." For the first time, the prosecutor gestured toward the table where Lincoln and Patterson sat, and the eyes of the jury followed the sweep of his arm.

"More particularly, listen to hear if there is *any* substance to what he says. Can Mr. Lincoln prove Dr. Patterson did not know each of the victims? Can Mr. Lincoln prove Dr. Patterson did not render each of them insensible with his foul potion? Can Mr. Lincoln prove—"

Lincoln was on his feet again, but before he could get the word "objection" out of his mouth Judge Thomas said, pointing at him with the burning end of his cigar, "It's only attorney argument,

Mr. Lincoln. I'm not going to stop him. You'll need similar latitude, I've no doubt. You may proceed, Attorney Prickett."

"Can Mr. Lincoln prove," Prickett repeated, a sly smile of triumph on his face, "that someone other than Dr. Patterson was the one who struck the fatal blows? Who killed Lilly Walker, and little Jesse, and finally the Widow Harriman? The answer is he will not be able to prove any of these things. Mr. Lincoln is a shrewd advocate, but even he cannot spin gold from dross.

"The truth—the unspeakable, unthinkable, and yet, you will soon see, unavoidable truth—is that Patterson did commit these crimes. The defendant did commit these murders, all three of them. And once you've spoken for the now-silent victims with your verdict, gentlemen, Sheriff Hutchason will hand Patterson over to the last man he'll see on God's Earth. The dispenser of final justice. The hangman."

Prickett took his seat as Jane slumped against Martha's shoulder. Shouts of approval and vigorous applause bounced around the spectator section. Judge Thomas sucked on his cigar for a few extra moments, letting the noise fill the courtroom. When it died down, he looked over at the jury and said, "We're in recess for the midmorning break, gentlemen. Feel free to stand and stretch if you'd like. Then we'll hear from Mr. Lincoln."

CHAPTER 30

During the fifteen minutes that followed, Lincoln did not speak to anyone, not even his own client. At one point, he rose from his chair and sat atop the wooden counsel table, his long legs dangling nearly to the floor. His socks, one black and the other a sort of grubby gray, were readily visible beneath his hitched-up pants. Lincoln leaned forward and rested his prominent chin on his palm in a thoughtful posture. He remained frozen in this position even when Matheny called the courtroom back to order and Judge Thomas ascended the bench.

"You may proceed, Mr. Lincoln," the judge said.

The gentlemen of the jury stared at my friend expectantly. He remained motionless and mute.

"Mr. Lincoln?" the judge said again. "If you've got anything to say by way of an opening statement, now's your time." Another pause. "Because otherwise, Prickett should begin—"

Abruptly, Lincoln straightened up and slid off the table to stand on the floor. There was a collective intake of breath from the courtroom, as if a marble statue of antiquity had suddenly sprung to life. Lincoln stared out at the gallery, then back at the judge and jury, like a man trying to gain his bearings upon waking from a long sleep.

"I was thinking . . . ," he began, before trailing off. He cocked his head back and forth and gesticulated with his arms. Then he seemed to win—or lose (it was impossible to say which)—the argument he'd been having with himself, and he began again.

"I was thinking of the first time I piloted a steamboat," Lincoln said. "I suppose it was the only time I've piloted a steamboat, but the way it lodges in my mind, it was the first time I'd done so. It was March, a few years back, the year eighteen hundred and thirty-two. I was living up in New Salem, right along the Sangamon River, where I was helping to run a small general store."

Lincoln was standing in the middle of the well by now, addressing himself directly to the jury, which looked back with an admixture of confusion and wonder. Both Martha and Jane gave me questioning glances. I shrugged my shoulders; I had no greater understanding of Lincoln's method than did they.

"Anyway—the steamship." He stood inclined forward in an awkward position, looking like a very tall tree that might topple over at any moment. "Word reached us in New Salem that a splendid, upper cabin steamer by the name of the *Talisman* had left Cincinnati on the Ohio River and was heading our way. Evidently, the captain of the *Talisman* had gotten it into his head he was going to demonstrate the navigability of our own little Sangamon River. Some of you who've been around for a few years may remember this," Lincoln added, looking down the row of jurors. Two or three of them nodded in response.

"So the *Talisman* headed down the Ohio, and then when it reached the Mississippi at Cairo, Illinois, it turned north, steaming upstream toward St. Louis. And then it went on past St. Louis, got to the mouth of the Illinois, and steamed up the Illinois toward the mouth of the Sangamon, over at Beardstown. And all the while, those of us in New Salem are getting reports on the ship's progress and we're getting more and more excited."

As Lincoln proceeded with his oration, his shrill, piping voice was becoming harmonious and his form straighter and more dignified. His face was aglow. It was as if he was shedding his natural awkwardness as he warmed to the occasion.

"Now by the by, we hear the *Talisman* is but a single day's steaming from Beardstown, and all of New Salem goes into a frenzy. Here's the ship that's going to connect us to the mighty Mississippi and broad Ohio—connect us to the rest of the world—and it's right on our doorstep."

Lincoln spread out his gangly arms in reverie at the wonder of that moment. From where we sat, looking up at him, the span of his arms seemed to reach from one side of the room to the other. On the bench, Judge Thomas sucked madly on his cigar. Prickett leaned back in his chair and stared up at his adversary with impatience. The silent gallery was transfixed—or more likely, I thought as I looked around, perplexed.

"Now, at this point in my tale," Lincoln continued, drawing in his arms and giving his head a shake, "I'm afraid I need to confess to a sin I committed. The sin of vanity. I thought, what a great day this will be for New Salem. But I also thought, what a great day this could be for *me*. What a great day this could be for Abraham Lincoln.

"So I gathered together a party of fellows and I led them to Beardstown and we spent the whole day along the banks of the Sangamon, cutting back the overhanging brush to make sure the steamer could pass upriver when it got there. And then, when the *Talisman* finally arrived at the mouth of the Sangamon, glistening with river water and belching smoke, I marched aboard the ship and said to the captain, 'I know the Sangamon and its bars and eddies better than anyone. Let me pilot your ship upstream.'

"And the captain, probably because he didn't know what to make of the overgrown oaf standing before him, hands thrust confidently on my hips"—Lincoln mimed this, and a few men in the audience chuckled—"the captain actually turned over his wheel to me, and so I piloted the ship up the Sangamon. In fact, I was so pleased with myself I took the steamer a lot further up the Sangamon than the captain or anyone else had in mind. Took it as far as Portland Landing.

"And the day we reached Portland Landing and docked there, we had a big celebration here in Springfield, on the green right outside of this building, in fact. We had fireworks and a band and a busthead cask or two. I know Your Honor was here," Lincoln said, nodding to the judge, who glowered back, "and Barton . . . and Sharp and"—Lincoln looked down the row of jurors—"Alkire. I reckon each of you was here that day too.

"Those of you who were here remember well, I'm sure— and I'm confessing to the rest of you—what happened next. How the wages of my vanity were paid. Because no sooner had I knocked out the head of the second cask of beer but a little boy comes running up to me, saying"—Lincoln took on the falsetto voice of a small child—"'Mr. Lincoln, Mr. Lincoln, you've got to come quick.'

"'Not now,' I said to him, 'because I'm celebrating my great accomplishment.' Notice I said *my* great accomplishment, not *our* great accomplishment. My accomplishment.

"'Taint no 'complishment at all,' the boy said back to me, "specially not since the river's dropping so fast that great ol' steamer is gonna be stuck here 'til the fall rains come.'"

Lincoln bent over, hands on his knees, and shouted with laughter. "Wouldn't you know it?" he said, looking with eyes crinkling with delight at the jury, then out toward the gallery, where many of the spectators were smiling along with him now, "but the little urchin was one hundred percent right. The river level was dropping. And fast.

"Those of you who were here know what happened next. Everyone at the spree galloped back to the river, back to Portland Landing. I jumped aboard the steamer, and as soon as we got the fire burning again, we cast off and I turned the boat around in the river, scraping the river-bottom with every fathom we moved. And we retreated down the river as fast as we could. But the river was dropping even faster. When we got to New Salem—*my* New Salem, the village I thought I was going to make famous with my exploits aboard the *Talisman*—we had to take ten sticks of dynamite and blow up the mill-dam, blow it to the high heavens, just to get enough flow in the river so we could limp back to Beardstown and the deep waters of the Illinois. We did make it back there in the end, but only barely, and I don't know how much thickness that poor, battered hull had left when we did."

Lincoln had been roaming around the well as he told his story, but now he came to a halt a few feet from the jury. Every member was looking up at him in rapt attention. "I was *sure* I knew what I was doing," he said, "taking command of the *Talisman* and steaming it so far upriver. I was sure of myself. And I was wrong."

Lincoln gazed up and down the row of jurors to make certain none had missed his meaning. When he had looked into the eyes of each of the twelve gentlemen, he turned on his heel and walked rapidly over to the counsel table where Dr. Patterson sat. Lincoln rested his large hand on Patterson's shoulder and faced the jury again.

"Now, I readily concede," Lincoln continued, "there is evidence against my client. My brother Prickett described some of it to you this morning, and I don't doubt we'll hear more this afternoon. Much more, I expect." I saw Jane Patterson stiffen. "There is evidence against Dr. Patterson, but I am not *sure* he's guilty." Lincoln paused for a moment and added, more quietly, "Are you?"

"All I desire, as you hear the evidence, is you ask yourself that question. Are you sure—do you know beyond all reasonable doubt—the doctor is guilty of the heinous crimes with which he's charged? Are you sure? Or are you like my younger self, feeling sure of something, *wanting* to be sure of something, when in fact it is not the truth?

"There was a fellow over in England in the last century who knew a thing or two about the law, and he wrote it all down in some big, heavy books judges like Judge Thomas up there like to take a look at, even today, when they're trying to figure out some complicated legal question. The fellow's name was William Blackstone, *Lord* Blackstone, in fact. And one of the most famous things Lord Blackstone said was, it is better ten guilty men escape than one innocent man suffers. Is Dr. Patterson part of the ten, or is he the one, the innocent one who should not be made to suffer?" Lincoln paused to let each juror think about the question. "Are you sure?"

Lincoln now gestured toward Prickett for the first time since he had begun his statement. "In his remarks," Lincoln said, "my brother said something about wanting you to focus on *substance*. 'Look for the substance, think about the substance.' That was his gist.

"I think my brother was suggesting you should set aside your common sense and focus only on the particular, individual pieces of evidence he wants you to look at." Lincoln gave a kindly smile. "But I don't know what's wrong with a little common sense. On the contrary, I suggest common sense is *all* you'll need as you listen to the evidence in this case. Common sense, and the question to ask yourself—are you sure?"

Lincoln turned to Judge Thomas. "That's what I have to say, Your Honor."

Thomas spit vigorously into his spittoon. "I was most certainly correct, Mr. Lincoln," he said, "that you'd need even more latitude than Prickett." To the jury, the judge added, "Let's take our lunchtime recess. Then we'll come back and hear from actual witnesses rather than windbag lawyers. We're adjourned."

CHAPTER 31

The green outside the courthouse resembled an enormous market fair when Martha, Jane, and I managed to file out a few minutes later. Saunders, Torrey, and several other innkeepers pulled around carts laden with sandwiches and roast slabs and tankards slopping with beer. Men smoked and argued good-naturedly about the opening statements; women unfurled brightly colored parasols and visited with neighbors; a few children got up a game of tag and ran through the crowd hither and fro, shrieking with laughter.

The two women and I stood together, an island of quiet amid the general gaiety. I saw Lincoln loping down the courthouse steps and I shouted out for him to join us.

When he approached, I stuck out my hand to shake his. "Well done," I said. "It was a little grim after Prickett spoke, but I think you turned the jury around, or at the least made them think carefully."

"It remains an uphill fight," he returned, "but I think it was a tolerable start."

"Did you have to admit there was evidence against Father?" Jane asked nervously. "It was unsettling to hear you say."

Lincoln gave her a severe look. "It doesn't do us any good to ignore reality, Miss Patterson," he said. "There is evidence against him. Plenty of it. That's why my argument was focused on certainty and reasonable doubt."

"Don't we have other arguments?" she persisted.

"In my judgment, they're not as strong," he replied. "If I have five arguments, but one is my best, it doesn't do any good to start with the other four. The jury will see right through them, and by the time I get to the one with merit, they'll be so against me for taking up their time with the first four, they won't give it a fair hearing."

"I'm sure Mr. Lincoln knows best how to argue the case," Martha said, putting her hand on Jane's arm.

Saunders pushed his cart by at that moment and Lincoln flipped him a dime and grabbed a meat pie. "I've got to go back inside and prepare for this afternoon's witnesses," he said as he gulped down a large bite. "Make sure the women get some refreshment, Speed."

As I watched him wade back toward the courthouse I spotted other familiar faces. Simeon Francis weaved through the crowd, notebook and pencil in hand, stopping every person or two to pose an inquiry. Major Richmond stood by himself to the side of the courthouse steps, a sandwich in one hand and a tankard in the other. His lips moved rapidly; he seemed to be engaged in a vigorous internal debate. Richmond's plumed hat was looking particularly forlorn in the bright sunshine.

A few paces away from Richmond slouched a circle of idle, vagabond-looking men, who were drinking heavily and leering at any woman unwise enough to get within spitting distance. One of the men, with a straw hat perched atop his head at a disreputable angle, turned and gave me a jagged, discolored grin. It took me a moment to recognize him as Hathaway, the poorhouse master. I wondered what he was doing here. Probably looking for incorrigible debtors whose labor he could procure for his fields now that the harvest was near.

There was a shout behind us. Herr Gustorf tottered our direction on his cast. He was managing to clutch a beer tankard in each hand, with a walking stick jammed under each arm.

"You're looking better," I said. The stitched-up scar on his forehead from the carriage accident had nearly closed.

"I'm feeling *much* better," he replied, taking a gulp from each of his cups. "Especially after yesterday's excursion." He raised one of his sticks and poked me in the ribs.

"What did happen yesterday, Joshua?" Martha asked. "You were gone all day, without explanation." Jane leaned in to hear my answer as well.

"Gustorf and I found evidence supporting an alibi for the doctor," I said. "Evidence of where the doctor was, most probably, on the night of Lilly's murder."

"That's exciting, isn't it, Jane?" my sister said. "How'd you manage?"

Herr Gustorf, a gleam in his eye, opened his mouth to respond, but before he could I interjected, "It's Gustorf's secret. But he's promised to reveal it in his book, if he ever gets around to writing one." Gustorf snorted with laughter, beer very nearly coming out of his nose.

Jane looked at the Prussian with disgust. "Take a turn with me, won't you, Martha," she said. She took my sister's arm and, without a backward glance, set off on a circuit of the bustling square.

"This whole process is such a spectacle to my eyes," said the Prussian, as we surveyed the scene. "Back home, this sort of trial would be conducted by the magistrates in secret. The first anyone would know about it would be when the chief magistrate leads the condemned man in chains into the main square and announces he's been sentenced to death. Then there's a large public procession, headed by the guild leaders, to a spot outside the town walls, and we all watch the poor fellow get his head chopped off." Solemnly, Gustorf raised one of his glasses to the condemned man and drank its remaining contents at a gulp.

"The end's not so different here," I said. "We'll all watch Dr. Patterson swing from the gallows within the fortnight if Lincoln can't manage to get him acquitted."

I turned to look for Martha and nearly collided with Sheriff Hutchason, who was lumbering away from the courthouse with great haste. "What's the matter, Humble?" I asked him, when I saw lines of worry etched on his face.

"Molly's just sent word her time's drawing near."

"Isn't my bondswoman Phillis at her side?"

"She is," Hutchason replied. "And she's been a great comfort, to both Molly and me, I must say."

"Then let them be. You'll only get in the way of the women as they do nature's bidding."

At that moment, Matheny hurried up. "There you are, Sheriff," he said, panting, his cravat askew. "The judge is looking for you. Says he has a question about Dr. Patterson's safety he needs you to address before we commence this afternoon."

"Very well," Hutchason said with a sigh. "I'm sure you're right, Speed. Don't want to unbalance Molly's good humors at a delicate moment like this. Lead the way, Matheny. Let's see what his honor wants this time."

CHAPTER 32

As we sat on the crowded front bench in the courtroom waiting for Matheny to call the afternoon session to order, I whispered to Martha the news that her friend would soon begin her labor of birth.

"Did the sheriff just realize that?" Martha replied with bemusement. "It's been apparent to the rest of us for the past week. I hope he's more observant on duty than he is around his own home."

As it happened, Hutchason was also Prickett's first witness. The thick-chested lawman strode to a witness seat wedged in between Judge Thomas's bench and the row of jurors. The chair seemed to vanish beneath his broad frame as he settled onto it. After Matheny administered the oath, Prickett began.

"You are the sheriff of Sangamon County?"

"I am," boomed Hutchason.

"And you viewed the bodies of all three victims in their places of final repose?"

"I did."

"Tell the gentlemen of the jury what you saw."

Hutchason cleared his throat and turned to the jury.

"Sirs, I've held my office for a decade," he began in a somber tone. "I've seen things no one should have to see—mutilation, scalding, eyeballs that have been gouged out, a man gored all the way through by the horn of an ox. I've even seen the inhumane savagery of the Red Man. But never have I seen such depravity as was inflicted on these three virtuous persons by this villain."

An ecstatic gasp arose from the teeming gallery. If a few weak-minded women, or men, had decamped after the graphic proceedings of the morning, their places had been filled five-fold by newcomers who had heard about those same graphic proceedings during the lunchtime recess. Not only was every seat in the gallery taken, but the ring of spectators standing against the walls was now three or four persons deep. The row of standees pressed against the wall even extended behind the gentlemen of the jury in the well of the courtroom, such that the jurors had been obligated to move their chairs forward a few feet to avoid being stepped or spat upon by the crowd.

The sheriff proceeded to describe the three murder scenes in blunt, exacting detail. Lilly Walker had been slain by a knife wound to the base of her throat, a cut that, the sheriff reported, looking over at Patterson for emphasis, had been made with the precision of a skilled hand. Jesse Walker had been killed by a single swift blow to the head. Rebecca Harriman had been strangled by someone with hands large enough to surround her delicate neck and wring the life out of it. Each of them, the sheriff testified, would have experienced great anguish in their final moments on Earth.

The audience shouted with outrage. A renewed cry of "String him up!" echoed through the courtroom. I felt sick to my stomach. My sister Martha rested her hand on my shoulder. In front of us, Dr. Patterson was erect and motionless, facing the witness. *If you did this*, I thought, boring a hole in his back with my eyes, *if you truly did this, then Prickett's right; facing the executioner only once isn't punishment enough.*

Under Prickett's questioning, the sheriff proceeded to relate that none of the victims showed any signs of having battled back against their assassin.

"No signs of struggle," repeated Prickett. "How can that be? Surely these three noble personages would have fought valiantly for their lives."

"I conclude each was incapacitated by the killer before the fatal blow was struck."

"How did he accomplish such?"

The sheriff shifted in his chair. "I wasn't present at the time, of course," he said, "so I cannot be certain. But it's my belief he induced them to ingest a potion rendering them insensible to the surrounding world. Once incapacitated, they had no ability to resist his deadly advance. I should note, in this regard, I detected a strong odor of alcohol near the bodies of Miss Walker and the Widow Harriman."

"And what of young Jesse?"

"A bystander reported finding a partially eaten cake not far from the boy's resting place," Hutchason said, his eyes flickering toward me for a moment before returning to the prosecutor. "I can only presume the villain had soaked the cake with his potion before malevolently feeding it to the boy. Unfortunately, as the gentlemen of the jury know, the Globe stable fired that very evening, so that evidence, along with who knows what else, was lost to us."

"I was going to ask you about the fire," said Prickett, giving his hair a well-practiced toss. "The gentlemen will remember well the night the Globe fired, I have no doubt. Do you accuse the defendant of arson in addition to murder?"

"Sir, it is my method to be judicious in the charges I levy. I am not certain I can *prove* he set the fire, and therefore I do not accuse him of such before this tribunal. However, the circumstances are suspicious in the extreme." He looked up at Prickett, who gestured for him to continue.

"Young Master Jesse was killed in the barn at the back of the Globe stables. We know this from the straw about his person. I believe the killer meant to dispose of the body but was interrupted in his design by some intervening event. Someone unexpectedly entered the stables, most likely. So he hid the corpse in a nearby carriage with the intention of driving it out of Springfield later that same night. When, instead, the Widow Harriman sounded the alarm and a search was launched for the missing boy, the killer decided to obscure his tracks by setting the fire. He was, in the end, only partially successful."

Jane leaned over and whispered, "The whole thing's speculation. Why isn't Mr. Lincoln challenging the testimony?"

"He's choosing his battles, as he told you he would," I returned. "Most of the sheriff's testimony concerns matters the jury will have heard plenty about before the trial even started. I wager Lincoln thinks there's not much profit in fighting to keep it out of evidence."

"On your view," Prickett was asking the sheriff, "how was the killer able to fire the stables before the search parties reached them?"

"By acting with alacrity, he was able to out-pursue the pursuers."

"Now, you mentioned earlier the Widow Harriman raised the alarm about her missing nephew," continued the prosecutor. "How, specifically, did she do this?"

"That's just the thing, sir," said the sheriff. "She did so by going to the house of this very man, the defendant." He pointed at Patterson. The crowd murmured. "In other words, calamitously, she told the one man who *didn't need* to be told, because he already knew of the boy's tragic fate, and the one man who *couldn't* be told, because it gave him time to spark the fire and thereby destroy evidence of his guilt."

A number of men in the gallery were now standing and yelling at Patterson. I recognized two of them in particular as men who had bravely stood on the roof of the Globe that night, fighting the insidious spread of the fire bucket by bucket. Judge Thomas pounded for order.

Once he could be heard over the din, Prickett asked, "You said the Widow Harriman tragically chose to go to the defendant

Patterson with news that young Jesse was missing. Did she later come to suspect Patterson himself was, in fact, the evildoer?"

"I believe she did," replied the sheriff.

"And the basis for that belief is what?"

"First of all, I spoke with a blacksmith up in Menard named Dickson, and he told me—"

Lincoln was on his feet. "Objection, Your Honor," he shouted, loud enough to drown out any recitation of Dickson's views. "Hearsay."

Before the judge could take the cigar out of his mouth to rule, Prickett coolly put up his hand and said, "Mr. Lincoln's quite right, Sheriff. Dickson himself is coming in tomorrow to give evidence. There's no cause for you to relate his words." Lincoln sat down, mollified.

"Let me put the question to you this way," Prickett continued. "Did you come into possession of a writing by the Widow Harriman, shedding light on her relations with the defendant Patterson."

"I did, sir," replied Hutchason.

Prickett took up a small packet of paper from his table and unfolded it carefully. "What's this?" he asked, handing it to Hutchason.

The sheriff made a show of reading the document carefully to himself. When he had finished, he looked up and said, "A letter. Authored by the Widow Harriman and intended for the defendant."

"I should ask, Sheriff, how you came into possession of the letter."

"The widow left it with an innkeeper in town, for delivery to Patterson. But the proprietor—to his credit—recognized the potential public importance of the document and delivered it to you, Mr. Prickett, instead."

At Prickett's prompting, the sheriff read the entire contents of Rebecca's note aloud to the jury, taking care to emphasize the words "confrontation" and "quarrel." Prickett then obtained permission from the judge to publish the writing to the jury, and each of the gentlemen examined it in turn. The spectators lucky enough to be standing behind the jurors stood on tiptoe and craned their necks to read the letter as it was passed down the row. The rest of the gallery murmured jealously.

During the entire spectacle Dr. Patterson sat straight at attention, occasionally moistening his fingers and running them over his moustache. What were his thoughts, I wondered, at hearing aloud the final words of his intended?

When the last juror had finished his examination, Prickett took up the note again and gave it back to the sheriff. "When did the Widow Harriman pen this communication, Sheriff, if you know?"

"It's dated last Thursday."

"And it refers to a confrontation, a quarrel, between the widow and the defendant occurring that same day, which is to say, last Thursday?"

"Correct."

"And when, Sheriff, was the widow slain? When did some blackguard immobilize her, stretch his fingers around her neck, and squeeze?"

The sheriff shifted in his chair. He looked very somber. I closed my eyes and tried to avoid imagining the moment of Rebecca's death.

"As near as I can tell," replied the sheriff, "she was killed the very next day. Last Friday evening."

A gasp rushed through the room. Prickett gave a satisfied nod and sat.

Judge Thomas called for a short recess, during which the courtroom hummed with excitement mingled with disgust. Then Lincoln rose to commence his cross examination.

Those persons, myself included, who hoped Lincoln would match Prickett's flair and forcefulness were disappointed. Lincoln established the doctor had not confessed to the charges and that Hutchason could not positively exclude the possibility another man had been responsible for the killings. And Lincoln got Hutchason to acknowledge none of the murder weapons had been owned by Patterson.

The only frisson of excitement came at the end of his questioning. "Is it fair to say, Sheriff," Lincoln said, his hands clasped behind his back and his long torso stooped forward, "you exhaustively considered all possible suspects before coming to lodge charges against my client, Dr. Patterson?"

"Very fair," returned the sheriff.

"You considered every possibility? You left no stone unturned?"

"Quite. I think the people of this county would expect nothing less of me."

"The people of this county expect when you determine to arrest a man for a crime, certainly for the most serious crime of murder, you will do so only after having reached the conclusion, as a moral certainty, of the man's guilt."

"Indeed," replied the sheriff. A ripple of uncertainty passed across his face; I guessed he was trying to figure out Lincoln's destination.

"The Widow Harriman's two wards, Lilly and Jesse, were the first two victims of this mendacious killer, isn't that right?" continued Lincoln.

"Yes."

"And you were well along into your investigation of those deaths when the tragic news came to you of the third death, that of the Widow Harriman?"

"Correct."

"And isn't it a fact you had determined to arrest the widow for those two murders—that you were, in fact, on your way to arrest her when you discovered instead she herself had fallen victim to the murderer?"

"That's right," the sheriff said. The crowd buzzed with surprise. On the bench, Judge Thomas blew out a large cloud of smoke and scowled at Prickett.

"What happened to your moral certainty the Widow Harriman was the killer of her own niece and nephew?"

Hutchason stared at Lincoln open-mouthed, as if he did not comprehend the question. "I changed my mind is what happened," he said at last. "The new evidence changed my mind. It's apparent, of course, she hadn't strangled herself."

"And what confidence," continued Lincoln, "can the gentlemen of the jury have, if they determine to pronounce a sentence of guilt, that you won't change your mind again based on some new evidence, this time about the guilt of Dr. Patterson—only this time after he meets his fate at the hands of the executioner?"

"That's not going to happen," sputtered Hutchason.

"How can you be sure?" Lincoln gestured to the jury. "How can *they* be sure?"

"Well, for one thing," said Hutchason, recovering his footing, "his guilt is apparent from the face of the widow's letter." He held up the folded packet of paper again. "I don't see what intervening fact could change the import of this letter. They quarrel, violently it would seem, and the next day she's dead."

"The letter," repeated Lincoln. "That's what I thought you were going to say. We'll come back to it in due course." And with that he resumed his seat next to the doctor.

CHAPTER 33

That night I dreamed repeatedly about Rebecca but never once glimpsed her. She remained in my nighttime world, as in my waking one, an invisible presence. A shade.

I awoke to bright sunlight. The other side of our bed appeared undisturbed. If Lincoln had made any use of it he had, uncharacteristically, tidied it before departing. As I crossed the green to the courthouse, a few minutes before nine, my sister Martha called out my name. From the red streaks in her eyes, it seemed she hadn't slept well either.

"How's Molly?" I asked. "Is there a baby yet?"

"The baby hasn't come," Martha said. "And do you genuinely want to know Molly's condition?" A brief pause, during which I remained mute. "I didn't think so. I'm going to spend the day at her bedside. I think I can be of use to Phillis."

"Let's meet for dinner at the Globe if Molly can spare you then," I said. "I'll let you know what happens in court today."

"Try to be kind to Jane," said Martha as she made ready to depart. "She was devastated last night after hearing her father attacked as a cold-blooded murderer."

"So was I."

Martha gazed at me appraisingly. She looked much older than her seventeen years. "But your pain is in the past. Hers is in the present. And the future."

Dickson, the blacksmith from Menard, was already seated in the witness chair when I entered the courtroom and took my place on the front bench. The smith was long and powerful, with a high forehead, receding curly hair, and a fiery red beard. His muscular forearms bulged out of his loose-fitting, soot-stained tunic. Simeon Francis and I had spoken briefly with Dickson on the day of our reporting trip, and I knew him to be a man of few emotions and fewer words.

"You operate a smithy a few storefronts down from Harriman & Co.," Prickett began without preamble while the crowd was still settling into their seats.

"That's right," replied Dickson. His deep, ragged voice was like an anvil dragged along a gravel path.

"And you came to know the Widow Harriman well during the time you and she were both in business in Menard?"

"Well enough."

"And you came to learn, over the course of time, about the deaths of the widow's two wards, the young woman Lilly and then her younger brother Jesse?"

Dickson grunted and gave what seemed like an affirmative nod. On the bench, Judge Thomas spit out his cigar and said, "You've got to answer with words, Mr. Dickson, not gestures. Do you understand?"

Dickson glanced toward the judge and said, "Yes." Then he turned to Prickett and repeated the same word.

A quiet laughter spread through the crowd, which was, if anything, larger than the previous day. Dickson did not react.

"Did you," said Prickett, nodding at his witness encouragingly, "have cause to speak to the Widow Harriman about her tragic losses?"

"No."

"Well," said Prickett, trying again, "did you and she have a conversation about the deaths and about her views about what might have happened?"

"No," said Dickson blankly.

In front of me, Lincoln looked over at the prosecutor with a bemused expression. In profile, his face looked weary. His frockcoat was rumpled and creased. Next to him, Dr. Patterson watched the witness attentively. There were no signs *he* had experienced trouble sleeping.

Painstakingly, painfully, Prickett pulled the story out of the smith. The day Rebecca had travelled from Menard to Springfield to see the doctor—and meet with me and Lincoln—she had stopped by Dickson's smithy first to ask him to keep an eye on her store. At the time, the smith relayed haltingly, she told him she was going to Springfield because she had figured out who was responsible for killing her niece and nephew.

"Those were her exact words?" Prickett said over the murmuring audience. "That she'd figured out who committed the crimes?"

"Right."

"And what did you say in response, when she told you this?"

"Don't think I said anything."

My mind was racing. If Rebecca had actually figured out who the murderer was, why didn't she tell me and Lincoln? Had she said anything to us that might provide a clue to her thoughts? The smith's story didn't ring true and yet—given the difficultly Prickett was having in pulling it from him—there was no indication he was fabricating.

Meanwhile, Prickett was trying without success to elicit additional details from Dickson. Finally, the prosecutor asked, "And do you know, in fact, that the Widow Harriman's destination that day, after she told you why she was traveling to Springfield, was the home of this man, the defendant Allan Patterson?"

"I don't," replied Dickson.

"Well, it was," said Prickett. "That's where she was going."

Lincoln shot up, saying, "Objection, Your Honor. If Attorney Prickett intends to testify himself, the least we can do is have Matheny swear him in first."

"Sustained," said Judge Thomas, before Prickett could respond. "Do you have anything else for this witness?" When the prosecutor hesitated, the judge said, "Then sit down and let Mr. Lincoln ask his questions."

Lincoln stood and walked in a big semicircle, passing in an arc by the jury box before coming to rest directly in front of the witness. "Good morning, Dickson," he said reasonably.

"Morning."

"Did you ask the Widow Harriman who it was she thought was responsible for the murders?"

"No."

"Weren't you interested in learning who the murderer was, or at least who she thought it was?"

"No."

"You don't know who she had in mind?"

"No."

"So as far as you know, the Widow Harriman could have intended to accuse Sheriff Hutchason, or Attorney Prickett, or even Judge Thomas up there on the bench of having committed the first two murders?" The crowd tittered nervously.

"True enough. Can I go now?" Dickson added. "I've said all I have to say."

"You can go," said Lincoln, resuming his seat.

After the judge called for the morning recess and left the bench to replenish his supply of cigars, I turned to Jane Patterson. She, too, was looking strained and tired.

"What did happen, between your father and Rebecca Harriman, the afternoon she showed up?" I asked, talking quietly so neither the spectators around us nor the doctor in the well in front of us could hear.

"I'm not sure," she replied. "I wasn't home at the time. But there was no scene, no long argument, I can assure you. My father was perfectly normal when I returned home later that day."

"Were you aware of the understanding between your father and the widow? Before the letter was read aloud yesterday, I mean."

"Of course," she said quickly. Something about the way she replied made me wonder, but the judge was back on his bench calling the proceedings to order.

"Your Honor," Prickett announced, "the People call Dr. Weymouth Warren." The doctor, one of Patterson's principal rivals in town, walked stiffly to the stand. He was long-faced and dolorous, with a flowing gray beard. Like Patterson, he wore a surgical coat stained with the insignia of his profession.

The contrast with the prior witness could not have been greater. Where the blacksmith struggled for monosyllables, Warren expounded in paragraphs and sometimes chapters. Warren's discussion of his background and experience in the medical arts extended at such great length that the judge was obliged to call for the luncheon recess in its midst.

A cynic might have wondered if Warren was more interested in recruiting patients from among the assembled multitudes than in providing his evidence. If this was indeed his goal, however, he had severely misjudged his audience, which looked on with increasing impatience as he expounded upon himself.

Midway through the afternoon session, Prickett had the sense—and the skill—to bring Warren to the nub of the matter. The rival doctor testified Dr. Patterson had often touted his self-brewed medicinal liquors as a reason his own medical practice flourished, while Warren's did not enjoy the full success his superior learning should have produced. Patterson had boasted, Warren relayed to the jury, that the strongest of his liquors was so powerful a few drops would dissolve any bodily ailment, and a few more would be sufficient to produce almost instant slumber.

As the gallery whispered excitedly about this new evidence of guilt, Lincoln rose to his feet. "Will you admit Dr. Patterson here is known for his modern methods and learning?" he began.

Warren stared out mournfully. "He, himself, has often said as much, Mr. Lincoln," he replied, his eyes blinking rapidly. "Indeed, there was a time he told me—"

"You've answered the question, Doctor," Lincoln said with a raised hand. "Let's see if we can't keep matters moving apace." Warren looked over at Prickett, but the prosecutor did not seem inclined to interfere with Lincoln's attempt to control his witness.

"Patterson has sometimes undertaken treatments you were unfamiliar with or hesitant to try, for lack of a certain result?" put Lincoln.

"That's true. He's been reckless, in my judgment. For example, there was the time—"

"But oftentimes, his patients have lived," continued Lincoln. "As a result of his innovative treatments, they've lived. Isn't that the case?"

"For every one such, I'd wager there are three who've died sooner than they've needed to," Warren returned. "For those three, if I had been privileged to be entrusted with their care, I suggest the results might have been conclusively different."

"You have been all these years a competitor of Dr. Patterson?" Lincoln asked.

"A colleague, I'd like to think," Warren returned, affecting an ill-fitting modesty. "There have been more than enough sick persons in the village—in the county, for that matter—to challenge all those of us with medical learning."

"But none who've been more prominent, or successful, than Patterson—wouldn't you agree?"

"Perhaps," said Warren. He shifted in his chair.

"If a man falls sick in Springfield, he's most likely to ask his wife to send for Patterson, isn't that the case?"

"Not in the last few days, I wouldn't think." Warren could not prevent a smile from creeping onto his face.

"I meant prior to these events of course, Doctor," Lincoln replied sharply.

"Perhaps."

"And would you admit your practice would be enhanced if Dr. Patterson were—well, if he were no longer ministering to patients in Springfield?"

"You can hardly believe, Mr. Lincoln, such a prospect would influence my testimony today."

"The jury shall be the judge of that," Lincoln returned, and he sat.

"At least Mr. Lincoln tried to undermine that witness," Jane whispered to me as Warren slowly made his way from the well of the courtroom.

Before I could respond, Prickett sprang to his feet and announced, "Your Honor, as the final witness of our case-in-chief, the People call Hiram Jenkins." As it turned out, the most damning testimony was about to arrive.

An older, tall man with well-tended whiskers made his way forward. The man and his name were vaguely familiar, but I had not placed either by the time Prickett began his examination.

"Were you, sir, at the general muster in Menard last weekend when the Widow Harriman's body was discovered?"

"I was," Jenkins replied in a deep voice.

"And did you view her body there?"

"Sheriff Hutchason sent for me," Jenkins said, "to give him a second opinion on the body and the *causa mortis*. We'd served together, you see, in the Indian War. He knew of my medical skill."

Startled, I realized Jenkins had been the drunk medic who'd tottered up to us from his tug-of-war games. That disreputable rogue was almost unrecognizable in the well-groomed man who sat on the witness chair now. I leaned forward with interest.

"Now, earlier that same day, did you happen to notice anything out of the ordinary?" Prickett asked. There was an undercurrent of excitement in the prosecutor's voice. He believes he's going for the kill, I thought.

"I saw a high-tandem gig, one of those sporting types, on the Springfield road," Jenkins replied.

"At what time was this, in relation to when you examined—at the sheriff's request—the Widow Harriman's body?"

Jenkins looked up at the ceiling and thought. "About six or seven hours prior, I'd judge. It was very early that morning. The sun had barely breached the horizon."

"How is it you happen to remember this particular gig?" asked Prickett. "After all, I expect there were a great many vehicles and beasts on the roads that day, it being the muster."

"There were, but the sporting gig was driving *away* from the muster—away from Menard. Everything else I saw that day was heading toward Menard."

"Did you recognize the gig, Mr. Jenkins?" asked Prickett.

The gallery was silent with expectation.

"I'd seen it plenty of times before," the witness said, nodding. "It belonged to Dr. Patterson over there." There was an explosion of noise, through which Jenkins added, "He cared for my little Jimmy, before he passed on. Must have seen that same vehicle coming up my road a half-dozen times."

The courtroom was in tumult. In front of me, Patterson's shoulders were tensed. Judge Thomas sucked on his cigar and pounded for order, though he seemed in no great hurry to have it restored. When it finally was, he gestured at Prickett to continue.

"Did you see Dr. Patterson himself in the gig?" the prosecutor asked.

"I saw him at a distance from behind—saw his back and hat," Jenkins said. "I'd recognize his surgical coat anywhere. There were too many times I watched in sadness as he drove away from our house after administering another purging to Jimmy."

"You yourself have medical knowledge," said Prickett. "Why was it you engaged another medical man to look after your Jimmy?"

"Patterson told me he knew of modern treatments that would keep the boy alive."

"Did they?"

"No." Jenkins blinked twice.

Prickett gave a respectful nod toward the witness and the jury. But as he turned back toward his table to sit, he had a wide smile of victory on his face. As Lincoln started to rise from his seat, Patterson put his hand out on Lincoln's arm and whispered something.

"Mr. Lincoln?" prompted the judge, who was looking over at their table with interest. "Do you have any questions for this witness?"

"A moment, if I may, Your Honor," Lincoln said hesitantly. He bent over next to Patterson and the two men whispered back and forth with growing animation. I leaned forward to try to catch their conversation, but the rest of the gallery was soon filled with noisy speculation about the same topic and I couldn't hear a word. A number of the jurors were whispering back and forth as well. As Lincoln and Patterson continued talking, Lincoln's expressive face became set in a look of dismay.

"*Tempus fugit*, Mr. Lincoln," Judge Thomas prompted, without sympathy, after a minute had passed. "Time flies."

Lincoln started to straighten up. He gave a last, questioning look at Patterson, who nodded vigorously in response.

"No questions for this witness at this time, Your Honor," Lincoln announced. Several gasps of surprise arose from the audience.

"We're adjourned for the day, gentlemen," the judge said to the jury. "We'll resume on the stroke of nine tomorrow to hear Mr. Lincoln's defense." I could almost hear the judge adding, silently, "If he has one."

As the courtroom filled with excited conversation, Lincoln strode to the railing and beckoned at me. "Come by Hoffman's Row after supper," he said, just loud enough for me to hear him over the din. "I'm sure I could use your good counsel then. Miss Speed's as well, for that matter. Patterson's finally agreed to tell me the whole truth."

CHAPTER 34

The Globe's public room that evening was full of men speculating confidently about the exact date on which Patterson would hang. More than a few wagers were placed. Martha and I did our best to ignore the chatter as we ate side by side. I described the day's proceedings in court and Lincoln's request to meet; in turn, Martha reported Phillis had said tomorrow would probably be the day the sheriff's child made his or her entrance into the world.

"And perhaps the day that seals Patterson's departure," I said.

"Show some confidence in your friend Mr. Lincoln," said Martha. "I'm sure he'll have a plan for the doctor's defense. Especially now that, as you've said, Patterson's confiding in him a fuller version of events."

"I'm not sure I want to have confidence in Lincoln," I returned. "If Patterson's in fact guilty . . ." I couldn't finish the sentence. "And, I'll tell you, having sat in court the past few days, it's getting hard to hold any other view. The evidence against him has been damning."

A few minutes later, we finished our meal and headed for the still, darkened streets. There was a hint of chill in the air. "Are you sure," Martha asked as we walked along, "your judgment about the trial isn't being clouded by your feelings for the Widow Harriman? From what I've seen, the question of Dr. Patterson's guilt is very much unresolved. And you must understand, Joshua, whatever happens at the trial isn't going to bring her back to life."

"Of course I know that."

"Perhaps you do as an abstract matter," returned my sister. "But that's not the way I've seen you reacting over the past few days."

I felt my temper rising. "So you're an expert, all of a sudden, on matters of the mind?"

"I'm an expert on you, dear brother," she said, putting a bare hand on my arm. Her touch warmed me. "At least I'd like to think I am. Do you realize, while the sheriff was testifying to the condition of the Widow Harriman's body, you looked up at the ceiling of the courtroom and started mouthing words? It was exactly as if you were trying to communicate with somebody."

"Did I?"

"Did you what?" called Lincoln through the open door of No. 4, Hoffman's Row.

"I'm trying to help my brother untangle his heart," Martha said as we entered the law office.

"In that case," said Lincoln, a warm smile crinkling the skin beside his gray eyes, "you're the only person in Springfield, Miss Speed, who's got a more thankless task than me."

Lincoln swept some papers off Stuart's lounge with a careless swing of his arm. As they fluttered about the disheveled office, he said, "Please, sit. I'm glad to see you both."

"How can we be of use?" Martha asked earnestly.

Lincoln lowered himself into his chair with a sigh and drew his buffalo robe around his shoulders. He looked tired. "You're going to get an answer to your question, Miss Speed," he said after a moment. "About what makes someone insane in the eyes of the law."

"What?" I exclaimed.

"I've spent the past four hours over at the jail cell, talking with Patterson," Lincoln said. "He's finally told me what happened. It would have been a lot more useful to his defense if he'd done so when he was first arrested, but he's done so now. He was waiting to hear the evidence against him, I suppose.

"Our defense in court tomorrow will be lack of sound mind. The Illinois statute books are clear a man's not legally responsible for actions committed in a condition of insanity."

"You can't mean it!" I cried, but Lincoln bobbed his head somberly.

"I don't understand," said Martha, looking back and forth between us.

I felt the blood pounding in my head. "What Lincoln's saying," I said, "is the doctor's now confessed to him he *is* the murderer. That it was he who killed Lilly and Jesse and Rebecca—all of them, I take it," I added, looking up at Lincoln, who nodded. "And now Lincoln's going to argue he's not legally responsible for the murders because he's mad."

I turned back to Lincoln and continued, with anger: "Which is *absurd*. The doctor's as *sane* as you or me. Depraved, to be sure, if he's now admitting he was the killer all along. Grotesquely depraved. But stone-sober sane."

"I wouldn't be so sure, Speed, until you've heard the whole circumstance," said Lincoln. "Wait for the testimony tomorrow and then you can come to a conclusion."

"There's nothing more to be heard," I said. "Nothing could change my mind. The man deserves to die. And the sooner, the better."

"I've never heard of insanity used as a defense in a murder case," Martha said. "Has anyone ever actually won acquittal on that basis?"

"More often than you might think," Lincoln said. "Do you remember reading of the case of the out-of-work house painter who shot at President Jackson a few years ago? Tried to shoot him in the portico of the Capitol building, in Washington, only both of his guns misfired?"

"Oh—wasn't the King involved somehow?" said Martha.

"That's right," Lincoln said. "The evidence at the trial showed the accused, a fellow named Richard Lawrence, believed himself to be the King of England. Lawrence believed President Jackson was preventing him from receiving the riches to which he was entitled. It took the jury all of five minutes to acquit him by reason of insanity. And that was for trying to kill the President of the United States."

"But he was a man who went around mad all the time, from the sound of it," Martha said. "That's obviously not Dr. Patterson's case."

Lincoln nodded. "Very perceptive," he said. "The testimony tomorrow will be that Patterson's been suffering from *transitory fits* of insanity. Maybe you should be reading the law after all, Miss Speed. Just because your brother couldn't endure the intellectual rigor doesn't mean there's not hope for you."

Martha gave Lincoln a pleased smile. I scowled; I was in no mood for Lincoln's humor.

Lincoln picked up a half-eaten apple from among the clutter on the table in front of him and contemplated it. He took a large bite and chewed loudly.

"Let me see if this one convinces you," he said. "There was a bizarre case in England recently. A sober, industrious tradesman was sitting calmly at home, reading his Bible, when a female neighbor came in to ask for a little milk. He looked wildly at her, instantly seized a knife and attacked her, and then attacked his own wife and daughter. His aim appeared to be to decapitate each of them, as he tried cutting the napes of their necks." Martha gasped in horror, and Lincoln gave a perverse grin.

"Anyway," Lincoln continued, "the man was subdued before he could inflict a fatal wound on any of them, and a doctor came at once and concluded he was in the midst of an epileptic fit. His complexion was a dusky red, his eyes starting from their sockets, and he was continually extending his jaws as if trying to yawn. The doctor tied him down and depleted him, both bloodletting and purging, and within three days he was back to normal. Had no memory of the acts he'd committed. Indeed, shocked to hear what had happened. He wasn't charged with a crime, for how could he be? How could it be said he had intended harm? As far as I know, he lives peacefully in Sussex to this day, if you want to go for a visit."

"Oh dear," said Martha, with a shudder.

"But that doesn't remotely describe Patterson," I objected.

"Or consider Hamlet," Lincoln said, taking another bite from his apple. "He acts rationally in contriving a scene by the players to test his uncle's guilt but irrationally in ordering Ophelia to the nunnery. When he kills Claudius at the play's end, is it an act of sanity or insanity? 'Here, thou incestuous, murderous, damned Dane / Drink of this potion. Is thy union here?'"

"But Hamlet's a fictitious character," said Martha.

"In many respects," Lincoln responded, "he's more fully realized than the men you'll encounter on the street tomorrow."

"It's an odd coincidence," she said. "Dr. Patterson himself mentioned Hamlet and King Lear at dinner on my first night here when he was talking about Major Richmond's condition."

"That's no coincidence," Lincoln returned. "I've talked to any number of modern medical men who swear the Bard provides the entire taxonomy of mental alienation and its proper treatment. It goes far beyond Hamlet's fits and Lear's melancholy. Macbeth and Lady Macbeth show the dangers of mania. Malvolio is imprisoned in *Twelfth Night* for being a lunatic. Stephano confronts Caliban's madness in *The Tempest* with methods material and psychological. And so on."

"You've certainly thought a great deal about diseases of the mind," said Martha.

"Perhaps I have," Lincoln replied. His face did not betray whatever inner feelings he had on the subject.

"Even the word 'lunatic' itself harbors the concept of an affliction waxing and waning, I suppose," Martha said.

"Just so," said Lincoln. "The idea of a person made insane only by particular phases of the moon."

Unsettled, I stood and walked over to the small window and squinted up at the glittering night sky. It was almost time for the luminous harvest moon to make its appearance. Even through my visceral anger, I could understand the intellectual force of Lincoln's argument, but—

"Doesn't it *dishonor* the dead?" I asked aloud.

"What do you mean?" said Martha.

"I mean, three vital persons have had their lives ripped away. That's an awful thing any way we look at it. It's a violation of God's plan for each of them, even though we can't know what His full plan was. And now, Lincoln's suggesting no one needs to bear guilt for these terrible acts if they were acts of irrationality. That the victims' pain, their abject fear at the moment of attack, the loss their loved ones feel"—I swallowed before continuing—"none of it matters depending on what was inside the mind of the man committing the crime. That the dead don't matter, only the villain."

"You're thinking like a philosopher, Speed," said Lincoln. "I don't have that luxury as an advocate."

"I am not thinking like a philosopher," I said as another jolt of anger raced through me. "I'm thinking like someone who lost a woman I cared for deeply."

"Of course you are," said Lincoln more quietly.

One of the two candles in the center of Lincoln's worktable had burned down to a stub. Lincoln wetted his thumb and forefinger and put it out. Immediately, the room was cast into shadow.

"It seems to me the most important point," said Martha, "is the law recognizes this as a valid defense. You're saying you can get the doctor acquitted with this argument."

"It's a fool's errand," I said. "The man's a liar—and a murderer. He deserves to hang."

"Let's let the jury decide the question, Speed," Lincoln replied. "That's their charge after all. Though I admit this defense reminds me of a story Logan told the other day, about when he commenced his law practice in Springfield. This is years ago, when he was but an eager young lad. Logan came upon an elderly gentleman in town and he said, by way of introduction, 'I'm from Kentucky, and a lawyer. What's my prospect here?'

"And the gentleman took one look at Logan and gave a discouraging shake of his head. 'Damn slim for that combination,' he said. 'Damn slim.'"

"Course, today, Logan's the leading lawyer in town," I said. Lincoln nodded.

CHAPTER 35

Lincoln stood tall and announced, "Your Honor, for my first witness, I call Dr. Allan Patterson."

As the courtroom gallery, if possible even more crowded than yesterday, clamored excitedly, Patterson arose from his seat at the counsel table and walked slowly to the witness chair. The doctor looked as if he had taken a little extra time on his appearance this morning. His thinning hair was combed back neatly, and his elaborate moustache was waxed into place. Even his surgical coat seemed less soiled than usual, although several dark splotches remained.

The judge looked over at Prickett to see if he planned to object. The law disfavored a defendant testifying on his own behalf. But Prickett, smiling a self-contained smile, remained mute. He's confident he can ruin him on cross examination, I thought.

"Good morning, Doctor," Lincoln said.

"Morning," Patterson managed in reply as his voice cracked. He damn well should be nervous, I thought, with what he's about to try to pull off.

"Tell the jury about yourself."

"I was born in ninety-seven on a farm near the settlement of Cincinnati, then in the Northwest Territory, now part of the state of Ohio. After grammar school, I showed an aptitude for medicine, and so I did an extended preceptorship with our neighbor, who happened to be the village doctor. That went well, so I enrolled in the Medical Department of Transylvania University, in Lexington, Kentucky. It was a brand-new medical faculty at the time, very interested in modern, innovative methods." He looked up at Lincoln.

"Go on," Lincoln prompted.

"After I'd completed the course of instruction at Transylvania, I heard about a shortage of qualified doctors in this state," Patterson continued, looking directly at the jury, who were listening with interest. The doctor's voice was strong now and his tone confident. He was regaining, sentence by sentence, the imperious bearing he carried before his arrest.

"So I moved from Lexington to Illinois, first to Albion, along the Wabash River, and then to Decatur. I ministered to the people of Decatur for nearly a decade. That's where I met my beloved wife," he added. For the first time in his testimony, the doctor looked directly at Jane, sitting near me in the gallery, and the two of them locked eyes for a moment.

"After my wife passed on," Patterson continued, "I decided to move to Springfield to continue my practice. And I've been serving the people of this community ever since."

"Have you done your best, at all times, to care for the people of this community faithfully and honestly?" Lincoln asked.

"I have."

"Have you ever intentionally harmed any of your patients?"

"Of course not. The human vessel's a mysterious thing, Mr. Lincoln. We can't always be sure how the body will react to a particular trauma or to a specific treatment. The best I can do as a modern medical man is to apply my learning and my skill to the cases I'm presented."

"You mentioned before the notion of 'modern' medical practices," Lincoln said. "What do you mean?"

"Too many of my brethren are stuck in the medieval epoch of medicine," Patterson replied confidently. "Knowledge of the medical arts has grown dramatically in the past few decades.

New surgeries and treatments have been devised. But too few medical men are willing to acknowledge these improvements or to make use of them in treating their patients."

"Such as what?" said Lincoln.

"Let me give an example one of the gentlemen of the jury is very personally familiar with," Patterson replied. He gestured toward juror Burton Judson, who gave a nod back.

"Last April," the doctor continued, "one of the sons of Judson over there was thrown from his horse and landed headfirst on top of a stone wall in their fields. When I reached him, the boy was insensible. His skull was swelling quite severely. The injury would have produced death within the hour had I not acted. In the event, I used my trephine to evacuate a hole half an inch in diameter in the skull in order to achieve an immediate reduction of the pressure.

"Most medical men would have stopped there, I daresay. But I knew, from my study of the lectures of great medical men such as Sir Astley Paston Cooper, President of the Royal College of Surgeons and the personal surgeon to the King, that it was also crucial to take a large quantity of blood, so as to reduce the ability of the brain to swell again. So I opened the boy's arm and took ten ounces, twice, over a one-hour period and took another eight ounces in the evening. My treatments produced a very favorable outcome. The boy regained consciousness, and he was able to converse with Judson, and with Mrs. Judson too. They were able to say a few words of love to each other."

Patterson looked over at Judson again. "Regrettably, even modern medicine has its limits," the doctor continued. "The boy passed the following day. But his parents will always have the memory of that final conversation, I'm happy to say."

As I studied Judson's face, I wasn't confident he would have described Patterson's treatment of his son in such favorable terms. Lincoln must have feared the same because he interposed, rather hastily, "Let me ask about some more of your modern methods,

Dr. Patterson, though perhaps it's best if you leave out the jury and their families from the cases you discuss."

Patterson proceeded to expound at great length on other modern treatments he had brought to the people of Springfield, including the application of blisters to the neck, sinapsims to the feet, calomel purges to open the bowels, a compound of lemonade and mercury to promote regularity, and antimonials to induce perspiration. Indeed, the discussion went on so long that Judge Thomas, chewing on his cigar with increasing agitation, was forced to call the morning recess. When, upon resumption of the proceedings, Lincoln continued the same line of questioning, the judge cleared his throat and looked at Prickett.

The prosecutor rose quickly from his seat and said, "I object, Your Honor. This testimony has got nothing to do with the three persons Dr. Patterson killed—is alleged to have killed."

"Yes, I think the objection is well taken," Judge Thomas said at once. "Move along, Mr. Lincoln."

"With respect, Your Honor," Lincoln said evenly, "we listened to Dr. Warren expound at length the other day. Seems to be a hazard of the profession." A few members of the jury laughed. "Moreover, this testimony by Dr. Patterson is very directly relevant to his defense, as you'll see shortly."

Judge Thomas waved his cigar irritably. "Move along quickly," he said. "I want to finish this case before I expire—or before another one of Dr. Patterson's patients does." The gallery laughed loudly, and Lincoln gave the judge an unhappy look before turning back to his witness.

"Now, Dr. Patterson," Lincoln said, "were you familiar with the three unfortunate victims in this case?"

"I was honored with the opportunity to treat all three of them as my patients."

"And during the course of your treatment, did you come to perceive a characteristic, a condition, shared by each of them?"

Patterson smoothed the ends of his moustache before responding. "They had each suffered terrible losses in their lifetime. The siblings, Lilly and Jesse, were orphans. They'd lost their parents, one after the other. And of course, the Widow Harriman lost her husband several years back. Each of the three of them bore a physical scar of their loss. Not one visible on the outside, of course, but a very real one, inside their bodies somewhere. I could tell from my examinations it affected them profoundly."

I watched Patterson with disgust. It was obvious he was fabricating the entire tale. It was true, of course, each of the victims had suffered losses, but it had hardly had the impact he claimed. I felt certain the Widow Harriman, for one, had come to view her husband's untimely demise as a liberation of sorts.

"In your experience, is there an established treatment for this condition?" Lincoln asked.

"There's not," said Patterson. "I'm convinced, from my study of these three persons, as well as others I've treated over time, that the depression of spirits, so to speak, is a very real phenomenon. But most of my brother physicians would deny its very existence. Certainly there's no agreed-upon cure for the symptoms."

"Now, the treatment of, to use your term, the 'depression of spirits'—is this a question to which you've devoted professional efforts, Doctor?" asked Lincoln. The jury and the gallery were listening with great interest. Prickett looked on with a suspicious glare. It appeared no one realized where the examination was heading.

"It's one to which I've given a great deal of study," Patterson said. "It has seemed to me there must be a way, a modern method, to effect a cure of the disease such that these persons can live a normal life free from the cares of their past."

"What methods of cure have you considered?" asked Lincoln.

"On many occasions, scientific knowledge advances experimentally," Patterson said. "By trial and error, one might say. For example, before we doctors came to realize bleeding patients in distress would often provide a complete cure for their symptoms, we tried many other methods, some less successful, some outright dangerous to the patients, as it turned out. But until some medical man tried it somewhere, it was impossible to know what might happen."

"And for the specific condition we've been discussing, depression of spirits, what treatments have you considered?"

"There are several. One is bleeding, of course, which produces wondrous results in so many areas. I've considered whether a special type of bloodletting, one that would produce a swift, dramatic drop in the pressure of the patient's blood, might be sufficient to occasion a reversal of the inner equilibrium. In turn, such a reversal might produce an immediate cure of the condition under discussion."

"Any others?" asked Lincoln amidst a few murmurs from the audience.

"The disease, the scar, appears to reside somewhere in the head. So I've wondered whether a sharp knock on the head might kill the disease in a single blow. And, of course, every living thing needs air to survive. So perhaps depriving the disease of air would kill it off." Patterson paused, then added, "Of course, as with any new treatment there are risks, *grave* risks, it would not produce the desired effect. Indeed, the treatment might make the patient worse."

The murmurings were louder and angrier now, as more and more of those present realized the defense Lincoln was laying. Several jurors, including Judson, were increasingly red-faced with anger. Judge Thomas sucked on his cigar with urgency. It was all I could do to keep from vaulting the railing and attacking Patterson with my bare hands.

"Now, you said you've been studying this issue," said Lincoln, who was determinedly ignoring the audience's reaction. "Have you done any more than merely study it?"

"I didn't think so," Patterson replied. He took a deep breath and expelled it loudly. "Until these past two days. As I've listened to the testimony here in court, I realized I must have done more than study it, although even now I have no memory of . . . of having done more."

"What do you mean?" asked Lincoln over the buzzing crowd.

"The ways in which the victims died . . . tragically, each mimics one of the methods of treatment for depression of spirits I've considered. The knife to Lilly Walker's throat—a sudden loss of blood pressure designed to reverse the inner equilibrium. The paving stone blow to young Jesse's head—an attempt to knock the life out of the disease. And, of course, hands around the Widow Harriman's neck . . . a loss of air . . ." Patterson choked on his words and buried his head in his hands.

The gallery was roiling now. There were angry calls from every corner of the courtroom. Major Richmond, his bulbous nose shining bright red, was on his feet two rows behind me, shouting over and over again, "Murderer! Murderer!"

Judge Thomas pounded his gavel and glared out at the gallery. "I'm going to have the sheriff arrest anyone who cannot hold their tongue," he thundered. "Mr. Prickett warned all of you at the outset these proceedings would be graphic. I'll not have my trial interrupted further. If there's another outburst, I will clear everyone but the jury from the courtroom." Silence prevailed.

"Thank you, Your Honor," Lincoln said. "What are you telling us, Doctor?"

Apparently genuine tears glistened in the doctor's eyes. "I realized yesterday, while sitting in court, I must have in fact tried out my proposed treatments. Unconsciously. In a fit of madness of some sort. And done so three times. With horrific, disastrous results, obviously. I've taken three innocent lives." Again the doctor's voice cracked and he dropped his head into his hands.

"And you have no memory of these actions you now realize you've undertaken?"

"None. I swear it, Mr. Lincoln."

"Are you telling the gentlemen of the jury you're mad?"

Patterson took a deep breath and smoothed his moustache. "Doctors are famously poor at diagnosing themselves,

Mr. Lincoln," he said, "so I am not sure I can testify to that. However, in these circumstances, I feel I have an obligation to disclose I've been afflicted, since my youth, with the vile though too-common disease known as gonorrhea."

There was a quick outburst from the gallery, which was immediately hushed by other audience members mindful of the judge's threat of expulsion. Patterson looked around the courtroom, his face wincing with discomfort, before continuing.

"Of course it embarrasses me greatly to have to admit this to the gentlemen of the jury, and as a consequence of this trial to the rest of the populace too. But it is well known, I fear, that men suffering from gonorrhea or other of the so-called venereal diseases can sometimes lose their minds and can do so in a creeping, progressive fashion.

"You ask, Mr. Lincoln, if I am mad. I am not fully so, I think it is clear. But am I slowly becoming mad some of the time, episodically, in fits? Before yesterday, I would have denied such, and done so vociferously. But after my realization of yesterday, I fear it may be so."

Patterson bowed his head and rested it in both hands. The courtroom was so silent I could hear the breathing of Martha and Jane near me, in rhythm with the pounding of my own heart. I studied the gentlemen of the jury but could not read their tense faces.

Lincoln looked as if he had additional questions, but he seemed to gauge the somber mood of the jury and the rest of the courtroom. Without another word, he took his seat at counsel table. Patterson remained in the witness chair, his head still clutched penitently in his hands.

CHAPTER 36

As soon as Judge Thomas called for the luncheon recess, he turned to Sheriff Hutchason, standing at his usual post to the side of the defense table, and said, "Remember what we discussed, Humble."

"But, Your Honor—" began Hutchason.

"Yes?" The judge, already halfway to his chambers, glared at the sheriff.

"Never you mind," said the sheriff. "It will be done."

It transpired that Judge Thomas had ordered the sheriff to remand Patterson to the jail cell during the luncheon recess for his own safety. The sheriff took Patterson firmly by the arm—the lawman towering over the doctor—and escorted him through the crowd. Lincoln walked with his client; Jane Patterson rose to follow closely behind.

"Let's go with them," said Martha. "I want to look in on how Molly's progressing."

"Very well," I said. "It's no wonder the sheriff wasn't keen on this idea. He's inviting the whole trial, or half of it at least, into his wife's birthing tent."

We made an odd little procession as we walked out of the courtroom and through the throng spilling onto the town green. No one in the crowd met Patterson's gaze as he marched along, eyes forward. When we reached Hutchason's backyard, the sheriff opened the jail cell door, led Patterson in, and carefully locked it behind him. Jane immediately thrust her arms through the bars to give her father an awkward embrace.

As they talked, Hutchason said, "Why don't the rest of you come inside. I asked Molly to lay out lunch, just in case the judge ordered us here."

"You didn't!" said Martha.

"Yes, I did," said the sheriff with genuine puzzlement. "Why wouldn't I?"

Martha gave an incoherent shout, threw up her hands, and hurried inside the house through the back door. The sheriff beckoned to Lincoln and me to follow at a more measured pace.

"We're content to stay outside if you'd prefer, Humble," said Lincoln. "We don't want to intrude."

"You'd do the same for me," returned the sheriff. "Come in and have a morsel and some ale, then you can come back out and talk with your client. He's a bold one all right. As are you, Lincoln. If you manage an acquittal somehow—well, I wouldn't want to have to guarantee *your* safety in town."

"Let's worry about one problem at a time," said Lincoln, patting the sheriff on the back.

We followed Hutchason into his kitchen, where indeed food and drink had been laid out on a table. The sheriff wolfed down his refreshment and excused himself.

"That went better than you had any right to expect," I said to Lincoln once the sheriff had left.

"So he convinced even you?" replied Lincoln.

"Certainly not. I still maintain he's a liar and a murderer. The murderer part he's admitted now. As for the liar part, I'll grant you he's an accomplished one. To falsely admit to a venereal disease in support of his false claim of madness was a masterstroke. If his facility as a doctor matched his facility with deception, he'd have a lot fewer deceased patients to testify about."

Lincoln snorted with laughter.

A bloodcurdling scream ripped through the house. There was an instant of silence, then we could hear my sister's voice offering encouragement to Molly Hutchason. Phillis appeared and, eyes downcast, she walked quickly through the kitchen and out the back door.

"I feel odd being here," I said.

"We're almost done," said Lincoln. "Besides, if the jailer of my client invites me into his home for a meal, I've found it prudent to accept."

I looked out the window into the backyard. Phillis was at the pump, drawing water for two jugs. Twenty feet beyond her, at the door to the jail cell, Jane and her father were engaged in an animated discussion. From their expressions and gestures, it seemed to be an argument of some sort.

I couldn't hear anything they were saying, but it was apparent Phillis could, because at one point she stopped her pumping and stared at father and daughter. As I watched, it appeared the Pattersons belatedly realized Phillis's presence, because Jane turned and said something to the old Negro woman. Phillis quickly looked down, shook her head, then rapidly finished filling her jugs. Soon she was walking back through the kitchen, head down, water sloshing about.

". . . don't you agree?" Lincoln was saying. He was oblivious to the drama I had just witnessed by the jail cell.

"Sorry. Agree about what?"

"This will be the hard part. Patterson surviving cross examination. I imagine Prickett only allowed me to call him as a witness because he figured he could thoroughly undermine the doctor through his own examination."

"What would you have done if Prickett had objected to him?" I asked.

"Tried to prove Patterson's madness through other witnesses. Though I doubt they would have been nearly as effective as the man himself."

"I still don't understand why lack of sound mind should be a defense at all. Certainly not to a charge of murder."

"I do agree," I said, "though I still don't understand why lack of sound mind should be a defense at all. Certainly not to a charge of murder."

Lincoln studied my face. "I'll not try to convince you further," he said, "but remember the law is clear in excusing actions taken in a condition of insanity. That's not *my* argument—that's the law."

"Perhaps the law's an ass," I said.

"Perhaps it is. You wouldn't be alone in thinking so."

As we were finishing our pies and tankards, Martha appeared to say Molly's labor of birth had reached a new, critical stage and that she would stay with her for the afternoon. I agreed to meet her for dinner at the Globe again, and Lincoln and I went outside to rejoin the Pattersons, who were now conversing in quiet, amiable terms. Lincoln said he wanted to talk to Patterson about a few of the finer points he expected Prickett to raise in his questioning.

"Will you walk me back to the courthouse, Mr. Speed?" asked Jane. "I'm sure no one will trouble me on the way, but I'd appreciate the escort. Just in case."

"Certainly," I said. I wanted no part of helping Patterson avoid Prickett's charge, even indirectly. "I'll see you back at court, Lincoln."

We set off in awkward silence. After a block, I managed to get out in a barely civil tone, "How is your father bearing up?"

"As well as can be expected," Jane said. "He's very embarrassed about having had to reveal his condition to the public at large."

"*That's* what he's upset about from this morning?"

Jane looked at me with knitted brows. "How would you feel if you had to admit carrying a vile disease?"

"I think I'd be a lot more upset about having admitted to murdering three innocent persons."

Jane merely sniffed in reply. Soon we reached the courthouse square. The green was swarming with spectators, though the mood seemed subdued in comparison to the initial days of trial.

"Mr. Speed," Jane said as we crossed the street to the square, "do you know who that old Negro woman was, the one who came out to draw water from the pump?"

"One of my family's bondswomen. She's a midwife. My sister brought her here from Kentucky to provide assistance to Molly Hutchason."

"Ah," said Jane. "I guess that explains it."

I spotted Simeon Francis's distinctive profile across the way. He was talking to Herr Gustorf, and as I watched they broke apart, laughing and shaking hands with mutual admiration.

"I'll leave you here," I said to Jane. "There's a fellow I want to visit before court starts up again." Before Jane could object, I hurried toward Simeon and hailed him.

"What was that about?" I asked.

"We were sharing notes on the curse of being a writer," he said. "Gustorf told me van Hoff has put his carriage back together, good as new. He's planning to leave in a few days to continue his tour of the West. I'll miss him—he's really a fine fellow." We watched as Gustorf dragged his casted leg along the green in slow pursuit of a cart of beer being pulled by one of the innkeepers.

Simeon turned back to me. "So how goes the conspiracy?" he asked good-naturedly. "Has Lincoln assured that everyone knows their roles for this afternoon?"

"I have no role whatsoever, I can promise you," I said. Immediately I thought back to the prior evening. Had I in fact played some role in trying to absolve Rebecca's killer merely by talking to Lincoln about his defense?

"My problem," Simeon was saying, "is no one who wasn't in court today will believe a word of it when I come out with my next issue. The local citizenry are always accusing me of printing the incredible. This time they'll actually be right."

"My problem is Patterson's trying to excuse three murders, and Lincoln's helping him."

"That too," said Simeon, "though I suppose it's the job Lincoln signed up for, isn't it?"

I didn't have a good answer to this, and I looked out across the green. On the far side of the courthouse I spotted a man with a slanted straw hat talking to Jane. The man turned slightly, and with a jolt I recognized him in profile as the poorhouse master, Hathaway. How could Jane have made *his* acquaintance? Perhaps their paths had crossed somehow in Decatur when Jane lived there with her father.

Before I could puzzle about this further, there was a murmur from the crowd, and I saw Hutchason leading the doctor by the arm toward the courthouse, with Lincoln walking by their side. A number of men spat in Patterson's direction. As they passed our position, I looked down in order to avoid making eye contact with the doctor. The three men went up the courthouse steps. A few minutes later, the sheriff reappeared at the top of those steps to throw open the door, and the crowd surged forward to find their seats for the afternoon's drama.

CHAPTER 37

As soon as Judge Thomas gaveled the courtroom to order, Prickett stepped to the center of the well. He straightened his frockcoat and fixed his most penetrating stare on the doctor.

"That was quite a tale," the prosecutor hissed.

Patterson met the prosecutor's gaze squarely but remained mute.

"Tell me, Doctor, are you pleased with your performance this morning?"

"If, by that," Patterson replied, "you mean am I pleased I admitted to the courtroom, admitted to all of Springfield in effect, I suffer from an unspeakable disease and, as well, acknowledged I may slowly, day by day, be losing my mind—no, I am not at *all* pleased, Mr. Prickett."

The gallery rumbled and groaned. While much of the noise was hostile, I realized with disgust that some portion was actually sympathetic to the doctor. The tenor of the reaction was not lost on Prickett, who took two aggressive steps toward Patterson.

"As I understand your testimony, Doctor," the prosecutor said, "you are admitting to having murdered all three persons."

"That's not what I said," Patterson insisted. The despair he'd shown at the end of his direct testimony had vanished. In its place had reappeared the doctor's usual self-confident mien.

"You are admitting to having caused their deaths."

"I am saying to the jury I can fairly reach no other conclusion but that I was, tragically, the agent of their deaths, however unwittingly and unconsciously so."

"You caused their deaths and you did so unlawfully," Prickett insisted. It was a statement, not a question.

"What is lawful and what is not is a matter to be determined by the judge, I suppose," said the doctor, keeping his poise. "And the jury, of course. I did not intend to harm them, any of them."

The audience was at attention watching the fierce exchange. Every man on the jury leaned forward on his chair. I turned to see Jane's reaction, but she was not in her usual seat near me. I craned my neck and looked around, but I couldn't spot her anywhere in the courtroom.

"You're claiming you did not intend to harm any of the three of them?" Prickett continued.

"That's right."

"Are you also saying you never harmed any of your patients intentionally, even the ones who died?"

"Certainly. No doctor can guarantee the continued good health of his patients."

"And your testimony is you've never intentionally killed anyone, isn't that right?"

"Absolutely that's the case."

Prickett nodded dangerously. He tugged on the sleeves of his frockcoat and arched his back, a strutting peacock getting ready to fan out his plumage.

"Now, you mentioned during your testimony the passing of your wife, when you were living in Decatur," the prosecutor said.

For the first time, Patterson looked discomforted. His eyes darted over to Lincoln and back to Prickett. "Yes," he said tentatively.

"I wonder if you could enlighten us. Were you referring to your first wife, or your second one? Because you've been married twice, haven't you, and both of your wives passed?"

The courtroom murmured.

"I'm not sure what it has to do with this matter, sir," Patterson said, "but I was referring to my first wife. My dear Jane's mother." The doctor shifted his gaze to where he expected Jane to be, near me, but when he found her absent he looked around the courtroom uncertainly.

"How did Miss Patterson's mother, your first wife, pass, if I may ask?"

Patterson stared at Lincoln, who rose hesitantly. "Objection, Your Honor," Lincoln said. "I don't see what this has to do—"

"No. Overruled," the judge said, pulling on his cigar and staring intently at Patterson.

"Dr. Patterson?" prompted Prickett.

"I'm sorry. May I have the question again?"

"How did your first wife pass?"

"She drowned herself," he said. "Shortly after Jane's birth."

There was *woosh* of sound in the courtroom. Judge Thomas banged his gavel once and called for order.

"You weren't the cause of her death?"

"Absolutely not," Patterson said. His face was contorted. "How dare you suggest—"

"Now, Doctor," Prickett continued blandly, as if he were carrying on a banal conversation about the weather. "Your second wife—how did she die?"

"I . . . I don't know. She went missing. Her body's never been found."

"You killed her, you bastard!" came an anguished voice from behind me. Major Richmond was on his feet, his plumed hat in hand, gesturing angrily toward Patterson.

"No, Syl, I didn't," Patterson said, his face pale. Judge Thomas pounded for order, but the doctor continued, "Truly. I had nothing to do with it."

"You killed her!" repeated Richmond in a shout above the roiling crowd. He strode down the central aisle of the gallery toward the gate, where Hutchason met him with the meaty-pawed grasp of a bear. Richmond was still yelling as Hutchason dragged him through the crowd and out the door of the courtroom.

It took Judge Thomas several minutes to restore order. Once he had, he said, looking from one side of his courtroom to the other, "Anyone else other than the lawyers and witness who so much as opens their mouth will be confined to the jail cell until well after the harvest. Is that clear?" The courtroom nodded silently.

"Proceed, Prickett," he ordered.

"If the body of your second wife has never been found, Doctor, then how do you know she passed?"

"It . . . it seems the most likely explanation."

"Maybe she tired of fixing your supper every day and went off." Patterson flushed.

"Your Honor," Lincoln said, rising again. "I'd ask that my brother be admonished to maintain a professional tone—"

Judge Thomas spit out his cigar and glared at Lincoln. "Let me make myself clear," he said. "In view of the testimony this morning from the witness, which I allowed you to put in unobstructed, I intend to afford your brother counsel every possible latitude in his questioning."

Lincoln sat, his shoulders slumping.

Patterson's face was red and his moustache starting to droop. "That's not what happened," he insisted. "She loved me—and I her. She just went missing one day."

"So you're saying someone killed her?"

"Yes."

"Did you?"

"No. I already told you—"

"Who then?"

"I . . . I don't know."

"So you do know she was killed by someone, but you don't know how or where or by whom?"

"Perhaps . . . perhaps it was an accident of some sort. I'm not sure."

"I thought you just told us the one thing you did know was your second wife had been killed by someone?"

Drops of perspiration lined his forehead. Patterson took out a handkerchief and mopped his brow. "Perhaps I was mistaken," he said.

"Now, this venereal disease of yours," Prickett said. He wrinkled his nose, as if he'd detected a particularly noxious odor. "You had it at the time of your first wife's death?"

"As I testified," Dr. Patterson replied quietly, "it has been my undesired companion since youth."

"Had it driven you mad by then?"

"No."

"Not even a little?"

The gallery chortled at Prickett's mocking tone.

"No," Patterson replied, wincing.

"What about at the time of the death—make that disappearance—of your second wife?"

"What about it?"

"Had your venereal disease driven you mad by then?"

"No." The doctor paused to consider, then added, "I don't think so."

"Not even a little?" Again the gallery howled.

"No."

"You're sure?"

"Yes, I'm positive," said Patterson, trying to rally to find his former confidence. "Not even the slightest bit."

"And the death or disappearance of your second wife—that was about four years ago?" Prickett asked in a soft, dangerous tone.

"That's right."

"Immediately before you moved from Decatur to Springfield."

"More or less."

"So you've had this venereal disease of yours all your life but it hadn't made you even the slightest bit mad four years ago, but now it's made you so mad you've gone and killed three innocent persons in some kind of accidental, unconscious fog. Is that what you're telling the jury?"

"I suppose it is." Patterson gave a nervous glance toward the gentlemen of the jury, who stared back with hostility.

"Perhaps," Prickett said, "you killed your second wife but don't remember it, just like you say you killed these three victims here but didn't remember it until, I think you said it was yesterday?"

"No. That's not possible."

"So you're saying it's not possible you killed your second wife in a fit of unconscious madness but it is possible—nay, it's a certainty, you've told the jury—you killed these other three persons in fits of unconscious madness. Do I have that all right?"

"I suppose you do," the doctor said over the mocking laughter of the crowd. He was leaning back in his chair now, making no attempt to engage the prosecutor or the jury.

Prickett continued to pound away. Lincoln rose on a few occasions to object to the prosecutor's tone, but Judge Thomas waved off each complaint before Lincoln could utter a full sentence, and eventually Lincoln seemed resigned to enduring the beating. He slumped further and further down in his chair at counsel's table. While I detested his client, I almost felt sorry for my friend.

Eventually Prickett concluded his ridicule of the doctor had reached a point of diminishing returns and, giving his hair a final triumphant toss, he dismissed the witness. Patterson sagged in the witness chair, spent. His surgical coat looked four sizes too large, as if the body underneath had wasted away. After a minute, he managed to rise and shuffle back to his table.

"What's next for the jury's consideration, Mr. Lincoln?" Judge Thomas asked. He gave an innocent smile toward the audience, which shouted with glee.

"A moment, Your Honor," Lincoln replied. He bent over next to Patterson and the two whispered back and forth at some length. Eventually Lincoln straightened and said, "We call Jane Patterson to the stand." He looked toward the audience.

An excited buzz arose from the crowd. Jane Patterson herself, however, did not rise. No one did.

"Miss Patterson?" called the judge, gazing out at his courtroom. "Miss Patterson?" He looked down at Lincoln. "Where's your witness?"

"I'm not sure, Your Honor," Lincoln said, glancing around with agitation. Dr. Patterson, too, was on his feet and scanning the audience, a perplexed look on his face.

"If I may have a minute," said Lincoln. He gestured frantically to the office boy Hay, who had been crouched in a corner of the well. Hay scurried over and, taking quick instruction from Lincoln, raced from the room as fast as his little legs would carry him.

In Hay's wake, the courtroom let down its guard. The gallery talked excitedly about Prickett's cross examination. The gentlemen of the jury stood and stretched. On the bench, Judge Thomas took out a new cigar and, having caressed it lovingly, struck a match.

Hay did not immediately return. Where could Jane have gone? I wondered. Surely she knew Lincoln intended to call her this afternoon. At length, the jury sat down again and started looking bored. Judge Thomas's pulls on his cigar became increasingly agitated. Several members of the crowd left the courtroom in search of a necessary.

"Mr. Lincoln," said the judge after some ten minutes had passed. "Why don't you call your next witness."

"I'm not sure I have one," said Lincoln. "I'd very much prefer to put Miss Patterson on next. I'm sure Hay won't be too much longer."

"I'll give him five more minutes," said the judge. He pulled out his pocket watch and laid it on the bench in front of him. Lincoln pulled out his own watch and studied it nervously.

Five minutes passed. Judge Thomas glowered at Lincoln. "Any minute now," Lincoln offered, hopefully. The crowd hummed with excitement. What might happen next if the witness was nowhere to be found? Perhaps, some wondered aloud, a hanging before nightfall. Seven minutes. Ten. Judge Thomas cleared his throat loudly.

"Mr. Lincoln—"

He was interrupted by the crash of the courtroom door as Hay burst through. The bedraggled boy was drenched in sweat. He raced up the central aisle and stopped at the gate, right next to me, seemingly unable to muster the strength to advance any further.

"Well?" said the judge.

The boy panted. The courtroom was silent, staring at Hay with anticipation. At last he managed to speak. "Miss . . . Miss Patterson has been . . . *abducted.*"

The courtroom was thrown into tumult.

Hay looked at me and added, "And your sister's gone too."

CHAPTER 38

About five things happened at once. Dr. Patterson, suddenly reanimated, shouted out, "My dear Jane!" and started to rush from the well. Sheriff Hutchason dove and managed to catch Patterson around the leg. Men shouted; women shrieked. Judge Thomas pounded madly for order.

But none of this mattered to me.

"What happened to Martha?" I demanded, taking Hay by the lapels of his jacket. The boy tried to wriggle free, but I pulled him closer, staring into his small, dark eyes and breathing in his stale, foul-smelling breath, and said, "Tell me. *Now.*"

"I only know what I learnt from Molly Hutchason in between her screamin'," he said. "And what some trades-fellow said he'd seen on the street in front their house."

"Tell me what you know," I demanded again. I was vaguely conscious of Lincoln beside us, listening to what the boy had to say.

"A slave-catcher snatched up the Negro midwife, right from Hutchason's yard," Hay said. "Asked to see her papers, and when she couldn't show him none, he bound her and loaded her into his cart. I guess your sister and Miss Patterson was there, and the catcher seized them up too. He drove off with all three of 'em."

"Don't tell me you neglected to register Phillis," Lincoln said to me.

I did not spare a glance for Lincoln but rather tightened my grip on Hay. "Who was the slave-catcher?" I demanded.

"I've no idea," said Hay. "Don't get too many 'round Springfield, do we? Maybe Billy would know."

"You didn't get a description?"

"The fellow on the street said he didn't recognize him neither. Said he had an ugly smile. Oh, and he was wearin' a straw hat, an old torn one."

"That was no slave-catcher," I said. "That was the poorhouse master, Hathaway."

"From what you've described," Lincoln said, "slave catching could easily be a side dish for him."

"As could kidnapping white women and passing them along." I shuddered. "I've got to go after them at once."

I released my grip on Hay, who staggered away and was immediately grabbed up again, this time by Sheriff Hutchason.

"Who's caring for Molly?" demanded Hutchason.

"No one, Sheriff," said Hay. "She was alone, shoutin' out the window for somebody to help, when I happened by lookin' for Miss Patterson."

The sheriff gave a loud, fearful wail—no one in town had ever considered that the massive Sheriff Humble Hutchason might be afraid of anything—and the singular noise put an end to the chaos. In short order, Judge Thomas adjourned court for the day, telling the jury to come back in the morning. The sheriff and Dr. Patterson made ready to depart for the Hutchason house, the doctor agreeing to Hutchason's plea that he avoid any of his modern methods in helping bring Molly's labors to a successful conclusion.

"Find them, Speed, and bring them home safely," Patterson said as he was led out by the distraught Hutchason.

"I fully intend to," I said, "but not for your sake. It's not Miss Patterson's fault she was burdened by a father like you." Patterson grunted, but I turned my back on him before he could say anything else.

"Let me walk with you for a moment," said Lincoln, taking my arm. We pushed our way through the departing crowd, which was rumbling with a combination of disappointment that there was to be no hanging tonight after all and excitement for whatever the next morning might bring. Outside, we found a comparatively deserted corner of the square.

"I haven't another moment to lose," I said.

"Your bondswoman Phillis is in great jeopardy," Lincoln said, giving me a severe look. "Without papers proving her identity, she has no rights whatsoever. And neither, I needn't remind you, do you over her, not in this state. I told you you were being reckless in the extreme in allowing her to be brought here."

"Whatever the slave's fate, I'll be fine," I said, my temper rising. I could not understand Lincoln's interest in her. "I barely know the woman. But if anything happens to Martha, I'll never be able to live with myself."

"I can hardly believe this fellow Hathaway took your sister and Miss Patterson," said Lincoln. "Seizing a Negro woman without papers is perfectly legal. But kidnapping a white woman is grounds for hanging. I've no doubt Hathaway is venal in the extreme, ready to prey on the unprotected at the slightest provocation. But I doubt he's that stupid."

"You haven't met Hathaway," I said. "Besides, you heard what Hay said."

"I need Jane as my next witness," said Lincoln. He worked his hands together with agitation. "She's going to corroborate Patterson's testimony about his creeping madness—at least the doctor said she would. Otherwise it's just his own say-so."

"I don't mind telling you I've no interest in helping your defense," I replied. "Not after hearing Patterson's testimony today. But I *have* to find Martha. And if by chance I locate Miss Patterson at the same time—well, I suppose I won't stand in front of her testifying."

I turned to leave and then asked, "Will the judge hold the trial for her?"

Lincoln shook his head. "I doubt it greatly," he said. "Either she's here first thing in the morning, ready to testify, or we'll go directly to closing argument. Either way, Patterson's fate will be sealed tomorrow."

"Good," I said, and I hurried off toward van Hoff's stables.

Fifteen minutes later, I set off astride Hickory. On horseback, I could make much faster time than Hathaway could in whatever sorry cart he was driving. But I didn't know how much of a head start he had.

As I raced through the prairie, I found myself repeating Lincoln's phrase in my mind. *Ready to prey on the unprotected at the slightest provocation.* The description applied to all too many people these days, especially in these economic times. The sun was fading behind us now, sending up lengthening shadows across our path. It would be dusk before long.

As Hickory and I pressed onward, I wondered about Hathaway. What had been *his* provocation to take Phillis? He could hardly have happened upon her in Hutchason's rear yard by accident. And then it hit me—hit me so plainly that in the next moment I wondered how I could not have seen it from the start. Jane Patterson had sent him. And in the moment that followed, the answer to the next logical question arrived as well: Jane had been afraid of whatever Phillis overheard during her argument with her father, and she encouraged Hathaway to spirit the Negro out of town before she could relate the knowledge to anyone else.

What had Phillis heard? Dr. Patterson boasting of the lies he had just foisted upon the jury? Perhaps he was confessing his guilt—and his sanity—all along. Or perhaps he had been attempting to suborn Jane into supporting his fantastical story with her own testimony. Whatever it was, if it was worth Jane instigating a slave-stealing over, it must have been truly damaging to her father's case. Phillis must have important evidence against the doctor. Suddenly my search for Martha was compounded by a considerable interest in retrieving the old slave woman as well. I spurred Hickory onward through the tall grasses with still greater urgency.

The sun had dropped to the tree line and the shadows in front of us were impossibly long as the farms surrounding Decatur finally began to materialize out of the prairie. Through the twilight we rode up to the poorhouse. In a small pen to the side of the house, a cheerless horse grazed next to an unhitched box cart. I went up and, murmuring sweet sentiments, put my hand on the horse's back. It was warm and damp. They hadn't been back for long.

As I turned toward the poorhouse, I noticed a single crow perched on the top rung of the pen, staring at me silently. Then it took off, a flutter of ink-black wings, screeching mercilessly at the heavens. Trying to avoid feeling shaken, I left Hickory in the pen and raced up the walk of the house.

The front door opened from the inside when I was five feet away.

"Thought I might see you," sneered Hathaway. His corncob pipe was stuck in the side of his mouth and his battered straw hat sat resolutely atop his head. He wore the self-satisfied smile of a steamboat gambler who thought he knew where all the cards lay.

"Where's my sister?" I demanded.

Hathaway shrugged. "I have no idea."

"You kidnapped her from Springfield," I said. "You must know." I could dominate the man, kill him easily if I had to, but that wouldn't get me any closer to finding Martha.

"She took an unauthorized ride in my carriage is more like it," he said. "I never wanted her along. Neither her nor the doctor's daughter. They don't do me any good. I only wanted the Negro."

I expelled my breath in relief. "Where's my slave then?" I said. "Give her back to me."

"*Your* slave? I don't know what you're talking about," he countered, smiling his gambler's smile.

"An old Negro woman who goes by the name Phillis. She's my family's property."

"Got anything to prove it?" he said. When I paused, he continued, "Didn't think so. She's my property now, and I'll dispose of her how I choose. In fact, I've done so already."

This statement knocked me back. "What do you mean?"

"Passed her along to a trader, as soon as I got back to town," Hathaway said. His grin stretched from ear to ear, his discolored teeth gleaming dull in the twilight. "Took pennies on the dollar for her, though I'm not sure how much she'll fetch down the river. Maybe there's a plantation owner near New Orleans planning a large family and in need of a midwife. One never knows what the market will be for them." He shrugged.

"You'll pay me compensation for my loss," I said. "But first, you'll tell me where you last saw my sister and Miss Patterson. If you don't, I'll strike you down on the spot." I clenched my fists and took two steps forward.

Hathaway was not, for all his bluster, a steamboat gambler, and he flinched. Perhaps the memory of the earlier time I'd hit him in the mouth, not far from where we now stood, weakened his resolve. In any event, he spat onto the ground near my feet and said, "I expect you'll find them at one of the public houses." He nodded over his shoulder toward the village. "After I made clear I wasn't giving back the slave woman, they went off in search of food and lodging. Your sister was hysterical about her slave when I first took her, wouldn't let go of her arm, but by the time we'd jolted all the way across the prairie, I think her sense of charity had vanished." He laughed harshly.

I doubted this, but I didn't doubt Martha's ability to make a tactical retreat while pondering her next charge. So I left Hathaway without another word and strode up the hill to Decatur's public square. One or two persons hurried along the far side of the green, but most of the populace of Decatur had, it seemed, headed inside this cool fall evening.

It had been a few years since I'd been in Decatur proper, and I thought I remembered two taverns plying their trade along the east side of the square. I headed off in that direction and saw, as I neared, that there were actually four public houses in a sorry row.

I walked into the first one I encountered. It was dimly lit and nearly deserted. "Martha?" I called out. "Martha, are you here?" The only person who responded was a young, ill-dressed woman standing near the entranceway, a glass in hand, who reached out to touch my arm and murmured, "I can be 'Martha' if you'd like."

"Not what I'm looking for," I said and quickly walked out.

The next public house in the row featured a large sign projecting sideways from the facade identifying it as the Hound's Breath. This tavern was much better lit inside, with squat candlesticks burning on each table. A Union Jack was tacked to the wall behind the bar—the citizens of Decatur evidently more willing than most to forgive our recent enemy. There were several dozen people inside the low-ceilinged room, and it fairly roared with conversation.

"Martha?" I shouted out.

"Joshua!" came a welcome call from the corner. I rushed forward and my sister leapt into my arms. Her lavender lace dress and gloves were filthy, and her hair had been blown around wildly, but she'd never looked better to my eyes. We held each other tight, our tears of relief mingling.

"Is Miss Patterson with you?" I asked.

Martha nodded. "She'll be back from the backhouse any minute. I'm so glad you're here, Joshua. We need your help in rescuing Phillis."

"I just came from talking to Hathaway," I said. "He told me he'd sold her down the river already."

"He's lying. I've no doubt he means to sell her, but he hasn't yet."

I looked around the tavern and saw no sign of Jane. "You do realize, Martha, it was Miss Patterson who put Hathaway onto Phillis?"

"Impossible," my sister said with emotion. "She would never do such a cruel thing. Besides, Jane's the one who risked her own well-being by remaining with me when I wouldn't leave Phillis's side. She's a heroine, not a villain."

"You're wrong," I said. "Jane's helping her father escape justice. She stayed with you because she didn't want to give Phillis a chance to tell you what she knows."

"What could Phillis possibly know that—"

"Mr. Speed," called Jane's voice from behind us. "I must say I'm glad to see you. I'm afraid we've found ourselves in a pickle."

Jane's costume was just as soiled as Martha's, but I saw a glint of steel in her eyes I'd never noticed before.

"Good evening, Miss Patterson," I said with a bow. "I'm relieved to have found you both unharmed."

"What happened at Father's trial this afternoon?" Jane said. "Is there still time for me to testify? Father told me I'd have to, but then I happened upon that horrible man trying to snatch away your bondswoman and I couldn't let Martha go after her unaccompanied."

"I'm very grateful to you," I said, ignoring Martha's *I-told-you-so* look. "As it happens, the trial day ended awaiting your testimony. If you're back in Springfield by daybreak, I think Lincoln can put you on the stand."

"What a relief," Jane said, expelling her breath. "Why don't you join us for supper and then the three of us can ride back together. I wasn't certain how we'd cross the prairie at night, just Miss Speed and I, but with you along to protect us, I'm sure we'll be in safe hands."

"I'm not leaving without Phillis," said Martha.

"I'm afraid you'll have to," said Jane. "You heard your brother—the trial won't wait for me. What if Father were to be convicted, where my testimony would have produced his acquittal?" Her voice rose with genuine emotion. "As soon as we eat, we must be back on the trail to Springfield."

"I'm not leaving without Phillis," repeated Martha.

"Dear, don't you think you're being a little stubborn?" said Jane. I could tell she was trying hard to maintain her composure. "And selfish. You've done all you can, especially in this state, where no part of officialdom will lift a finger to protect your rights. Molly will have given birth by the time we're back. And you won't need a midwife yourself for several years now, will you? Meanwhile, my father's life is at stake. Tonight."

"Martha's right," I said. "We need to reclaim Phillis before we return."

Jane looked at me with great surprise. "But Mr. Speed—my father . . . Mr. Lincoln's client. Surely you share my interest, at the least, in seeing to it Mr. Lincoln is positioned to advance his best possible defense. His professional reputation depends on it, I would think."

"Whatever interests we do or do not share," I returned, "is beside the point right now. My sister's correct. We can't leave our bondswoman in the hands of a blackguard. We've got to reclaim her, if she's still in Decatur."

Jane was at a loss for words.

"She's still here, all right," Martha said. "Surely it would take time for Hathaway to locate a slave dealer in these parts. When we arrived, he dragged Phillis into the poorhouse and locked the door, preventing us from following. She must be hidden away inside somewhere."

"I bet I know exactly where," I said. "Supper can wait. Let's go." I paused. "Unless you want to stay and dine, Miss Patterson. We'll be happy to come back and collect you after we've found the slave woman. Returning to Springfield tonight is the plan. I'm in full agreement with you on that score."

Jane shook her head. "I'll accompany you," she said. "I'm as invested as Miss Speed in righting the injustice of Phillis's capture." Jane gave a gracious smile to Martha, who did not return the same.

I gave a cold stare to the proprietor of the Hound's Breath, who had come to complain we were taking up a table without ordering any food, and the three of us hurried out of the tavern and across the dark square. A thin layer of clouds dimmed the moon and obscured all but the most persistent stars.

"I'm so proud of you, Joshua," Martha whispered as we walked down the hill toward the poorhouse. "I knew you'd see, in the end, that rescuing Phillis was the honorable thing to do."

I hesitated; Jane was watching us closely, trying to hear whatever might pass between us. But I realized it didn't matter if she heard my response.

"Honor's got nothing to do with this."

CHAPTER 39

Martha stood in the dark at the poorhouse door and knocked loudly. And again. And then again. Finally we heard footsteps echoing inside and Hathaway's rough voice: "Who is it?"

"It's Martha Speed. May I come in?"

"No."

"Please, sir, it's a matter of urgency. I'm trying to find my brother. Have you seen him about today?"

"Of course I haven't. Now go away. I warned you when you insisted on coming along that I'd show you no mercy."

From my hiding place, flattened against the wall beside the door, I motioned for Martha to get on with it. It was so dark, I had no idea whether she could see me. Jane was standing a step behind Martha; I could hear her quick breathing.

"Please, sir, Miss Patterson and I have no place to spend the night. All the inns are full."

"That's your problem, Miss Speed. Not mine."

"We have money. Lots."

There was a pause. I readied myself to break through the door with my shoulder if necessary. But then we heard the sound of two locks being snapped open. The poorhouse master opened the door and, without looking to either side, took a step out. I'd have to tell Lincoln that Hathaway was that stupid, after all, I thought, as I brought down a rock on the scoundrel's head with as much force as I could manage. He dropped to the ground, a limp sack of potatoes, in front of the young women. Jane gave a gasp.

"He'll be fine soon enough," I said. "Martha, find some twine to bind him, in case he wakens before we're finished. I know he keeps his keys in here somewhere." Martha went off in search of supplies while I rummaged through Hathaway's pockets until my fingers struck a ring of keys.

I took the candle that had been in Hathaway's hand and walked into the house. At once, I was hit by the stench of decay and suffering. A few residents were peering out from their doors on the long hallway, drawn by the late night disturbance. I saw them gape in wonder as they realized it was their master who was lying unconscious in the entranceway. I didn't stop to ask their views on the matter, but Martha seemed to have procured with great speed enough rope to tie Hathaway up three times over.

By the time Martha had secured his arms and legs, pulling the rope especially tight, Hathaway was moaning softly. "Where to?" my sister asked.

"Perhaps I'll stay to make sure he's bound securely and then catch up with you," suggested Jane.

"No, we need to stick together," I said, thinking there was no longer any doubt Jane and Hathaway had been in league. "It's a labyrinth inside. Follow me."

Jane looked at me warily but did not argue. I led the two women along the dank hall, through the closed door at the end, and down the narrow flight of stairs to the long infirmary. Most of the persons there were sleeping, and we walked through the room quietly in order to avoid waking them. I noticed several were covered by blankets once in the inventory of A. Y. Ellis & Co.

As quietly as I could, I tried the various keys from Hathaway's ring in the door at the end of the sickroom. Finally one inserted and turned, and I opened the door and beckoned Martha and Jane to follow me into the small, pitch-black space.

The two women looked around the empty room with confusion. "I thought you said you knew where he'd hide her," said Martha.

"I do. Hold this for a minute." I handed her the burning candle, then dropped to my knees and felt around until I found the hidden lever in the floor. I pulled open the panel, revealing the Idiot's pit and the top of the ladder. A great smell of waste erupted from the hole. Martha gulped.

"I'll be right back," I said, taking the candle from Martha and descending the ladder. Jane took half a step to follow after me, but the odor must have hit her with full force as she gagged and stepped back.

When I reached the bottom of the pit, it was hard to see anything at all. If I looked at the candle, it blinded me to the rest of the dug-out room; if I looked away, the refracted light was too faint to make out anything. But gradually my eyes adjusted, and I perceived Fanning asleep in his man-cage, a sighing, foul heap of rags, skin, and bones. Stooping to avoid the low ceiling, I squinted around the room. Where was she?

"Over here, Master," came a quiet voice.

I knelt beside a shrouded figure, bound in a burlap sack under the eaves opposite the man-cage. I held the flame up to Phillis's eyes and she blinked rapidly. There was a bruise below her right eye.

"Did he hurt you?"

"No, sir."

"What's happened to your face, then?"

"It's nothing. But that one over there is crazy. Hollering at me until he fell asleep from the effort."

"Phillis?" called Martha's voice from above. Lifting the candle, I saw Jane peering down anxiously beside her.

"I've got her," I said. "We'll be up in a minute." I put the candle in my teeth and, working quickly with both hands, managed to loosen the sack and untie Phillis's arms. The Negro neither smiled nor thanked me but merely stood there, rubbing the welts on her arms and awaiting my further direction.

"Can you make it up the ladder by yourself?"

"Imagine so," she said, and she did, slowly. As I trailed behind her, I tried to figure out what to do next. Jane seemed determined not to let Phillis out of her sight. There was no need to bring the issue to a head here in unfamiliar territory. After we'd returned to Springfield, there would be plenty of opportunity to learn what Phillis had overheard.

When she reached the top of the ladder, Phillis was swept up by Martha in an exuberant embrace. "I told you I wouldn't let you go," Martha said, her arms gleefully around Phillis's neck. The slave stood limp; her arms remained at her side. "I told you she was still here," Martha continued, looking at me and Jane with triumph, seemingly unaware of the bondswoman's lack of affect.

"Now can we get on the trail for Springfield?" Jane asked. "We've lost nearly half the night as it is. I need to be back in time to testify for my father."

"We can," I said, but then I stopped short. Phillis was staring at Jane with determined, hostile eyes. Jane noticed the stare a moment after I did, and her mouth dropped open with disbelief. Martha realized as well something was afoot, and she released Phillis from her embrace and stepped back. The slave stared at Jane, and the other three of us stared at the slave and her remarkable act of defiance. The room was silent; the flickering candle in my hands casting all of us in its dancing light.

"I'll not cover for your madness again," said a voice. Even though I was looking right at Phillis, it took me a moment to realize the words had come from her mouth.

"Excuse me?" I looked at the slave incredulously.

"'I'll not cover for your madness again.' He said that."

"*Who* said that?" I asked, looking back and forth between Jane and Phillis. Jane had one hand to her mouth and the other near the folds of her skirt.

"Dr. Patterson, to his daughter here. 'I'll not cover for your madness again.'"

Jane gave a nervous, high-pitched laugh. "Don't be ridiculous," she said. "I said nothing of the sort."

"What *he* said," repeated Phillis, still staring at Jane with dark, unblinking eyes.

"You're misremembering the words I used," insisted Jane.

"Not you. Him. That's what *he* said."

"But surely, Phillis dear, you're mistaken about who said what," said Martha. "Surely it was Jane who said that to her father, if anyone said anything at all. Her father's the one who's admitted to having a creeping madness."

"That's right," said Jane. "Perhaps I did say it, but to my father. My father's the one who's mad."

"He said it to you," repeated Phillis firmly.

I was staring at the three of them, open-mouthed. *Jane was mad.* Suddenly that made sense to me, where nothing else had made sense for a very long time. Not since I'd stumbled upon Rebecca's broken body and my mind filled with grief and fog had I had such a coherent, definite thought. *Jane was mad.*

"You have no idea what you're saying," said Jane. "Mr. Speed, I'm warning you, your bondswoman is far over the line. I won't stand for it. I demand you correct her at once."

I took two steps toward Phillis, and finally she shifted her gaze from Jane to me. "Are you quite sure," I said, "the phrase you're remembering is something Dr. Patterson said to Jane and not the other way around?"

"I'm sure."

I turned and looked at Jane. Her face was twisted in the flickering flame.

"Don't be ridiculous," said Jane. "You're not actually giving any credence to what this illiterate slave is saying, are you, Mr. Speed?" When I did not answer, she continued, her voice fluttering ever higher, "You're going to take her word over mine? You cannot be serious."

I wondered at the slave's fortitude. Even now she showed not the slightest concern whether I believed her.

The proposition put by Jane would have seemed absurd to me just a half hour earlier. Accept the word of an illiterate Negro slave over the word of a doctor's daughter? I would have laid a hundred to one—nay, a million to one—odds it would never be so. And yet—

"I believe her," I said.

Martha started to open her mouth to say something, but before she could, Jane jerked up the hand that had been resting in the folds of her skirt. In it shone the barrel of a small lady's muff pistol, with an ebony stock and silver frame. She grabbed Phillis around the neck and shoulders with one arm and dragged her a few paces back into a corner of the room. With her other hand, Jane held the pistol to Phillis's temple.

"Jane—no!" shouted Martha.

"Father gave it to me," Jane said with an unnatural calmness. "After they found the dead girl. He told me I needed to be careful with a killer about." She gave a high-pitched laugh.

"My father's wrong, you know," Jane added, looking at Phillis, who remained tightly secured by her other arm. "Completely wrong. I'm not mad. I'm the sanest person I know."

The midwife, who was not struggling against her captor, did not respond. Her face was calm and clear, as if secure in the belief she was protected by some higher presence.

Meanwhile, my mind was working furiously. *I'll not cover for your madness again.* How far back did Jane's madness extend? Her mother had died shortly after her birth. But her stepmother had disappeared only four years ago, right before the Pattersons had moved to Springfield. Had the doctor known his daughter was responsible for his second wife's disappearance in Decatur and moved to Springfield to give her a new beginning?

I had the sense I was missing an important connection. Something else had happened in Decatur at about the same time. Then I remembered: the young woman Abigail had told my sister that

Lilly Walker and her family had been thrown into turmoil when their neighbor and landlord in Decatur, a land speculator, had suddenly sold off their property.

I hastened to piece together the events. What if Patterson himself had been that neighbor and speculator? Lilly and Jane, about the same age, would have been neighbors—acquaintances surely, likely friends—at the time of Jane's stepmother's disappearance. And then earlier this summer Lilly, newly rescued from the poorhouse and determined never to return, had visited Springfield with her aunt and walked about town. And soon thereafter she'd been murdered.

"You must have been surprised to see Lilly Walker again," I said.

Jane's face gave no reaction, but I saw her grip on the pistol tighten. The gun would carry only a single shot. If I could get her to discharge it, we would all be safe.

"You two had been close, hadn't you, when you lived next door to each other in Decatur?"

"She was a poor girl with a runny nose and dirty, mended clothes," said Jane. "We were never friendly."

"But she knew what you'd done to your stepmother, didn't she?" I continued. I heard Martha gasp quietly behind me. "How, I wonder? Did she see it happen? Help you, even—two thirteen-year-old girls whispering and plotting? Or did you boast about it to her afterward? 'A poor girl with a runny nose.' I'll bet she would have been impressed with you, for your daring. I'll bet that's exactly who you would have wanted to share your deed with."

A tremor ran across Jane's face. She did not answer.

"So then she tried to blackmail you when she encountered you again in Springfield after all those years," I continued. Everything was becoming clear now, like the morning mist melting away to reveal the new day. "Threatened to reveal your secret if you didn't give her money."

I had always wondered about Jane Patterson and Lilly Walker. Their lives had seemed mirror opposites of each other; in fact, they had been far more intertwined than I ever could have imagined. And, in the end, Lilly's instinct for financial independence—the very characteristic that had so pleased Rebecca—is what had gotten her killed.

"She was a greedy wench," said Jane. "She was nobody. She didn't mean anything to anybody."

"Except her aunt," said Martha. "And her little brother."

I started moving slowly toward one side of the room and inclined my head slightly at my sister. At once she understood and began drifting toward the other side.

"Her brother was a pest," Jane said. Her eyes were focused tightly on me.

"He was an innocent little boy," said Martha.

"He was a nosy little brat," Jane responded. "He didn't know his place. And I wasn't sure what he might know. Or might have seen."

"But Rebecca Harriman figured out that you were responsible for the two murders," I said. "That's what she came to confront your father about. That's why they quarreled."

"Father had no true feelings for her," said Jane. "He didn't need her. He's never needed anyone else. He's always had me."

At that moment, a dark shadow streaked across the room. Belatedly I realized it was Martha charging at Jane. I shouted and took a running jump toward Jane from my side of the room. As I leapt, the candle dropped from my hand and extinguished on the dirt floor. I felt myself landing atop a tangle of writhing bodies in the pitch-black room.

A single shot rang out.

CHAPTER 40

"Martha?" I shouted. "Martha, are you harmed?"

For an instant that seemed to stretch without end, there was no answer. Then, from somewhere beneath me, my sister's voice. "I'm fine, Joshua. It didn't hit me."

"Miss Patterson?" I called out, at the same moment Martha was saying, "Phillis? Are you all right?"

"I will be once everyone gets off," came the hoarse voice of the slave.

Jane did not answer.

I struggled free from the pile of bodies and felt around on the floor in the darkness until I found the candle, which I lit with a match from my pocket. Martha and Phillis were each standing and brushing dirt from their clothes. All three of us looked down in the candlelight. Jane Patterson's body lay motionless on the dirt floor. There was a dark stain spreading out on the ground beneath her.

Martha screamed.

I knelt beside Jane's body. Her eyes were wide and frozen and her chest was still. I lay my fingers on the inside of her wrist, feeling for a pulse that did not come. The fabric of her dress by her heart was torn apart and some of her insides spilled out horribly. I looked away and saw the muff pistol still clenched in her right hand.

"Is she . . . ," began Martha.

"She's dead," I said, rising to my feet.

"Did we do that?" cried my sister. "Did *I* do that?"

I held Martha against my chest and stroked her hair. "It's all right," I said. "You're not to blame."

"But—"

"*Shhhhh.* She shot herself, most likely. I doubt we'll ever know fully what was in her mind."

My sister nodded, her resolution flooding back.

We heard shouting from the infirmary room and banging on the door. A female voice called out: "Who's there? Was that a gunshot?"

"What do we do now?" asked Martha.

"Take back one of my blankets, for starters," I said.

Twenty minutes later, we had loaded Jane's body, shrouded in a checkerboard quilt, into the cart in the front yard of the poorhouse. With the help of Martha's acquaintance Abigail, we'd managed to exit the house through a side door without drawing any more attention than necessary. The poorhouse residents seemed used to persons coming and going in the dark without explanation. I helped Phillis climb into the cart next to Jane's body and started to hitch up Hathaway's horse.

"Where are you taking my horse and carriage?" came a harsh voice from behind me. "And my slave?"

I turned and saw Hathaway standing unsteadily at his front door, a shotgun clutched in his hands. Given the iron hand with which he ran the poorhouse, I supposed it was no wonder he had an ally somewhere in its depths who had freed him.

"I'm simply borrowing the horse and carriage," I said. "I'll return them tomorrow and pay you twice the market rate. As for the slave—you know full well she's mine, not yours."

"She's mine in this state," said Hathaway. "And I'll not let her go." He swayed before steadying himself on the doorframe. "Not for nothing, anyway."

I sighed and asked Martha to finish hooking up the cart. Martha nodded, her eyes flickering back and forth between Phillis and Hathaway. I took a few steps toward the poorhouse master. With everything else we still had to accomplish that night, paying the venal man a few coins in exchange for an unobstructed departure seemed the better part of wisdom.

"You yourself said you'd take pennies on the dollar for her," I said. "At her age, with her physical condition, I can't imagine her fetching fifty dollars on the St. Louis quay. I'll pay you two dollars to be done with it."

"She's worth at least two hundred," he said, clutching his shotgun tightly, "but I'll take forty."

"How about five dollars, then? That's the best I can do."

"Thirty."

I stopped to consider the absurdity of the situation. Here I was, bargaining over how much to pay for the right to take away a slave who had belonged to my family since her birth in the prior century. What would my father say if he could see me engaged in such folly? But I looked again at Martha and realized such concerns would have to await another day. Over Martha's shoulder, I could just make out Phillis's impassive face in the dim moonlight. She seemed to be watching our negotiations closely.

"Very well," I said, turning back to Hathaway. "Ten for the lot—the slave and the horse and carriage rental."

His face broke into a jagged, discolored grin. I noted with pleasure that the area around his eyes was swelling with the same black and purple hues of his teeth.

"I always say I'm open to business twenty-four hours of the day," Hathaway said. "Throw it on the ground and be off with you." I did so, noting with even greater pleasure his determination to stay far away from my right hand.

We set off through the prairie, me astride Hickory and Martha sitting sidesaddle atop Hathaway's nag, which pulled the rickety cart. But after about fifteen minutes, we came to a halt.

We were traveling at the pace of a snail; the tired nag was struggling with the weight of the cart and the two bodies it carried.

"We'll never reach Springfield at this rate," said Martha. "And if we don't get there by morning . . ."

"We'll have to leave the cart here with Jane's body," I said. "We can come retrieve it tomorrow. You and Phillis ride atop Hickory. I'll take the nag. I think there's still a chance we can make it by sunrise."

Working quickly, we detached the cart from the horse and dragged it some fifty feet into the tall grasses. It would be perfectly visible to someone looking for it, but someone who wasn't might miss it. And for anyone who did find it, perhaps the dead body inside would prevent scavenging.

We set off again, cantering side by side through the dark prairie. With the moon and stars providing only a dim illumination of the treacherous, uneven carriage path, I pushed the horses as fast as I dared.

"I misjudged her greatly," said Martha after a while.

"We all did," I replied. "But if you think of it, it's the only thing that makes sense of Patterson's conduct since his arrest."

"What do you mean?"

"From the start, the doctor never put up a strong defense. He's never stood and shouted 'I didn't do this.' You heard Lincoln complain about it himself. Why? Because if he did, he was afraid someone would figure out it was Jane who'd slit Lilly Walker's throat with surgical precision, Jane who'd borrowed his surgical coat and hat and high-tandem gig and gone to Menard on the night before the muster, Jane who'd used his medicinal liquors to subdue her victims before she killed them. If it wasn't him, she was the only person it could have been."

"I suppose you're right," Martha said.

My horse whinnied and pranced sharply to the right, and I saw he had narrowly avoided a gaping hole in the dark path.

"*And* it illuminates why insanity was the defense Patterson dreamed up in the middle of trial, once he saw how much incriminating evidence Prickett had," I continued. "It's one of the few defenses where the defendant acknowledges he did commit the crime. The usual defense says, 'I didn't do it.' But insanity says, 'I did it, but I'm not responsible under the law.' If Patterson denied having been the one who killed the three of them, then the sheriff might keep searching for the person who did, and Patterson feared the sheriff might come to realize it had been Jane."

"When do you think Patterson knew she was the killer?" asked Martha.

"He must have suspected it after Jesse's body was found. And he must have realized then that he had, in effect, unwittingly facilitated Lilly's murder. Remember, Patterson told Lincoln he was out of town on the night of the first murder, but he was vague about the circumstances. We assumed he didn't want to tell Lincoln because he didn't have an alibi. The truth was the opposite—he didn't want to say because he *did* have an alibi. He was with the Widow Harriman at the inn near Salt Creek that night. The inn's log proved it. He'd realized his absence from Springfield had given his daughter the freedom to act. To murder."

I closed my eyes and felt the cool breeze against my skin and my horse's shoulders working up and down along the trail. I listened to the rhythmic beat of the two horses' hooves. We rode in silence.

"What do we do when we get back to Springfield?" asked Martha a little later.

"Go straight for Lincoln. He'll want to call me as a witness, I think. Once the judge and Prickett hear the truth, the charges against Patterson will be dismissed."

"I wonder if that will be enough," said Martha. "If you think of it, Jane never confessed anything to us. She was careful in what she said. If she was truly a lunatic, she was a calculating one."

"Then Phillis shall be Lincoln's witness," I said. "She can say what she overheard at the jail cell."

This whole time, Phillis had been balanced behind Martha on Hickory's broad back, her legs crossed and her hands clasped in her lap, looking off blankly across the dark prairie. If she was grateful to us for the great effort we'd exerted in rescuing her from Hathaway's clutches, she'd given no visible signs of such.

As I glanced at her, I was reminded of the fortitude she'd shown in challenging Jane Patterson. Even now, the slave's boldness at that moment amazed me. But for the Negro's actions, Jane might well have gotten away with her crimes.

"Will you testify to what you heard, Phillis?" I asked.

"If you bid me to, Master."

"I may have to. Let's see what Lincoln says."

Before long, the shadowy forms of Springfield emerged ahead of us, black on black. We'd been pushing our horses much faster than I'd realized. Glancing toward the sky, I judged an hour or so remained until the sun breached the horizon. As we neared the square, I could see a dull light in the window that looked down from No. 4, Hoffman's Row. We tied the horses to a post and, weary and stiff-legged, I led Martha and Phillis up the stairs.

Lincoln was bent over at his table, scratching away in front of a candle almost burned down to its nub.

"It's nearly morning," I said.

"I can sleep after the trial ends," he replied, still hunched over. "Have you brought my witness?"

"Your witness is dead," I said. "And your client is innocent."

Lincoln looked up sharply. It took a second for his eyes to focus, and they widened as he realized who was and was not standing before him. "Why don't you all have a seat and tell me what's happened," he said.

He struggled to his feet and pushed aside various piles of paper to make three places to sit. Martha and I sat; Phillis remained standing diffidently, eyes downcast, even after Lincoln gestured toward the empty place he had cleared on Stuart's lounge. After a moment's pause, Lincoln let the Negro be and turned back to me. "So?"

Hurriedly, I told him everything that had transpired, Martha interrupting me on occasion to add a detail here or there. When we had finished, Lincoln sat silent, his thumb and forefinger running over the stubble on his chin.

"That's an amazing tale," he said. "I believe every word you've said. And I have absolutely no way to prove it in court when the sun comes up."

"Is it because Jane never confessed directly to us?" I said. "We've thought of that. Phillis can testify to the argument between Patterson and Jane at the jail cell. Everything else follows."

"Phillis won't testify," Lincoln said evenly.

I looked back and forth with indignation between the slave and my friend. "Of course she will. And she should. She's the one who figured out the truth, after all."

The slave made no reaction.

"You're not following me, Speed," Lincoln said. He seemed to have an odd light on his face. "Judge Thomas won't allow her testimony. No judge in Illinois would, or could. She's a Negro."

"What of it? Is it because she's a slave? Fine, I'll free her in the morning then restore her status in the afternoon, when Patterson's charges have been dismissed."

"Free or slave has nothing to do with it," said Lincoln. "No testimony from any Negro is admissible in the courts of Illinois in a case involving a white person."

"That's absurd," I said, my temper rising. Martha, too, cried out in disbelief.

"I do agree," Lincoln returned with a bitter smile, "though I'm rather surprised to hear *you* say so."

"Very well," I said, still convinced there must be an easy way around the obstacle Lincoln seemed intent on throwing up. "Phillis can tell me what Jane said and I'll testify to it. She already has, in point of fact. I'll be your witness."

"That won't help," said Lincoln. "If evidence has passed by a black tongue, the State of Illinois doesn't want to hear it."

"But the life of a white doctor is at stake!"

"Even so."

I gaped at him, feeling completely flummoxed. "That's absurd," I repeated.

"The slave is not the only one imprisoned by this institution," said Lincoln, shaking his head. "Do I take it you're becoming a convert to the cause of civil rights for the Negroes, Speed? Perhaps emancipation, even? Congratulations. I knew it was only a matter of time."

"Of course not," I said. "Don't provoke me. She should be able to testify here. That's all. It's only common sense."

"I'm not provoking you," said Lincoln seriously.

"But there must be something we can do," said Martha, wringing her hands. "Surely you're not suggesting we need stand by mutely while the jury convicts the doctor on faulty evidence."

We looked at one another helplessly.

"I've heard it said, in times like these, you should find a stiff glass of brandywine," murmured Lincoln, as if to himself. "No matter how far away you have to travel to find it. I've heard the Prussians, in particular, believe in this cure."

Martha turned to stare at Lincoln while I said, "This is no time for your jests. Patterson's head is on the block."

"What about the baby?" came a hoarse voice. All of us turned to Phillis.

"That's right—Molly!" exclaimed Martha. "In all the confusion, I'd totally forgotten. I feel terrible. What's happened with Molly, Mr. Lincoln?"

"Last I knew, she was still in her labors of birth," he said. "Dr. Patterson was at her bedside around midnight, when I left the sheriff's house to return here to write out my closing argument. Hopefully he'll have delivered of her successfully by now."

"I doubt it," said Phillis. "The man's ignorant. And a butcher."

Suddenly Martha's face lit up. "We must go to her at once," she said. She was on her feet, grabbing Phillis by her arm. "We haven't a moment to lose. The sun's almost already up as it is."

She hurried from the office without another word, the slave midwife in tow.

"I do admire her enthusiasm," said Lincoln in Martha's wake.

"She's impetuous," I said. "Rushing around before she thinks. You saw what trouble it got her into with Hathaway yesterday."

"Did Jane Patterson really take her own life?" Lincoln asked.

"There was a scuffle in the dark, and the gun she'd been holding against Phillis's head went off," I said. "The bullet went straight through Jane's heart. No one will ever know exactly what happened. But I think, all things considered, assuming that Jane shot herself is the only sensible conclusion."

Lincoln thought about this, nodded, and resumed scrawling out his notes. "I'll leave you in peace," I said. "You'll need to reach new heights of eloquence in your argument in the morning. Unless we can somehow convince the judge to hear the new evidence."

Rather than head back to my lodgings, I paced the dark, deserted streets. I was bone tired from the exertions of the past day and night, but my mind was restless. There had to be a way to persuade Judge Thomas to receive the evidence we'd uncovered. For all his bluster, I knew the judge, at bottom, sought to discover the truth.

Surely *I* could make him see it. As a man of the law, Lincoln seemed encumbered by the strictures of the Black Code. But I was not. I would stand before the judge at the start of trial in the morning. I would proclaim the truth: that Jane Patterson had killed the Widow Harriman and her two wards and that she'd taken her own life in front of me rather than take responsibility for her crimes. I would lead the judge and sheriff to her body. I would explain that Jane had a motive for these horrendous acts and that her father's confession of madness was, in fact, a false note of paternal love. I would lay before the court the details proving that Jane and Jane alone could have been the villain.

Rebecca's killer was dead and yet justice was not done. If Dr. Patterson swung for a crime he did not commit, Rebecca's memory would be tainted. I would not let it happen. I'd told my sister honor had nothing to do with going back to rescue Phillis, but honor had everything to do with this.

As the plan of action coalesced in my mind, I turned around and headed home to get an hour's sleep. The faintest hint of the coming dawn glowed in the eastern skies. In the distance, I could hear the sounds of the town slowly coming to life.

As quietly as I could, I opened the door to the store and crept through the storeroom and up the back stairs. Hurst and Herndon were snoring in syncopation in the other bed. Silently I unlaced my boots, undressed, and lay down in our empty bed. I was exhausted. My plan was bound to succeed, I thought as I closed my eyes. I would stand tall in front of the courtroom when the trial recommenced. I would be the herald of the truth.

The last thought I had before my mind went blank was that I should leave a note for Herndon asking him to wake me in time.

CHAPTER 41

"There you are, Speed. I've been looking all over for you."

"What time is it?" I mumbled. I opened my eyes a crack and saw bright sunlight flooding our bedroom. In an instant, I recalled my plan from the prior night and I flung myself out of bed, feeling around for my clothes before I'd even hit the ground.

"You're too late," said Lincoln with a laugh. "The trial's over."

"How can it be? But I was going to—what's happened? Did you win?"

"The doctor has, it appears."

"What?" I sat down on the side of our bed and tried to shake the slumber out of my pounding head.

"You slept through quite some excitement. Dr. Patterson was gone from his jail cell this morning. And that foreign fellow, Gustorf, had disappeared too. Vanished—the both of them. You'll be glad to hear your sister suffered no lasting harm, though."

"What happened to Martha?" I demanded.

"It's a funny thing, in the end," said Lincoln. "She was found in the jail cell this morning. Tied up and gagged. And clad in the doctor's coat, with his boots shoved onto her feet. She told the sheriff she'd happened upon the scoundrels as they were sneaking away in the dark and they detained her and threw her into the cell so she couldn't raise the alarm."

"Did they?" I had the sense I was missing something, but in my groggy state, I couldn't quite put together the various pieces of what Lincoln was telling me.

"Proved to be crucial for them, I think," Lincoln continued. It seemed unlikely, but it was almost as if there was amusement lurking behind his wide-set eyes. "The sheriff looked out at the cell at dawn, as he always does, but when he saw what he thought was Patterson's sleeping form under the surgical coat, he didn't actually go outside for a close view. So it wasn't until several hours later, when he went to make sure the doctor was ready for court, that he realized it was your sister under the coat. And by then, the rogues had vanished.

"Half the town's out looking for them," Lincoln added. "The sheriff's posted a bounty. But I doubt highly they're around to be found. It's a good thing I thought to get my fee from the doctor up front."

"I can't believe it," I said.

"Neither could Judge Thomas," said Lincoln. "You should have seen it. He threw a fit. Shouted at the sheriff so loudly I feared the old walls of the courtroom might collapse then and there. But what can he do? Nothing, unless they find the fugitives."

"Well, I suppose it's all worked out for the best, somehow or other," I said. "You're sure Martha's unharmed?"

"I just saw her with my own eyes over at the sheriff's house. She's never looked more spirited."

"That's saying something." I yawned. "In that case, I think I'll close my eyes for another hour. It was an awfully long day yesterday." I lay back down on the bed.

"You'll have to get up soon, though," said Lincoln. "Now that court's been cancelled, Hutchason has promised to start his spree on the stroke of twelve noon."

"Why is he celebrating? He's lost his prisoner."

"But he's gained a child. Molly gave birth to a little daughter early this morning. Phillis reached her side just in time. She may not have been able to testify, but her knowledge proved invaluable nonetheless."

I could only shake my head in wonder. Lincoln and I agreed to meet in the storeroom shortly before noon to head over together to Hutchason's spree. He turned to leave, but before he ducked out of the bedroom door I called after him. "You know, Lincoln, I've just realized—this keeps up your record in murder cases."

His face broke into a broad, toothy grin. "You're right, Speed," he said. "Still haven't lost one yet."

★ ★ ★

Between the spree and the continuing commotion surrounding Patterson's disappearance, it was not until two days later that I first got the chance to speak alone with Martha. She suggested we pick wildflowers to place by Molly Hutchason's bedside. We walked out of town arm in arm and headed into the waning prairie.

"You must be pleased with yourself," I said. The puzzle pieces of Patterson's flight had long since come together in my mind.

She giggled. "Of course. Aren't you pleased with me? Dr. Patterson did wrong by trying to cover for his daughter's madness, but he didn't deserve to hang for that mistake."

"I agree, though I can't figure out why you willingly courted such danger to ensure he didn't," I said. "If the sheriff had discovered your scheme . . ."

"When we got back to the house that night it was chaos. Molly was screaming in pain, Humble bellowing with worry. Phillis took charge immediately, directing everyone about. The last thing anyone possibly would have noticed was me taking the keys to the jail cell from the hook inside their back door. And if someone had, I would have said I was going out to ask Dr. Patterson a question about Molly's care."

Martha bent down and picked a few stems of striking smooth, blue asters. When she straightened up, she added, "Besides, it was apparent you weren't going to take up Mr. Lincoln's hint."

"I plumb missed it at the time," I admitted, "if he indeed meant it as a hint. Prussians travelling far for brandywine—what nonsense. Even now, I'm not completely sure he meant it as a suggestion rather than it being merely another of his absurd sayings."

Martha laughed and skipped ahead, making a beeline for a spectacular stand of ox-eye sunflowers and compass plants, a riot of yellow, orange, and gold. "You can believe that if you want," she called over her shoulder. "But I think I know your Mr. Lincoln better."

I knelt and cut off several long stalks of Indian grass and little bluestem. The cold nights had already started to turn the bluestem a reddish bronze. I ran my fingers up its spine and the silvery-white seed heads scattered to the winds.

"What did you tell Patterson about Jane?" I asked.

"The truth. That Phillis had overheard their argument the prior afternoon, that Jane tried to have her stolen, to silence her, but that you'd tracked her down and learned what had happened. And that when Jane realized as much, she took her own life. I told him where we'd left her body, so he could recover the remains."

"He must have been devastated."

Martha nodded. "At first, he refused to leave the cell. But I convinced him that his senseless death wouldn't do anything to reverse hers. And that he had a chance to do for others what he'd failed to do for Jane by covering for her madness for so long. In the end, he promised me he would."

"I'm most surprised you were able to enlist Herr Gustorf in your scheme," I said. "And to do so with such speed."

"I wasn't too sure I'd be able to," Martha said, chewing on her lip seriously. "On my way over with his team and calèche carriage, I'd figured out all manner of ways of trying to wake him without disturbing the Pattersons' hired girl. But when I got there, he was already on the porch, smoking his pipe in the murk."

"But how did you get him to go along? It was quite a risk for him too."

"A girl knows what a man wants," said Martha, smiling at me slyly.

"Martha!" I exclaimed. "Don't tell me that you—what did you do for him? Or promise to him?"

My sister bent over double, laughing so hard tears came to her eyes. "Not *that*," she said when she finally recovered her breath. "He didn't want that. Well, he probably did, but not as much as he wanted something else."

She looked at me expectantly, but when I failed to supply the answer she continued, "His *cast*, Joshua. He wanted the doctor to be able to remove his cast, so he could go back to a normal existence. At first, he absolutely refused my suggestion he drive the doctor away in his carriage, but then I pointed out that if the doctor left without him, so too would the only medical man in the West with the knowledge of how to remove the cast without sawing off his leg. He tamped out his pipe at once and set off."

I laughed and Martha smiled with satisfaction. We turned to head back to town, linked arm in arm. Martha carried a bouquet overflowing with the long stems of yellow and blue and purple wildflowers. She glowed vibrant and fresh against the slowly decaying prairie.

"I've decided to organize proper gravestones for Rebecca and the two children," I said. "It isn't much, but I think it'll provide a final measure of honor to their lives. And deaths." Martha squeezed my arm and I felt her warmth.

A little further along I added: "And you need never worry again that I won't take you seriously. To have done everything you did—and before the sun even rose. No one else could have managed it." I paused. "It *was* quite a risk you took, you know."

"There was more peril in not acting," she said. "That's what I thought, anyway. You can't go through life merely focusing on the risks of acting, Joshua. You might never get anything done."

I looked at her with pride and wonder and thought how much more I had to learn from my younger sister. "Martha?" I began. "Do you want to stay—"

"Oh, yes, please," she shouted, dropping her bouquet to the ground and throwing her arms around my neck. "Yes—yes—a thousand times yes. I was hoping you'd ask. I'll stay here in Springfield forever."

"No one's said anything about forever," I said, returning her hug and then slipping free of her embrace. "Let's take it a season at a time. But I will write to Father and ask that you be allowed to stay here through the winter, at the least."

"That'll do, as a start," said Martha. She bent down and carefully gathered up her flowers and then she gaily linked arms with me again. "As long as, next spring, you write him to say you've discovered you need my company through the fall. And so on. I'll tell you this, Joshua. I'm never going back to the strictures of Farmington. Not after I've discovered what I can do—what I can be—here."

"We'll see," I said. "As I said, we'll take it a season at a time."

When we reached the Hutchason yard again, Phillis was at the pump, filling two earthenware jugs. Martha hurried up to her.

"Phillis dear," she said. "I've decided to extend my stay in Springfield. Indefinitely. You shall stay here with me as my housemaid. I'm sure that'll be pleasing for you, to be of further service. Besides, you'll enjoy much more freedom here than you have at Farmington.

"Joshua will write to our father to sort things out with him. And we can register you as an indentured servant, which you'll be, of a sort, so all the formalities will be taken care of. It shall be a tidy arrangement for us all."

"Yes, Miss Martha," Phillis mumbled after a brief pause. She had finished filling her jugs and stood, eyes downcast, next to the pump.

Martha gave a broad, pleased smile and started to continue into the Hutchason house, but when I took another look at Phillis, I came to a halt. Something about her posture, per-haps the strong carriage of her shoulders, recalled the fortitude she'd shown when confronting Jane Patterson in the darkened poorhouse.

"What is it?" I asked.

Phillis turned partially in my direction but remained mute.

"You may speak your mind," I said.

"Sinderella needs me," came the slave's hoarse voice.

"Who's Sinderella?"

"My gran'baby. Just turned one year. Her momma can't care for her, not properly. She needs me."

"And where does Sinderella live?" Martha asked. "Some-where in Jefferson County, I'd guess. Near about Farmington?"

"*At* Farmington. She belongs to your papa. Like me."

"Don't you think one of the other girls on the farm can take of her?" asked Martha.

"I suppose, ma'am," Phillis replied, her eyes focused on the brimming jugs that rested at her feet.

"Good, then it's settled—"

I held up my hand. "Wait," I said. "Are you saying, Phillis, you would rather go back to Farmington, to the conditions of your bond, than to stay here in Springfield with Miss Martha, where you'd enjoy so much more latitude?"

Phillis turned and looked me directly in the eyes. The expe-rience was so unfamiliar that I found myself taking a half-step backward. "For Sinderella's sake, Master," she said quietly. "She needs me. Meaning no offense to Miss Martha."

"Miss Martha takes no offense, I assure you," I said. "She'll manage here just fine without you. Won't you, Martha?" My sister nodded resolutely. "We shall do as you ask."

Phillis's eyes had reverted to the ground. She gave no out-ward sign of gratitude but rather picked up her jugs, slopping with water, and walked through the back door and into the Hut-chason house.

★ ★ ★

The following week, I encountered an engaging young woman with vivid blue eyes and rose-red lips who was returning to her native Kentucky after spending the summer visiting with her older sisters in Springfield. The woman seemed a responsible sort—she told me she was returning home to become an apprentice teacher—and I entrusted Phillis to her custody. She later wrote to confirm that she'd deposited Phillis at Farmington before completing her journey home to Lexington.

As it turned out, that woman, Mary Todd, would soon come back to Springfield—this time permanently. But that's another story for another day.

CHAPTER 42

The letter arrived at the Department offices nearly two years later. Postmaster Clark himself brought it over to me at A. Y. Ellis & Co. to collect the postage due. As I handed him the coins, I knew at once whom it was from, even though the block handwriting on the outside flap was unfamiliar.

I slit open the envelope with a letter knife and took out a single folded sheet, covered on both sides with the same block writing. Inside the fold were several large denomination banknotes issued by a New York bank. I put these aside and read the letter:

> *My Dear Speed—*
>
> *I am safe and sound. Due to the daring of our mutual friend from the Continent, and aided by your dear one's quick thinking as the cocks began to stir in their coop, we got out of town well before anyone knew to give chase. I collected the package where you'd left it for me and we made it north to the little village of Chicago unmolested. From there, I set sail among the "Great Lakes."*
>
> *You will be glad to know I've kept the promise I made to your dear one when we last spoke. The tragic circumstances in Sangamon, which I abetted by my wishful blindness and inaction, increased my fervor to bring modern methods to*

the care of the ill. Especially for those who suffer from true afflictions of the mind.

With the assistance of some enlightened friends here in New York, and with the proceeds I'd managed to amass from my real estate schemes, I am organizing a new sort of hospital. It will be a "lunatic asylum," supported by the state, where disturbed persons, regardless of their material circumstances, may be sent to receive moral treatment leading to their rehabilitation or, should that prove impossible, at least live out their days without posing any threat to their fellow man.

Had my daughter lived, she would have been our first patient. As it is, there are two men and a woman from the surrounding towns who are residing with us now. Several more sufferers are expected to arrive shortly. My daughter rests in eternal peace in the ground outside my window. A small sapling from an apple tree has recently taken hold above her. I am hopeful it will bear fruit in the coming years.

I have one final debt to pay, for which I humbly beg your assistance. My former brother-in-law was wrong in his belief that I caused the death of his sister, but he was right about everything else. I realize my sudden departure prevented him from securing the compensation he was due for my unworthy attempt to renege on our land transaction. The enclosed notes represent the full agreed-upon purchase price. Kindly see to it they reach his hands.

I have taken certain precautions to obscure my origins. Nonetheless, please destroy this letter for your safety and mine.

Yours sincerely,

Dr. Amariah Brigham
Founding Superintendent
New York State Lunatic Asylum at Utica

When I finished reading, I looked up and saw my sister Martha watching me closely from across the storeroom. Martha and I had since moved on to other adventures together, but not a month had passed where one of us had not wondered aloud about the fate of Dr. Patterson.

"He made it, then?" she asked.

"He did," I said, as I struck a match and held the letter over the flame. "Thanks to you." The fire ravenously tore its way up the sheet.

"What are those banknotes for?"

The fire had consumed the entire letter now, and once the flames licked my fingers at the very top of the page, I held the envelope to the flame until it, too, had all gone up in smoke.

"The doctor asked that I deliver them to Major Richmond, the so-called mad major. To make amends for his wrongdoing in the land dispute between the two of them."

"I'd long ago forgotten all about Richmond," my sister said. "Do you even know where to find him now?"

I nodded my head. "He's at rest in the churchyard behind the Episcopalian Church," I said. Martha's eyes widened. "Passed on last year, from an ailment of the stomach, as I recall."

"What are you going to do with the notes?" she asked. "That's quite a sum."

It took only a moment for the answer to come to me. "There's to be a general muster next month, on the field south of town," I said. "I'll stand the entire regiment of the Late War with Great Britain. And I'll tell them I'm doing it in Richmond's honor."

And that's exactly what we did.

HISTORICAL NOTE

These Honored Dead is a work of imaginative fiction, but it is grounded in fact. Joshua Fry Speed and Abraham Lincoln shared a bed in the room atop Speed's general store, A. Y. Ellis & Co., from the day Lincoln arrived in Springfield in April 1837 until the spring of 1841, when Speed returned home to Louisville. The two men remained close lifelong friends. Lincoln's presidential secretaries John Nicolay and John Hay (the latter the nephew of Milton Hay, "young Hay" of the novel) wrote in their 1890 biography that Speed "was the only—as he was certainly the last—intimate friend that Lincoln ever had."

Indeed, Lincoln would become close to several members of Speed's large family during his life. Speed's older brother James, depicted in the opening pages here, was named U.S. Attorney General by President Lincoln in 1864 and served in that position at the time of Lincoln's assassination. He is best known to history for issuing the legal opinion that the Lincoln conspirators should be tried by a military commission rather than in civilian courts. Speed's sister Martha was the youngest of the Speed children who survived into adulthood.

As portrayed in the novel, 1837 was a momentous year. The nationwide currency crisis, sparked in part by the closing of the Second Bank of the United States, set off the Panic of '37, which would mire the country in a deep depression until the early 1840s. Meanwhile, in Springfield, only the lonely capitol cornerstone—laid on July 4, 1837—marked the coming arrival of the state government, which was moving there from the previous state capital, Vandalia. The state legislature, with Lincoln a prominent member, would first meet in Springfield in December 1839.

The trial at the heart of *These Honored Dead* is inspired by a number of actual cases Lincoln handled during his long and varied legal career. A surprisingly large number of Lincoln's cases involved questions of insanity. And several defendants in Lincoln's cases disappeared before justice was served. Among the murder defendants Lincoln represented was one Melissa Goings, charged with killing her abusive husband by striking him on the head with a piece of firewood. Goings fled during a recess in her trial. When the trial judge accused Lincoln of having encouraged her flight, Lincoln is said to have responded: "Your Honor, I did not chase her off. She simply asked me where she could get a good drink of water, and I said Tennessee has mighty fine drinkin' water."

Beyond Lincoln and Speed, many of the characters in the novel are drawn from life. At the time the novel is set, Judge Jesse B. Thomas Jr. presided over the Circuit Court for Sangamon County; David Prickett was the state's attorney; Stephen Logan was the senior lawyer in Springfield and Lincoln's patron; Henry van Hoff was the carriage maker; Cyrus G. Saunders ran the Globe Tavern (where Lincoln and Mary Todd would later live during their first years of marriage); and Speed and Lincoln's circle of friends included the newspaperman Simeon Francis, Billy the Barber, the court clerk James Matheny, the young office boy Milton Hay, and the store clerks William H. Herndon (later to become Lincoln's final law partner) and Charles Hurst, who shared the other bed in the room above Speed's store.

Eighteen-year-old Mary Todd spent the summer of 1837 in Springfield, lodging with two of her older sisters, Elizabeth and Francis, who had previously moved there from their home in

Lexington, Kentucky. After returning to Lexington to work at Ward's school as an apprentice teacher for two years, Mary would move to Springfield permanently in June 1839.

Frederick Julius Gustorf was a young, well-born Prussian who toured Illinois in the 1830s and kept a journal he intended for publication in his native land. Earlier during his American journeys, he had tutored Harvard and Yale students in German; by some accounts, he was the first-ever German-language instructor at Harvard.

Shortly after the time when the novel ends, Dr. Amariah Brigham founded the New York State Lunatic Asylum at Utica, New York. It was one of the first modern insane asylums in the country.

The 1840 federal census counted 116 African-Americans among Springfield's total population of 2,579, including 6 "slaves" (notwithstanding the fact that slavery did not, as a legal matter, exist in Illinois) and 110 "free colored persons." A number of these "free colored persons" were bound in strict contracts of indentured servitude, a system explicitly allowed by Illinois's Black Code.

Separately, an 1840 "inventory of the slaves" at the Speed estate Farmington near Louisville, Kentucky, listed the first names, ages, and "value" of some 56 enslaved persons owned by the Speed family. Among these was Phillis, then age 43, with a "value" of $300, and Sinderella, then age 4, with a "value" of $250. While the inventory does not indicate familial relationships among the slaves, it is a likely reading of the information the inventory does provide that Sinderella was indeed one of Phillis's granddaughters.

ACKNOWLEDGMENTS

I was a trial lawyer for two decades before embarking on writing a novel. It's been a long road, and I have a lot of people to thank.

My sister Lara Putnam, an eminent historian, currently chair of the History Department at the University of Pittsburgh, tirelessly read successive drafts and contributed her keen historical knowledge and editorial sense. Lara also gave me the key narrative insight for how to tell this story.

My college roommate Joshua F. Thorpe, one day older than me and therefore forever wiser, was also present at the creation. Josh patiently read draft after draft and consistently gave me on-target feedback. As a fellow trial lawyer, he also helped me shape the courtroom scenes.

In Michael Bergmann and Christin Brecher, I found two fellow writers who shared my passion for puzzling out the mysteries of storytelling (and the storytelling of mysteries) while eating mediocre Italian food. I am very grateful to both of them for their countless insights that have greatly improved this story.

My many friends and colleagues at the leading international law firm Kirkland & Ellis LLP, where I was a partner for many years and am delighted to remain of counsel, taught me everything I know about being a trial lawyer and have been remarkably supportive of this new venture.

Carolyn Waters and her staff at the incomparable New York Society Library (NYSL) gave a home to my writing life and provided me with so many invaluable resources. Chief among these were my colleagues in the NYSL fiction writers' group, who read drafts of many different versions of my story and always gave me insightful and sympathetic feedback. My fellow NYSL writers included Jamie Chan, Lillian Clagett, Susan Dudley-Allen, Janet Gilman, Hurd Hutchins, John Koller, Jane Murphy, Alan Siegel, Helena Sokoloff, Victoria Reiter, and Mimi Wisebond.

This book is based on extensive historical research. I'd particularly like to thank for their assistance the staffs of the Lincoln Presidential Museum, Old State Capitol Historic Site, Lincoln Home National Historic Site, Lincoln-Herndon Law Offices State Historic Site, and Edwards Place Historic Home, all in Springfield, Illinois, as well as Diane Young of the Farmington Historic Home site in Louisville, Kentucky. Dr. Dennis C. Dirkmaat of the Department of Applied Forensic Sciences at Mercyhurst University and Professor Thomas D. Morgan of the George Washington University Law School generously gave me insights into their areas of specialty (dead bodies and legal history, respectively).

In addition to the people mentioned elsewhere in these acknowledgments, this and previous versions of my story have benefitted greatly from the editorial input of the following people: Cordelia Francis Biddle, Gail Brussel, Catherine Hiller, Patrick LoBrutto, Alonso Perez-Putnam, Nike Power, Amy Ross, Mark Stein, and Alina Tugend.

While nearly everyone I know has been incredibly supportive of this venture, I need to specifically thank the following additional people for their support, encouragement and assistance along the way: Robin Agnew, Nancy Almazar, John Robert Anderson, Ruby Barrios, Shannon Campbell, Stephanie Altman Dominus, Andrew Dominus, Steven Everson, Shiva Farouki, Andrew M. Genser, Tom and Julie Gest, Marc Goldman, Atif Khawaja, Laura Kupillas, Wyman Lai, Laura Lavan,

Jay P. Lefkowitz, Janet Lopez, Nancy Pascone, Mario Perez, Gabriel Perez-Putnam, Miriam Perez-Putnam, Michelle Pfeffer, Mark Pickrell, William H. Pratt, Joel and Jane Schneider, Joseph Serino Jr., Ed Steinfeld, Lee Ann Stevenson, David Thorpe, Megan Tingley, Jeff Wang, Jennifer Warner, Caroline Werner, Doug Wible, Nancy Winkelstein, and Dan Zevin.

My fantastic agent Scott Miller of Trident Media Group said "maybe" when other agents were saying "no," and he has been an unerring guiding light throughout this process.

My editor Matt Martz, the editorial director of Crooked Lane Books, also said "maybe" when others said "no." Eventually we got to "yes" together. I've learned a tremendous amount about storytelling from Matt, and I'm thrilled to publish my debut novel with him.

My parents and parents-in-law, Robert and Rosemary Putnam, Donna Gest, and Joel and Carla Campbell, have been a constant source of support. I often tell the joke that my parents may be the first in history who, upon learning that their son was resigning from his New York City law firm partnership to try to become a novelist, reacted by saying, "Thank God. It's about time." It's not actually a joke.

My three sons, Gray, Noah, and Gideon Putnam, have been incredibly good-humored about joining me on research trips, giving me focus-group insights into my story, and making room for a late-to-the-party stay-at-home dad.

Finally, this book is dedicated to my wife, Christin Putnam. During one of our first dates—thirty years ago, when both of us were still teenagers—we sat along the scruffy banks of the Charles River in Cambridge, Massachusetts, and discussed a shared future together in which I was a writer. I am overjoyed, at long last, to have made that vision come true with her. Christin has been my first and last reader of every word in the novel and an inexhaustible source of love, encouragement, and—not least—plot points. The book would not have existed without her.